ALSO BY JEANINE CUMMINS

American Dirt

A Rip in Heaven: A Memoir of Murder and Its Aftermath

The Outside Boy

The Crooked Branch

Speak to Me
of Home

Speak to Me of Home

A NOVEL

Jeanine Cummins

Henry Holt and Company
New York

Henry Holt and Company
Publishers since 1866
120 Broadway
New York, New York 10271
www.henryholt.com

Henry Holt° and 🅗° are registered trademarks of
Macmillan Publishing Group, LLC.

Copyright © 2025 by Jeanine Cummins
All rights reserved.
Distributed in Canada by Raincoast Book Distribution Limited

"Hurricane" by Mary Oliver
Reprinted by the permission of The Charlotte Sheedy Literary Agency as
agent for the author.
Copyright © 2012 by Mary Oliver with permission of Bill Reichblum

Library of Congress Cataloging-in-Publication Data

Names: Cummins, Jeanine, author.
Title: Speak to me of home : a novel / Jeanine Cummins.
Description: First edition. | New York : Henry Holt and Company, 2025.
Identifiers: LCCN 2024052414 | ISBN 9781250759368 (hardcover) |
    ISBN 9781250759375 (ebook)
Subjects: LCSH: Puerto Rican women—Fiction. | Puerto Ricans—Fiction. |
    Families—Fiction. | Women—Fiction. | LCGFT: Domestic fiction. |
    Novels.
Classification: LCC PS3603.U663 S64 2025 | DDC 813/.6—dc23/
    eng/20241202
LC record available at https://lccn.loc.gov/2024052414

Our books may be purchased in bulk for promotional, educational,
or business use. Please contact your local bookseller or the Macmillan
Corporate and Premium Sales Department at (800) 221-7945, extension
5442, or by email at MacmillanSpecialMarkets@macmillan.com.

First Edition 2025

Map and family tree by Laura Hartman Maestro
Designed by Meryl Sussman Levavi

Printed in the United States of America

This edition was printed by BVG, Fairfield.

1   3   5   7   9   10   8   6   4   2

This is a work of fiction. All of the characters, organizations, and events
portrayed in this novel either are products of the author's imagination or are
used fictitiously.

For my dad,
who fashioned bedrock
out of sand.

But listen now to what happened
to the actual trees;
toward the end of that summer they
pushed new leaves from their stubbed limbs.
It was the wrong season, yes,
but they couldn't stop.

—Mary Oliver, "Hurricane"

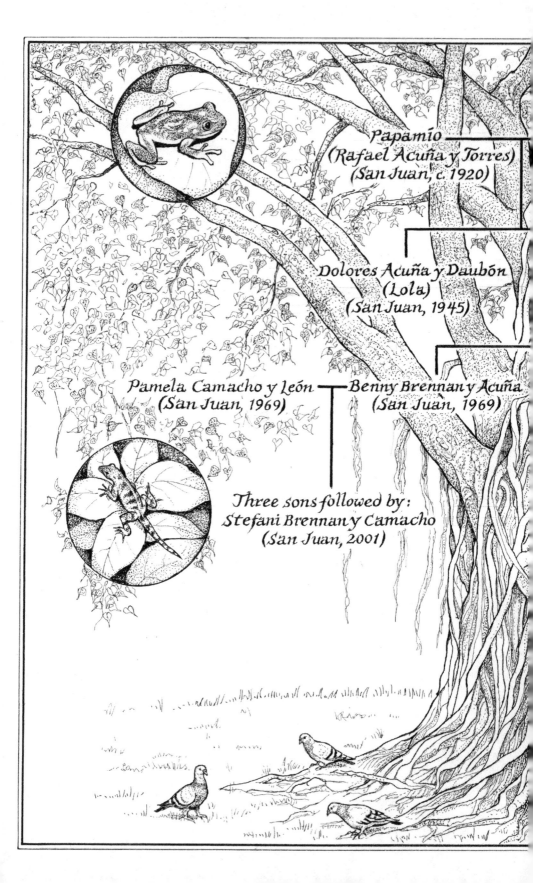

Papamío
(Rafael Acuña y Torres)
(San Juan, c. 1920)

Dolores Acuña y Daubón
(Lola)
(San Juan, 1945)

Pamela Camacho y León
(San Juan, 1969)

Benny Brennan y Acuña
(San Juan, 1969)

Three sons followed by:
Stefani Brennan y Camacho
(San Juan, 2001)

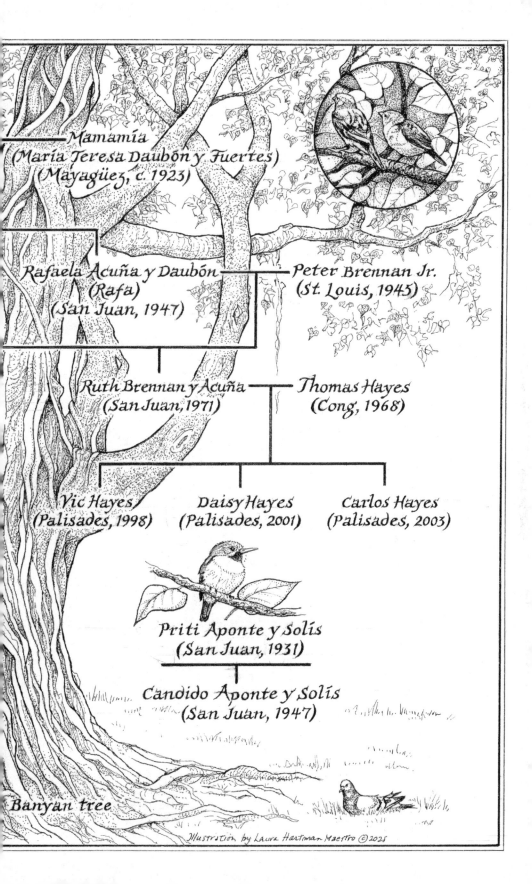

Mamamía
(María Teresa Daubón y Fuertes)
(Mayagüez, c. 1923)

Rafaela Acuña y Daubón
(Rafa)
(San Juan, 1947)

Peter Brennan Jr.
(St. Louis, 1945)

Ruth Brennan y Acuña
(San Juan, 1971)

Thomas Hayes
(Cong, 1968)

Vic Hayes
(Palisades, 1998)

Daisy Hayes
(Palisades, 2001)

Carlos Hayes
(Palisades, 2003)

Priti Aponte y Solís
(San Juan, 1931)

Candido Aponte y Solís
(San Juan, 1947)

Banyan tree

Illustration by Laura Hartman Maestro © 2025

Speak to Me of Home

Chapter One

～

Palisades, New York
2023

Afterward, Ruth will say she knew the moment the phone rang, even before she picked it up. She will say there was something calamitous in the sound. No one ever calls the house line anymore.

It is 8:14 P.M. on a Tuesday evening in June and in truth, despite Ruth's eventual perception to the contrary, she feels no ominous pang when the ringer asserts its shrill voice into the room. What she feels is annoyed that she forgot to unplug the phone before her shoot. She always tries to make these videos in one take, because if she has to scrap the first effort and start again, a rehearsed note sometimes creeps in. Despite having a career that requires her to maintain a constant presence online, Ruth isn't a person who's particularly good at pretending. So when the phone rings, the video captures her irritation in the form of a wince before Ruth slips from the stool. She doesn't stop to hit pause on the camera, so the video captures all of it: Ruth, barefoot in her jeans and linen tunic, padding across the slate floor, retreating into the background of the frame. She answers the phone, which is an antique, wall-mounted contraption with a mother-of-pearl face that Ruth selected mostly for its contribution to the decor, and because her daughter, Daisy, has convinced her that old, impractical things can sometimes be more fun than their convenient modern counterparts. The phone does look beautiful on the wall, but is ill-suited to conducting actual conversations.

From this distance, it's easier to discern how small Ruth is, how slender her shoulders. She is in profile as she lifts the earpiece, on tiptoe with her neck craned as she speaks into the mounted cone mouthpiece on the front of the phone.

"Hello?"

Just as she loops the cord around her finger there's a shift in her body. She flings one hand out to steady herself against the counter and submits to an unflattering curl of her posture. The room around her still appears just as she designed it to appear, the first iteration of the aesthetic that accidentally made her famous (or at least *fame-ish*, as her kids insist): high ceilings, exposed beams, enormous tropical vegetation in earthenware jugs. You can tell just by looking at this room in pictures that it smells like lemon cupcakes and sandalwood, maybe a trace of mint. But within the careful diorama, Ruth is just a small woman in a large room receiving terrible news.

"Wait, oh my God," she says into the phone, leaning her forehead against the outstretched arm on the counter. "No, no," she says, but whoever's on the phone can't hear because she's too far away from the ridiculous mouthpiece. "No, I don't know." She stands up again and makes an effort to throw her voice toward the phone. "I'm her mother! Yes, of course. What do you mean, her medical history? Oh my God, wait. How . . ."

Her forehead leaves a dark smear of foundation on the unbleached sleeve of her tunic. She stands up straight and uses the flat of her hand to smack herself over the heart.

"Yes, she has insurance. Of course, yes. The card should be in her wallet. What?"

Ruth curls into an even tighter knot while she clutches the phone.

"I will, yes," she says. "Of course."

She makes an effort to uncoil herself, propping a hand on her hip and tipping her head back to gaze through the skylight above. Darkening blue. A rind of moon. She tries to speak again but finds the effort trapped in her throat. She pushes past it.

"I need to take down your number and call you back," she croaks, opening a nearby drawer.

She fishes out a pen but can't find paper. She uncaps the pen with her teeth and writes on her hand.

"Okay," she says. "Yes, okay."

After she replaces the earpiece into its cradle, Ruth makes a sound that's foreign to her own ears. It is a mammal sound and it comes from the crypts of her lungs. Then she cries softly in a huddle for a few moments before remembering the camera. The instant of remembering is visible: the alertness drops into the frame and stands her up. Ruth tries to shake clean air into her body, pushes her shoulders away from her sternum, and strides across the room. But some things she cannot hide, and the mascara turns to mud beneath her eyes.

Outside, there is a tumult in the trees, a wind so sharp it startles a few summer leaves from their too-dry branches. It whips away and south and south, to where her daughter is.

The sweep and tumble of Ruth's mind goes with it.

Chapter Two

~

San Juan, Puerto Rico
One hour and forty-three minutes ago
2023

In the lobby of her building, Daisy turned the key in the little metal box with her name on it, Apartment 2B, and retrieved her mail from inside. A book of local coupons on cheap newsprint, the weekly letter from her grandmother, perfumed and handwritten on lavender stationery as if they were conducting a Victorian romance, and—yes!—the envelope she'd been waiting for all week. Daisy bumped the mailbox door closed with her elbow, provoking the satisfying click. Behind her, the main door to the building rattled in its frame, and Mrs. Fernández in 1A opened her apartment door to stick her head out.

"Ay, Daisy, you're not going out in that weather, are you?"

Daisy turned. "No, Mrs. Fern, don't worry!" she said. "I'm in for the duration. Just grabbing my mail." She waved it between them like evidence.

"Good, good," Mrs. Fernández said. "You be safe!" And she closed the door.

If there was one thing Daisy appreciated about Mrs. Fernández, it was her friendly brevity. Daisy took the stairs to her apartment two at a time. She'd left the door open. Not just unlocked, but standing open, because she knew all seven of her neighbors, none of whom were thieves or delinquents. Daisy could smell something delicious coming from upstairs,

probably Mr. Kurtzweiler's place. Maybe he was trying to cook up everything he had in the fridge and freezer before the power went out and it all
spoiled. Hopefully he'd bring her a small tower of Tupperware later, or at
least a plate covered in Saran Wrap. She closed her door, kicked her flip-
flops under the coffee table, and folded her legs beneath her on the couch.
Her little backpack yawned open beside her, spilling out the contents of
her life: wallet, ChapStick, extra hair ties. She threw her keys on top and
settled herself on the cushions. She stared at the envelope and paused long
enough to check the time. If she waited for Carlos, she knew he'd find some
way to turn this moment into a ceremony. But he wouldn't be out of
rehearsal for another hour at least, and honestly, Daisy didn't have that
kind of patience. She slid her finger beneath the top flap and tore in.

The two DNA reports inside were several pages thick, folded in thirds.
She took a deep breath, allowing her curiosity to swell for a moment while
she unfolded the pages across her bare knees. The mantel clock ticked
loudly in the quiet room, and Daisy felt the rhythm of her heart attempting to steady itself into that cadence. Instead, as confusion descended,
Daisy's pulse went in the other direction. She turned the pages over, as if
she'd find a different explanation, one that made more sense. The back of
the packet was blank. She flipped to the front again, and then to the second page, third, and fourth. Each was filled with pie charts, graphs, and
colorful maps, easy to read. And yet Daisy was confounded by the data.

"What the heck?" she said out loud. Daisy unfolded her legs, sat forward on the couch. "This doesn't make any sense."

She groped for her phone, still studying the pages in her hand. She
glanced at the time again and knew Carlos was still in rehearsal, his phone
on silent, but she called anyway. It went to voicemail and she blurted her
message after the beep.

> *Carlos, this is the weirdest thing, you're not going to believe it.*
> *Obviously I couldn't wait for you and I opened the DNA results*
> *and HOLY SHIT, I'm still trying to wrap my head around it.*
> *Call me the moment you get this! Call me, call me, call me!*

As soon as she hung up, she dialed his phone again and said, *Don't*
worry, we're still related! and hung up. Her eyes were fixed on the pages in

front of her, and she started to read them again, more carefully this time. The phone in her hand began to ring, and Daisy answered it without looking.

"Carlos!" she said. "You won't believe this, it's so crazy."

"Who's Carlos? Is that, like, your boyfriend?"

Daisy pulled the phone away from her ear. *Ugh.*

"Hi, Brandon," she said, her voice dropping. "What can I do for you?"

Daisy's Tío Benny had about a dozen rental properties in San Juan, and even though Daisy's own business had been thriving for over a year now, she still managed a couple of the properties in Condado for her uncle. The apartments weren't far from where she lived in Miramar, and besides, every successful entrepreneur Daisy knew in San Juan had at least one side hustle, and this was hers. Daisy liked sharing insider knowledge about which cafés had the best lunch specials, which beaches were quietest on weekends, and which galleries featured the hottest local artists. Before Brandon and his pals arrived, Daisy had purchased a pretty box of alfajores from Paulina's bakery and arranged it on the kitchen counter alongside a bag of freshly ground Yaucono coffee. With the exception of the occasional nightmare guest, she really enjoyed this second job.

Brandon had showed up almost a week ago with four of his fraternity brothers and a half-empty bottle of tequila. They traveled with their own shot glasses, whether from home or the airport, Daisy couldn't say. They suggested she take a shot, poured her one anyway after she declined three times, and then began making not-quite-out-of-earshot comments about her body as she tried to show Brandon how to work the electronic locks and alarm system. She'd never been so happy to finish a check-in.

She hadn't spoken to them again until she called two days ago to alert them that the storm warnings had turned serious, that tourists were evacuating the island ahead of the weather, and that if they wanted to get on a flight, they needed to act now. Brandon swore they were prepared.

"We're from the Gulf Coast, sweetie. We're not afraid of a little weather."

A little weather. She closed her eyes briefly to see if she could submerge the little bubble of rage that was rising in her, aerated by his moronic hubris.

"You know the power will definitely go out," she said. "There will be no air-conditioning."

"You think we have AC on the bayou?" He laughed. "As long as we have beer and Doritos, we're all set!"

For days, the island meteorologists had employed their most climactic turns of phrase, and the people had listened to those reporters on the television, but also to their neighbors, to the rising and flattening birdsong, to the aching joints that were reliable messengers in times like these. They gathered sensory information from all these sources and more, and then, having acquainted themselves with the particulars, they set about making preparations. They purchased batteries and bottled water, collected cash from ATM machines, packed their picnic coolers full of ice, and charged their cell phones. At this late hour, all across the Puerto Rican archipelago, all that was left was to close the hurricane shutters if you were lucky enough to have them, to hunker down against the growing breeze and greening sky. With a great suction of wind, the storm was coming.

But here was Brandon on the phone again, too late to be having second thoughts. Daisy felt her previous excitement and confusion receding to make room for whatever nonsense Brandon was about to unleash. It wasn't her fault he'd failed to heed her warnings, that he hadn't prepared for the storm. She pushed the stack of paperwork off her lap and onto the open backpack beside her as she stood to stretch her legs. She peered out the window at the green-gray sky, the color of raw clay.

"Listen, turns out we're gonna make a run for it," Brandon said.

Daisy flinched. "Wait, what do you mean?" She was almost giddy with disbelief. "Have you looked out your window? It's too late to leave now."

"Yeah, we don't wanna take any chances, we're getting out."

"You mean your *mom* doesn't wanna take any chances," Daisy heard one of the douchebag friends say, and then they all laughed like they'd heard something witty.

"Listen, being from the Gulf Coast," Brandon said, "we got mad respect for the weather. We know a storm when we see one, and this bitch is comin' in hot."

Daisy placed her palm on the warm pane of glass in front of her and looked at its shape outlined by the alarming color of the sky.

"Is the airport even open?" she said.

Soon she would roll down her own hurricane shutters and pray the

AC would stay on for as long as possible. It gets hot fast in a sealed concrete box.

"Yeah, I think we got the last Miami-bound flight," Brandon said. "But we have to make two stopovers. Can you believe that shit?"

One of his friends belched loudly, and then Daisy heard a woman's voice.

"Sir, I need you to hang up the phone now, please."

"Wait, you're on the plane now?" Daisy heard the alarm in her own voice.

"Yeah. I gotta run," he said, "this lady is freaking out cuz I'm on my phone."

"Wait!" Daisy said. "Did you bring everything in from the balcony like I asked? Did you close the hurricane shutters?"

There was a full suite of patio furniture out there. An empty beach cooler, an umbrella, four folding chairs. A gas grill with an extra propane tank. There was a small hibiscus tree in a heavy pot, a perfect airborne projectile. If any one of those items took flight from the fourteenth-floor penthouse, it could kill someone.

Brandon put a hand over the phone, but she could hear him asking his friends if anyone had done these simple things. There was laughter.

"I remembered to bring the rum!" one of the friends said.

"Sir, you need to put your phone in airplane mode," the flight attendant said. "Now."

"Yeah, I don't know," Brandon said to Daisy.

"Sir!" The flight attendant.

"I gotta run."

Then it was just the click.

And Daisy's worry, her insistent worry, like a buzz in her brain, crowding away everything else.

"Shit," she said, stepping through her sliding door and out onto the balcony to assess the sky, which was low and changing, a color between pink and green now, the color of a healing bruise. She knew she had no choice. She had to go.

The rain hadn't started yet, but Daisy could feel it heavy in the atmosphere, the wind kicking visibly through the emptying streets. A bad time to venture out on her scooter, an idiotic time, truly. There was a heavy sort of crackle in the air, and an earthy, metallic scent. On the balcony, the weather raked through Daisy's hair and pulled a tendril loose from her ponytail. No lightning yet, but it was coming. She could be out and back in half an hour. If things got really bad in the meantime, she could just crash at the other apartment. She could be there in ten minutes. Eight, maybe, if she was really fast. Back inside, she rolled down and latched the hurricane shutter, closed the sliding door, grabbed her backpack, and stuffed her things inside. She double-checked that her keys were there, and double-knotted her sneakers on her way out the door.

Outside, the wind was strong enough now that the traffic lights were dancing lightly on their wires. Strong enough that the public-use scooters had all been rounded up and tucked into their warehouses or wherever it was they went when they weren't littering the streets.

Daisy went to unlock her own scooter from the shed in the gathering darkness. It beeped its electronic response when she stepped aboard. The headlight flickered once and then shone onto the hot asphalt in front of her. She snapped the chin strap under her helmet, and fixed her mini backpack onto both shoulders, checking that the reflective tape was still clean and visible on the back. She pulled the accelerator and eased into the bike lane, expertly swerving around the three potholes on her block as she gathered speed. Behind her, a passenger van rattled and bounced as it hit a pothole she'd avoided, and she smiled at the acknowledgment that, over the course of her time in San Juan, she had become someone different. She'd become someone who rode scooters in the wind, in the almost dark, someone with a small catalog of potholes in San Juan. Did that make her Puerto Rican now, had she finally achieved it? What an embarrassing thing to wonder. No matter how comfortable Daisy became with her life in this city, no matter how at home she was here, she could never quite evict from her brain the unhelpful questions her mother had instilled there. She remembered the DNA results she'd just received, and there was a quizzical, unfamiliar feeling as her brain tried to reconcile the new information with all the ways she'd attempted to define herself throughout her twenty-two years on Earth. It felt like fizz in her veins. Overhead, light ripped through the darkening sky in flashes, and the boom that followed was almost immediate. Daisy crouched on her scooter, pulled harder on the accelerator.

When she arrived here two years ago, Daisy had been terrified of the scooters. She watched them zip and weave through traffic, their riders invariably helmetless, often wearing flip-flops, a beach bag slung carelessly over one shoulder, sunglasses deflecting the bugs. The riders never seemed to signal, rarely stopped at red lights. Daisy remembered one woman in a red evening gown and glittering high heels gliding down avenida Ashford behind her date, who was wearing a tux. The woman's black hair was pulled into a sleek side-part pony, and the gauzy trail of her gown fanned out behind her scooter like a crimson wing. Daisy caught herself staring, her mouth literally hanging open, her hand fluttering toward her neck. She was consumed by a fear, a *certainty*, that the dress would catch in the wheel, the scooter would crash, and the glamorous woman would be flung to her bloody death beneath the wheels of a passing truck.

But the scooters were so ubiquitous here that Daisy soon found it difficult to maintain her apprehension about them. As with most unfamiliar things, Daisy eventually got used to them. And then came the day when, after fortification in the form of a coffee and quesito, Daisy downloaded the app, reserved a scooter, and double-knotted her sneakers before gingerly stepping aboard. Within the first half mile, she was in love.

She loved balancing on the scooter with both accelerator and brake in the grip of her hand. She began to crave the rough stickiness of the board beneath the soles of her shoes, the warm wind whipping her T-shirt against her body, drying the sweat from her neck even while the sun shone on her outstretched arms. She enjoyed the reasonable speed, the ease of the velocity, how quickly the city blocks went by beneath her wheels. She appreciated the way it still felt like walking, almost, but without exertion. She listened to flashes of laughter and the boom bass of reggaeton while she flew modestly through the streets. The guy who worked at the smoothie stand began calling out to her, a greeting every time she zoomed past. *¡Buenas, linda!* And sometimes she would answer him.

Daisy rode the public scooters for several weeks before she decided to buy her own so she could make sure the battery was always charged, the brakes dependable. She also purchased a helmet, and in all the time she'd been riding since, she hadn't seen a single other rider wearing any kind of safety gear at all. She thought they were all nuts.

Daisy wasn't naturally fearless, but she was self-aware, so she pushed herself into doing scary things. Like a water diviner, she had an innate sense that the fear was where the good stuff was hiding. She knew that if she listened to the trembling apprehension in her body, and went toward it instead of running away, there was often a payoff. Of course there were notable exceptions (dark alleys, questionable men, riding her scooter in a hurricane), but Daisy knew the difference, and she learned to fashion the healthy fear into a catapult. That was how she'd landed here at twenty years old, far from her mother and brothers back home on the East Coast, far from the college she was supposed to go to on Long Island and the predictable, orderly life that had been expected of her. She'd pushed herself here instead because she wanted courage to be a thing she could ingest, a seed she could eat that would grow roots and bloom within her.

She really didn't need the scooter anymore, now that she had the truck for work, but she'd grown to love both the adventure and convenience of riding this little zipper through the streets. For a moment like this, it was perfect—she wouldn't have to worry about traffic or parking. It would be much faster than taking the truck.

In the quickening wind, she kept her knees slightly bent to absorb the bumps as she flew down calle José Martí and turned left up the hill where she could see a fog of drizzly light hanging above Condado. At the highway intersection, she dismounted so she could walk across. Tourists often whizzed past her at this corner while she lingered at the crosswalk, but Daisy knew that being brave and being foolhardy were not the same thing. She always waited for the light.

The cat appeared as if by magic then, as if he were himself only a trick of light. He was black and gleaming, and only his yellow eyes were visible enough to assert that he was not imaginary in the darkness, which was earlier and more oppressive because of the arriving storm. The traffic lights were kicking up their colors in the wind, but the intersection beneath was slow, quiet. Very few cars remained out on the roads now. All the non-idiots were safe at home, filling their bathtubs with water and charging their devices. A single car eased through the intersection toward her, and Daisy began to fear for the cat.

"Here, kitty," she said softly. He paused on three legs to look up at her, unwilling to advance any farther. "No, don't stop," she said, her voice mounting in volume. "Come out of the road!" The cat twitched a whisker. "Ven, gatito," she tried, realizing that perhaps the cat didn't speak English. Still, he did not move, and Daisy recognized that he was like her: a worrier out flitting around in the hot night, pretending to have his shit together. She took two steps back, and the cat padded forward like it was a waltz. Just as the car slid past behind him, he leaped to the curb and dashed past Daisy through a nearby fence. As his tail was swallowed up by the hedge on the other side, it seemed to suck the last impression of daylight with it. When Daisy turned back around, the corner appeared even darker than before. Full night had fallen in the time it had taken to turn her head. She stepped down from the curb then, holding the handlebars of the scooter in both hands, trusting and adjusting as her headlight lit the pavement below. Her body knew something was about to happen before her brain did. There was no sound except wind, no sensory information to serve as a warning, yet still, Daisy's body flexed with a feeling of tremendous foreboding.

It appeared in her peripheral vision as a growing shape, a swift and hungry shadow, impossible to comprehend, black and silent as it hurtled toward her through the darkness. A car with its headlights off. Noiseless and fast. But Daisy was visible in her light-colored clothing, her scooter, the light, the reflective tape! She wasn't even fully onto the road yet, so it made no sense that the car would reach her here, just off the curb, that it seemed to be accelerating toward her. She could not move. Like a nightmare, she was stuck. And though it happened almost instantly, the moment seemed to stretch into an hour, a year. Daisy watched herself from above, unmoving, frozen in panic. She willed herself to flee, but there was no movement at all. Only a scream as she released her grip on the handlebars and her arms flew uselessly up in front of her face, as if they could stop the car from coming.

Terror does not wear the conventional costume. It's not a monster with fangs and claws that swoops in screeching with blood on its breath. True terror is walking into a room where you've lived alone for forty years and finding that your chair is not precisely where you left it. Terror is the smallest detail, just slightly askew: a car where a car should not be. Just before impact, Daisy understood that some people are not as philosophical as they expect to be about death. They experience no profound review of their life's most exceptional moments, no series of flashing images, no survey of love or regrets. Sometimes, in the instant just before the crash, the only thought that appears in the mind is this one: *Oh, God. I'm about to die.*

The rain was starting now with rigor. It sent no emissary droplets ahead, but gathered itself into a dark and spirited wall that galloped into the city all at once, the way it often did on this island, thundering down the streets and across the expanse of Daisy, or at least across the expanse of her crumpled body, which was set at an unnatural angle beneath the deluge, one leg tossed up against the fence, the creamy color of her top quickly changing with the splatter of muddy water. The car, too, had lodged itself at an unnatural angle, one headlight now on, bleating into the ropes of rain, its driver slumped over the hollering horn. Did Daisy's chest rise and fall with the tenacious effort of breath? Did her warm fingers twitch across the surface of a gathering puddle?

It was too dark to tell.

Chapter Three

~

San Juan, Puerto Rico
1968

On a blazing summer afternoon in 1968 less than a mile from that very intersection, Daisy's grandmother Rafaela Acuña y Daubón stood before a heavy oval mirror. She was visible through the picture-frame window of a freshly painted, powder-blue hotel of modest renown. Outside, the sun was just beginning to lower itself into the hot bath of the sea, stretching its slow, golden light across the rooftops and cobblestones. This was another June in Santurce, Puerto Rico.

Rafaela's black hair was pinned through with red roses, and she wore a white peineta and mantilla above. The bell sleeves of her gown were lace and her own grandmother's drop pearls swung lightly from her earlobes, something borrowed. Rafaela had never cared much for simplicity, and certainly not on her wedding day.

Her sister, Dolores, was there too, in a panic, which provoked a profound tranquility in Rafaela. Beads of perspiration came to stand in the crevice of Dolores's chin, and Rafaela was glad her sister's rose-colored dress was silk, so dark circles wouldn't spread beneath the arms. The sashes of the tall windows were thrown open so the blushing evening sunshine would flood the room. Outside, someone rang the bell on a passing bicycle, and the sound cheered Rafaela. She would not let her sister ruin the splendor of this day. She deserved one perfect day after the stretch of turmoil from which their family was only beginning to emerge. Rafaela's bridal heels made no sound on the thick carpet as she crossed the room and set the letter down on the table beside the standing mirror. Behind her, Dolores opened a hand fan with a sound like a rolled *r*, and Rafaela watched its colors flash while her sister fanned herself.

"Well, Rafa?" Dolores said.

Rafaela fitted her fingers into a long white glove and began drawing the satin up her slender arm.

"Help me with the other one, Lola," she instructed.

Dolores sighed and clicked her fan closed, placing it atop the still unfolded letter. That letter was so unimportant Rafaela wouldn't even bother refolding it. She wouldn't bother ripping it up or burning it. She would just abandon it there on the small marble table. Then she would forget it had ever existed.

"But never mind the gloves, Rafa!" her sister said as she picked up the second glove anyway and held it open for Rafaela to snake her arm into. Dolores smelled like the orchids in Rafaela's bouquet, just at the trembling peak before decay. Dolores pulled the top edge of the glove up over Rafaela's elbow and grabbed the letter from the table once more. "What are you going to do?" She waved the letter in front of Rafaela like a second fan.

"Oh, don't be so dramatic." Rafaela checked her makeup in the mirror, making sure the red lipstick hadn't strayed onto her teeth during the minute and a half since she'd last checked. She gathered her mantilla to one side and turned to inspect the trail of white buttons stretching from shoulder blades to waistline. Satisfied with what she saw, she settled her mantilla lightly around her shoulders and turned to smile at her sister. "I'm going to marry him," she said.

Rafaela didn't have a single remaining doubt in her mind. Of course there had been the usual misgivings of any courtship, but that was all behind her now. They were in love, and this union wasn't so much a decision as an inevitability. God had created her for this man, and even though he bore almost no resemblance to the future husband she may once have imagined for herself, surely that was only because the limits of her former imagination had been circumscribed by the perimeter of this island. That was no longer true. And so, in less than one hour, Señorita Rafaela Josefina Acuña y Daubón would become Mrs. Peter Brennan Jr.

"I'm ready," she said.

Dolores stood with her lips parted, her panic suspended by bewilderment. "But . . . you have to at least talk to him about it."

Rafaela lifted the bundle of white orchids into her gloved hands. Their stems were wrapped with a dark pink ribbon and fixed with a pearl head pin. "Talk to him about what? There's nothing to discuss, Lola."

Dolores shook her head. "But . . ."

Twenty-one years they'd known each other, and Rafaela was still the only person who could truly stun her sister. Dolores was speechless.

"Look, even if I wanted to talk to him, how would that work?" she asked. "I waltz into the church in my wedding gown and ask him to step outside for a moment?" Rafaela waved a hand vaguely in the air. "We will discuss it later."

"But later will be too late," Dolores said. "Later you'll already be married."

Rafaela crossed the small space between them and grasped her sister's hands. She leaned her face toward Dolores as she had done since they were small, when the eighteen months that separated them had been a visible distinction, two matching moon-faced girls, two halos of black curls, one head slightly taller than the other. Rafaela had learned this trick when she was still in diapers, to face her big sister, to cast her eyes into Dolores's eyes, to hook and reel. When she'd established the steady gaze of her sister's focus, Rafaela could always make her understand.

"Sister, listen," she said. "It's not as if Peter wrote that disgusting letter himself, right?"

Dolores took a deep breath and nodded. This was true.

"That would be different," Rafaela continued. "But maybe he doesn't even know about it."

"But maybe he does," Dolores said. "And you won't know how he feels about it until you ask him."

Rafaela's shoulders drooped in frustration. "So what if he does know about it, Lola, who cares? He obviously doesn't think that way or he never would've agreed to move here, right? He asked me to marry him! He loves me!"

"Of course he does, Rafa, but you don't marry only him, you know that. You marry all of them, the whole family."

"Ay, please—such a cliché!"

"It's a cliché because it's true! And if you marry into a family that doesn't accept you—"

"Stop," Rafaela interrupted, a new disquiet warping her voice. She dropped her sister's hands. "Enough, Dolores, please. This is my wedding day."

Rafaela seldom called her sister Dolores.

She felt Lola searching her face for a crack of doubt, a fissure where she might slip in, but Rafaela knew her sister wouldn't find a foothold there, because Rafaela's certainty was resolute. Peter was the one. She lifted the heavy hem of her gown to check her shoes, which were Vaccari, silver, and a gift from her cousin Clarisa, who had worn them only twice. The shoes were gorgeous but not enough to distract her from the worry on her sister's face. Rafa sighed, dropping the weight of her hem back to the floor.

"They'll have to accept me once I'm his wife," she said. "They'll have no choice. And besides, once they meet me, they'll see how they misjudged me." She grinned now, turning her attention back to her sister and pinching Lola's waist. "They'll see how lucky he is. Just look at me!" Rafaela threw one arm up over her head and did a hip-rocking twirl, the dress swooshing around her legs.

Dolores couldn't help but laugh at the force of Rafa's joy, her self-certainty. Dolores tucked her lips inside her mouth and nodded her head. Rafaela could see the resignation settling over her sister's features. Lola had told herself she would try, and try she had. Now that the effort was behind them, Rafaela could count on her sister to march through the front door of Sagrado Corazón de Jesús and face the long stretch of that church aisle with a smile. She would disregard the empty pews on the groom's side and pretend nothing was amiss, that the absence merely reflected the challenges of geography, that here were two happy families uniting their children in holy matrimony.

"Okay." Lola forced brightness into her face, and then sincerity followed. Rafaela could see the moment it shifted, the way her sister softened, so that when she opened her arms, they were the petals of a maga flower unfurling. Rafaela folded into Lola's embrace and clung there.

"You are the most beautiful bride!" Lola whispered into her mantilla.

Rafaela pressed her eyes closed once, and then straightened herself to arm's length, squeezing Lola's hand. "Well." She could feel her rib cage rise beneath her bodice. "We have a wedding to attend!"

When Dolores paused on the landing and decided to dash back to the suite for the letter, she didn't consider why she was keeping it. Perhaps it might one day serve as evidence, a reminder, an insurance policy of some kind. Perhaps one day she'd have occasion to slap it down on a table along with a demand for explanations. Or maybe it was just the possibility of someone else finding it, the shame of its existence. When Dolores snatched it up from that marble table, when she folded and stashed it beneath the wire of her bra where it would pulse against her skin throughout the ceremony like a second heartbeat, maybe she was only hiding it to protect Rafaela, as if she could neutralize its contents through the damp assertion of her humanity.

Rafaela followed her sister beneath the arched double doors of the church she knew as well as her own bedroom, and heard the sober snap of her heel against the tile floor. She allowed her eyes a moment to adjust. Papamío was waiting just inside the vestibule, and when Rafaela peeked through the small arched window of the interior door, there was Peter waiting for her, too, tall and beautiful in his dress blues, gold buttons gleaming, two stripes on the cuff. His blue eyes were so light they were almost white, and the sight of him there, standing hopeful and alone at the foot of the altar, aroused a flame of tenderness in Rafaela. His cheeks bore a hint of red, like the roses Rafaela had fixed beneath the curve of one ear. Her heart throbbed inside her corset, either with love or apprehension. Perhaps both. Lola went first down the aisle. And then Papamío squeezed Rafaela's hand and did not ask if she was ready. It was too late for all that. What he said was, "Here we go." And the doors opened.

At the end of the aisle, Peter's eyes flashed in the late-day church, and Rafaela could see that he was everything she wanted. She could see the life she would have, as the wife of such a man. He was hers, with a smile like daylight, and she loved him. She did. Surely her trepidation was natural. True, stepping down the aisle felt something like walking the plank, but when she reached its end, Rafaela would drop with a splash into her new life, and Peter would catch her.

At the foot of the altar, Papamío was patient while she clung to his arm. If he sensed any reluctance there, he betrayed nothing. He only smiled and breathed, unmoving until she was ready to let go, so he could kiss her cheek and hand her over to the husband-to-be. The moment trembled and expanded while Rafaela failed to let go of her father's arm. She could feel the joy radiating off Peter only three feet away. It was heady, buoyant. Her groom stepped forward awkwardly, and this was the moment then, it was really time. A different life awaited, a very different life. At last she turned to her father, who embraced and kissed her. Over Papamío's shoulder, Rafaela scanned the pews and faces. She took inventory of that church while her father turned to shake Peter's hand.

Because there was one face that might have changed everything, one pair of green eyes that might've supplied the errant domino that would have diverted Rafaela onto a totally different path. But that face wasn't there—of course it wasn't. Papamío rubbed the bumps of her knuckles once more through the satin glove. Rafaela squeezed his fingers. And let go.

Chapter Four

~

St. Louis, Missouri
1978

Ruth had only been to St. Louis once before, when she was four years old. Grandpa Pete wore a straw hat, and took her to the county fair. He smelled of Rolaids and Old Spice, and she knew this because he carried her on his shoulders, her little arms wrapped around the brim of his hat, the heels of her sandals tucked into his armpits. He stood beside her on the carousel and looped his arms around her waist, making himself a human seat belt to keep her safe. The pony she chose had a turquoise mane and a studded golden saddle. She'd never had cotton candy before. And even though she didn't speak English then, Grandpa Pete communicated easily with her. He used funny faces and elaborate gestures. He crossed his eyes and made her laugh. So when her parents told her they were moving to Missouri, it sounded to Ruth like a great place to live. Not as good as San Juan, maybe. But carousels, cotton candy, her other nice grandpa? All good.

Ruth was three weeks shy of her seventh birthday when they moved from Puerto Rico to St. Louis, and later she would have no memories of the move at all. She wouldn't remember packing her toys and books into cardboard boxes, or emptying the white dresser with the painted-on roses in her room, or stacking her clothes into neat rows in her suitcase: socks, undershirts, shorts, skirts. She wouldn't remember her mother pleading with her father to delay the move just one more month so they could celebrate Ruth's birthday in San Juan with friends and family. "There's always another reason to put it off," she wouldn't remember Dad saying. All the preparation, and any feelings that may have been attached to it, would become an insistent blank in Ruth's memory. Yet the days and weeks immediately following that void would be vivid.

The very first morning she woke up in their new bungalow, in their new subdivision in North County, to the familiar scent of coffee and bacon. Ruth was glad to have that recognizable aroma to cover the new house smell of lumber and fresh paint. Her room was smaller here than the one she'd had in San Juan, but also painted yellow, and in the center of the ceiling it had a pretty little chandelier with pink flowers and green leaves. The sunlight coming through her morning curtains was dim and shadowy, causing Ruth to wonder on that first morning whether perhaps her room sat beneath the shade of a spreading tree she hadn't noticed the evening before. But when she opened the curtains to look outside, she realized she was not in shade at all. The sun was simply different here. A different angle, a different distance.

She had three more weeks to be six years old, and though Ruth did not remember feeling sad before moving away from San Juan, she was melancholy then upon discovering the unreliability of the sun's position in the sky, which she had never questioned before. She felt that this was a thing she should've been able to avoid knowing until at least her seventh birthday. She felt it was an injustice that a six-year-old child should be exposed to such a discovery. She could hear her parents talking and laughing in the kitchen. Ruth frowned at her reflection in the not-very-bright glass of her new window and shut her curtains.

Benny was nine then, and it was worse for him because he'd been in school longer and had more friends to leave behind. They hadn't been able to bring his bike to St. Louis either, so Benny had given the bike to his best friend, Tiago, and their dad had promised to buy Benny an even better one when they got to St. Louis—any color he wanted.

On Monday, Dad walked them to the bus stop, and the four other children who were already waiting there started talking to Ruth and Benny all at once. Their words were garbled and loud, and Ruth thought they all sounded like they had trumpets in their mouths. Ruth and Benny were already accustomed to hearing English because back in San Juan, their father had spoken to them frequently in his native tongue. If asked, Ruth and Benny would both have answered that, yes, they spoke English. They spoke quiet, careful, precise, slow English in the manner of their father back home in San Juan, the style of English he used when he read their bedtime stories, his finger following the words along the page. They knew how to say, "May I please have a glass of water" and "This hamburger is delicious" and "The Yankees are overrated." They knew what action to perform when their father said, "It's bedtime now" or "Please pass the salt" or "Go find your shoes." But these children at the bus stop spoke an entirely different English from the one Ruth and Benny knew. All their wordsrantogether-likeonebigword and the kids never even breathed between their twangy sentences. Ruth could feel her eyes getting bigger, gaping in an effort to contain all the noise. She was wearing her new turquoise backpack with the red-and-white stripes. She'd chosen a pink seersucker romper, which her mother thought would be fine for September, until they had a chance to go shopping and buy some warmer clothes. But Ruth already felt cold, so she leaned down to hoist her socks over the knobs of her kneecaps. She wished for a cardigan. Dad was in his shirtsleeves and didn't seem to notice the chill in the air. He laughed at something one of the children said, and then answered in his own trumpet voice. He placed a hand on each of their heads in turn, saying their names.

"This is Benny." Dad's palm was flat on top of Benny's head, lightly squishing down his boisterous black hair so it pushed over his forehead and crept toward his eyebrows. Benny looked aghast. He frowned at Ruth. Then it was her turn, but her black curls were tightly braided into two ropes that hung down her back. Her father's hand felt warm against the part on her scalp. "And this is Ruth. Say hello, Ruth!"

"Hello, Ruth!" she said. Her first English joke.

All the kids laughed, and Ruth felt a little warmer.

Whatever volume the children had employed at the bus stop was amplified by a factor of a thousand once they got on the bus. Benny, who always left for school five minutes early back home so he could walk with Tiago and pretend he didn't have a little sister at all, nestled in beside Ruth and leaned his forehead on the seat in front.

In the first-grade classroom though, Ruth had an easier time following the words of the teacher, who spoke more carefully than the children. Within a few days, Ruth was able to recite her shapes and colors in English; she could sing the alphabet and count to one hundred. And she quickly identified her mortal enemies in the classroom: Timmy O'Brien, who had a broad, pink face and blond hair that was always damp around the front, and laughed every time Ruth tried to pronounce a word with an *r* in it. Their classroom was fraught with squares, triangles, green trees, red roses, her own name, for God's sake—a veritable minefield of *r*'s. And Alice García, who Ruth initially mistook as a potential friend because of her black hair and her last name, but who eagerly disabused Ruth of this notion by flipping her hair literally into Ruth's face whenever Ruth had the misfortune of being behind her on the walking line. Nevertheless, by the end of the first week, Ruth already felt less shy speaking English, and she had made three sweet friends: Kathy, Jennifer, and Jenny. On the playground, they skipped rope together and admired Ruth's braids. The questions they asked about her life before St. Louis were minimal and inoffensive. Their interests tended more toward hopscotch and cookies than intimate personal history.

But Benny still sat beside Ruth every afternoon on the bus, and even began insisting on the window seat, using Ruth as a human shield between him and the other kids. She tried asking him how it was going, how he liked third grade, if there were any boys like Tiago who liked baseball, but Benny wouldn't respond to her English efforts. So she switched to the comfort of Spanish, to see if she could draw him out and soothe him, but he shushed her sharply, looking quickly around the bus to determine whether anyone had heard her.

By the end of their second week, it was clear that Benny was not adjusting well. Their parents were summoned. Mama wore a lime-green linen dress with a slim belt at her waist and high heels, and Dad wore a suit. It didn't help.

It was a Friday afternoon, and class had been dismissed for the week, but Ruth and Benny stayed behind to await their parents' meeting with the principal, Mr. Parnacki. They sat on chairs just outside the closed door of Mr. Parnacki's office, but they could hear every word the grown-ups exchanged inside. The principal felt that Benny needed to move back a year, to the second grade.

"He's such a smart kid, though," Dad insisted. "He was a top student at his school in San Juan."

"Well, I don't know what their curriculum is like over there," Mr. Parnacki said, "but he's way behind his third-grade classmates here."

Their mother was uncharacteristically quiet.

"But he's already one of the older kids in the grade. If you move him back, he'll be more than a year older than his classmates." Their father's voice was grim behind the door. "That would be mortifying for him."

"Well, perhaps a little embarrassment will provide the motivation he needs then," Mr. Parnacki said, "to learn English."

Benny leaned over nervously, elbows on knees. "What are they saying?" he whispered to Ruth in Spanish.

She paused. Then shrugged.

In the car on the way home, Benny fiddled with the roll-down knob on the window handle, flicking it repeatedly with his finger. Ruth watched the black plastic wheel spin, and wondered how much Benny understood of what their parents were discussing in the front seat. She wondered if he was even listening, or if he was really as entranced by the window's mechanics as he seemed to be.

"I know it's difficult, Rafaela," Dad was saying, "but you have to learn English too."

"I already know English," their mother snapped. "I am speaking to you in English right now, am I not? Is this not English?"

The light ahead was about to turn red, and their father stepped on the brakes harder than he needed to. Ruth noticed his fingers grow paler as he gripped the steering wheel.

"You know what I mean, Rafaela! Damn, I'm not your enemy. I'm not trying to make you miserable."

Their mother sighed loudly, and the noise of her breath was almost a shape in the small Datsun. It crowded the car.

"Of course you already speak English." Dad's voice was softer now, the best version of her father, who Ruth recognized from the bedtime stories. "You speak English very beautifully," he said in Spanish. He lifted her mother's hand and kissed her knuckles. Then he returned to English. "But you haven't practiced in years. And the kids are struggling, Benny especially. You heard what the principal said. They need more practice, we all need to practice if we're going to make this work."

Mama did not respond, but Ruth watched her swivel her face away from their father and toward the window. The car radio was off and Benny was still spinning the plastic wheel. *Click. Whirr. Click. Whirr.* Their father glanced into the rearview mirror and lifted his voice to address all three of them.

"So that's it," he said, "I have to put my foot down, it's the only way everyone is going to learn, okay? No more Spanish at home. From now on, we all speak English. Solamente inglés, Benny, ¿me entiendes?"

Click. Whirr. "What about the bike you promised me?" Benny said in Spanish.

Their mother leaned forward and rolled her window down, propping her elbow on the ledge. "I have a headache," she said, her English clipped and precise.

Ruth felt something like a strangulation in her throat, but she knew it was only sadness. Even at six years, fifty-one weeks, and three days old, Ruth was a pragmatist. She knew that tight, uncomfortable feeling she had when she swallowed wasn't actually going to kill her.

Ruth enjoyed her seventh birthday party very much despite its overarching social failure. They held it at a nearby park on a sunny Saturday afternoon, and Kathy, Jennifer, and Jenny all showed up on time. But in a confusing twist, they all piled out of the same station wagon, and Jenny's mom waved goodbye from the parking lot, beeping her horn twice before pulling away.

"Where is she going?" Ruth's mother wondered aloud while the three girls scampered across the grass in a cloud of excitement to embrace the birthday girl. They deposited their brightly wrapped gifts on the crowded picnic table and dragged Ruth away to the monkey bars without greeting Ruth's parents. Ruth stole glances at Mama and Dad while she hung upside down by her knees, her braids sweeping the mulch beneath her. Ruth's father stood at the grill holding a spatula, staring into the meat and pretending not to notice her mother's growing turbulence behind him. He tipped a brown bottle into his mouth and took a swig. Meanwhile, her mother turned in circles, fussing around the table, attempting to disguise the fact that she'd prepared way too much food. She rearranged some of the bowls and platters on the table, hid a few things away in the shopping bags and a cooler that sat in the shade nearby. Then she called Benny over and loaded him down with items to return to the car. Benny, who'd been kicking his soccer ball against the fence at the tennis court, did not complain because doing so would have required him to speak English.

Ruth watched while Benny walked back to the car with his arms full. Behind him, their mother folded her own arms tightly and began talking to Ruth's father, whose only response was to take another sip from his brown bottle. Ruth's mother gathered more words and ejected them through the upturned line of her mouth, shaking her head, and gesturing tightly from the knot of her folded arms. Ruth was glad the monkey bars were far enough away that she and her friends could not hear what was being said, though Ruth suspected from her mother's body language that the words were being spoken in Spanish anyway. Ruth's father finally turned and shrugged, said something in response, causing Ruth's mother to renew her attack on the bowls and platters across the table, and this time, the sounds of slamming and banging did carry to where Kathy and Jennifer were now taking turns spinning on one knee, whirling impossibly around the parallel bar like the second hand of a clock. Ruth returned her attention to her friends because how could she not? It seemed impossible to spin like that, seemed to flout the laws of gravity, that neither of them flew off and slammed their head into the ground, fastened onto the bar only by one crooked knee. Ruth was awestruck. She righted herself and dropped down into the mulch, bouncing on her toes.

"Teach me!" she said, climbing up and cocking one bent leg over the bar like her friends.

Jenny's mother returned promptly at five o'clock, and Ruth's three friends all hugged her, wished her a happy birthday, thanked her parents, and then scrambled back across the grass and into the waiting station wagon at the curb. The mother honked and waved again, and Ruth's mother managed to lift her own hand in salute, but did not manage to fix the appropriate expression of friendliness onto her face when she did so. Once the guests were gone, Mama was finally free to give liberal expression to the dismay she'd been attempting (failing) to conceal all afternoon.

"I've never seen anything like it," Mama said. "Who drops their small children to a party without even coming in for a drink or a bite to eat? Without even coming over to say hello? She's never even met us!"

Ruth's father held the black garbage bag open while Benny collected paper plates and cups from the table and tumbled them in. Dad tossed his empty bottle in too. No one answered Mama because they understood that her questions were not meant to be answered.

"For all that woman knows, we could be axe murderers," Mama said. "They might have returned to find their daughters had been axe-murdered on the playground!"

Ruth wondered whether all four of them were axe murderers in this scenario, but she kept the question to herself. She knew from experience that she might be able to short-circuit some portion of her mother's outburst if she made herself excessively helpful and asked for nothing in return. So she scampered all around the table, snapping lids onto Tupperware, screwing tops onto glass bottles. She drained her own cup of orange soda before tossing it. Ruth's mother directed the operation using only one finger to point here and there. She did so while packing up the enormous leftover supply of napkins and plates, and without taking a break from her rant.

"But at least this woman came close enough to observe that her child was in fact attending a birthday party!" Mama said. "What about the other mothers? Did they even know where their children were today, or who they were with?"

"I'm going to need another beer," Dad said quietly to Benny, who set down the cooler he was hauling to the car so Dad could retrieve another bottle.

"You knew about this!" Mama finally articulated the accusation that had been simmering just beneath her words.

"I what?" Dad used a contraption from his keychain to pop the lid off his beer.

"You knew! You must have known that this is what birthday parties are like here."

Dad flicked the bottle cap toward the nearby garbage bag.

"Rafaela," he said, in a tone that indicated the exhaustion of his patience. "All birthday parties are different. Just the way not every party in Puerto Rico is the same, not every party in St. Louis is the same either. Sometimes the families come, sometimes it's just the kids. Did you tell the mothers? That they were all invited, to bring the whole family? Or did you just assume?"

Ruth and Benny both stopped moving because they could sense the shift their father had just incited, and they knew that when Mama was enraged, she was like a pterodactyl, laser-focused on her target, but also highly attuned to any peripheral movement. Mama closed her lips tightly for a moment, as if she might wish to stop the words that were gathering like a storm in her mouth, but really she was only giving them a moment to amass strength.

"Oh," she said after a beat. "So this is my fault? I should have known? That these crazy people send their children off to spend whole afternoons alone in the park with strangers? How would I know that, why would anyone know that?"

"Christ, Rafaela, I'm not blaming you. It's no one's fault, there's no fault here. Calm down."

Ruth closed her eyes. *Never, ever tell Mama to calm down,* she silently admonished her father.

"Calm down?!" Mama's voice now could only be described as a shriek. "You dragged me away from my home, brought me to this ugly place, failed to help me adjust, failed to warn me about the simplest, most idiotic things. You watched me cook for the last three days—you knew I was making enough food for two dozen people, and you didn't think to warn me that the families wouldn't come, that we might only have three guests? You let me humiliate myself, Peter! And now you tell me to *calm down?*"

Benny broke his frozen posture just enough to swivel his head around, to see if anyone else was close enough to witness this domestic carnage. There were two blond teenagers lobbing a ball back and forth on the tennis court, but they didn't seem to notice the warfare in the picnic area. Dad slung a hand into the pocket of his jeans, tipped his head back, and drained his beer in one long gulp. Then he tossed it with a clank into the bag.

"All right, that's enough," he said quietly. "You're being ridiculous." He leaned down to tie the handles of the bag. "It's one thing to feel confused, but it's another thing to blame me. The party was great. Right, pumpkin?" He looked at Ruth, who attempted to freeze even deeper into her body. "You had fun?"

Ruth moved her head perhaps an inch, though she couldn't say herself whether the movement constituted a shake or a nod. She'd had so much fun. It was the best day she'd had since they left San Juan. In fact it was the best day she could remember. But wasn't it some kind of betrayal to admit that in this context?

"Grab those two bags, Benny, let's pack up the car." Her father pointed to the remaining shopping bags on the table. "I'll bring the cooler. Ruth, bring those beautiful presents from your friends. We'll get 'em home and open 'em."

Their father took the garbage bag and cooler, turned, and headed for the Datsun, but Benny and Ruth did not move. They waited for Mama to sanction their father's instructions. The beat expanded into a few seconds, and Ruth felt herself stretching toward the three colorful packages on the table. She would not step toward them, would not lift them into her arms.

"Go on," Mama finally released them from the spell. "Do as your father says."

Chapter Five

~

Palisades, New York
2009

Three days after her thirty-eighth birthday, Ruth came in from work and was unbuckling her heels by the door when her phone rang. She sighed, glancing at her watch. A call at this time usually meant that Thomas was going to be late to pick up the kids from after-school care, so could she please do it this evening, and he'd make it up to her tomorrow? She had to dig around in her purse to find the phone, and sure enough, it was her husband.

"Let me guess," she said.

Except it wasn't Thomas. There was an unfamiliar voice on her husband's phone.

"Hi, is this Thomas Hayes's wife?"

"Um." Ruth pulled the phone briefly away from her ear to double-check the screen, an attempt to relieve her confusion. "Yes," she said. "Who's this?"

"My name's Travis, I'm the manager at Future Fitness." It took Ruth a moment to remember that was the name of Thomas's gym. "I'm sorry to say this, but your husband is on the way to Nyack Hospital."

"Wait," she said, because that was always Ruth's first word in a crisis, a plea against time. Wait. Then, "How . . . why do you have his phone?"

A stupid question, precipitated by her first wave of assumptions: a sprained ankle, a torn ACL, a concussion, none of which might explain this stranger's voice on Thomas's phone.

"I'll bring the phone with me and meet you at the hospital," the stranger said. "I'm following the ambulance."

Ruth's capacity for language dried up at the word *ambulance*, which did its job of escorting her brain in the correct direction. She didn't respond, didn't ask what happened. She grabbed her keys from the bowl by the front door where she'd tossed them not one minute earlier, and slipped her feet back into the recently abandoned heels. She didn't need to ask questions anyway, as she pulled the front door closed behind her and realized she'd forgotten her coat. Travis was still talking.

"He collapsed on the treadmill," the man said. "We called 911 immediately, and the paramedics were there within minutes."

Ruth could hear a strain in this man's voice now, the things he was hesitant to say. She could hear the hard pulsing of his adrenaline through the phone line.

"I did CPR until the paramedics arrived."

Ruth made it to Nyack Hospital in just under nine minutes, but it didn't matter. Thomas was dead before the ambulance arrived, before they needlessly unloaded his stretcher into the emergency room. He was dead before his forehead bounced off the end of the treadmill, even, before his body was flung away from the machine and into the wall behind. Thomas was dead almost a full second before his collapse.

"A brain aneurysm," the medical examiner later explained. "Not a heart attack after all." There seemed to be some suggestion that this information might be a comfort to Ruth. She couldn't imagine why.

When she called her mother from the emergency room to ask her to pick the kids up from after-school care and bring them home, Ruth could not bring herself to say why. She was not yet able to form the nightmare words, *Thomas is dead*.

"Please, Mama," she said instead. "I'm at the hospital with Thomas. Can you get the kids home and feed them dinner?"

When Ruth arrived home alone, her mother was in the kitchen with the boys, and Daisy was in the bath. Mama took one look at Ruth's face and whisked the boys into the family room to watch some unprecedented school-night cartoons. The flowers Thomas had bought for Ruth's birthday three days ago were still in their vase on the counter. They hadn't yet started to wilt. Ruth knew that technically the flowers were already dead when Thomas presented them to her in all their raucous colors on the evening of her birthday. She knew, despite the brightness of their scent and the springy resilience of their petals, that the flowers were dead the moment they were separated from their roots and cut from the soil. Of course, none of this had occurred to her until Thomas was also dead, and then it seemed impossible to reconcile the two discordant truths. Her mother returned to the kitchen, and Ruth crumpled into a silent howl in her mama's arms. It lasted a very long time, or so it seemed to both Ruth and her mother. And during the moments when Ruth thought she might get ahold of herself, when she dried her face and took some breaths, it was then that she'd catch sight of those fucking flowers, and lose it all over again. She could not come to terms with the sheer audacity of them, being dead but still here, fragrant and vivid. Some derailed and broken part of Ruth's brain kept trying to swap one death for the other, to bring Thomas back. There grew a kind of grinding in her ears, and the panic was like nothing she'd ever known. It had the quality of falling and falling without landing, a constantly renewing cycle, the insistent terror of waiting for an impact that had, in fact, already arrived.

Vic was almost eleven. Daisy was eight. And five-year-old Charlie was just small enough that he still requested "uppy" when he didn't want to walk, but plenty big enough that the clinging weight of meeting this request was difficult for Ruth when she was wearing heels. The children didn't understand that Thomas wasn't coming back. Even Vic, who was perhaps old enough to perceive the fundamental permanence of death, didn't seem to grasp the finality of their new family circumstances. So those first few days also had a surprising condition, a kind of cottony ease. It was awful, and Ruth was besieged by the constant rumble of horror, but the children were more manageable than she would have expected. Through the funeral and burial, the kids barely cried. In fact they smiled and laughed and played with their friends. Daisy wore a little crown of flowers at the church and a navy-blue dress, which Ruth had never seen before. She didn't know where it came from, who had dressed her daughter that morning. Charlie squeezed Ruth's hand and swung her arm while they followed Thomas's casket down the same aisle where she'd walked in her wedding gown just thirteen years ago. Yes, the kids held up well, even in the moments when Ruth did not.

Right up until those birthday flowers began to droop, until they turned brittle in their vase and fuzzy along their stems. Ruth couldn't bring herself to throw them away, of course, even as the scent of rot crept out of the vase and permeated the kitchen. Throwing them out would mean accepting the time that had elapsed since Thomas had drawn his last breath. These were the last flowers her husband would ever give her.

"These flowers stink, Mom," Vic told her one afternoon while he sat at the kitchen counter with his math notebook in front of him. She'd taken a leave of absence from work, but she had yet to learn all the harrowing new things she'd need to learn in Thomas's sudden absence. The 401(k)s, oil changes, how to work the pressure washer, when and why to work the pressure washer. Ruth's inner feminist was aghast at how much she'd left to her husband, how much she hadn't even noticed she'd left to her husband. Thomas had also been the one to tackle math with the kids. Vic reached out and touched one of the dried flower petals, which quietly clattered to the counter in a small shower of pollen. Even this minor disruption amplified the odor.

"I know, sweetie," Ruth said.

"So why don't you throw them out?" He swiveled on his stool.

"Let's just focus on your fractions."

Of course, the suspended nature of her children's grief did not last, and when the dam did burst, no one was spared. There was Vic on his knees beside the open dishwasher, both sobbing and somehow refusing to cry all at once, the scene infused with the sour-milk stink of the dirty dishes. There was Charlie breaking the binding on his favorite storybook, rending the sewn pages from their spine and whipping them across the room against the wall. And there was little Daisy standing stock-still in the grocery store with a box of cereal in her hand, her tears making tiny, starshaped splats on the linoleum, her pink sneakers frozen in place. Ruth's own grief was a marathon, characterized mostly by filthy sweatpants and a grueling, shuddering exhaustion.

In time, Ruth learned to mold herself into a vessel both steely and soft, learned to cleave open her own heart so her children could throw in their sorrows. She learned about the 401(k)s and how to check the oil in her own car. She sold the pressure washer to a neighbor who promised to loan it back if she ever needed it again. Why would she ever need it again? Some things Ruth had no desire to learn.

There was a small life insurance policy that Thomas had insisted they buy.

"We don't need life insurance because you're not allowed to die," she'd told him when he first suggested it.

"Ah, you'd miss me," he said.

"Of course! Plus I'd never be able to quit my job if you were dead."

"Joke's on you, missus," he answered. "You can't quit your job anyway!"

They'd laughed then, the two comfortable idiots they'd been. The policy payout wasn't nearly enough. Ruth and Thomas had both made decent money, and Ruth had inherited a good sum from her aunt when she was still in college too. But they'd spent most of that on a house they otherwise could never have afforded, in the best school district, right on the banks of the Hudson River, with the property taxes to match. They even had a boat dock where they tied up kayaks in the summertime. If Ruth and Thomas had lived almost anywhere else in the country on their salaries, they'd have been rich. But here in the barely suburbs of New York City, the money went as fast as it came, so their lifestyle was much the same as any other fortunate family with two working parents, a steep mortgage, and three kids: mostly great with a solid undercurrent of constant worry.

When she started *The Widow's Kitchen*, Ruth hadn't intended for it to generate income. After all, she was no longer a woman who could afford to indulge impractical ideas, even if she'd previously been inclined to that sort of thing, which she had not. And now, if she hoped to successfully raise three kids on her own, she'd have to be intentional and pragmatic in all of her goals. Goal number one was to keep their life and their home intact. Ruth would have to invest the life insurance payout perfectly. She'd have to reach for and earn every possible promotion at work. She'd have to budget and scrimp—no more organic veggies, no more ordering in on Friday nights, no more piano lessons or vacations. And she'd have to have lots of help at home.

Mama moved in to Charlie's old room without even pretending there were other alternatives. Just for a year, they said, until Ruth could find a new rhythm, like learning how to run with one leg. Mama would be her prosthesis. They bought bunk beds for Vic's room, which then became the boys' room, even though Charlie never slept there because he climbed into Ruth's bed every night, often even before she got there herself. She'd come in to find him sweating beneath the covers in his footed pajamas, radiating heat into Thomas's side of the bed. She would rearrange his limbs and stroke his hair away from his sticky forehead, and Charlie wouldn't stir. She never carried him back to his new bunk bed.

The year went by, and then another two. They found their rhythm. The kids learned to eat Mama's cooking without complaint, and Ruth helped by doing whatever meal prep she could on weekends. At work, Ruth wondered if she got the first promotion because they felt sorry for her, but when she got the second one she knew she'd earned it, and perhaps she wouldn't have earned it if Thomas were still alive. Perhaps she wouldn't have worked so vigorously and with as much purpose. She brought that same level of energy to their domestic life, where she budgeted and saved and managed and planned while Mama flew around behind the scenes like the energetic new wife she'd never been when she had actually been a new wife. But Ruth didn't know that then. What she knew was just boundless gratitude to Mama, for doing all the invisible work that made it possible for Ruth to earn those increasing paychecks.

During that time when Mama lived with them, *The Widow's Kitchen* was only for weekends. It was their together time, when the kids were still small, and it helped Ruth cope with the amnesia of grief, the fact that she could no longer recall her husband's flaws, the way he left his whiskers in the sink after shaving or used his knife to ferry crumbs into the butter. On his worst days, Thomas had refused to articulate his emotions, which did nothing to impede the actual existence of those emotions, which then presented themselves in all sorts of subtle physical cues, ones Ruth had to interpret like some kind of magical diviner. A slammed cabinet might mean it was his deceased alcoholic father's birthday. An extra intense session at the gym might mean something had gone wrong at work. The one time she'd suggested he might benefit from therapy, to talk about his difficult childhood, Thomas rolled his eyes and called her a real *American* as if the word were a slur. Yes, sometimes this marriage had been exhausting, exasperating, but now that it was over, all Ruth could remember was the love.

So she would bake or build or paint or meal prep with her mama and her kids, all five of them together, and Ruth would document their projects in photographs she uploaded online. The pictures were artful, beautiful, and anonymous. She never showed her children's faces, but there might be a dimpled hand stealing a warm cookie off one edge of a cooling rack. Or the curve of Daisy's ear with a tendril of hair hanging down might frame a shot of some charred tomatoes with a brick of fresh mozzarella by a rainy windowpane. Or five colorful aprons hanging on their hooks by the paneled pantry, the sixth hook, Thomas's hook, always empty. The empty placeholder became their trademark, a reminder of why the beauty they were seeking together was so important. A spare plate, an empty seat at the table, a single dry paintbrush amid the splashes of color.

For Ruth, *The Widow's Kitchen* became a kind of Instagram meditation, a rumination on absence, a way to document the dynamic nature of their grief, how it changed and expanded and contracted and made room for new adventures, but never ever disappeared. She didn't dream that a project that felt so intimate and personal to her would develop a following, that it would mean anything to anyone else. Ruth wanted only to identify beauty in their lives, to insist on it, to remind herself and her children that beauty was still possible after annihilation. Sometimes she was so good at this artistry that the kids barely recognized their own experiences when they looked back at Ruth's photos.

"But wasn't that the day the smoke alarm went off?" Daisy would ask, confused by the loveliness of her mother's posts. "Wasn't that the morning Charlie threw up in my cleats?"

This was a sentiment that would become more strident and pointed as Daisy grew older and more critical of Ruth, but in those early days it presented mostly as bafflement. Still, the enterprise wasn't artificial. It was simply that the force of Ruth's need for beauty created a whole new and separate reality from the one in which they were living (and sometimes barfing). In the photographs, nothing was ever stained or streaked or smeared. The sink was never piled with dishes, Ruth never skipped a shower. Vic never burned the flat of his arm taking a tray of homemade croutons out of the oven, never dropped the tray, never sent breadcrumbs scattering to the four corners of the kitchen, beneath the fridge and the range, attracting a family of mice that would take weeks to evict. On Instagram, Ruth never cried or sighed or became irritated when her children didn't follow simple instructions. She never said *shit* or *damn* in front of them. In *The Widow's Kitchen*, everything was perfect. Ripe, juicy, colorful, clean.

When she reached a hundred thousand followers, Ruth was amazed. When she ticked over four hundred thousand, she started to wonder if this crazy little project might have some staying power. The day she reached a million, she and the kids made and photographed a whole row of little white cakes with fireworks on top sculpted from colored sugar, and then ate them for dinner with their hands.

Eventually, Ruth would understand the mostly wonderful reality that her online life had become more lucrative than her full-time job. She would study how best to negotiate with vendors and advertisers, how to use analytics to increase her engagement, how to navigate the minefield of being beholden to a fickle public for her livelihood. Where once she shot video whenever and however the mood struck, Ruth would now spend time developing *creatives*. She'd learn to use the word *creative* not only as a noun, but as a noun that was not a person. She would weigh the benefits of being her own boss, setting her own schedule, working from home, and making more money, against the fearful prospect of giving up a steady paycheck and good healthcare benefits at the same moment when her three kids were losing interest in participating in *The Widow's Kitchen*. She would opt for the hustle, remain fluid and attentive. She would have lean years and flush years, but would work relentlessly, adapt relentlessly, and never lose sight of the risk. Mostly, it would pay off.

While her unexpected fan base grew, so did the kids. Charlie went on being Charlie, though he did eventually stop demanding "uppy," which Ruth did not miss at all, despite Mama's predictions to the contrary. He devoted himself to tiaras, pirouettes, and glitter. When he and Daisy broke into Ruth's makeup cabinet, Daisy went for the corals and nudes while Charlie slathered on the brightest colors he could find. He'd emerge from the bathroom like a full Pegasus, and he never met a rhinestone he didn't love.

Charlie never came out to his family because he didn't have to; it was always clear who he was, from those earliest diapering days. But he did rebrand himself in the seventh grade, during his middle school production of *Beauty and the Beast*. The night before the final dress rehearsal, Charlie brought home the program, and in the space just to the right of his character Lumiere, instead of Charlie Hayes, he was listed as "Carlos Hayes-Acuña."

Ruth was sitting at the kitchen counter with the program opened in front of her, staring at her son's modified name, not only the latinized first name, but also the addition of her mother's maiden name, tacked onto the end like a vestigial tail. Charlie leaned on his elbows across from her, looking from her face to the paper and back, trying to gauge her reaction while she adjusted her glasses and cleared her throat. As was often the case, Ruth found herself stalling for time while she tried to craft an appropriate reaction to her youngest child. She had no idea what to make of this.

"Well?" Charlie grinned. "What do you think?"

Ruth cleared her throat again, an unconscious signal of her displeasure that caused both Daisy and Vic, who usually only feigned interest in Charlie's plays, to come peer over her shoulder. Ruth thought she was being subtle with her bewilderment, but her kids always let her know when she was wrong, which was pretty much all the time.

Vic looked down at the program and then clapped Charlie on the shoulder. "¡Ayyy, Carlitos!" her oldest child said approvingly.

It was true that they called Charlie *Carlitos* sometimes, and when he cried: Bendito Carlitos; and when they thought he was being an annoying little shit: Pendejito Carlitos; and when all the teachers immediately fell in love with him: Guapito Carlitos; and when time was of the essence, sometimes they called him just Lito. But more often they called him Charlie. Never Charles, and certainly never Carlos. So, as monikers go, Ruth thought it was a stretch. She took a noisy breath, a sigh she performed at least a dozen times a day, and which could indicate pleasure, irritation, hunger, or exhaustion. Her kids called this sigh El Suspiro, and they were forever lampooning it.

Vic nudged Daisy and nodded at their mother. "El Suspiro!" he whispered.

They leaned in.

"But don't you want people to know it's you who's playing Lumiere?" Ruth asked carefully.

"Everybody knows it's me," Charlie said. He did a little jazz dance with invisible top hat and cane. Then he shrugged. "Anyway, I've always been Carlitos."

It was true.

"Yes, but Carlos?"

He shrugged again. "Sounds more grown-up."

Was it silly for her to feel slightly abandoned by this? What Ruth's kids didn't know (because not even Ruth herself knew) was that, when her parents got divorced in the Midwest in 1982, there had been endless grown-up discussions about what to do with Mama's name.

For Ruth's mother, the married last name would've been infinitely harder to part with than the man. When they first got engaged, Rafaela had balked at the idea of trading her family names for Brennan. She'd never known a woman who'd changed her name after marriage—that just wasn't a thing women did in Puerto Rico. But her groom had insisted, so after lengthy conversations about why this was so important to Peter, they reached a compromise wherein Rafaela and their future children would have Peter's name, but would also retain Papamío's. In legal documentation then, Rafaela and her children became Brennan y Acuña. But in St. Louis, because the second surname was unconventional, because it confused and sometimes alarmed people, they'd fallen out of the habit of using it. In St. Louis they became the Brennans. And then after the divorce, Rafaela had wanted to carry on sharing her children's name, but more than that, she knew because she'd witnessed it: the name Brennan provided all of them with a small measure of protection against prejudice, or at least it bought them some time. So after deep consideration, Mama had chosen not to return to her maiden names. They all remained Brennan.

Then in college, Ruth had briefly considered resurrecting the family name she'd left behind in Puerto Rico when she was six years old, the name she'd been born into. In her angsty, romantic youth, she toyed with the idea of reclaiming the lost Acuña half. But then she met and married Thomas anyway, and swapped the whole messy business for Hayes, and she did so without any of the cultural dissonance her mother had endured. In fact she did it without much deliberation at all. And yet, Hayes was a name Ruth had felt ambivalent about until Thomas died. In her grief, though, she wore her husband's name like a devotion, a talisman. She would never take it off.

So seeing it hyphenated there in a theater program for a middle school production of *Beauty and the Beast*, shoehorned between "Carlos" and "Acuña," in such a way that the reader would have almost no choice but to mispronounce Hayes as "Ay-ez," caused a little ribbon of alarm to unfurl itself across the back of Ruth's neck. It felt like a minor sacrilege. She couldn't explain this properly to Charlie because she wasn't fully aware of it herself. She knew only that it made her uncomfortable. She slid the program back across the counter to her son and tried to shake some bright energy into her voice.

"Whatever makes you happy," she said.

Charlie looked back at her blankly, and Ruth knew she had failed some test she'd been unaware she was taking. She reviewed her previous statement. *Whatever makes you happy.* Supportive. Innocuous. What had she missed?

"What's wrong?" she asked.

Charlie scrunched up his mouth and forehead. "Just, it seems like you don't understand."

He was right, Ruth did not understand.

The lesson motherhood was now teaching her was that it was no longer enough to placate your kid, even though when she was Charlie's age, no adult in her life would've dreamed of placating her. Ruth grew up, as all previous generations had done for the breadth of human history, at a time when kids were expected to appease their parents. But then, when it was her turn to be the parent, she discovered that in the space of a few years, the balance had tipped entirely; her kids were not interested in appeasing her in the least. For Ruth and her peers, it was never going to be their turn. And worse, she realized it wasn't enough that she'd mastered the art of mollifying her own children. Now she had to do it convincingly, internally. It wasn't enough to say what they wanted to hear. She was required to believe it.

"It's my heritage," Charlie said simply.

His heritage! Ruth was aware of an unreasonable internal voice suggesting, *Your heritage is contemporary, suburban self-indulgence!* She knew that voice was unfair. She muzzled it, duct-taped it, kicked it in the ribs, and threw it off a cliff. She reached for a more reasonable voice instead. She would've liked to invoke Thomas, the miraculous joy of choosing baby names together, the lilt of his voice the day he first said *Charlie.* But that memory was so sacred Ruth couldn't quite call the words into her mouth.

"It's just, changing your name is a big deal," she said instead.

"It's really not," Charlie said flatly. "Lots of kids do it nowadays."

Ruth shook her head, her mouth barely open, empty of anything reasonable to say. What a humiliating time in the world to be a parent—when, after millennia of value, generational wisdom was suddenly meaningless.

Her son picked up the program and read his new-and-improved name out loud, *Carlos Hayes-Acuña.* The sound of it produced a tiny flare of anger in Ruth, which surprised her. She couldn't fully interpret that feeling, but here was an ember: she had lost *Acuña* at a time when she had no choice. It was a name that meant something to her, and not only because it was Papamío's, but also because in a single mouthful it contained all the music of Puerto Rico, of home. She'd lost it or it had been taken from her, but in any case, the name was gone. So what right did Charlie have to take it up so carelessly, to try it on as if it were a costume?

"I'm proud of it, Mom," he said. "It's cool to be Puerto Rican."

Which struck Ruth as such a confounding non sequitur that she was unable to respond at all. Charlie took advantage of her silence to seal the conversation shut.

"Anyway, the program's already printed."

Chapter Six

~

San Juan, Puerto Rico
2023

Daisy's soul is still in her body, but she can't tell if that body is still fit for the world. She doesn't feel cold or hot. The amplifying intensity of the storm does not exist on the same plane where Daisy truly is. There is no weather here. No blasting gale of wind. No sheets of hard rain. There is no pain either, in the wreckage of bones and skin that encase her. She is both conscious and unconscious because she can sense some of what is happening to her, even though she is unable to respond in any of the customary human ways. She can almost see the flashing of the lights when the ambulance arrives. There are voices, masculine and feminine, that she can hear but not apprehend. There are hands on her skin, which she is aware of but can't exactly feel. There is a thin-drawn quality, a warp of space, a perception of herself as a rubber band, pulling taut and then loosening into a dangerous and terrifying wobble. Her soul ascends and descends with hideous speed, over and over, shooting into the atmosphere and then plummeting back into the stillness of her body, as if she's trying to defibrillate herself. Back on Earth, the hands that are working on her body affix her to some kind of board, and when the board is lifted, her soul falls out of her again. Heedless of gravity, it plunges upward, and this time, it feels too far.

They are sliding her body into the back of the ambulance. There is the clicking and beeping of some medical machinery nearby. Daisy understands that her soul has to return now, right this instant, that they can't close the ambulance doors yet, that they cannot leave without it or it might never find her again. *Not yet, not yet. Wait!* Daisy wants to scream.

Her voice is not available.

§

When Daisy arrived in San Juan almost two years ago, she brought some secret, far-fetched plans and a solitary suitcase of secondhand clothes with her. It was her second attempt to move to Puerto Rico in as many years, and despite her mother's rigorous grievances, she had every intention of making this one stick. Her cousin Stefani, whose entrance into college in Florida was delayed by the pandemic, had finally gone, leaving a vacant bedroom behind.

"You'll take Stefani's room, stay with us!" Tío Benny said.

When Daisy was little and they'd come to visit on summer vacations, she would cry whenever it was time to go home. On the last night of the last visit before her dad died, Daisy and Stefani made a set of handcuffs for themselves out of gray construction paper and a stapler. They chained themselves together. They ate dinner and brushed their teeth that way, slipping out of the handcuffs only momentarily when it was time to wriggle into their nightgowns. They went to sleep wearing them, and then woke up heartbroken when they discovered they had ripped their paper chain during the night. Mom was unable to conceal her impatience with the whole display.

"You can't pack wearing handcuffs!" she said. "Even paper ones!"

It was Dad who took Daisy onto his lap, smoothed her hair, and kissed the top of her head. He allowed her to make a damp spot on his clean shirt with her tears.

"We'll come back again real soon," he said.

But he never did come back. That was his last time, his last sunburned nose. Daisy remembered that every time she arrived in Puerto Rico and then again every time she left. She would never take it for granted that there would be another trip. She was bereft every time, just in case. Mom tried telling her that it wasn't necessarily Puerto Rico she loved.

"It's only because we're here on vacation," Mom reasoned. "We spend our time here doing all this fun stuff together, sleeping in, going to the beach. Of course you love it. If we lived here, things would be different. I'd have to work, you'd have to go to school. You wouldn't be having sleepovers with Stefani every night."

But Daisy had always known Mom was wrong about this. Or actually that she was right, but it didn't matter. Because for as long as she could remember, Daisy had wanted to move to San Juan. The draw was partly Stefani and family and fun, yes, but it was also the fizz of energy, the light, the language, the flavors of the food. The chorus of nighttime sounds, the smell of hot asphalt and rain and flamboyán trees. It was the gestures and mannerisms she'd always presumed were particular to her own family, her own self, until she began to see them in abundance here: the way her mom always scrunched up her nose when she wanted Daisy to repeat herself, the way the stockperson at the grocery store might place her hand on Daisy's forearm before directing her toward the olives she needed in aisle seven. It was the way communal pride emerged here in hard times, as a consequence of autonomy in a place that was supposedly not autonomous. It was grit and determination in balance with an ease of joy seldom seen in New York. It was the evolution of Daisy's understanding of this place that was just foreign enough to be an adventure and still familiar enough to feel like home. Daisy knew that it was Puerto Rico she had always been in love with, no matter what Mom thought. She felt more alive when she was here.

On her twelfth day of her second time moving to the island, Daisy went to see an apartment Benny was thinking of buying. The apartment was not on the market, but a friend of Benny's in Miami had inherited it from an elderly aunt, and wanted to sell it quickly with all of its contents. Benny was the guy for a purchase like that. He'd take care of everything and earn a significant price reduction for the effort of cleaning the place out, and then he'd earn even more when he sold whatever items were worth selling, and then he'd earn more again when he renovated and added the property to his rental portfolio, which had become an extremely lucrative second line of work for him. The deal was more or less done over the phone, so Daisy's only job was to show up at the building, meet the neighbor who would let her in, and then take some pictures for her uncle.

Despite the simplicity of this task, Daisy felt unqualified for it. But

Benny was busy and she was not, so he gave her a checklist and sent her on her way. She was to run water from every tap, locate every outlet and plug her phone charger into each one to test that they worked. She was to photograph the pipes beneath the sinks and the casings around the windows. She was to check the floorboards for warping or discoloration, any signs of water damage, search every corner for the tiniest hint of mold—even a single spore was unacceptable.

Daisy arrived at the small art-deco building with its curved balconies and geraniums in every window box, and she pressed the buzzer that said *Fernández*, waiting until a glamorous older woman appeared behind the glass. She was tall and stately with striking cheekbones, and her white hair had the personality of a skating cloud. She smiled warmly at Daisy, but refrained from opening the door until Daisy produced identification. After Daisy satisfied that requirement, the older woman twisted the handle and pulled the heavy door so Daisy could step inside. The woman smiled somewhat formally before turning to glide down the hallway, her loose hair and silken garments trailing behind her.

"You're much younger than I expected," Mrs. Fernández remarked over her shoulder. "You're thinking of buying this place?"

"Oh, not me," Daisy said. "My uncle. I'm just the eyes and ears."

"Oh, you're much more than that, I'm sure." The older woman winked at Daisy, pausing at the bottom of the steps and gesturing upward. "Second floor, it's the door on the left. Apartment 2B."

"Thank you!" Daisy said, but her hostess had already disappeared.

In front of apartment 2B there was a welcome mat in the shape of a sunflower, where Daisy slipped out of her sandals. She closed the door behind her and hung her tote bag from the knob. When she flicked the kitchen switch, she didn't expect it to generate light, but there was a pop followed by a mild hum as the long fluorescent bulb in the ceiling flared to life. Electricity was still on, and Daisy, too, felt suddenly lit from within.

This apartment was pristine and glorious and looked like a place where a woman wearing matte lipstick, kitten heels, and an apron might prepare a Bundt cake. The kitchen cabinets were a sunny yellow with chrome hardware, and the Formica countertops had the kind of sharp, pointy corners that hardly existed in Daisy's lifetime. Beyond the kitchen, the wall-to-wall carpet was orange and plush, and the sofa was olive-green velvet with doilies on both arms. Daisy stared at the living room wallpaper for a full three minutes, trying to determine whether the cascading geometric shapes were waterfalls or rainbows or fruit trees.

She stood transfixed for some further number of minutes, barely aware of the passage of time until she felt a gathering of sweat at the nape of her neck that reminded her she was here to do a job. She roused herself, retrieving her phone from her tote bag. But first, air-conditioning. She found the modern window unit, the apartment's only concession to the twenty-first century, and when she turned it on, it filled the small apartment with both cold air and enough white noise to stifle the passing traffic on the street below. Daisy unfolded her checklist and flattened it out against the counter. She was diligent in working her way through the list, but felt a stab of yearning each time she opened another cabinet and discovered inside a stack of plates ringed with palm leaves, or a set of colored glass tumblers in a weird miniature cart. Benny had to buy this apartment, he had to, and then she could rent it from him. *I need to never leave this place*, she thought. When she was finished and slipped her feet back into the sandals outside, she realized the welcome mat wasn't a sunflower at all; it was a daisy.

That night at home in Tío Benny's kitchen, she waited impatiently for her uncle to ask about the apartment. She'd already helped Tía Pamela clear the table and load the dishwasher. Benny was tired after a full day at the garage, but his energy for new real estate was inexhaustible. Daisy had been staying here for less than two weeks, and already she could tell that Benny and Pamela had an understanding: Benny could invest their savings in property as long as it was profitable and Pamela didn't have to hear or worry about it, ever. So Daisy waited.

"I'm taking Karl Marx for a walk." Her aunt kissed Benny on top of the head. Karl Marx was the French bulldog who filled in as their child now that all four of their kids had grown up and moved out, three to the mainland (including Stefani, who they all hoped would return after college), and one to Vieques. Daisy's arrival had done nothing to threaten Karl Marx's current position as favored child, and they all knew it. The door had barely clicked shut behind his stubby little tail before Benny asked to see the pictures of the apartment. Daisy opened her photo app and handed over the phone, trying to keep the tremor from her voice.

"It's in great condition." She stood up so she could look at the pictures again over her uncle's shoulder, as if she hadn't been staring at them all afternoon, as if she hadn't memorized every detail. "The whole building is in good condition, but the apartment itself is mint."

"Hmm." Benny made a noncommittal noise while he swiped through the pictures, pausing longer than necessary on the most boring ones, zooming in on pipes, on the spaces beneath the pipes. "Is that water?"

Daisy leaned down with a squint. "No, it's just a shadow. It was bone-dry."

"Wow, that is some wallpaper!" He said this without a trace of admiration.

Daisy nodded solemnly. He zoomed in on the carpet.

"Is that wall-to-wall?"

She nodded again.

He sighed. "I guess we could do laminate flooring in there." He zoomed in on the countertops, the cabinets. "But it'll be expensive enough to replace all the rest of this stuff."

"But why would you need to replace it when it's good as new?" Daisy asked.

He looked up at her with an arched eyebrow and did not reply until he came to the pictures of the bathroom, which was tiled to eye level with pink squares. The tub, toilet, and sink were also pink, and there were enormous pink flowers on the shower curtain.

"It's like a life-size version of Barbie's Dreamhouse," Benny said.

"Yes, exactly," Daisy said reverently.

"It's almost a shame it's in such good condition," Benny said. "No one's going to rent it like this."

"I will!" she answered too eagerly. Daisy swallowed loudly enough that they both heard the gulp in the otherwise quiet kitchen. "I'll rent it exactly like this, if you buy it. You wouldn't have to change a single thing. Literally nothing."

Benny looked from the screen to Daisy and back again, as if to gauge her seriousness. He zoomed in on the back of the pink toilet, where a crocheted cozy in the shape of an elaborate cake hid the spare roll of toilet paper. "Not even that?"

Daisy looked at him. "Especially not that."

He set the phone on the table and sat back in his chair, folding his arms.

"And what about all the old lady's stuff?" he asked.

"What about it?"

"Everything's still in the apartment, right? Like, everything? Her clothes, shoes?"

It was true there were prescription bottles in the medicine cabinet, clothes in the closet, books on the shelves, a definite odor coming from the fridge.

"I can take care of it," Daisy said. "I'll take care of all of it."

Benny nodded his head in an ambiguous way that didn't mean yes. It meant he was thinking about what she'd said.

"I mean, I really love it actually." Daisy said this because saying what she really meant would make her sound insane. *There is a newly formed cavern in my soul that will only be satisfied by the presence of this apartment in my life, by the presence of my life in this apartment.* "I would be really happy there," she said instead, reaching for an articulation that would make sense to a normal person. "The location is perfect, and you wouldn't have to invest time or money renovating it. You'd have it rented from day one."

She had a plan for the contents, too, but she didn't need to get into all that just now. Benny clicked her phone off and placed it face down on the table in front of him. Daisy sat back in her own chair and hopefully watched her uncle's face.

"Tell you what," he said after a few moments of quiet contemplation. "The asking price is more than fair. I'll make an offer, get the deal done. You'll take care of cleaning out the old lady's stuff, right?"

She nodded, her breath quickening.

"Then, if you agree to manage the other vacation rental in Miramar and the two in Condado, and I mean everything, from booking to check-ins, cleaning, dealing with guests, all of it. If you do that, I'll let you live in this one." He pointed a finger to the phone. "Rent-free."

Daisy felt a leap in her chest. "For real?"

"For real. I'm tired of fighting traffic in Condado every time we have a guest arriving. Parking over there is a nightmare. This is a win-win. It's a solid investment."

Daisy felt her rib cage rising and expanding. Benny held up a hand between them, a calming gesture.

"Just for now, though," he said. "We'll give it six months. See how it goes."

Daisy's face was a mess of suppressed emotion. She tried to keep it together.

"Maybe you'll get tired of living in 1965," Benny said.

"Never," she whispered.

The only thing Daisy changed was the sheets on the old lady's bed, which she laundered along with the lemon-embroidered hand towels she found in the linen closet. After the closing, Daisy stayed on in Benny's house while she worked on the cleanout. When Stefani came home for Thanksgiving break, they tackled the old lady's closets together. Daisy bought a bottle of cheap wine for the occasion, which she poured into two amber-colored glasses she found in an upper cabinet.

"This place is incredible." Stefani sipped from her glass and then set it down on the heavy wooden nightstand in Daisy's soon-to-be bedroom. Daisy rushed to get a coaster, trying not to make it obvious that she was rushing to get a coaster. Stefani kicked off her Converse beside the bed and pulled open the accordion doors on the closet, bending inside to retrieve a pair of tan loafers with a Velcro strap. "What size shoe we got going on here?"

Daisy surreptitiously slipped the coaster beneath her cousin's wine glass and then bent down to retrieve the other shoe.

"Six and a half." Daisy fiddled with the Velcro strap.

"Too small." Stefani dropped both into the cardboard box they'd marked *thrift* and then reached back into the closet, pulling out a silk kimono-style robe covered in peacocks. "*This* though!"

"Gorgeous." Daisy whistled. "That one goes in the *keep* pile."

Stefani tossed the colorful silk down on the bed. Two hours later the single *thrift* box was only half-full, dwarfed by an enormous heap of new, old clothes. The girls tried on everything: bell-bottoms, a host of belted miniskirts, shirts with enormous pointed collars. Wristbands, head-bands, leotards, leg warmers.

"We can't keep all of it, though!" Daisy said.

Stefani pouted into the mirror.

"We have to be reasonable," Daisy said.

"Exactly what is it about this outfit that you find unreasonable?" Stefani gestured the full length of her figure-hugging, powder-blue leisure suit, and Daisy found herself at a loss.

The girls knew that their benefactor's name had been Gloria Jiménez, so they began to reference her, as in, "Gloria really knew how to rock a silk turban," or "I wonder where Gloria found this caftan."

When they were finished, they retreated to Gloria's living room, Stefani in a terry-cloth minidress, and Daisy in a gold lamé jumpsuit. They sat together on Gloria's olive-green sofa and ripped into a bag of Chifles.

"I clash with the couch," Stefani said.

"Nonsense." Daisy held the bag out to her cousin, who plunged her hand in. "This couch goes with everything."

Stefani made a dubious face but did not reply.

"What a cool old lady Gloria must have been," Daisy said, kicking her shimmery gold legs up onto the coffee table.

"When are you gonna move in here?" Stefani asked.

Daisy shrugged. "We could stay here tonight? It's pretty much ready now. I still have to bring my stuff over from your house, but I don't have that much."

Stefani shook her head, talked with her mouth full. "I'm only home for four days. Mom would murder us both if we don't come home."

"True." Daisy tipped some Chifles into her hand and set the bag on the coffee table beside her cousin's feet. "So I'll move over here when you go back on Sunday."

"Awesome." Stefani leaned forward and began rummaging through the drawers in the coffee table. "Where's the remote for this thing?" she said, gesturing at the television, which was an enormous box that stood on four spindly, gold-capped, mid-century legs, although the screen itself was no more than fourteen inches across.

"No remote." Daisy smiled. She stood up and walked over to the box.

She pulled a knob outward with a click, and the screen began to glow. It was several more seconds before fuzzy images began to appear there.

"No cable?" Stefani asked.

Daisy shook her head. "But there are a bunch of VHS tapes." She squatted down to check the shelf beside the television. "We could watch an old movie."

It took them a half hour to figure out how to work the VCR, but after consulting Google on Stefani's phone, they eventually got it running. They watched *Guess Who's Coming to Dinner*, and when it was finished, they stayed there, in Gloria's clothes, with their feet stretched out across Gloria's coffee table while the credits rolled.

"We should get back," Stefani said. "Mami won't sleep until we're in for the night."

"In just a minute," Daisy said. "I want to show you something first."

Stefani stayed where she was on the couch while Daisy went back to the bedroom and rummaged around beneath the bed. She pulled out three large pieces of poster board and an overstuffed green binder, and hauled everything back to the living room.

"What's all this?" Stefani said, straightening up from the couch and stretching her arms overhead. "Looks like a middle school art project."

"Just wait," Daisy said, tossing the binder down on the recliner and then walking across the living room, where she propped the three posters up against Gloria's sideboard.

"Oh!" It began to dawn on Stefani what she was looking at. "Girl!" She stood up.

"Pretty good, right?" Daisy said, standing back to admire her handiwork.

"Yes!"

Daisy had told no one except her cousin about her plan to start her own business here in San Juan, and her secrecy was born mostly as an avoidance strategy against having to bear her mother's opposition. When Daisy anticipated all the possible reasons her fledgling business might fail, a lack of foresight or aversion to hard work would not be part of the equation. She had contingency plans for every scenario.

"You know there's perfectly good software available that will do this work for you," Stefani said, stepping closer to inspect the posters. "But, wow, doing this mood board thing the old-fashioned way is so much better. Look at this!"

Daisy watched as her cousin leaned in to admire the images she had mostly glue-sticked to the poster board. The almost-transparent edges of some scotch tape were visible in a few stubborn places where the glue wouldn't hold.

"It's so tactile, so cool!" Stefani knelt down for a better look. "It's amazing. You're a straight-up visionary, prima."

Daisy grinned, and when Stefani stood, her kneecaps were criss-crossed by the indentations of the shag carpet.

"And what about this?" Stefani grabbed the green binder up from the recliner and collapsed back onto the couch with the heavy book on her lap. "What kinda analog situation we got in this three-ring dinosaur?"

"That's the business plan." Daisy sat down beside her and pulled open the cover so the binder spilled across both of their laps.

Daisy was quiet then, watching as Stefani flipped through the binder, shaking her head in admiration, asking occasional questions, expressing some degree of wonder when she noted that Daisy had ready, multilayered answers for every possible concern.

"This is incredibly impressive, Daisy," Stefani said, looking up. "It's like you've thought of everything."

Daisy took a breath and made a small, tentative nod. "Yeah, I think so," she said. "I've worked really hard on it. I think I'm ready."

Stefani dragged the heavy binder closed and slid it off their laps and onto the waiting coffee table. "All right, then," she said. "We better get some rest if you're going to take over the world tomorrow."

Stefani turned and reached out to Daisy, who allowed herself to be hauled up from the couch.

"I'm gonna change back into my clothes before we drive home," Stefani said, retreating briefly to the bedroom.

Daisy took one last look at her vision boards and felt the quiver and thrill of determination, a new adventure. She was barefoot on the shag rug, the orange fibers coarse beneath the soft arch of her foot.

§

In the ambulance, Daisy is wearing only one shoe. Her sock is drenched, and the paramedic peels it from her foot. There is a rubbery, disconnected sensation, a stimulus against the arch of her foot. Rather than sensing the fingers against her skin, Daisy feels as though the fingers belong to her. She is the one animating them, pinching, tapping, flicking, probing for signs of life. The foot is cold and wet to the touch. The toes, which Daisy painted lilac just this morning, are pruned. Outside there is another bolt of lightning, the flash briefly changing the pallor of Daisy's tepid skin, silver/gold/silver.

Chapter Seven

~

San Juan, Puerto Rico
1953

When Rafaela was seven and Dolores nine, their friend Candido and his mother, Priti, lived with them in the big house on calle Américo Salas. That's how both girls thought of it—not that their housekeeper, Priti, lived there with her son, but that their friend Candido lived there with his mother, in the downstairs bedroom of the house where she happened to cook and clean. There were four larger, empty bedrooms upstairs, but it didn't occur to the sisters to wonder why their friend and his mother shared the small, spare room beside the kitchen when there were so many better ones to choose from upstairs. Their upbringing did not encourage that manner of question.

Priti was always up first, dressed, and humming around the kitchen, brewing coffee, sizzling eggs, popping toast, no matter how early Rafaela came down. Priti dipped and twirled around her frying pan, and if Rafa came into the kitchen without her dressing gown, Priti would swipe at her backside with the spatula.

"Where are your slippers?" she'd say. "You'll catch a foot fungus!"

Rafaela would laugh and screw up her nose, thoughts of mushrooms sprouting between her toes. Even though Candido was the same age as Rafaela, he never came out of their little room in his pajamas, never ever walked barefoot on the cool tile floor. He helped his mother polish the railings by the steps, dust Papamío's jade chess set, burnish the bone-inlaid wood of Mamamía's vanity with lemon oil. Rafaela liked the way it smelled in there when Candido was done polishing. Once, she asked if she could try, and Candido nodded silently, passing her the bottle and rag, but she spent more time smelling it than wiping it around. She left a thick smear of fingerprints behind, so he had to do it a second time when she'd finished, but he didn't seem to mind, or if he did, she didn't notice.

Both children knew, without understanding why they knew, that no one should ever catch Rafaela with the rag and polish. In fact, no one should observe the mutual fondness between them at all, despite the fact that they were secretly best friends. So Rafaela was quick to cover her teeth and concentrate elsewhere when any of the adults were nearby. Still, sometimes she hid behind the potted palm in the corner of Papamío's study so she could watch Candido open wide the double doors to the courtyard and sweep the gathered dust outside, a grace in his movements, an elegance in the flex of his arm as he reached to unlatch the top lock. Sometimes she admired the way his honey-colored hair curled just so behind his ears. Even when they were little, she had noticed the smoothness of his skin and the deep green of his eyes, the same color as the crown of a perfectly ripe pineapple. She felt it was a pleasure just to look at him, to stare at him, and whenever she could do so unobserved, she did. Dolores caught them together in the pantry once, squatting on the checkerboard floor, chins resting on knees, playing with a spinning top. Candido could make that top go for a full three and a half minutes with one spin. He was teaching her the technique, how to whip the cord for maximum torque, but Dolores pulled Rafaela out by the ear, didn't let go until she'd dragged her little sister upstairs to her bedroom.

"Oh my God, if Papamío saw you with that boy!" Lola said.

Rafaela rubbed her ear. "We were only playing," she pouted. "He's nice."

"He's very nice," her sister agreed. "And that's why you have to leave him alone. You'll get him in trouble."

"Look what you did to my ear!" Rafa pulled back her hair to examine the damage in the mirror, but the pink was already fading, and with it, her irritation.

On Nochebuena that year, Rafaela and Dolores had to stay home while Mamamía and Papamío went to dinner with the governor's family at La

Fortaleza. Rafaela had never been inside the governor's palace herself, but it made her giddy to think of her parents being ushered inside, past the tourists who gathered to take pictures by the front gate. Such was Rafaela's despair at being left behind on the evening of such a glamorous event that she didn't know how she'd survive it. She and her sister sat together on their mother's bed while she got ready. Mamamía's black hair was bundled and coiled and looped dramatically all over her head, and then fixed in place with golden combs. Her dress was made of emerald-green brocade, and her matching gloves came up to just beneath her elbow. Mascara black, lipstick red, shoes golden to match the combs stuck through her piled hair. When Mamamía smiled, she was radiant like the sun. Rafaela ached just from looking at her. Jewels dangled from her mother's ears and reminded Rafaela of heavy fruit straining the limbs of a mango tree. Lola was stretched out on her tummy reading *Pérez y Martina* for the thousandth time, and Rafaela sat beside her with her legs crossed, her mother's latest issue of *Vogue* spread open across her lap. Mamamía was just as pretty as any of these blond ladies in the magazine. *Prettier*, Rafaela thought, as she flipped idly through the pages.

"When will we get invited to the governor's house?" Rafaela asked.

Dolores marked her place with her finger and looked up from the page. Mamamía turned on her vanity stool to look at her girls. In the mirror behind her, Rafaela admired how the back of her mother's green dress scooped low to emphasize the delicate brown wings of her shoulder blades.

"Only the older children come," Mamamía said, bending to adjust the strap of her shoe.

"But we're older," Rafa said.

"Speak for yourself, I'm still a baby," Lola said, returning her attention to the book.

Mamamía stood up and walked over to the bed, where she settled her weight between them. "I think the youngest ones there will be twelve or thirteen." She smiled. "A few years yet, for you two."

Rafaela groaned and flopped onto her back. "I'll never be able to wait that long!"

Mamamía flipped the magazine closed before hauling Rafaela onto her lap. "I'll tell you a secret," she said.

Rafaela reached up to touch the dangles hanging from her mother's ear. "What?" she whispered.

Lola pretended to keep reading beside them, but Rafaela could feel a shift in her posture and knew her sister was listening too.

"These fancy dinners?" Mamamía said, stroking the soft skin beneath Rafaela's chin with the fingers of her satin glove. She leaned her face in so close that their noses were touching. "*Dreadfully* boring."

"What?" Rafaela was aghast. "No!"

"I knew it!" Lola slapped the book closed and sat up on her knees.

"So boring," Mamamía confirmed, crossing her eyes.

"But what about all the dresses and the fashion?" Rafaela asked.

Mamamía thought about it, nodding her head this way and that. "Sometimes the ladies are beautiful, sometimes they're smart and interesting," she said. Rafaela tipped herself back in her mother's arms like a baby, and Mamamía caught her in the crook of her elbow, swinging her legs up over the other arm. "But the most beautiful ladies, the smartest and most interesting ladies live right here in this house!" She reached back and squeezed Dolores's ticklish knee with one hand. Lola squealed. Reclining in her mother's arms, little Rafa was unconvinced.

"What about the food?"

"Who's a better cook than Priti?"

This was a valid point.

"The music?"

Mamamía sighed, tipping Rafa back up to a sitting position. She stood out from beneath her daughter's weight, and Rafaela slid off, landing on her feet.

"Well, the boleros and guarachas are magical," Mamamía admitted. "And your father is a marvelous dancer."

"Will there be an orchestra?" Lola was unable to hide her curiosity any longer.

"Of course," Mamamía said. "Maybe Rafael Hernández and his band."

"Wow!" Lola was sufficiently dazzled, and both she and Rafa began to sing their favorite Rafael Hernández song, which, they all agreed, was the real national anthem even if it wasn't the official choice Governor Muñoz Marín had signed into law just last year. *Yo se lo que son los encantos de mi Borinquen hermosa, por eso la quiero yo tanto, por siempre la llamaré ¡PRECIOOOOOOSAAAAA!* Rafaela clutched her heart, and Lola threw her head back to better belt out the lyrics.

"Ay, my little chorus of angels!" Mamamía laughed. "See? How much I would rather be home with you, practicing our aguinaldos and getting ready for the parrandas!"

Mamamía shimmied her hips. The parrandas were one of Mamamía's favorite Christmas traditions. Even in San Juan, she always said the parrandas reminded her of growing up in Mayagüez, when the carolers would go from door to door all through the town and surrounding campo, singing and dancing and playing instruments both crafted and improvised, clapping their hands, shaking their skirts, sharing pitorro and coquito and food. Everyone was rich in the parrandas, never mind who had money and who didn't. It was a spirited swell of community gathering joy and commotion as it rolled through the streets from one house to the next and the next. For all their glamour, the festivities at La Fortaleza paled in comparison to the liveliness of the parrandas.

"Anyway, I'm sure it will be fun." Mamamía convinced neither herself nor her daughters.

She tucked a tube of red lipstick into a tiny mirrored box and stowed it in her handbag.

"How do I look?" She checked her reflection in the mirror.

"So beautiful, Mami!" Lola said.

"The prettiest lady who ever lived," Rafaela said with absolute sincerity.

Mamamía smiled at them both, and delivered their hugs carefully, so as not to smudge her makeup or wrinkle her dress. She wasn't a naturally fussy woman, but when she attended these events, her physical appearance was of utmost importance. She strived to look immaculate, to leave no opening for the suggestion she was slovenly. To her daughters, she would not yet mention the subtle resentment of the other wives, the backhanded compliments about her *sophistication* and comportment, the straying hands and breath of their men. She couldn't begin to explain the verbal gymnastics some of these women performed in order to arrive at the point: the lineal purity of their Spanish ancestral blood. A purity, they implied, Papamío himself had enjoyed until he'd chosen to dilute the line of his progeny by marrying una jíbara morena, even though

Mamamía would've described herself as parda clara, had anyone bothered to ask. (Of course, people seldom did ask directly, and no one had asked recently, not since the census taker two years prior, who listened politely as Mamamía explained how absurd it was, trying to distill the question of race to just two or three options when anyone in Puerto Rico could see that race was a spectrum with at least a few dozen distinct and beautiful designations. The man had nodded and sipped from his teacup, and then ignored Mamamía's assertions, recording his own assessment, *mulata*, on the clipboard in front of him.)

On one previous occasion at La Fortaleza, a lady who considered herself genteel to a fault had lightly touched Mamamía's elbow, and nodded to her feet, remarking on the height and beauty of Mamamía's heels.

"Was it difficult," she asked then, "to become accustomed to wearing shoes?"

Mamamía had taken an extra beat to chew and swallow her canapé before answering. In the right mood, she enjoyed inflaming this manner of ignorance.

"The shoes weren't much bother," she replied, turning one leg in and lifting the heel to admire her own foot. She dropped her voice and added, "But I don't suppose I'll ever adapt to imprisoning my magnificent breasts in this damned brassiere!"

Mamamía briefly appreciated the woman's scandalized expression before turning to deposit her empty champagne flute on the tray of a passing waiter. She took a solemn pleasure in meeting these women in the ugliest corners of their conceit, but she was determined to protect her daughters from having to do the same. When it was their turn to stand in these gowns, in these ballrooms, suffering these excruciating conversations, Dolores and Rafaela would face some potentially reduced version of this ignorance, Mamamía knew, because her daughters had the half entitlement of their father's pedigree to bolster them. Mamamía would arm them with impeccable manners, with an outstanding education, and with the beauty that was their birthright. Her daughters, she determined, would own these rooms. But not before they had to.

Although young Dolores and Rafaela knew nothing of this social blood sport, knew only the scent of their mother's gardenia perfume, the elegance of her posture, the smile she aimed at Papamío when he proffered his arm, they could feel Mamamía's absolute sincerity when she said she'd rather stay home with them. They knew it to be true. They kissed her powdered cheek at the door and then scrambled up onto the balcony to watch Benicio pull the yellow 1949 Buick Roadmaster out of its arched carport. Benicio got out of the car in his guayabera and walked around to the other side to open the door for Mamamía and Papamío. In the driveway, all three grown-ups turned their faces up to the girls standing above.

"We'll be back in time for the parrandas!" Mamamía said. "And if you eat your dinner, Priti has a little surprise for you after."

Lola bounced on her toes, and Rafa tried to guess what it might be. Perhaps mallorcas from La Bombonera—swoon!

After dinner, Priti let all three of them—Lola, Rafa, and Candido—have two servings each of her homemade tembleque, which was cold and perfectly set, and which she always garnished with a few shavings of fresh, raw coconut and just the right amount of cinnamon. Then in the living room, she carefully opened the lid on Papamío's record player and slid a 45 out of its sleeve and onto the center post where, with a small crackle, it began to turn. Candido slicked his hair back, tucked one arm behind his waist, and bowed deeply in front of Rafaela, who giggled on the couch.

"Señorita," Candido said in his deepest, most formal voice. "Will you do me the honor of granting me this dance?"

Priti laughed and Lola rolled her eyes, but Rafaela stood up and tucked her fingers into Candido's waiting hand. His fingers were warm and dry. She curtseyed, and then pitched her voice up three octaves to a ridiculous falsetto, and answered through her nose.

"The honor is all mine, kind sir!"

They all laughed, but that sound disappeared beneath the rhythms of "El Cumbanchero," and even Lola couldn't sit still. They all danced, didn't stop dancing, even when the song ended and Priti had to start it again and again. Rafaela could feel the heat of her own skin like an answer to the air around her. They danced until the room spun beneath them.

Twelve days later, on Three Kings Day, Rafaela awoke to discover that the magi had left her a flute, a new kite in the shape of a hawk, and most exciting of all, a heavy golden brush and hand-mirror set with trails of stars all along their pearl-studded handles. They were as beautiful as Mamamía's, and very grown-up. Rafaela put on her favorite dress and took the hand mirror out to the balcony to admire herself in the sunshine. Whenever a young girl passed by on the street below, Rafaela angled the mirror to direct a sunspark into the girl's face so the girl was forced to look up and see Rafaela standing on that balcony like some tropical Juliet, dark-eyed and luminous with her resplendent new mirror.

It was Priti who interrupted her amusement. "Come inside, you have to get changed," she said, closing and fixing the tall shutters as she ushered Rafaela inside.

"What do you mean? This is what I'm wearing today," Rafaela protested, gesturing to the fabulous dress.

But Priti had already crossed to the wardrobe and was rummaging deep on the bottom shelf. She emerged with Rafaela's sole pair of Bermuda shorts.

"Here." She turned and proffered them to Rafa. "These still fit?"

Rafaela winced. "No?"

"Try them."

"I don't—"

"Put them on!" Priti almost never raised her voice, not even with Candido.

Rafaela grabbed the shorts and quickly wriggled them up to her hips beneath her dress.

"There," Priti said. "Perfect." Then she whipped Rafaela around and dragged her long black curls into a ponytail while Rafa stood trying not to grouse. She saw Lola flit past in the hallway outside, also dressed strangely, in shorts, a T-shirt, and her old saddle shoes.

"What's going on?" Rafaela asked, while Priti tugged at her hair.

"A surprise," Priti said, tightening the ribbon around Rafa's ponytail. "Come on."

Rafa still had the dress on over the shorts, so she returned to her wardrobe and emerged with a short-sleeved blouse with a lace collar. It didn't exactly match the shorts, but Rafaela hoped the lace would provide the elegance the shorts lacked. She buttoned it up, glanced disapprovingly in the mirror, and grabbed last year's saddle shoes off the bottom shelf of the wardrobe.

Priti sat in the front seat beside Benicio just like she had last week when Benicio drove all seven of them to the Vanderbilt for their annual holiday lunch. Rafaela had perched on Papamío's lap that day, and Candido had squeezed in between Benicio and his mother in front. When they got home later that afternoon, Benicio had presented Papamío with a jug of pitorro, and all four grown-ups disappeared into Papamío's study to have a festive afternoon drink that lasted until the sun went down and Priti had to make sandwiches for dinner.

But today it was just the five of them in the car, so there was plenty of room for the three kids to sprawl out across the back seat. Rafaela sat in the middle, behind the ashtray, but there was no worry about getting her shorts or shoes dirty with soot, because Benicio emptied that ashtray every single time Papamío got out of the car, and then he'd even wipe it out with a damp rag. Priti had a blue scarf tied over her hair and was wearing the new sunglasses Mamamía had given her for Christmas. Dressed like that and smiling the way she was, and looking so at home in the Roadmaster, Priti could've been mistaken for Mamamía's younger sister. When they reached the bridge along calle Arecibo, the Roadmaster slowed to a crawl, and Priti leaned forward in her seat. Ahead of them, traffic wasn't moving at all. Wherever they were going, it seemed like all of San Juan had decided to go there too. Benicio leaned out over the edge of the driver's door, but there wasn't much to see. Priti glanced at him.

"How far from here?" she asked.

"Half a mile maybe?"

She opened her door with a squawk.

"You going to walk with all three of them?" Benicio asked.

"If we wait, it'll be all melted before we get there!"

Melted! This was a clue, for sure. Rafaela turned her head from her sister to her friend and back.

"Piraguas?" Lola asked.

"But why would all the piraguas melt?" Rafaela wondered, her mouth already watering as she considered the flavor options. Cherry, china, papaya.

Candido shrugged.

"Let's go, no time to waste!" Priti said, yanking open the back door as well.

They were in the middle lane of the roadway, near the center of the bridge, but there was no danger as they piled out of the car, because none of the other cars were moving either. All around them, other kids were climbing out of other cars with other ladies.

"If I can get out of here, I'll wait for you at that café on the bottom of avenida Miramar," Benicio said. "The one with the yellow umbrellas."

"Maybe two hours?" Priti said.

"Take your time—boss has me finished for the day after this. I'll sit and have a coffee while I wait."

Priti grinned and ushered them up onto the sidewalk like wayward ducklings to a pond.

"Where are we going?" Rafaela asked for the hundredth time.

Again, Priti's only answer was to hurry ahead, all three kids tagging along behind her. A nearby woman holding a small boy by the hand smiled over at Priti.

"You have such beautiful children!" the lady said, and Rafaela could see how pleased Priti was to receive this kind of praise, the misapprehension that her son was here in the company of his two pretty sisters. It was a mistake that happened with some frequency because, with the exception of Candido's green eyes (inherited from Priti), the three children all did look rather alike. As usual, Priti stood up a little taller and did not correct the assumption that these three little beauties all belonged to her. In a way, she thought, they did.

"Thank you!" Priti said. Then to the kids, "Come on, hurry!"

They joined the growing crowd of other children, all dressed as strangely as they were, shorts, T-shirts, raggedy shoes. A lot of the boys wore their baseball uniforms with caps and striped tube socks. Priti stepped down off the sidewalk to pass a slower-moving family in front. They followed the crowd, but when they finally arrived, Rafaela still didn't understand what they were doing there, in a crowded park on the eastern end of El Viejo San Juan.

There was a large knot of people in the center of the park, and all around this nucleus, Navy airmen stood back, handsome and smiling in their caps and reflective sunglasses. Candido understood before the girls did, and he broke away from his mother's hand to run toward the center of the crowd. Rafaela tried to follow, but Lola was hanging back, cautious. Rafa tugged on her sister's arm, but when Lola wouldn't budge, Rafa broke free, too, and followed Candido into the crowd. There were elbows everywhere, and Rafa couldn't see much, but she kept her head down and ducked between the swinging arms and bodies. There was screeching and squealing, too, and as she got deeper into the mass of the crowd, Rafaela realized it was all children. The mothers hung back around the perimeter, matching smiles and chatting with the uniformed men. The next thing she noticed was the crunch of something wet beneath the flat sole of her saddle shoe, like brittle gravel that popped beneath the weight of her steps.

"What is that?" she said out loud, stooping to touch the gray-white pebbles beneath her feet.

Cold. It was ice cold. Beside her, a boy in a Cangrejeros jersey was packing the white stuff into a ball. It crunched as he squeezed it together, dripping its icy water down his wrist. He saw her staring.

"It's snow!"

Her mouth dropped open.

"How?"

This mantle of freezing slush beneath the hot blue sky could not have been more different from her one previous experience of snow, a hushed evening flurry during a family visit to New York. It had been magical, had delighted all of them. Even Papamío had turned a little waltz beneath the weightless sprinkles in front of their hotel on Fifth Avenue.

"Doña Fela flew it in from Vermont for Three Kings Day!"

Rafaela blinked as she tried to take the information in, but it made no sense, it was too grand a gesture for her imagination to hold. Later, on the way home, Benicio would buy them all piraguas, while Priti explained that the beloved mayor of the city, Doña Felisa Rincón de Gautier (who happened to be a personal friend of Mamamía's) had organized the snow delivery as a Christmas gift for the children of San Juan. Much later still, decades hence, academics would re-examine this day, this immoderate offering, and declare it to be an act of psychological colonization. But that judgment would happen in some remote, alien future. Today, the piraguas would turn the children's tongues red and blue and green with icy syrup while they spoke reverently of Doña Fela: her pearls, her immaculate braids and enormous sunglasses, her implausible generosity.

But before any of that, first, there was snow! A fleeting miracle, gritty with sand. Rafaela dropped into a squat and plunged her hands into the mess, sending a spike of cold up her arms. She found herself squealing like all the children around her, great peals of laughter while the boys pelted each other with their hand-packed snow nuggets, and the girls tried to skate across the surface on their slippery shoes. One kid lay flat on his back in the middle of everything, flapping his arms and legs wide, making shapes in the melting slop. When he stood up, his back was a wet shambles of sticky grass, his reddened skin dripping with the cold.

"Rafa!" She heard her name, and when she looked up, there was Candido standing beside an airman who was holding open a pristine bag of fresh snow. "Just for us, come here!"

She pushed through the small space between them, but by the time she got there, four other kids had already noticed the fresh bag, and they were all shoving in around Candido to be first to get their hot hands on the clean snow, like greedy piglets at their mother's teats. Rafaela squirmed and pressed, but she couldn't reach. Candido went up on his tiptoes then, stretched out across all the grabbing hands, and found hers above the fray. He pulled her across and folded her in front of him, between himself and the bag. He was no bigger than she was, but she felt the safety of him even then, the way he made his small body like a barrier around her. The way he folded her hand in his and then plunged their fingers together into the waiting snow.

Decades would swim by in an instant. Rafaela would live an expansive life. She'd know love and suffering and pleasure and wonder. She would experience many snowfalls. And then Lola would die, and Rafaela would find within herself a new capacity for despair. She'd hire a psychologist who'd teach her to relieve her grief-borne anxiety by instructing Rafaela to close her eyes and breathe deeply, to breathe into her happiest memories, to locate the *feeling* of those moments. When, in her life, had she felt safest and most cherished? Go there. Be there. Breathe.

Rafaela surprised herself by turning up here, over and over again. This simple city park in El Viejo San Juan. This bolt of feeling when Candido stood behind her, tangled their warm fingers together, and burrowed them into the cold.

Chapter Eight

～

St. Louis, Missouri
1979

Ruth knew her parents would divorce before they knew it themselves. She knew before she learned the English word for "divorce," before she even fully understood divorce as a concept, that married people could choose to no longer remain married. No one in her life, on either side of her sprawling Catholic family, had ever been divorced. Not in Puerto Rico, nor in Missouri, and it wasn't even legal in Ireland. The marital unions of the Acuña and Brennan families were permanent ones, or lasted at least until death, and a person's long-term happiness or unhappiness was not typically a relevant consideration in the arrangement. And yet it was clear to Ruth before her eighth birthday, almost three years before her parents would finally report the decision to Ruth and her brother, that the marriage was untenable.

Ruth's moment of early clarity occurred the summer after they moved to St. Louis, when she spent almost every day at Jennifer's, Jenny's, or Kathy's houses. She never invited them to her house, not exactly because she was ashamed of anything there, but she did worry actively about the snack situation. Her mother did not buy the Fritos and onion dip that Jenny's mom always had on hand. She never purchased Oreos or Doritos. There was nary a Twinkie to be seen in Ruth's house.

"Why don't you invite your friends over here for once?" her mother asked at least twice a week.

But Ruth would eye the towering fruit bowl with apprehension, and then hop on her bike. At Kathy's house on hot days they used the Slip 'N Slide. At Jenny's, where her mother kept the air-conditioning turned up as high as it would go, they stayed in the carpeted basement where there were no fewer than a hundred blond Barbie dolls, most of whom had their own homes and luxury vehicles, even if they did keep daddy long-legs for pets. Jennifer's mom worked part-time, so they didn't congregate at her house as often, but when they did, her mom would make popcorn and close the curtains in the middle of the day, and they'd each get their own beanbag (Ruth always took the yellow one), where they'd sit and watch movies on Jennifer's Betamax.

Ruth was vaguely aware that her mother and brother were not adjusting as well as she was. Benny had finally made a single friend, but then that kid went away to boy scout camp, so Benny was on his own again, at least for the first couple weeks of summer, which is an eternity when you're ten. His English was improving, but he was still largely joyless, and he spent most of those gaping days trying to convince their parents that it wasn't too late for them to send him back to Puerto Rico for the summer, that he still had another *blank* number of weeks before he had to be back in school, that Titi Lola had repeatedly said he could stay with her as long as he liked.

Ruth overheard her parents talking about it many nights after Benny went to bed. Perhaps *talking* wasn't the right word—she shared a bedroom wall with them, and it was the urgency of raised voices she overheard, Mama insisting it would be good for Benny to go back, to spend time with Tiago, to see that his life there still existed, that they still loved him and he wasn't forgotten. And Dad arguing with equal intensity that all of Benny's progress would evaporate if they let him go back, that he'd forget what English he'd learned and they'd have to deal with even greater anger and resentment when he returned.

But however challenging things were for Benny, they were worse for Mama. Ruth had no idea how her mother spent her days, but Ruth knew she didn't spend them playing bridge or canasta with the other moms, or scrubbing the bathroom fixtures until they shined, or packing picnics into the Lil' Oscar and taking her children on cultural outings. Neither did she spend them sitting on her sister's balcony in San Juan drinking coffee to the soundtrack of Héctor Lavoe and the distant surf. And that, more than anything, seemed to define her mother's current existence: it was the neither/nor.

Dad seemed to understand the desolate emptiness of Mama's new life in St. Louis. He seemed to understand it as a corrosion that would eat their family if he could not find a way to contain it. So it was the effort, the spectacularly failed effort, in that direction that signified to Ruth the coming collapse.

It was a Friday evening when Dad came home from work and announced that they were joining the country club. Mama had made merciless pork chops for dinner, shoe leather on a plate. Ruth sat behind her striped place mat and thought wistfully of Kathy's house, where it was pizza night on Fridays. Benny was sitting beside her, and Dad to her left, while Mama was still fussing around the table filling everyone's glasses. At first Mama didn't respond to Dad's news, not even with her face. Ruth wondered if her mother had heard.

"The Maguires and Powells are already members there," Dad continued, "and actually a lot of my clients."

Dad was already cutting his meat, but Mama gave him a sharp look, so he set down the knife and fork. She turned to hang her apron on a hook beside the back door, smoothed her hands over her skirt, and joined them at the table. She served herself from the bowl of wrinkled peas before reaching her hands out on either side of her. They all joined hands and briefly prayed over the meal. When the prayer was finished, in her mind Ruth added, "Dear God, please teach Mama about pizza night, amen."

Dad returned to sawing at his pork chop, popped a bite in his mouth, and kept talking. "But the real reason to join is for you." He reached over and squeezed Mama's hand. She allowed the intimacy before retracting herself toward the business of her meal. Dad was undaunted by her remoteness. "They have luncheons and card games. Lots of opportunities for volunteer work. It'll be great for you—you'll get to meet so many new people. Make some friends."

Dad took a break from the pork to work on the peas, which he shoveled into his mouth rapidly until they were all gone. Ruth was amazed by his resolve: he set his mind to eating those peas, and just like that, they disappeared. Not a single pea was left abandoned on the plate. Ruth tried a forkful and chased them with a shudder of milk. Mama toiled delicately over her dinner.

"Oh! And wait till you see the pool! You'll love it. Tennis courts too. And hey, maybe we'll take up golf? Would you like that? I could get you a set of clubs for your birthday?"

Mama finished chewing and lifted the cloth napkin from her lap to dab at the clean corners of her mouth. She took a deep breath and replaced the napkin on her lap. Ruth could see that her mother was suppressing something, but she couldn't tell what it was. There was some ambiguous emotion there, beneath the stony facade. Was it excitement? Hope? Irritation? Mama was impossible to read.

"It sounds lovely," she said without inflection.

Dad leaned back in his chair. Sniffed. Nodded.

"Really," Mama said, reaching to squeeze his hand back. "It sounds nice. When can we see it?"

Dad grinned, placated. "Tomorrow!"

"Oh?" Mama's eyebrows went up, which was the closest she came to revealing any real sentiment in the conversation.

"Yeah, I stopped by today with Bob—we had a game of golf this afternoon, and he showed me around. It was so incredible, I went ahead and signed up on the spot. They'll have our membership cards ready tomorrow morning. We can go for the day, check out all the amenities."

"Me too?" Ruth asked. It sounded like a dream.

"Yes, of course," Dad said. "All four of us. And there's a full restaurant overlooking the golf course, but I have a feeling you and your friends will be spending your time at the cantina by the pool."

"My friends can come too?!"

"Sure, sweetie! Anytime you want."

"What do they have at the cantina?"

Dad had nearly finished his pork chop, Ruth noticed enviously. Meanwhile, discussion of other food—food that was not rubbery pork chops and overcooked peas—was both a palliative and a torture. Dad began to list the menu items from the cantina across his fingers.

"Pizza."

Oh.

"Hot dogs."

Oh.

"Hamburgers, french fries, ice cream."

Ruth was in raptures. Benny didn't respond because he seldom spoke at the dinner table unless there was a question posed to him directly. But he ate quickly, as he always did, and Ruth could read in his posture that he was excited about the country club too.

In the morning, Mama made scrambled eggs and bacon, and took extra care with her hair and makeup. She wore a light-blue skirt and a fitted, button-down top that she tied into a crop knot at her waist. Her lipstick was the color of dulce de leche, which made her teeth look even whiter and more dazzling than they were. She fixed simple pearl earrings into her ears and strapped sandals onto her pedicured feet. Ruth's mother was so much more beautiful than the other moms that it would've been embarrassing if there were less pride in it. Ruth wriggled into her favorite pink bikini with the ruffle across the top, and threw on jean shorts until her mother turned her around by the shoulders and sent her back to her room to hide the bikini beneath a sundress.

The excitement in the Datsun felt like a contagion despite Mama's immunity. Ruth watched the little clock on the dashboard because she wanted to know for future visits how long it would take to drive there. Seventeen minutes. Just off the highway, they pulled down a tree-lined boulevard with white gravel that crunched beneath the tires. A black sign all in gold cursive welcomed them to the SHORT HILLS BABYLON COUNTRY CLUB. Before the property even came fully into view, Ruth was enchanted by the arching canopy of trees, the manicured grass beneath, the symmetry of the gates that opened as they approached. They came to a stop at a guard booth of red brick, and an older man wearing a cap and uniform greeted them. Dad rolled down his window.

"Morning, Mr. Brennan!" the guard said. "Back already!"

"Morning, Carl!" Dad said, as if they'd known each other forever. "Yes, I'm here to show my family around."

"Very good, sir." Carl waved his clipboard at Dad, and the gravel crunched beneath the tires once again.

Ruth was first out of the car, bouncing on her toes while she waited for Dad to pop the hatchback. She pulled out her beach bag and tried to steady her feet beneath her, but she could already spot a sliver of the crystalline blue pool between the trees, which felt like a salve against the racket of the cicadas beyond the tree line. Mama was taking her time, a maddening thing she sometimes did when all around her was eagerness. She slowed, forcing her family to match her pace, holding them captive while she pulled down the visor and checked her reflection in the mirror. She touched the pearl on one earlobe, pressed her lips together, smoothed an invisible stray hair. Ruth knew better than to run ahead or to make any comment that might be interpreted as impatience. Benny stood with his hands in his pockets while they waited.

And then she was out! She was out of the car! Mama and Dad walked ahead, Dad's voice detailing the locations of things, his arm outstretched, his finger pointing this way to the clubhouse, that way to badminton and lawn bowls. Benny stopped in front of Ruth and bent down so she could hop onto him like a backpack, her beach bag thumping against his hip. She pressed her cheek into her brother's neck and realized that the scent of his skin was different now than it had been in San Juan. Not better or worse, just different, as if some element of heat that was there before had now cooled.

At the clubhouse there were double staircases, one on each end, leading up to the sweeping front porch, where Benny finally set Ruth down. Their father reached for the handle, but before he could open the door, a staff member did it for him, tipping his hat.

"Morning, Mr. Brennan."

How did everyone already know his name?

But then there was a falter, a flicker, which the man attempted to conceal as he replaced his hat. It was too late. They had all seen it, although Ruth didn't know what that flicker meant.

"Mrs. Brennan," the man said quickly, standing aside and holding the door while they all passed through into the clubhouse.

Ruth immediately forgot the strange moment because of the elegance and comfort of the clubhouse: golden lighting, a full bank of tall windows with white panes overlooking the golf course beyond, the carpet so plush it came up over the edges of her sandals. She could feel the softness of it against her toes. There was a room to one side with leather armchairs and mahogany desks and an enormous fireplace and tons of bookshelves lined with gleaming leather spines. There was a scent like firewood, which felt incongruous indoors, in the heat of the summertime. Even Benny let slip an appreciative "Whoa."

Thus enraptured, Ruth failed to notice the flurry of anxious glances and cleared throats being bandied about behind the welcome desk. The manager of the club wore a smile but no hat. It was his job to liaise, to greet members on the level of their own social status, and then to translate their needs and desires to the staff. As such, his uniform was a suit and tie. He leaned forward, bent slightly at the waist.

"Good morning, Mr. Brennan, how nice to see you again so soon." He wore thick glasses with a double gold bridge across his nose. His eyelids were pink, and he was blinking heavily at them just as Ruth turned to take him in. "And who do we have here?"

His mouth was making the shape of a smile.

"This is my wife," Dad said. "Mrs. Brennan."

"How do you do," Mama said.

"I see," the man said, blinking ever more furiously.

There were two other staff members standing behind the desk as well, both white, and both staring openly at the Brennan family. They did not pretend busyness, did not hide their flagrant interest. Their boss straightened his posture and then moved himself around the edge of the counter.

"Mr. Brennan, do you mind if we have a word?" he said, gesturing with an upturned palm to the book room. "Privately?"

Dad frowned with his whole face, his whole body. It started in his forehead and traveled at least as far as his fists. He turned to Mama, kissed her fragrant cheek.

"I'll just be a moment," he said. And then to Benny, "Check out the view over there, sport!"

But Benny's optimism had curdled. He moved himself instead to nuzzle beneath his mother's arm. Ruth checked out the view, though, drawing herself to the bank of windows, letting the sunlight fall on her face, watching the way it shot through the trees outside. She could see the pool much better from here, its eight sparkling lanes, its big, roped-off diving well, its two lifeguard chairs and its swoopy curl of a slide. The cantina wasn't yet open for the day, so there was a grate pulled down to the counter, but Ruth could see two teenage girls moving around inside, wearing white golf shirts and aprons, their hair gathered into neat ponytails. Ruth focused all her attention on the ponytails in an effort to not hear the words that her father and the manager were exchanging "privately," just a few feet away. The book room had a door. Even Ruth understood that, if the manager hadn't meant for everyone to hear this conversation, he would've closed it.

"It's a very exclusive club, Mr. Brennan," the man said.

"I'm aware," Dad responded. "As evidenced by the rather exorbitant annual dues which, you will remember, I paid in full just yesterday."

"Yes, sir, but the bylaws are clear on the point of membership requirements. This club is for whites only."

"Yes," Dad said. "And?"

The manager made a sound that could only be described as a scoff, and Ruth caught the two young women behind the desk exchanging a silent giggle. Ruth's mother stood tall beside Benny, her back perfectly erect, the pearls white in her ears. She stared at the large oil painting on the wall behind the welcome desk. Three men in top hats on horseback, chasing some dogs that were chasing a fox.

"I'm afraid I could not have approved your membership had I known that your wife was . . . not white."

"Don't be ridiculous, of course she's white!"

Again, the scoffing sound. "And where is it she's from, if I may ask?"

"I don't see what that has to do with—"

"It may help us to determine—"

"She's from Puerto Rico. From one of the finest and wealthiest families in Puerto Rico."

"I see."

"This is outrageous."

"Mr. Brennan, please. You must admit it's a highly unusual situation. Surely you can understand that you've put me in an uncomfortable position. I'm sure your wife is a lovely woman from a fine family, and it's not a personal slight against her. But there are other dues-paying members to consider as well, families who've belonged to this club for generations.

My job is to administer the standards they expect. I don't make the rules, but I am obliged to enforce them on behalf of the board. I do my best to keep everyone happy."

"Well, so far you're doing a bang-up job."

The manager cleared his throat loudly, buying them both a moment to gather themselves, to calm down, but Ruth could hear their hearts skidding and thudding in the attempt at silence. She could hear veins throbbing in necks.

"You can perhaps provide some documentation?" the manager asked then. "Some proof that she's white?"

"Can you prove she's not?"

"Mr. Brennan, anyone with eyeballs can see that she's not!"

Ruth had eyeballs. She turned to look at her mother, whose skin was a similar color to the two white women behind the welcome desk. Ruth had never considered her mother's whiteness (or non-whiteness?) in terms of her actual pigmentation. Mama was perhaps less pink, Ruth conceded. But these two women were certainly not *whiter* than her mother, were they? And then something else occurred to Ruth for the first time, and she found herself extending one arm to study her own color. She'd been out on her bike all summer, out flying down the Slip 'N Slide, playing hopscotch, jumping rope. Her arm was brown, brown, brown. She turned it over to note that her skin was whiter underneath, but she was already worried. She clamped her hands over her arms, suddenly cold in the air-conditioned clubhouse. She wished she'd thought to bring a sweater.

"Outrageous," Dad said again, his voice spiking into fury, accompanied by the smack of his palm against some hard surface in the other room. "My father-in-law could buy and sell this club."

Ruth knew that this claim was Dad's misguided effort to defend Mama, to defend the very existence of their family. But she was equally aware that, though perhaps it was the kind of argument that could reach a man with pink eyelids at a St. Louis country club, and though perhaps it had once been true, it was certainly not true now. Ruth knew the stories of Papamío's once legendary family wealth, but she had not seen evidence of that fortune in her lifetime, so as a means of justification, it smacked of both dishonesty and humiliation. Ruth didn't apprehend this particular sliver of shame with her brain, could not have articulated its presence, but she could feel it all the same.

"Well," the manager said. Ruth could hear the noisy breath he drew in through his elongated nose. "Mr. Brennan, it is certainly not my intention to offend. Let's see if we can come to some compromise, shall we?"

The men emerged from the book room a few minutes later, both having given up the ruse of smiling. Behind the desk, the two lingering staff members now wore brazen smirks, which their manager addressed.

"If you have nothing better to do than to stand around gawking at our newest members, then perhaps we are overstaffed, and your shifts should end early."

Then he turned back to the Brennan family, addressing Mama specifically. "Mrs. Brennan, please," he said, gesturing with a sweep of his hand. "Allow me to give you a tour of the grounds."

Mama lifted her chin higher, narrowed her eyes. Benny reached for her hand.

"Get me a glass of lemonade," she said.

"I'm sorry?" the manager stammered.

"I'm thirsty," she said. "Lemonade with ice. And for my children as well."

The manager turned and snapped at the one staff member who remained behind the desk. She flinched and scampered off to retrieve the lemonade, which was delivered, icy and cold, into their waiting hands no more than ninety seconds later.

"Anything for you, Mr. Brennan?" the manager asked.

"No."

The new member tour was awkward and stiff, and though Ruth still felt a nominal thread of excitement quivering through her limbs when they walked the pool deck, she had a primal understanding that it would be disloyal to express anything approaching happiness. Back in the clubhouse, it was quietly agreed among the men that the Brennan family could retain their membership, but the manager had to draw the line somewhere, and it just wouldn't do to assign Mrs. Brennan a locker in the women's locker room, where the other wives would surely object.

"We will give her access to the staff locker room, and we'll direct the staff to clear out whenever she needs to use it. Like her own private dressing room. Even better than the communal women's room, right?"

That's when it happened. The instant Ruth knew with every certainty that her parents' marriage was terminal. Although the lights were dim on the lower level of the clubhouse, Mama had not removed her sunglasses.

"That will be fine, Brian. Just fine." Dad shook the manager's hand and clapped him on the shoulder. "Right, Rafaela?"

"There's always a compromise to be found among gentlemen," the manager said.

Both men turned to look at Mama then, her face stoic. Through the mild tint of her glasses, she held their gazes each in turn. Mama glared silently until the moment grew long enough for both men to squirm and whither. Ruth watched without breathing. She perceived the towering shape of her mother's dignity in that wordless exchange. Ruth determined to absorb her mother's strength, to make it her own. If Mama was an oak tree, Ruth would be a sapling. She understood that this moment was only rain.

But Ruth knew even as it was happening that this memory would grow roots in the turned earth of her mind, that one day it would come to define something important about Mama that Ruth did not yet fully understand. Years from now, Ruth would return frequently to this memory like a sepia-toned slide. She'd hold it up by the edges, watching the colors filter through the translucent skin. It would be a very long time before the shadows of the image were clearly illuminated, before Ruth would understand that it was not simply the existence of unmistakable bigotry that infuriated Mama that day in the country club. What Mama really couldn't abide was the fact that, for the first time in her life, that bigotry was being aimed *at her*.

In the perfumed silence of the Short Hills Babylon Country Club, Ruth was motionless in her ruffled bikini, sundress, and flat sandals. She'd been still for long enough to drain the color from her peripheral vision, and yet, she kept her eyes on her unblinking mother, who had ensnared the two men using nothing but the weight of her gaze. When Mama was done, she held her empty glass out toward the manager without taking a step toward him. When it was clear that her arm did not extend quite far enough to hand him the glass, she waited for him to close the space between them, to step forward and lift the glass from her hand. He did. Then she turned and ushered Benny and Ruth back toward the stairs.

"Three towels," Mama said, without looking back. "We'll be at the pool."

Chapter Nine

~

San Juan, Puerto Rico
1964

Priti's mood was evident the moment Rafaela walked through the squeaky front gate on calle Américo Salas and clanged it behind her. Through the open windows at the front of the house, Rafa could hear the banging of cabinets. She paused silently and looked down at her saddle shoes against the broad red steps beneath her. She set her books down beside the front door and tiptoed over to the window, wrapping her fingers around the wrought-iron bars and hauling her weight up to peer through. In the dining room, the long, formal table was already set for dinner, but through the arched doorway at the back, Rafa could see into the kitchen, where Priti was stalking back and forth, muttering to herself. Rafaela lowered herself back to the ground and crept to the edge of the porch where she could lean over the low wall leading to the carport. Papamío's car wasn't there. She hopped over and sat on the edge of the wall with her feet dangling down. Maybe she could wait it out.

It wasn't that Rafaela was afraid of Priti, exactly. She loved Priti like a second mother. But her moods, though rare, were formidable, and stirred in Rafaela some deep, uncomfortable, and confusing feelings of guilt.

When she was little, Rafaela had presumed that Candido's father had died, and that was why he and his mother had to come live with them and work in their house. It was an arrangement she believed suited them all equally: Priti and Candido earned money and had a nice place to live, and Rafaela's family had all the help they needed. But by the time she was seventeen, Rafaela knew enough to understand that Candido's father was not dead at all, but neither was he married to Priti. And while Rafaela did not expend a lot of energy trying to imagine how such a predicament had befallen Priti, and she felt personally responsible for neither Priti's misfortune nor her deliverance, she gleaned that most other well-to-do families in San Juan society would not have hired Priti. Still, Rafaela knew that, despite what other people might think, she was tremendously lucky to know Priti, to eat her food every day, to hear her humming in the kitchen, to stand each morning beneath the exacting scrutiny of Priti's hairbrush and palm oil. Were Rafaela given to rumination of this sort, she would even have considered herself lucky to receive the back end of Priti's spatula from time to time, for she knew that Priti's insistence on good manners and moral rectitude—and her occasional, well-placed, and largely painless smacks— were designed to bring forth Rafaela's better self. Priti was not given to unreasonable tempers; there was always a specific and justified cause.

So Rafaela had hoped to get the scoop from Papamío before she entered the house, but he wasn't home, and she couldn't sit out here all afternoon; she had homework to do, plus she was expecting a phone call from her friend Claudia at four o'clock. She heard another bang from the kitchen—a pot on the stove, perhaps—and winced lightly. Rafaela had spilled three drops of coffee on the ruffled white collar of her school pinafore that morning too. She always tried to keep her clothes clean not because of how much she disliked the stains herself, but because she knew their appearance created extra midweek work for Priti. She dreaded adding this problem to whatever was going on inside. Maybe she could sneak up to her room and change her clothes before Priti noticed? Maybe she could try soaking the pinafore herself, if she could figure out how Priti did it, which one of the mysterious bottles she tipped onto the fabric before placing it in a bucket of warm water to steep. Or maybe she could dig her other rumpled pinafore out from the bottom of her hamper and make it work until laundry day. Surely Rafaela could figure out how an iron worked.

"Hey!"

Rafaela looked up and shielded her eyes from the sun. Candido was above her on the second-floor balcony off her parents' bedroom.

"You hiding from Mami?" he asked.

Rafaela pushed herself away from the wall. "That's crazy," she said. "I was just looking to see if Papamío was home."

Her father often was here in his study when Rafaela got home from school in the afternoons. His work hours were relatively predictable, usually at the office in the mornings and early evenings, home by seven or so. He took an extended lunch hour most days to eat at home with Mamamía, and might work in his study for a few hours before returning to the office to wrap up the day.

"Benicio took him back to work an hour ago."

Candido went to the public school only two blocks away. He left an hour after Rafaela did in the mornings, and got home before her in the afternoons, so in Rafaela's experience, Candido was almost always home. He received excellent grades despite the fact that he never seemed to study, and always had ample time to help his mother around the house. He was holding a soiled rag in one hand and leaning on his elbows on the balustrade above. He tossed the rag down and it landed at Rafaela's feet.

"O Romeo." He threw one arm up and across his forehead. "I hath dropped mine handkerchief."

"Weirdo." Rafaela laughed, and bent down to pick it up. She could feel Candido watching her from above, and she wondered what he saw as she leaned down, straightened herself back up. She put one hand on her slender waist. "I hath retrieved thy unclean doily, Juliet!" She pinched the dirty rag between two fingers.

"Bring it up!" he said.

She stepped away from the wall, but then paused and looked up at him again. "What's up with Priti?" she asked.

An unfamiliar flame briefly darkened Candido's face, but as Rafaela watched, he doused it. "Come up," he said.

That's how it happened then, that unbeknownst to Papamío, Candido saved him from being the one to break the news to Rafaela that everything in their life had changed in a single day. Candido hadn't planned to tell her, but neither did he feel that he was overstepping by so doing. She was his oldest friend, and wasn't it his trouble too? They would share the burden between them.

Often, in times of crisis, it feels impossible to assess the extent of the damage from within the moment, and it's only in hindsight that one is able to determine the true measure of the destruction. Such was not the case with the downfall of the Acuña y Daubón family on November 8, 1964. Their collapse was instant and absolute, and though it took Rafaela and Dolores some time to understand how and why it was all happening, they understood the following immediately.

Some money had disappeared. A vast sum of money, gone, under Papamío's watch, so Papamío lost his job as municipal treasurer of the city of San Juan, effective immediately. There were no answers to the questions of why or how or where the money had gone, but the scarcity of facts did not stop the people, the press, the neighbors from conjecturing.

There was a suggestion of impropriety. Accusations but no evidence of wrongdoing, gambling, embezzlement, fraud. In his statement to the press, the governor was tepid in his defense of Papamío, insisting that he'd always known Don Rafael Acuña y Torres to be a man of good character, but confessing with some measure of implication that he could not, in fact, explain where the missing money had gone.

"Whether it was a series of bad investments or simple mismanagement or something more nefarious than that is rather beside the point," the governor said at that evening's press conference, amid the snapping and flashing of cameras. "The money is gone, and so, too, must go the man responsible for keeping this city financially stable and viable. Rest assured we will get the budget back on track and we will implement safeguards to ensure nothing like this ever happens again."

Everyone in San Juan understood how important it was for the Partido Popular government to respond swiftly and decisively to any potential scandal. It had been only a dozen years since the United States had (ostensibly) ended colonial rule on the island, granting the people of Puerto Rico the right to elect their own governor. But Puerto Ricans remained United States citizens who had no representation in congress and could not vote for president. They remained second-class citizens who, according to the Supreme Court, "belonged to but were not part of the United States," and as such, the political scene in San Juan was boisterous and fraught. Opinions were strong and loud and varied. People wanted statehood or independence or to maintain their relatively new status as a US commonwealth and a territory of the United States. Some felt that the adjustment in status to commonwealth was nothing more than an illusion, that Puerto Rico was still a de facto colony. In any case, there was very little overlap among the various opinions, and this question of sovereignty for Puerto Rico would remain the primary political concern for decades to come. But in 1964, the citizenry did not know that yet. They knew only that they intended to prove, to themselves and the world, that they had the capacity and inalienable right to self-governance. There was no room for the tolerance of corruption, or at least no room for its plain visibility.

Papamío had to go. His family would move out of the seven-bedroom house where they lived on calle Américo Salas so the new city treasurer and his family could move in. They would sell the yellow Roadmaster too. And of course, all of this meant that Papamío could no longer afford to pay Benicio or Priti. Candido and his mother would have to leave, they would all have to leave.

Finally, even if the abrupt change in their social status hadn't guaranteed Rafaela's and Dolores's urgent expulsion from Las Madres, Papamío could no longer afford to pay the fees at the finest school in Puerto Rico and perhaps all of the Caribbean. The girls' elite education was over.

On a regular day, the two resident seventeen-year-olds, Rafaela and Candido, would never have found themselves alone on the second floor of the house, and if they did happen to find themselves in that unsuitable situation by chance, one or both of them would rectify it by returning to the ground floor immediately. But on a regular day, Mamamía also would not have closed the thick curtains in her dressing room, taken a headache powder, and lain down on the chaise longue with her door closed at three o'clock in the afternoon. On a regular day, Priti would not be slamming pans around in the kitchen cupboards, cooking away her rage to make room for the sorrow that would come in its stead. This was not a regular day. So there was no one to notice the two teenagers sitting side by side on the small couch at the end of Mamamía's and Papamío's bed, their knees touching, their faces close.

"But where will you go?" Rafaela asked. She hadn't yet arrived at the neighboring question: Where would *she* go?

Candido leaned down on his elbows and shrugged. "Maybe I'll go find my pops. Nueva York."

Rafaela shuddered.

Unlike Rafaela, Candido had never been off the island. He had no real knowledge of blustery, hardscrabble New York, and he probably harbored some romantic notions about it, the same way everyone did until they went there and saw it for themselves. The gray buildings, the gray streets, the gray skies, the gray faces of the people whose color bled from them in that cold, discordant place. Rafaela had been there twice, once in 1951 when she was so young she had only two memories of the visit: disembarking from the ship in the port of New York perched on Mamamía's hip, craning her little neck at the terrifying height of the buildings, and clinging so hard to her mother that she'd accidentally sunk a fingernail into Mamamía's breast. Mamamía had yelped, and then felt chagrined when the woman in front of her turned to look. Her second memory was ethereal—only a dark sky, muffled by the silence of drifting snowflakes, little pinpoints of cold that turned to water the moment they touched her skin.

Rafaela had much more vivid memories of her second trip to New York just four years ago, in the spring of 1960. Papamío had been dispatched on business, so he brought the whole family with him. They stayed at the Plaza Hotel, which was elegant and luxurious and, despite the abruptness of the front desk staff and occasional bewildering scowls of the other patrons, felt something like home when they turned the key in the lock of their suite and closed the door behind them.

Rafaela and Dolores looked forward to the daily visits from their housekeeper, who was a Puerto Rican girl not much older than them, who made them laugh with stories of her adventures in the city while she changed their sheets, dusted their sconces, wiped down the sink in their bathroom. The two sisters sat cuddled up on the overstuffed armchair together, their eyes unselfconsciously following the housekeeper while she talked and worked, the familiar notes of her Spanish landing like colorful birds in the ivory-hued bedroom, unexpected and delightful.

"You two are like part of the furniture," she told them one day, tickling their feet with her feather duster. If there was any resentment in the remark, the sisters had failed to detect it.

During the workdays when Papamío had his meetings, Mamamía took the girls shopping on Fifth Avenue, to morning mass at St. Patrick's Cathedral, and to a matinee showing of *West Side Story* at the Winter Garden Theatre, where the Puerto Rican characters were dangerous and electrifying and completely unlike anyone Rafaela had ever known.

But Rafaela's most enduring memories of that trip were from the one afternoon her mother had shuffled them into a taxi and taken them to Spanish Harlem, where they trudged up four flights of steps into a garlic-scented apartment to visit Mamamía's cousin and her five children, who all thundered in from school about halfway through their second cup of coffee. Rafaela and Dolores both felt conspicuous in their ribbons and starched, bright dresses. Their cousins swarmed around them, jostling them at the small table, elbowing for attention and peppering them with questions about their lives in San Juan.

What was their school like?

Did they have boyfriends?

Did they go to the beach every single day or only on weekends?

Did they have pizza in San Juan? Or had they tried the pizza in New York yet? What did they think?

Mamamía smiled at the interrogation and gracefully intervened. "Rafaela and Dolores are studying English at Las Madres, but they don't get a lot of practice, so I'm not sure if they can keep up with all the questions!"

The cousins switched seamlessly to perfect, if accented, Spanish and started again.

What Rafaela remembered most from that day, from the entire trip, was how comfortable Mamamía appeared to be in that unfamiliar place. The way the redolence and ruckus of that tight apartment seemed to dissipate around her. Her smile never strained, her posture was that of a woman entirely at ease, one elbow slung up on the table in a manner Rafaela had never observed in her mother before. She was almost a different person inhabiting Mamamía's body. She leaned her forehead close to her cousin's and did not stop talking or laughing until the brick wall opposite the room's one small window seeped from red, to dark brown, to purple, indicating that Papamío would be back from his meetings soon. He'd expect to find his three girls at home in the Plaza. Mamamía embraced her cousin for a long time before they bundled back into the narrow stairwell and down to the street to find a taxicab.

On the gold brocade couch at the foot of the bed in her parents' opulent bedroom, Rafaela tried to imagine her friend Candido in that faraway place. She tried to imagine his tongue slowing and loosening, finding the lethargy of English. Candido eating pepperoni pizza. Mounting endless flights of stairs into a noisy apartment. Sirens, neon, sky-high pavements that crowded out the sun. The lively clamor of Spanish Harlem. Rafaela's memories of New York were all blaring noises, sharp edges, hard surfaces. She couldn't make room in that landscape for the softness of Candido. The softness of his voice, his eyes, his skin, his laughter, his mouth. New York would obliterate him, she thought.

"I guess if there's ever a time to do it, this might be my last chance," he said. And then he wrapped his cool hand around the back of Rafaela's neck beneath the tumble of her curls, and without closing his eyes, he kissed her.

When he drew back, she was afraid she would cry and he'd mistake her tears for regret. So she kept her eyes on their entwined hands instead, and she lowered her voice to match his softness.

"Don't go to New York," she said.

Later that same evening as Mamamía returned from an unknown errand, the next-door neighbor, a dowdy, needling woman, cast a sidelong glance at Mamamía from her porch, and declared loudly her observation that Papamío had long demonstrated a rather acute shortcoming in terms of his ability to make sound decisions. Priti, who had spent years cultivating an uneasy self-restraint, overheard the remark through the kitchen window and, realizing that her employment with Mamamía was at an end and she was no longer required to silence herself in the face of ignorance, dried her hands, untied her apron, and draped it over the edge of the sink before going to the front door and opening it. Priti met Mamamía coming in, and stood aside for her employer before going out to the porch railing with her arms crossed.

"Oye," Priti called to where the neighbor sat in her rocking chair with her fan and her glass of lemonade. Just being addressed this way would be enough to shock the neighbor into reticence, but Priti, who had waited a long time to say her piece, would say it fully. She would say it without raising her voice, too, she decided, because she would not concede that potential distraction, would not provide an excuse for the woman to misinterpret her as a kook. So Priti walked down the steps and crossed the driveway, past Benicio, who was polishing the back bumper of the Roadmaster with a clean rag, and she didn't stop until she was on the neighbor's porch, in front of the no-longer-rocking chair.

Priti unfolded her arms and held her hands together behind her back. She spoke quietly and urgently. She said, "It has been a long number of years you've been under the misapprehension that you're somehow above Doña María Teresa. And why? Because of that limp yellow hair? Because God played a joke on you, giving you that pink skin that burns if you walk outside uncovered? Because your rich, bloodless family inbred with all the other European families on this island instead of invigorating your prospects with a little sangre fuerte local?"

The neighbor's lemonade trembled in its glass, and the fan hung still in the air.

"I have held my tongue these long years while you made your back-handed compliments. But, gazmoña, I tell you now, those bitter insults only drew attention to your envy." Priti raised a hand and pointed back across the driveway, toward the door where Mamamía was still standing just inside, biting her knuckle in amazement. "It is my pleasure to inform you," Priti said, "now that I am finally free to say it, that the woman in there has more grace and elegance in the mole on her backside than your whole family and your pig-looking kids could muster in a generation."

The neighbor's eyes and mouth were wide-open circles, but there was no verbal response beyond a gasp, so Priti turned to go, shaking her head and muttering as she walked away.

"We will not miss your ugly ass one little bit. God gave us one reprieve here, at least we'll get away from this flock of turkeys."

Mamamía was waiting for Priti just inside the door. They closed it behind them together with a quiet click, and then collapsed at the bottom of the staircase, where they recounted every word they could recall, and laughed until they cried.

§

So many things fell apart in the weeks that followed that it was impossible for Rafaela to place them in any sensible order in her mind. There was no hierarchy to her loss, it was just loss, upon loss, upon loss. A partial list of what she lost: friends, status, routine, home, security, the ability to sleep past sunrise, her sense of herself, her place in the world.

At Las Madres, Rafaela had been an excellent student, better liked by her teachers than her peers who, without testing the theory, presumed that Rafaela's beauty and wealth made her arrogant. Rafaela hadn't cared much, because the assumptions about her arrogance weren't totally unwarranted, and luckily, that mild little ego of hers shielded her from noticing the worst of her peers' judgment. If Lola and Candido had been her only friends, she'd have counted herself lucky enough, but she did have a few other friends besides them, and anyway, school wasn't for making friends. It was for learning physics and calculus and French and English, and reading classic novels and writing persuasive political essays. Education at Las Madres was a portal, a preview of the complicated and fascinating life that awaited them.

In the first days following her expulsion, then, Rafaela tried to imagine that her early exit from school might mean only that the complicated and fascinating part of her life was beginning ahead of schedule. Everyone around her was in a plan-making scramble. There was tremendous activity at the house. Buyers, sellers, movers, men in ties with briefcases coming and going at all hours, men in uniforms with trucks and hand trucks, hauling things away. It felt like heady choreography, like a bad dream where everyone had learned the dance except for Rafaela. She stood still in the middle of the ballroom while the waltz of decomposition gained terrifying speed around her. Her arms hung loosely at her sides.

In Papamío's study, she and Dolores sat on boxes that had been packed with books. The furniture was gone, all except for Papamío's tufted leather desk chair. He looked strange and small sitting in it now with no desk in front of him, like a turtle without its shell. All these years in this house, and Rafaela never knew that chair had wheels. She'd never once sat in it herself. There were many things she hadn't known, had never even wondered about. For example, she didn't realize that Papamío, whose family had been extraordinarily wealthy some generations before, was almost bankrupt before he married Mamamía, whose own once-humble father had prospered in agriculture and real estate. Neither did Rafaela understand how much of her mother's inheritance was gone now, how much of her family's extravagant lifestyle had been financed in recent years by her father's government position. And certainly no infinitesimal part of Rafaela's brain could ever have dreamed that Mamamía was already at work developing the business plan (curating and renting out high-end fashion, positioning herself as the first one-stop luxury stylist in San Juan) that would eventually see them through the worst of this financial catastrophe. Even if Rafaela had known some or all of these things, that knowledge would have done little to mitigate her current disorientation. It was simply too much change, too fast.

Papamío's voice echoed back to them from the empty, sun-stained walls.

"We can manage school until graduation, but you will have to go one at a time, and not to Las Madres," Papamío was saying, the words only adding to her sense of turbulence. "Dolores will be first, obviously, as she's in her final year already."

The girls were holding hands.

"First to what?" Rafaela gave voice to her confusion.

"And what about Rafa?" Lola asked.

Rafaela squeezed her sister's hand, but not in gratitude. Whatever Papamío had to say, Rafa didn't want to make it any harder for him. He leaned forward in the chair and rolled himself closer to the boxes where the sisters were perched, side by side. He put a hand on Rafaela's knee, on the linen of her skirt; his moustache twitched when he smiled, and for one horrifying moment, Rafaela thought he would cry.

"Rafa will have an adventure." Papamío smiled thinly, and she nodded to encourage him. He cleared his throat. "We have secured a good job for you, Rafaela. For one year, just until Lola graduates, and then Lola will go to work while you come back and finish school."

"Come back?" both girls asked at the same time.

"Where is she going, Pa? Where's the job?" This was Lola. Rafaela couldn't bring herself to ask.

Papamío rolled himself back a few inches. A buffer. He leaned his elbows on his knees.

"The job is in Trinidad."

Lola gasped, and Rafaela could feel her sister crushing her fingers in her hand.

"On the Navy base there."

Rafaela nodded. She smiled at Papamío, but she could feel her heart beating in all her extremities, a wobble in her peripheral vision, the edges of her known universe giving way.

"You can't send Rafa to Trinidad!" Lola stood up abruptly, and they both looked up at her. Neither girl had ever spoken to Papamío that way before. Not even in their dreams or their nightmares. But these were unprecedented times, and all kinds of things were happening for the first time ever. Lola lowered her voice into sorrow. "Where will she live?"

Papamío blinked rapidly. "Mamamía has a niece there already. She lives in a civilian boarding house right on base, and there's room for Rafaela."

Rafa nodded again. "It's good. That's good," she tried to convince herself. "What's the job?"

Lola sat down again with a thump.

"It's secretarial work. For the Navy."

Rafa was still nodding. Her brain felt like rusty machinery. She was trying to engage the gears, trying to imagine herself in an office somewhere, but the chain wouldn't budge. She didn't even know what a secretary did. Papamío came to the rescue.

"To begin with, it'll be very light administrative work," he said. "You'll answer the phone, you'll type memos, you'll do some filing." Perhaps her terror was visible on her face because next he said, "Don't worry, they will show you what to do. You'll pick it up."

Lola was holding her head in her hands, but now she sat up quickly, sparked into energy by the idea she'd just had.

"I will go!" she said. "I'm older, more experienced. Rafa is too young to leave home." Lola did not say out loud that Rafaela would be disastrously bad at the job her father was describing, but the sentiment was plain enough on her face, and they were all thinking it anyway.

The sigh that escaped Papamío then appeared to physically pain him. "It's already arranged for her," he said.

"I'm sure we can change it!" Lola waved her hands between them like she was conducting a magic trick. *Voilà!*

"They need English-speaking personnel only, Lola," Papamío said.

"I speak English!"

Papamío smiled at her sadly. "Rafa got top marks in English two years running. They were impressed by those grades, that's why they agreed to hire her so young."

"But they won't know the difference if you send me!" Lola said. "I can be Rafaela for one year! Who will know?"

"No," Rafa said.

They both turned to look at her.

Rafaela stood up and clasped her hands behind her back. She began to pace the empty length of the study while they watched her push a little harder on the rusty machinery in her mind, which finally sprang to action. There. She could see herself in a warm, bright office next to a window. Her hair tied back in a bun. A pencil skirt like Lois Lane, maybe some glasses. A glass of water on a coaster beside her clacking typewriter. She'd speak English and she'd say things like, "Yes, Captain Browning; right away, Captain Browning." She'd reach for the phone when it rang, all business. She'd ask, "How may I direct your call?"

Lola sniffed on the box behind her, but Rafaela would not turn to look. Lola's tears were known to be contagious.

"It will be fun, maybe," she said, convincingly, she hoped. She could learn to take orders instead of giving them, right? She could learn to be humble, to hold her tongue. And she could be the one to save her family, to earn money and see them through.

Papamío reached into his breast pocket and flicked his handkerchief out of its little square. He handed it to Dolores, who honked into it.

"You will meet a lot of new people," Papamío said. "Do you remember Clarisa? Mamamía's niece? She's only a year older than you."

Rafa shook her head.

"She hasn't been to San Juan since you girls were little." He slapped his hands on his thighs and pushed himself to standing. "But you'll be reac-quainted in no time. It will be nice, you'll have family there."

Papamío walked toward her with his hands outstretched, and Rafaela stopped pacing so he could take her in his arms. He held her by both shoulders, blinked again, and looked briefly to the floor before locking eyes with her.

"Mija," he said, and then two words she'd never heard from her father before, and hoped to never hear again for as long as she lived. "I'm sorry."

Chapter Ten

~

Palisades, New York
2023

Daisy.

So far, the calamity exists in only one word because Ruth cannot bring herself to place that word in a larger context, to surround it with other words. It is Daisy.

Ruth stands in the guest bedroom in front of the open closet where the large suitcase is stored. She opens her phone and scrolls through her list of saved cities until she finds San Juan. A technicality, really, because she knows the weather in Puerto Rico. The predictable twelve-degree window, the rain, the increasing annual terror of the hurricane season. But it's only June now, so there won't be the threat of a storm for at least another month, more likely two or three. And in any case, none of it will much affect what Ruth needs to pack anyway. She'll be spending her time there in a hospital room. If she's lucky.

So it's only the comfort of habit that leads her to check. A quick glance at the forecast will allow her to pack without thinking. There's so much to do. Airline tickets. Calling the boys. She has to tell Mama, too, and Dad. She can't think past the immediate next steps. She checks her breath to keep herself present.

But what she sees on the phone screen produces a sort of clicking in her spinal column. She feels herself straightening up as she stares at the phone in her hand. The string of stacked sun icons is not there on the lefthand side of the screen where she expects to see it. In its place, the phone background is gray, filled with tiny lightning zappers. Ruth touches the top of her head to see if she'll find her glasses there, because she's now of an age where she can get only a vague sense of things without them. They're not shoved into her hair. She turns in circles, pats her left-hand pocket where she sometimes finds them, gropes at her neckline to find that neither are they hanging there at her collar by one stem. She feels like a cartoon character in some macabre animation.

"Shit," she says out loud.

She starts back to the kitchen still clutching the phone, where she finds the missing glasses abandoned beside her computer, of course. She always leaves them within arm's reach when she's shooting a video. That damned video seemed so important an hour ago. She slams the laptop closed and pushes the glasses onto her face. The weather app springs open in her hand: 100 percent chance of thunderstorms, 100 percent chance of thunderstorms, 100 percent chance of thunderstorms. For three days.

"Unusual," she says quietly, because she always has had a gift for understatement.

Ruth makes her way back to the bedroom while peering at that dismal forecast, and feels a line of worry mark its usual crease in her forehead, feels her lips purse out from her face. But that's it. Nothing more penetrates the whole-body cloak of composed fear she's already wearing.

She stares into her phone and scrolls back up to the top where all is explained in the box with the tiny red exclamation point in the corner. *Severe Weather Warning*, it says. Ruth clicks "see more," and watches her screen fill with bold red urgency, box after box. *Hurricane Warning. Tornado Watch. Flash Flood Watch. Storm Surge Warning. Mudslide Warning.*

Ruth backs up without looking until she feels the backs of her legs make contact with the bed. She thumps herself down there, and clicks on each of the warnings in turn. Even as she reads them and rereads them, she can't locate the uptake button in her brain. It doesn't make sense.

"It's only June," she says to no one.

Instead of processing what she's reading, her mind is unhelpfully focused on denial and other futile pursuits. Why hasn't she been paying attention? How can she be so thoroughly disconnected from Puerto Rico and her daughter that this storm wasn't even on her radar? And most distressing of all, why, for the love of God, hasn't she tried harder to work things out with Daisy? Whenever she and her daughter try to talk about Daisy's life, they revert to a calcifying script where Ruth demands recognition from her daughter, and Daisy tells her mom to butt out so she can live her grown-up life on her own terms. Beneath this pattern of vexation, what Ruth really feels is rejected, because the modest college fund she worked so hard to establish is still rotting in the bank. She is hurt by Daisy's dismissiveness, and hopes her daughter never has to learn how grueling it is for a single mom to raise three kids, let alone to save that kind of money for their education. But they haven't been able to discover the tender parts of this feud because they're both locked into the anger instead.

"I can literally hear you rolling your eyes," Daisy said the last time they spoke on the phone, and then they bickered about the word *literally*.

When was that? Two weeks ago? Three? What a waste of precious breath, of time. Why hadn't she said to her daughter, *I love you beyond reason and none of this matters at all and every day that you breathe is a gift*? The words on Ruth's screen run together. They tumble and whip and swirl, but they also bolt into her consciousness and temporarily blow everything else away.

Threat to life and property includes typical forecast uncertainty. Potential for winds greater than 120 miles per hour. Plan for extreme conditions. Prepare for catastrophic destruction including devastating structural damage to sturdy buildings, complete destruction of insecure buildings. Prepare for life-threatening storm surge up to 12 feet in coastal areas. Prepare for peak rainfall amounts to exceed 20 inches across the interior of the island causing extreme flooding where rivers may overflow their banks. Prepare for flood waters to overwhelm control barriers and escape routes. Situation favorable for tornadoes. Urgently bring emergency evacuation plans to completion.

Just a sliver then, the width of a knife blade. A tickle of horror that asserts itself as goosebumps across her arms, a hot wash of tingles across the back of her neck. A new layer of fear on top of the previous layer of fear, neither of which Ruth has yet begun to grasp. She has to get to Daisy immediately. And here is a monster in her path.

When the phone rings again, it wouldn't be right to say that it startles Ruth from her thoughts, because Ruth is already in such a heightened state of alarm that it would be impossible to shock her further. She drops her cell phone on the bed and runs to the kitchen, to the phone that never rings anymore, which is now ringing again for the second time this evening. She does not say hello when she picks it up.

"Daisy?"

"Ruth Hayes?"

It is not Daisy, of course.

"Yes?" Ruth feels breathless and wild. She steadies herself against the wall with one hand.

"It's Kevin, calling from the administrative office at the trauma hospital in Río Piedras." The man on the phone is barely audible behind the loud internal thrum in Ruth's ears. "We spoke a little while ago," he says, as if Ruth might have forgotten.

"Yes." She holds her breath, squeezes her eyes closed. Whatever questions are ready to fly from her mouth, she is not ready for the answers, so she swallows them. She will let this man talk.

"I'm sorry to bother you again," he says. "I'm sure this is a lot to take in, and you must have your hands full making arrangements."

Ruth does not like the sound of the word *arrangements*. She strains her ears to see if she can hear anything happening in that faraway room where Kevin is sitting, but nothing except his voice crosses the threshold of the distant mouthpiece. Ruth wonders if he has seen Daisy. Have they been near enough to mingle oxygen? Daisy is still breathing, still trading air with the people around her. Ruth would know if she wasn't, because Ruth would stop breathing too.

"Is she—" Ruth cuts the question off right there because the confirmation she's seeking is that Daisy is still alive, and she cannot bring herself to articulate the possibility that there's an alternative.

"I don't have anything new to report on your daughter's condition, I'm afraid," Kevin says. "I'm sorry."

Ruth closes her eyes, an act of timid prayer in her eyelids.

"I'm just calling to ask about secondary medical insurance," he says.

The words he is saying do not make sense. They don't sound like Spanish or English.

"The what?" Ruth says.

"Does she have additional medical insurance?"

"She has Pinnacle. The diamond plan."

"Right, we did find her insurance card, but I'm just wondering if there's secondary insurance?"

"I don't—" Ruth pauses to consider the question, not because it's possible that Daisy has secondary medical insurance, but because she's so confused by the sudden appearance of the question. Her brain is on a lag. "No," she finally says. "No, that's her medical insurance. I know because I pay for it myself. She has four more years before she ages out. It's Pinnacle."

"Right, but, I just thought she might have travel insurance as well?"

Ruth shakes her head, but the confusion doesn't clear. "No, she's, she's not traveling. She lives there."

"Oh!" The pitch of his voice shifts and then, almost more to himself than to Ruth, he says, "Oh, they had her home address listed in Palisades, New York."

"That is where she's from, it's where I live." Ruth presses the flat of her palm against her forehead, but she can't get through the skin and skull to placate the uncomfortable spinning that's happening underneath. "Can we, could we take care of this later?" she asks. "When I get down there?"

"Of course," Kevin says. "Of course, we're going to provide your daughter with the best possible care in the meantime. You don't have to worry about that."

She hadn't been worried about that. But now she kind of is.

"Thank you," she says.

"Just . . ."

Ruth can hear him moving papers around, and then some keyboard clicking.

"Just, if you can, Ms. Hayes, I would recommend calling your insurance company as soon as possible, just to verify coverage."

"Verify coverage?"

"I'm sure it's the last thing you want to be dealing with right now."

There are worse things, Ruth knows.

"It's just, Pinnacle is telling us your daughter isn't covered in Puerto Rico."

"What." The word comes out without any upward inflection.

"Maybe it's just because we're out of network." He sounds neither convinced nor convincing. "I'm sure it's just a misunderstanding. I hate even asking these questions right now."

He's trying, bless him. But his kindness is only making things worse. Ruth recognizes this brand of kindness, she remembers it from when Thomas died. Surely hospital administrators are not this gentle when an uninsured patient comes in with a sprained ankle or a bump on the head. Surely they save this level of empathy for the truly imperiled.

"It's okay," she says. "I'll figure it out. I have to pack, book my flight. When my brain can make room for this, I'll call."

Rafaela sets her small table with a place mat and silverware. She places her crystal wineglass on a coaster because even though she lives alone, she's not an animal. She dims the lights over the dining room table and is carrying her plate in from the kitchen when she sees the shape of her daughter appear outside the glass door on her little porch. Although they live about fifty yards apart, it's unusual for her daughter to drop by without sending a text first. Still, Rafaela doesn't think much of it as she waves Ruth in. She sits down and takes the first bite of her dinner just as Ruth opens the door and steps inside. Her daughter does not move into the room, which seems unmannerly to Rafaela until her eye lands properly on Ruth for the first time. She is crumpled, haggard-looking. Her breath seems to be stuck in her neck and shoulders, her face contorted with some unnameable emotion. Rafaela drops the fork on her plate and stands quickly from the chair.

"What's wrong?" She crosses the space between them in a few quick strides, and gathers Ruth into her arms.

She knows even before Ruth confirms it that it must be one of the kids. Ruth has trouble forcing the words to exit her body. There is no wind to carry them. Only a single word escapes.

"Daisy."

No.

No, no, no, no, no.

"What?" Rafaela says, now fully in the grip of dread. "What happened to Daisy?"

The odor of blackened fish and scalded oil sour the room. Rafaela has taken only one bite, but now she fears it will come back on her. Ruth is tense inside the fortress of Rafaela's arms, a shuddering knot of grief and fear. Rafa's hands are firm on her daughter's shoulders. She holds Ruth at arm's length and tries to peer into her daughter's face. She needs to coax this horror into the light.

"What is it?" she says again. "What's happened to Daisy?"

"An accident," Ruth croaks.

Rafaela's breath stops too. She can feel the clobber of her heart within her.

"Is she—" Rafaela sucks the beginning of that sentence back in. "Where is she?" she asks instead.

She steers Ruth to the couch. They sit down on the edge together, perched and curled.

"At the trauma hospital in Río Piedras."

The assertion again of her skidding heart. So her heart still works, then. It does acrobatics.

"Okay," she says. "Okay, let's go. Let's pack."

She stands up, but her daughter is still seated, reaching into the back pocket of her jeans and pulling out her phone. She opens it, hands it miserably to Rafaela. Ruth crumples over her own knees. Rafaela looks down at the screen, at the icons of doom, the whole impenetrable parade of them.

They will not be able to go, there will be no flights. They are stuck here, and that feeling of imposed stasis brings with it a sort of panicky claustrophobia. Rafaela feels the rush of determination fizz from her body, and in its place an alarming void opens up. The fog begins to filter in.

Ruth sits up quickly, suddenly, and takes the phone from Rafaela's hand. "Benny," her daughter says. "We have to call Benny. He can get to her."

Ruth is trembling, opening her phone app, but Rafaela is momentarily blank. Benny. Benny. It takes her a minute. The blankness can be insistent, but it never lasts more than a few seconds, a minute. Rafaela patiently drops the bucket once more into the well of her memory, and it comes up empty. She tries again. And again. There. *Shit.* It feels like a pop, the onset of a secondary terror.

Benny. Of course, Benny.

Her son.

Chapter Eleven

~

St. Louis, Missouri
1980

Two years before the divorce, Benny made his second friend in St. Louis, a new boy at school.

"That's great, sport!" Dad said from behind his newspaper at the breakfast table. Ruth knew when Dad was taking a sip of his coffee because one hand would disappear from the edge of the paper and the barrier would begin to droop. She'd hear the cup go back into its saucer, and then her dad would whip the paper upright again.

Breakfast was Ruth's favorite meal of the day, least likely to be overcooked, most likely to be inoffensive. Ruth was able to make and butter her own toast, and she was allowed to salt and pepper her own eggs until they tasted the way she liked them.

"Hurry and eat so I can do your hair before the bus comes," Mama said.

Ruth was nine, and her mother had stopped putting her hair in braids every single day, but she still insisted that Ruth wear it up, despite the fact that Jennifer, Jenny, and Kathy all wore their hair down and flowy, with pretty little barrettes on the sides.

"Well, they can have pretty little barrettes and they can have lice," Mama said. "Meanwhile, my daughter will be clean."

"That's right, pumpkin," Dad said, lowering the newspaper long enough to wink at Ruth. "Gotta wear it up."

Ruth interpreted the wink to mean that her father didn't actually care how she wore her hair, but he was eager to find innocuous opportunities to agree with Mama.

"Anyway, I was wondering if I could go ride bikes with him after school," Benny said.

"Ride bikes with who?" Dad lowered the paper again.

"With the new kid. Eddie."

Dad frowned, as if this were the first time he was hearing of Eddie.

"The boy I was just telling you about? Who just moved here?"

"Oh right." Dad definitely did not remember. "Sure thing."

Mama was standing at the sink rinsing the frying pan, but Ruth could see her disagreement before she even turned around. Her arms stopped moving in the soapy water. Her shoulders were still. She took in a deep breath and shook her head before she turned, drying her hands on her apron.

"More information, please," she said to Benny, coming to stand beside him at the table. One hand on the back of Dad's chair, the other perched on her hip.

Benny had already finished his scrambled eggs and was shoveling his second bowl of Life Cereal into his mouth because, as Ruth had observed, eleven-year-old boys almost never stopped eating. He swallowed before he answered.

"What do you mean?"

"I mean, if you're going to go out with this boy I don't know, I need more information!" Mama said.

"What kind of information?"

"Last name, where does he live, where are you going, what time will you be home?"

"Oh." Benny looked crestfallen. "I don't know. I don't know him that well yet. I can find out. But then."

Dad folded his paper and set it on the edge of the table.

Ruth watched Benny try to work through a solution in his head, where he could get his mother the information she wanted but still go bike riding today, this afternoon, directly after school. This was 1980. Logistics were complicated and friends were in short supply. Benny couldn't afford to miss an opportunity with his Huffy.

"Rafaela, it's fine," Dad said, snapping his last slice of bacon in half with one bite. "It'll be good for him."

Benny grinned up at Mama, his face a plea.

"And it will be good for me to have more information so I don't have to worry. I'm not asking for much." Mama turned to Benny. "Why don't you stop by here for a snack after school so I can meet him? Then you can go out and ride your bikes."

Benny tried to hide a cringe, but Ruth caught it. Their mother and father both missed it because they were preoccupied attempting to conceal their mutual irritation instead of looking at Benny. Ruth took another bite of her toast and waited to see what would happen next. Although she sometimes felt bad about her parents' fights, they were also a reliable source of domestic intrigue, and she could feel this one building right in front of her.

"Just stay between the school and the park, and don't go farther north than Midway Avenue," Dad said, rolling his paper into a little tube. "Right, Rafaela? That way you'll know where they are."

"Peter." Mama's voice was full of reproach. "I don't even know this child."

"Ah, they're just boys," Dad said, standing up and draining the last of his coffee. "They're all the same. Right, sport?"

Ruth looked at Benny, who was too smart to agree with their father at a moment like this. Benny lifted his spoon and worked a heap of Life Cereal into his mouth instead, before saying something completely unintelligible. Dad used the rolled-up paper to pat Benny and Ruth on the head, once each. Then he leaned in to kiss their mother, who stiffened. If her mother had leaned in even an inch, even a centimeter, Ruth might have felt some hope for them. Or if Mama had leaned back, even, away from Dad. Mightn't that have been an indication of some feeling? It was her very stillness, the fact that Mama didn't even bother to move away from him, that was the most damning thing of all. Like she took leave of her body just long enough to endure Dad's kiss. Ruth watched Dad grab his keys and his briefcase from their spot by the back door. She could almost see her mother's spirit alight and return after he was gone.

Ruth and her friends were on the swings behind the school that afternoon when her brother and the new kid came by in a cloud of bike dust.

Benny flicked out his kickstand and left his bike upright at the edge of the playground, but the other boy stayed astride his mount for an extra minute or two doing tricks. He popped a wheelie, spun his handlebars around and around. Then he did a reverse wheelie and some bunny hops on his front tire. Ruth could feel her friends watching him.

"Hey, dweeb," Benny said to Ruth.

"Hey, loser," she responded.

Jenny was on the swing next to her, stretching and pumping her legs to increase her momentum. Ruth was twisting in circles, making her swing chains into a tight coil, stretching her toes down as far as they'd reach so the chain could reach maximum corkscrew above her. She stopped with one toe extended beneath so she could watch the new kid do his tricks. When he was done showing off, he dropped his bike in the dirt and followed Benny to the monkey bars. Jenny waited until he was looking before she jumped, arcing her body high into the air, the abandoned swing loose behind her, her blond hair winging out like a cape, arms and legs windmilling through the sky. Ruth leaned back and watched her fly, held her breath on the hard thump of the landing. But Jenny landed perfectly, two feet and one hand in the mulch before she moved seamlessly from crouch to handstand. Jenny dropped to her feet and then brushed the mulch from her hands, pretending not to notice the boys watching her. She stuck her hands in the back pockets of her Jordache jeans.

"¡Mira, Evel Knievel!" the new boy said.

Ruth couldn't be entirely sure. She thought that was what he said, and there was a small wiggle of feeling that came with the sound of it, something she couldn't quite name. She leaned back until her body was parallel with the ground before removing the lock of her toe from the mulch. She arched her back while the swing spun her like a top. She loved the dizziness of it. She kept her eyes open and watched the upside-down world spin past.

The boys were talking quietly, but she couldn't hear them because Kathy and Jennifer were doing their handclaps super loud. So Ruth waited for her swing to come to a stop and then she hopped off. She ambled dizzily over to the monkey bars, where Jenny was already hanging by her knees on one end. The new boy and her brother were standing on top, balancing on the two outside bars, and when Ruth started across, the boys pretended they were going to step on her fingers. She squealed, but raced across until she bumped into Jenny on the other side. She turned and raced back, Jenny giving her a push from the hips as she went. When she reached the far side, she climbed up the ladder to the top and leaned against the rail where her brother was still standing with his new friend.

"What's your name?" she asked the boy.

He turned to look at her. "Eddie," he said.

She gleaned nothing from this exchange. She leaned out, making her body into an acute angle: feet, bottom, hands.

"You just moved here?" she asked.

"Yes."

There. There was something in that syllable. An almost *j* where a *y* should be. Actually, a whole *yes* where a *yeah* should be. She knew she hadn't imagined it.

"Where'd you come from?" she asked.

He looked at Benny for a translation, and Benny obliged.

"¿De dónde vienes?"

He looked back at Ruth. "De Puerto Rico," he said.

"Oh."

She slid her eyes back to Jenny, still hanging from her knees with her blond hair draping down like a yellow curtain, long enough that it almost swept the mulch beneath her. It was impossible to read Jenny's upside-down facial expression. Eddie moved his body so he was sitting on the top of the monkey bars, and then he dropped down. Her brother followed. Ruth did another lap across and back, and then she watched while the boys got back on their bikes and took off.

The girls met up on the merry-go-round to discuss the new boy. It was Kathy's turn to push, but she was taking her time, sitting on the edge and lazily pushing with one foot.

"That was cool what he could do with his bike," Jennifer said.

"My brother can do way more than that," Kathy said. "He can do jumps and spin around in the air."

"What was his name?" Jenny asked.

"Eddie," Ruth said.

"Yeah," Jenny said. "That's right."

"Seems nice," Jennifer said.

Kathy shrugged. "I dunno. Did you see how rusty his bike was? And his sneakers were totally busted. Who starts a new school with raggedy sneakers?"

Ruth wished she had looked more carefully at the sneakers, but she also couldn't intuit what their condition had to do with anything.

"Well, I think he's cute," Jenny said.

"Ew, gross!" Kathy said, trying to suppress some twist of feeling from displaying itself across her mouth. Jennifer and Jenny weren't looking, but Ruth examined Kathy's face, and there was no hiding the pink that climbed up her cheeks. Kathy saw Ruth notice.

"Anyway," Kathy said, jumping off the edge of the merry-go-round to begin pushing. "I think he's, like, foreign or something." She put an ugly slant on the word so they all understood the unspoken modifiers attached, and eyeballed Ruth when she said it.

Ruth froze. That small feeling she'd experienced as only a tingle now expanded within her. All in a rush, it spread to every part of her body, and it was made of many different pieces. It was both pride and shame, anger and joy, loss and leverage, alienation and belonging. It was nausea, and it was calcified by a tangential feeling that gathered up all the others and displaced them. This largest feeling was much easier to identify: fear.

Ruth wanted to say something. To agree with Kathy, to make some declaration that would illustrate her recognition that Eddie was indeed *foreign*. But the sentiment stuck in her mouth. Because Benny. Because the comfort of Eddie's speech, familiar but distant, like awakening in the morning and feeling the remnants of a dream just at the edge of your mind, where you can feel its presence, a vague sense of it, and a prolonged precipice where it may return if you don't try too hard, if you don't lift your head from the pillow and sit up. The trick is in a stillness of mind. You can't want it too much, can't look too directly, can't beckon it. With patience and breath, the details may return in sharp relief. The access point may be a single element, a door kicked open, and the sudden unspooling of the whole thing at once. *¡Coquí!* Or just as often, *poof!* The door is sealed shut. All is irretrievable, gone.

Ruth held herself very still on the metal deck of the merry-go-round. The sun ducked behind a shelf of clouds, and she zipped her red hoodie all the way up to her chin.

Ruth went home early, told her friends she didn't feel well.

Dad was still at work, and Mama was playing solitaire at the kitchen table, a mug of coffee at her elbow. Ruth dropped her bag by the kitchen door.

"Hang it up," Mama said without looking up from her card game.

Ruth lifted the backpack onto her seat at the table instead, unzipped it, and pulled out her homework folder and pencil case. Then she went and hung the bag on its hook beside the back door.

"How was your day?" Mama asked.

"Good," Ruth said.

"You're home early." Now she looked up, and Ruth stood close to her mother, leaned against her, and kissed her face. Mama pulled her chair back a few inches so Ruth could squeeze onto her lap.

"I didn't feel well," she said, picking up Mama's ten of spades, and placing it on top of its jack.

"Oh?" Mama wrapped a cool hand across Ruth's forehead, checking for fever.

Mama leaned into her back then, folded her arms around Ruth's waist, and kissed the nape of her neck. Ruth felt herself loosen in her mother's arms. She felt that new mantle of confusion rolling away. She tipped her head back onto her mama's shoulder.

"Okay, mi amor?"

Mi amor. Only when they were alone was Ruth still mi amor. The tears came hot and fast, and Ruth didn't understand them, didn't know their source exactly, even though it was clear they had arrived with Eddie. She didn't really think that boy was to blame.

"Oh." Mama held her tighter, and rocked them both lightly in the kitchen seat. "Shh, shh. It's okay," her mother hummed. "What happened? Did something happen?"

Ruth took a deep breath and sat up. She wiped her eyes on the sleeve of her red hoodie. "No, nothing happened. Not really. I don't know. I just don't feel good."

Mama turned Ruth on her lap so she could investigate her face for the truth. A few seconds passed before her mother determined that Ruth was telling the truth, as best she could.

"Okay," Mama said, pushing her off her lap and standing up from her card game. "Sit."

Ruth pulled out her own chair and sat behind her homework folder while Mama got up and pulled a Snoopy glass out of the cabinet, filled it with Hawaiian Punch. She set it down in front of Ruth and then sat back down beside her. She picked up her eight of diamonds run and moved it onto the nine.

"You have much homework tonight?"

"Just math," Ruth said.

She did the first problem and then pulled her sharpener out of her pencil case. "I met Benny's new friend," she said. Totally casually, while she stuck the point of her already-sharp pencil into the little black gadget and began to turn.

"Oh?" Her mother matched her nonchalance. "Was he nice?"

Ruth shrugged. "I guess."

A delicate curl of wood peeled from her pencil and landed on her workbook. She did two more math problems. They were learning long division, and Ruth didn't care for the numbers, but she liked drawing the little garage with its roof and door.

"He's from Puerto Rico," Ruth said quietly.

"Oh." Mama held the draw deck in her left hand, her fingernails painted the faintest pink. The inside of a seashell. The soft glow of a cloud during a sun-shower. The color of their little house in Santurce, their first house. Home.

"Where is he from, in Puerto Rico?"

Ruth shrugged again. "I don't know." She traced a little squiggle in the margin of her math workbook.

Mama drew three more cards from the top of her pile. Ruth could feel the next question brewing, and she knew it was the big one. No way to disguise it, despite the quiet hush of her mother's voice.

"Is he white?"

There it was.

Another shrug. "I guess." Ever since that day in the country club, Ruth had lost her ability to distinguish who was considered white. She also didn't understand why it mattered, but there was no question that it mattered. It mattered in Puerto Rico and it mattered even more here. "Like us, you know? Like, in between."

Her mother nodded. Relief in her posture. And the swamp of Ruth's bad feelings returned with a rush. Deep down she knew that Benny had withheld this information on purpose, that there was some reason he hadn't told his parents or sister that the new kid hadn't just moved here, but that he'd moved here from Puerto Rico. Ruth didn't understand what Kathy saw when she looked at Eddie or why, or what her brother was hiding from Mama or why, but when it came to matters of loyalty, Benny was no match for Mama. They weren't even in the same universe. So in that way, it didn't really feel like betrayal.

"He doesn't really speak English, though," Ruth reported.

Mama took a deep breath. "Oh dear," she said.

Dinner that night was intense, and not only because Mama made tuna noodle casserole (an abomination in four ingredients: a can of unseasoned tuna, a can of condensed soup, a scrum of wet noodles, and a sad population of flaccid Velveeta). Even Dad had a hard time getting it down, but Benny finished his plate and went for seconds. It was unthinkable.

Mama swirled the long noodles onto her fork, but didn't lift it to her mouth. "Did you have fun with your new friend today?" she asked Benny.

"Yeah." Benny nodded. There was a glob of Velveeta on the side of his plate that looked for all the world like something he'd just liberated from his sinuses.

Ruth still felt queasy from earlier.

"Not hungry, sweet pea?" Dad asked.

Ruth shook her head.

"She's not feeling well," Mama said, reaching over to tuck an escaped curl behind Ruth's ear. Mama stroked her cheek, and Ruth felt pleased that her wellness was the one topic substantial enough to move Mama to deliver a spoken sentence directly to her father, rather than into the void around him.

"What's the matter, pumpkin?" Dad asked.

"I don't know. Just a tummy ache."

Dad looked down at his plate and nodded in solidarity. "Just try a couple bites," he said, then turned his attention to Benny as a way of offering her a reprieve, she thought.

Ruth picked up her fork, but without conviction.

"So what did you and your new friend get up to?" Dad asked.

"We just rode around," Benny said. "We stopped at the playground but then we went over to the tennis courts on Wooster Place, and nobody was playing, so we rode bikes over there."

"What, on the tennis courts?"

"Yeah, because Eddie has a BMX bike and he does all these tricks and stuff. He can do a wheelie with no hands. And he can keep it going, like, forever, without even moving really. He just pushes the pedals back and forth and the bike barely moves and he just stays up like that."

"Wow," Dad said. "Can he teach you any of that stuff?"

"Yeah, well, some of them you need a trick bike for," Benny said. "But he showed me how to do a regular wheelie."

"That is great," Dad said. "Can you show me after dinner?"

"Yeah." Benny grinned. "He can do a kind of handstand on his handlebars, too, but I don't think I can do that one." It was the most Ruth ever remembered Benny talking at dinner.

"I don't even think I could do a handstand on the carpet," Dad said. "Never mind on a bike!"

"Yeah, it was so cool. And then after we left the tennis courts we went to 7–Eleven and he bought a Slurpee." Benny paused long enough to register Mama's disapproval. "Don't worry, Mama, I didn't have one because I didn't want to spoil my dinner. I didn't have any money, anyway. Look, look at my tongue." He stuck out his tongue for their mother's inspection because everyone knew you couldn't sneak a Slurpee.

"Your father said not to go north of Midway."

"Oh."

"Don't be such a stickler, Rafaela," Dad said. "The 7–Eleven is on Midway."

"Technically, it's on Upton Street." Benny shoved another bite of tuna noodle casserole into his mouth.

"It's on the corner," Dad said.

"On the north corner," Mama said, "and Benny, I do not want you crossing that major intersection on your bike!"

"I didn't, Mama, we walked them across," Benny said. "I promise."

The information wasn't sufficient to walk Mama back from the glare she had trained on him. Dad took a bite of the tuna noodle casserole, and Ruth watched the experience of it wash over his face. Mama stood up from the table, walked to the counter, opened a drawer. She pulled out a box of Saran Wrap and brought it over to the table where she unrolled a piece and fitted it over the edges of Ruth's plate. Ruth had never felt more love for her mother than in that moment of deliverance.

"Is your homework all done?" Mama asked.

Ruth nodded.

"Okay, sweetie," she said. "You're excused. Why don't you go lie down on the couch in the den? I'll bring you an afghan."

"Thanks, Mama," Ruth said.

She stood slowly from her chair, stretched, and yawned. She didn't want to eat, but she also wasn't ready to be alone. She needed the comfort of her family around her. Ruth stopped by her dad's chair on the way out and leaned her chin on his shoulder. He kissed her cheek. Mama lifted Ruth's covered plate from the table and deposited it in the fridge.

"So where is your friend from, in Puerto Rico?" Mama asked, returning to her seat.

"What?" Benny snapped his eyes at Ruth, who straightened up from Dad's shoulder and turned for the door.

"I hear he's Puerto Rican."

"Yeah," Benny mumbled.

"Oh, that's great!" Dad's voice filled the room.

Ruth stood just outside the doorway behind the wall, listening. There was a diagonal line on the carpet where the light from the kitchen was cut from the room. Ruth stood in shadow.

"Funny you didn't mention that first thing!" Dad said.

Another mumble from Benny.

"Well, we'd like to meet him right away," Mama said.

"Absolutely," Dad agreed.

How seldom they agreed on anything, how unusual it was for this confluence of opinions to occur at her family's dinner table, Ruth realized. She understood, too, that her parents' reasons for wanting to meet the new boy were likely very different. Dad would be eager to meet a new Puerto Rican family so he could socialize and drink rum and impress them with his Spanish. He'd be hopeful that a friendship might evolve there not only for Benny but also for Mama. But Mama's reasons would not be social in the least. She'd be interested only in reconnaissance; she'd want to assess this boy and his family. To make sure they were the right *kind* of Puerto Ricans for Benny to befriend. It didn't really matter though, because the rare convergence of her parents' desires meant there would be no escape for Benny regardless. They were going to meet this kid.

"Maybe we should invite the whole family," Dad said, and Ruth could almost feel Benny's discomfort radiating through the wall. She pressed her cheek against the wood paneling there. "What do you say, Rafaela? Be fun, right?"

"Yes, I think it's a wonderful idea."

Benny had gone quiet, and Ruth could hear only the scraping of forks on plates, and then a moment later, a scraping of chair legs on the tile floor, and a firm but quiet declaration from her father.

"I can't eat this, Rafaela."

Chapter Twelve

~

Palisades, New York
2023

Daisy sat cross-legged on her grandmother's couch with a floppy pillow on her lap and a video game controller in both hands. Grandma sat next to her, kicking her ass in Mario Kart. Daisy tried not to be distracted by the knock on the door, but it didn't matter anyway. Grandma had just lapped her.

"It's open!" Grandma called without taking her eyes from the screen.

Daisy's mother walked into the room and came to stand behind the couch. She leaned over and watched them play. Onscreen, Grandma pitched a squid at Daisy, whose windshield was immediately covered in black ink. Daisy drove off the road.

"Well, what are you two up to?" Mom asked.

It seemed pretty obvious to Daisy what they were up to, but she refrained from saying so because she was only here for two more days before she had to return to San Juan. Half the reason for this trip was to try to patch things up with Mom, which efforts so far had not flourished. The other half was to celebrate her grandfather's eightieth birthday. Daisy had found him a mint-condition vintage Gamboa panama hat for his gift, and had carried it here on the plane because she didn't want it to get crushed in her suitcase. She'd wrapped it in tissue paper and placed it carefully into a paper shopping bag, which she held on her lap the entire flight. She didn't know where Grandpa would have the chance to wear it in Missouri, but maybe that would be all the encouragement he needed to come visit her in San Juan. Grandpa and his second wife, Trisha, were still good travelers, they enjoyed their little getaways. They were flying in from St. Louis this afternoon, and Vic was on his way to the airport to pick them up.

"Oh, just the usual," Grandma finally answered the question just as she collected her checkered flag at the finish line. She placed her controller on the coffee table. "Just destroying my granddaughter's dreams of being a winner."

Daisy was still a full lap from reaching the finish line herself, and had just driven off the road again.

"Oh, give me that." Grandma reached over and relieved Daisy of the controller.

Daisy was happy to see it go.

"I thought you might like to give me a hand with the cake, Daisy," Mom said.

"Sure." Daisy stood up and yawned, stretched her arms overhead. "You making tres leches?"

"Dad's favorite," her mother confirmed.

"And then what's on the docket for the rest of the weekend, Ruth?" Grandma asked.

They both watched Grandma drive the cartoon motorbike while Mom talked. "Vic should be back here with them by five, and we'll have an early dinner on the back deck before he takes them to the hotel to get settled in. Benny and Pamela and the kids get in super late tonight, so they're taking a cab straight to the hotel. Then the party tomorrow is at one o'clock. Everybody will be here. Even Vic's girlfriend is driving down from Boston later tonight."

"And Peter knows, right?" Grandma said. "This isn't like a surprise party or anything? Because he's eighty, Ruth, which is a far cry from the youthful seventy-six of yours truly. I don't want him having a heart attack before we get him back on the plane."

"Mama, you know well he's in great shape. And anyway, until Sunday he's still seventy-nine."

"I'm just saying—"

"He knows about the party, Mama."

"Good."

"You want to help Daisy and me with the baking?"

Grandma crossed the finish line for the second time, and turned the system off. "What do you think, Ruth? You think I want to help bake?"

Daisy laughed.

"I didn't like baking his cakes when I was married to him! Why would I do it now?"

"Okay, Mama."

"Wake me when it's ready!" Grandma locked the door behind them and waved through the glass.

Daisy was at home in Mom's kitchen, and as they fell into the familiar choreography of baking prep, the tension between them eased for the first time since Daisy's arrival two days ago.

"You want a cup of coffee?" Mom asked.

"Sure. Thanks."

Mom refilled the water carafe and set the thing to brewing while Daisy hauled the pink stand mixer down from its shelf in the pantry. She tied on her favorite apron with the cows all over it, collected their ingredients, and lined everything up on the counter: flour, baking soda, salt, eggs, sugar, milks, cream, vanilla, cinnamon. Apart from the two cans of milk (one evaporated, one condensed), nothing in Mom's kitchen was still in its original packaging. The dry ingredients had all been transferred to labeled jars or canisters shortly after purchase. The milk, cream, and vanilla were in matching glass jugs of various sizes. Even the cardboard egg carton was long gone, its inhabitants re-nestled into a pale-blue porcelain tray that photographed beautifully against the white countertops. And while grown-up Daisy found this rehoming of products to be slightly ridiculous, even she could admit that the aesthetic result was strangely soothing, probably because it called to mind a time when all these products might have been purchased or procured somewhat closer to their natural state, without all the synthetic packaging, bright colors, artificial sweeteners, and additives. The soothing appearance was an artificial trick, Daisy understood. But it worked.

Mom set Daisy's coffee mug down and took a sip from her own.

"Thanks," Daisy said, and joined her.

The coffee was good, and they were ready to bake. Daisy pulled her hair into a ponytail and turned to wash her hands.

"Just. Move your mug over there," Mom said. "Out of the shot."

Daisy stood still at the sink, the too-hot water running over her hands. After a moment, she adjusted the temperature and finished her rinse. She dried her hands on the apron, lifted her coffee from the counter, took another sip.

"The shot?" she said.

Her mom looked at her but didn't say anything. She was rearranging the way Daisy had lined up the ingredients on the counter, so Daisy repeated herself.

"The shot, Mom?"

"Daisy, don't start."

"You're shooting this?"

Still, Mom did not answer.

"Are you serious?" Daisy said.

Mom shook her head and Daisy untied the apron.

"What are you doing?"

"Taking off my apron."

"Come on, Daisy."

"Mom, I have no interest in this."

"Yes, you've made that abundantly clear," Mom said. "For years now, actually. The good news is that you don't have to be interested in it. You just have to do it."

"I have to do it?"

"I mean, you don't have to. But you're only here for a few days and we've hardly spent any time together."

"So this is your idea of spending time together?"

"We're baking! You love to bake!"

It was true that Daisy loved to bake, mostly because the end result was baked goods, which she could then eat.

"I'm not here to be your pretend-daughter, pretend-baking and pretend-smiling for the camera with you."

Mom switched on one of her wireless ring lights and maneuvered it into various positions, checking for shadows.

"You're my real daughter, Daisy. And we're baking real cake."

Daisy discarded the apron on the counter but then, anticipating her mother's complaint, moved it out of the shot and stuffed it back into the drawer where she'd found it.

"You know what I mean," she said. "It's all fake."

Mom took in a deep breath and then let it escape noisily between her lips. El Suspiro.

"Daisy, don't you ever get tired of this argument? Isn't it exhausting, lugging all that around, being so judgmental of me all the time?"

Daisy did not answer. She leaned back against the farmhouse sink and crossed her arms.

"This is my job, Daisy. This is how I pay the bills, how I have paid the bills since your father died. I know you don't like it. But the truth is, two things can be true at once: we can spend quality time together, baking your grandpa's birthday cake. And while we are doing that actual thing, which will be delicious, by the way, I can also take pictures to use later in a blog post that my advertisers will pay me for. So that I can continue to fund your useless, fallow college account."

"Oh, here we go," Daisy said.

"And pay for your health insurance, by the way," Mom said. "And your cell phone."

"I already told you to cancel the cell phone if you want! I don't need it."

Mom shook her head. She walked over to the drawer where Daisy had stuffed her apron, and Daisy thought for a moment that her mom was going to bring it back to her, slip it over her head, put her hands on Daisy's shoulders, and look her in the eyes. But instead she shook the apron out of the crumpled ball Daisy had left it in, refolded it, and returned it neatly to the drawer. She turned back to Daisy.

"Surely there must be some other way to have this conversation," Mom said. "We've tried it this way a thousand times. It gets a tiny bit worse every time."

"This we can agree on," Daisy said.

"I just. I know it's too late for you to come back here now, I get that the Stony Brook ship has sailed, you have tanked that particular opportunity."

Daisy snorted.

"I know you've signed a lease down there, Daisy, and for whatever reason, you've decided to stay. Fine, I won't even argue that part. But there's no reason you can't go to college in San Juan. UPR is a great school, and—"

"Where's Carlos?" Daisy interrupted.

"What?"

"Your son? Carlos?"

The skin in the middle of Mom's forehead drew itself into the shape of a cross. Mom didn't usually abide interruptions, but she was so confused by this one that it threw her off course.

"He's . . . at rehearsal. Why?"

"Just." Daisy shrugged. "He's nineteen years old. Seems like he should be in college."

The cross in Mom's forehead collapsed.

"Oh my God, Daisy, please," she said, leaning over the counter on her elbows in a posture of utter fatigue. "Daisy, your brother is a totally different scenario."

"Yes, he's a Broadway actor and a dancer. He's in one of the most notoriously unstable professions in the world. Why would he possibly need a college degree?"

"He will go!" Mom said. "But his trajectory is different from yours. He can't waste his youth, his best dancing years—"

"Mom, *my* trajectory is different from mine!" Daisy unfolded her arms and held her hands out in front of her as if she could draw her argument in the air between them and finally make her mother see. "It's a total double standard! And you have this idea that Carlos is a special case because he's some Broadway big shot, but you're so busy being impressed by him that you haven't even noticed that I am killing it in San Juan, that unlike your *working actor* son, I can actually afford to pay my own rent. If you would come and see, if you would support me for five minutes instead of always criticizing."

Daisy ran out of steam at the end of her sentence, and Mom stood up, pushed her curls away from her forehead.

"I don't know, Daisy," she said. "I worked so hard to give you kids the best chance. It was so hard to do that after your dad died. And now you don't even want it."

They were talking in circles, as always.

"You know, when I was your age, I had a fork in the road too." Mom swiveled one of the stools at the kitchen island and sat on it. She hooked her bare feet around the footrest. "For a while, I went down the wrong road. I ran down it. Almost made the biggest mistake of my life."

Mom was not looking at her. Her gaze was resting on the porcelain egg tray, but Daisy didn't think she was really looking at that either. She was somewhere else, and for a moment, Daisy considered going with her. All she had to do was ask. Daisy kept her mouth closed, her arms folded, and after a thick silence, Mom returned.

"I just want you to know it's never too late to make a course correction," she said. "To choose a different path."

Daisy did not help with the cake, but the party was a success anyway, and Grandpa loved the hat. On Sunday, Daisy was under the duvet in her old bed reading a paperback novel when Carlos knocked on her bedroom door.

"Come in." She tossed the book aside, happy to be briefly back under the same roof with her baby brother, double standard be damned.

Carlos swung the door open, but stayed in the doorway.

"Happy birthday!" he sang out.

"My birthday was two weeks ago."

"Yes, but you were far away, and now you're here," Carlos said. "So it's your birthday now."

Daisy smiled. "Okay then. What, no dancing? No fireworks?"

"I have something way better than fireworks." He grinned, still in the doorway.

Daisy waggled her eyebrows.

"I have to give it to you now, before Ruth gets back from shopping."

Daisy sat up the rest of the way and gathered some extra pillows behind her. "Okay, I'm ready. Lay it on me."

He stepped around the doorframe then, dangling the little gift bag from one outstretched arm. He hopscotched across Daisy's backpack and the pile of dirty clothes she'd left on the floor.

"Oh, the intrigue!" she said, reaching to take the bag from him. It was a reused Christmas bag that Carlos had dug out of the attic because he knew Daisy thought buying new wrapping paper and gift bags was wasteful.

He perched beside her on the bed, bouncing the mattress beneath them. "Open it!"

She peeled back the crumpled paper layers very slowly. "It's so nice you found the red and green tissue paper to match the bag," she said, stopping to admire the wrapping.

"Oh my God, would you just open it!" he said.

Daisy laughed, reaching past all the paper layers and drawing out the first of two flat, book-shaped boxes from inside. These were also wrapped in paper and haphazardly taped. She peeled back the tape and slid the first box out of its wrapping. She grinned then, looking from the box to her brother.

"It's a DNA test!" he said, in case she couldn't read what it said on the box. He couldn't wait for her any longer; he reached into the bag, grabbed the second papered box, and ripped it open too. "Actually it's two DNA tests. One for you, one for me."

"Wow, no wonder you don't want Mom to see." Daisy laughed again.

"Yeah, she would totally hate this," Carlos said.

"But why'd you get two of them?"

"Vic said that some of the information you can only get if you're biologically male. You have to have the Y chromosome, I guess. So he said I should do a test too, so we can get the largest amount of genetic information. All the tea!"

"Thank goodness we have such brainiac DNA in the form of our eldest sibling with his chromosome advice," Daisy said. "Vic didn't want to do his too?"

"Nah, wasn't interested, same as always. Said if he wanted to know, he'd just look at ours. It'll be more or less the same as mine."

Daisy tore open the box and tipped the contents across the bed while Carlos watched.

"You're so messy," he said. "How are we even from the same gene pool?"

There was an accidental moment of pause amid the levity then.

"Come on, no chickening out." Carlos slapped her arm. "We're doing this."

"Wait, just one minute," she said. "We're definitely doing it. But come here first."

She pulled her brother closer, and then swung her legs over the edge of the bed. She wanted to look at the two of them sitting side by side in the full-length mirror.

Carlos's skin was olive, while Daisy's was pale and freckled, a difference that was exaggerated every summer when he tanned and she did not. Her hair was lighter and thinner, and there were other things, too, not quite as obvious. Carlos had an elegance about him that Daisy couldn't even mimic. He was musical; she couldn't carry a tune. She loved spicy food; he couldn't tolerate it.

So Daisy wanted the pause to remind herself that those disparities were not acute, especially when compared with the flip side. Because there in the mirror she could plainly see the similarities too. The shapes of their noses, the curves of their eyebrows—Daisy's wild, Carlos's meticulously groomed, but the little crook on the outside corner was the same. They each had a stray dimple in their lower left cheek, the same long, slender fingers. They made the same clownish honk on the inhale when they hiccuped, and Vic too. So, okay. It felt safe then, to conjecture what could never in a million years be true.

"Imagine I turn out to be Mom's love child?" Daisy said.

"Oh, please," Carlos said. "I'm clearly the love child in this scenario."

She smacked him lightly in the chest with the back of her hand. "Why do you get to be the love child?"

"Come on," Carlos said. "Have you seen me? Everything about me screams love child."

She nodded at him in the mirror. "You do scream love child."

"*Love child!*" he screamed. "See?"

Daisy laughed.

"Besides, I'm the baby," he reminded her. Then he stage-whispered, "It's always the baby."

In the bathroom, they swabbed their cheeks and sealed their samples, and then Carlos smeared a blue clay mask all over his face while Daisy leaned over the counter and filled in the paperwork. On both forms, she checked the little box that said *Please send my results by postal mail*, and then filled in her own name and the address of her apartment in San Juan.

"Are you kidding me?" Carlos said, peering over her shoulder. "Results by snail mail? That's extreme even for you, Daisy."

"I hate email, Carlos, you know that."

"I mean, you can hate it and still be a member of the twenty-first century, though."

"I am," Daisy said defensively, licking the first envelope. "I'm extremely modern. I'm so modern I'm postmodern. Anyway, it's not like I don't have email."

"It's exactly like you don't have email. If you never use it, that's pretty much the same as not having it."

"I do use it." Daisy shrugged. "For work and stuff. I use it when I have to. But when I have the option, I prefer to do it the old-fashioned way."

Carlos pushed his lips all the way to one side of his face and blinked out at her from behind the blue clay.

"Imagine how cool it will be," she went on, "the day the results arrive in the mailbox and we get to rip open the envelope and read them together!"

"Um, hello, we can't open the envelope together. You'll be back in San Juan, and I'll be all alone here in the burbs with Ruth, waiting impatiently for my DNA results."

"Oh, please," she said. "You'll be at some glamorous rehearsal not even thinking about it."

"Oh, Daisy." He shook his head. "You know rehearsals aren't glamorous. They're absolutely laborious!" He threw one arm dramatically across his forehead, careful not to actually touch the blue clay. "Unless you're the star, of course."

"Well. You'll be the star soon enough." She believed this.

"I know." He grinned.

"*Anyway*," she said. "We can video chat!"

Carlos shook his head. "You are an enigma," he said, scanning the paperwork for the fine print. "It already takes six to eight weeks to get the results back, and you can add at least two more weeks for snail mail, Daisy. Maybe three, for it to get all the way to San Juan!"

"Well, lucky for me, it's my birthday gift, so I can do it however I want." She folded the second set of forms and slid them into their envelope along with her brother's sample, double-checking the numbers on the tube and form to make sure she'd kept everything straight. "Good thing you love me."

"Do I, though?" Carlos leaned into the mirror to inspect his mask, and then washed the leftover clay from his hands, turning his head this way and that, following the eyes of his reflection. "God, I'm so good-looking blue. Maybe I should be blue all the time. Look at my cheekbones!"

Daisy fanned his face with the envelopes. "You're breathtaking."

Carlos lifted his phone from where he'd left it on the toilet seat and opened his calendar app. "Okay, today is April twenty-seventh." He scrolled through the weeks, counting as he went. "So we should have the results before the end of June."

"Too bad we won't have them in time for Mother's Day!" Daisy laughed.

Carlos locked his phone and returned it to his back pocket.

"Is she going with you to the airport?" he asked.

Daisy leaned back against the doorjamb. "I don't know. Probably not."

He turned his blue face to look at her. "Don't worry, Daisy. She can't stay mad at you forever."

Chapter Thirteen

~

Trinidad

1964

Her ship was out of Ponce at four o'clock on a Thursday afternoon. Rafaela would arrive in Trinidad Friday morning, and she'd have the weekend to get settled before beginning her new job, her new life. Her letters would be cheerful and light. She'd write them faithfully every week, one each to her parents, her sister, and Candido. She would not write about her awkwardness with the other girls in the secretarial pool, who took orders easily, without prickling, and who demonstrated a bombastic informality with each other that Rafaela found both coarse and alluring. Rafaela appreciated some of these girls, but found herself unable to relax with them, unable to mimic their bonhomie. Neither would Rafaela mention in her weekly letters her homesickness, or how bad the food was in the canteen, or whatever flowered on this island that made her sneeze so loudly she sometimes startled a passing officer, causing him to wonder aloud how such a clamor came out of such a *pretty little thing*. Her English improved to include all kinds of curiosities. And there was plenty that felt familiar here, in Trinidad, so she focused her attention on those comforting details instead: the whiteness of the clouds across the warm blue sky, the Latin hymns in mass on Sunday mornings, the nighttime lullaby of el coquí outside her bedroom window.

When she received the news from Dolores, rather than from Candido himself, that Candido had booked a one-way ticket to New York, it happened again that Rafaela felt the wobbly blur at the edges of her vision. She wrote to him at once, and when his reply came, it had the feeling of a chronic affliction in that it both distressed her and felt so already-accustomed that the disquiet it provoked in her felt almost indulgent. *My dearest friend,* he wrote, *what is the difference between an absence of a few hundred miles or a couple thousand? You are not here. New York on its worst day can be no drearier than San Juan without Rafaelita.*

Candido was right that it made no real difference, she knew. Even if they'd both remained in San Juan, or if he'd come to Trinidad, or she to New York, even that wouldn't have changed things. Because in that case, she would've had to examine the feelings he roused in her. And even if she did that, next she'd have to acknowledge that those feelings meant she was in love. And well, what then? She and Candido could never be together. She'd understood that from childhood, as clearly as she knew that Mamamía should never catch her with the polish and rag. Their incompatibility was as evident as the pink of her ear that day Lola had dragged her out of the pantry and up the stairs, away from him. Rafaela was attracted to Candido because they were young and he was beautiful. That would surely pass. This is what she told herself when she lay tangled up in the hot sheets at night, alone and thinking about him. *It will pass,* she insisted. Because what choice did she have, now that she was here, earning money for her family? There was no room for childish indulgence among the new responsibilities of her life.

And anyway, even though it was never explicitly spoken aloud, Rafaela had always understood, even before Trinidad, that it was fine for a man (like Papamío) to choose anyone he wanted (like Mamamía) as his spouse, no matter what his beloved looked like or where she came from or who her parents were. Men from certain bloodlines could do as they liked, and any attendant scandal for the man would be swift and light and quickly forgotten. The same was not true for Mamamía, nor would it be true for Rafaela. She knew it was different for women because, although no one ever said so, she had breathed and consumed and absorbed it since infancy: falling in love with a boy like Candido would ruin her. And despite the new circumstances of her life, she was not yet willing to concede that she might, in fact, already be ruined. It had not yet occurred to Rafaela that *ruin* and *liberty* were the same word. So the quavering of her heart notwithstanding, the possibility of Candido did not exist, and the ache that remained in the shadow he cast there only served to confound her.

In Trinidad, Rafaela learned how to flirt, and even more important, she learned how *not* to flirt. She learned how to subdue her smile, turn her face away, cave in her posture ever so slightly from the shoulders, to remove herself out from under the notice of a young man's undesirable attention. For a girl as beautiful as Rafaela, a US naval base in the deep southern Caribbean was a veritable minefield of young men's undesirable attentions. Her cousin, who was a lesser beauty, went out on dates three or four nights a week, but Rafaela stayed in and listened to the radio or wrote her letters, which grew more meandering with each passing week. Sometimes she wrote an extra letter, or two or three, to Candido in a given week. These extras she tried to imagine as simple narratives, a dispassionate chronicle of her time here, but that ruse was not sufficiently convincing. She never mailed more than one.

"All I'm saying is there's much better food on this island than what they're feeding us in that godforsaken canteen!" Clarisa would joke, wiggling into her stockings. "So, you have to tolerate some goofy fella looking down your top for an hour or two. At least you can get a decent pelau out of the arrangement."

But Rafaela was only weeks out of saddle shoes and poodle skirts, weeks out of her school pinafore and lace socks. Never mind that some of these enlisted men were only eighteen, only a year older than her. They seemed decades older. Maybe it was the haircuts, the uniforms, the husky deepness of their voices. Maybe it was the way they swaggered when they asked if she had plans on Friday night, their yanqui presumptuousness, their aggressive cologne. Whatever it was, it wasn't because she was hung up on Candido.

"Well, how about Parcheesi at Pat and Lorraine's place tomorrow night then?" Clarisa asked, slipping into her heels.

This was tempting only because Rafaela did love games. Pat and Lorraine, like many of her cousin's girlfriends, Rafa could do without. She appreciated Clarisa trying to include her, but it was clear to Rafaela, during the few evenings she did join in, that her tepid feelings about the girls were reciprocal. Rafaela didn't know how to talk to them. She didn't enjoy trying. Whenever she noticed two or more of her cousin's friends sitting together in the canteen at lunchtime, Rafaela would hold her book an inch higher and pretend not to see them.

"Whattaya say?" Clarisa asked. "We can make sangria."

Rafaela stood to help her cousin with the zipper on the back of her dress. "We'll see," she said.

Rafaela's daily lunch break was thirty minutes, and that included a three-minute walk each way in the high heels she was still getting used to, then perhaps five minutes waiting in line for her food, which left her twenty minutes to eat. Luckily, the meal was reliably disagreeable enough that she didn't mind leaving some portion of it behind on the tray. The dining room smelled of antiseptic and boiled tomatoes, but it felt like a glory to sit down for those twenty minutes, to quiet her mind. Sometimes the effort of hearing and speaking English all day left her with a mild head-ache, which she could often alleviate during these twenty blessed minutes just by briefly closing her eyes while she chewed her unpleasant food, by breathing deeply, and by temporarily evicting the foreign words from her brain. She eased into her Spanish thoughts like a warm bath.

But for the past several days in a row, a very persistent young man with red hair and freckles stood up from his table when he saw her com-ing, and robbed some number of those precious minutes from her. She felt them slipping past, one, two, while this man smiled in front of her with his yellow teeth and yellow skin and bright orange hair. Rafaela was tired and hungry, and the tray of food was heavy. She didn't like balanc-ing her milk on the tray, carrying it through the crowded canteen. She worried someone would bump her or the milk would slide off the edge, that she'd spill it all over herself and end up in a sour stink for the rest of the day. The milk trembled in its glass.

"Please," she said, "I need to sit down."

The name patch on the young man's breast said "Busby." She tried again to walk past him, but he stepped into her path. This was his favorite move. When she tried a different route, he blocked that way too. Rafaela blinked slowly, telling the headache just to be patient, she would be there soon with the remedy. And then, for a moment, she imagined letting herself fly with the tray. She imagined how the hum of conversation in the room would arrest itself at once, the only remaining sound the sizzle of meat on the kitchen grill, followed immediately by the clatter of her flying silverware and falling tray. She imagined Busby's shocked face, his freckles hidden beneath a dripping white veil, eyelashes sticky with milk. She accidentally smiled.

"See? I knew you had a smile in there for me!" he said. "Rafaela, right? I'd never forget a name like that, and on such a knockout."

She didn't even need to answer him anymore; he knew what to expect, and there seemed to have been a shift: he no longer hoped to charm or convince her, but instead to wear her down, to find a way to leave her no choice. She looked at his face again, and lamented that it was clean and dry.

"Foxy girl like you can't say no forever. Come on, you gotta be lonely, right? Just one date. Come out with me for one date, and I'll have you begging for a second!"

Rafaela didn't have it in her to respond, so instead she turned, and was about to collapse into the nearest chair, but even as she made this decision, she was aware of the risk. There was an empty chair directly across the table, and they both knew he would take it as an invitation. He would colonize her blissful, important minutes with his idiotic freckles and wretched voice. Her shoulders drooped, and the milk began to slide, and just as she felt that a scream might make its way out of her throat and into the air without her expressed permission, there was an arm reaching across her, a hand that caught the sliding glass of milk and lifted it up, lightening the weight of the tray. And then a second hand that lifted the tray right out of her arms.

"Bug off, Busby." The man who belonged to the hands had spoken. "That's an order, Private."

Busby's cheeks reddened beneath all those freckles, and Rafaela could see the struggle that it was for him to close his mouth and obey, but after a moment, he did.

"Aye, sir," Busby said, saluting before turning on his heel to retreat to his table.

What prevented Rafaela from smiling at the man who was now carrying her tray in one hand and her glass in the other was her worry that a new antagonist had simply replaced the first, that the newcomer might believe his chivalry had earned him the right to sit across from her during her remaining balance of dwindling minutes. Still, she meant it when she said, "Thank you."

"It's that clown who should be thanking me," the man said. "For rescuing him from further disgrace."

Now she did smile.

"Where would you like to sit?" he asked.

She pointed to her favorite table, by the window. There were crumbs on it, but she would take it anyway, as it was half-hidden by a large pillar and she liked the view beyond, of the sea. Sitting there, Rafaela could almost see Port of Spain across the bay, and she knew if she looked in the other direction, and her eye followed the spits of land that flaunted themselves out into the sea, if she allowed her gaze to travel across those islands and out toward the wider Caribbean beyond, if she could stretch her gaze long enough, magically enough, to six hundred miles, then Rafaela would see Puerto Rico.

The man walked with her toward the table, and then set her tray down with the glass on top. He pulled the chair out for her, just as if he were Papamío and she were Mamamía and they were having dinner on Nochebuena at La Fortaleza.

How odd, she thought to herself, but she sat into the chair and lifted her fork. She tried to steel herself for the moment when he pulled out the opposite chair and sat, to regale her with his clamorous English. But he didn't pull out the chair, and he didn't sit. Instead he rested his hands on the back of it and nodded his head at her somewhat formally, so that she was able to admire, for the first time, the unexpected appeal of that head. Tanned skin, an impressive whip of wavy black hair, and thick black eyebrows above the most piercing blue eyes she had ever seen. He clicked his heels together lightly and almost bowed.

"Have a lovely day, Miss," he said.

And she was so surprised by this that when she opened her mouth to respond, she found nothing inside to say. He was leaving her in peace, this gallant man. He wanted nothing from her, had no plan to plunder her time, to take what was hers and fill it with noise.

"Thank you!" she said again, but he was already on his way. She caught a glimpse of his name patch just as he turned to go.

Brennan.

§

The chapel on base at Chaguaramas was small and spare, and although Rafaela attended ten o'clock mass there every Sunday, she felt that the damp, soupy aroma of the carpets made it difficult to discern the voice of God. She got nothing out of the service except the wafer, and so finally one weekend she didn't bother going at all, a decision that felt risqué and thrilling altogether on the morning she made it, but which later resulted in a case of homesickness so acute that she was filled with remorse, and ended up saying nine rosaries in the effort to restore her good humor. The following Sunday morning, Rafaela rose early and full of contrition. She put on a cap-sleeved pink dress, silk stockings, and black pumps. She wore a simple pearl in each ear and a lipstick with a reasonable shimmer. By 7:30 A.M., she climbed aboard the bus at the gate that would carry her away from base and into town.

Although Rafaela had never been there before, the Cathedral Basilica of the Immaculate Conception in Port of Spain was familiar the moment she stood in the plaza and watched the white clouds float behind the imposing twin spires. It was an elaborate wedding cake of a church, but when she stepped inside and breathed the scent of salt and stone and the smoky memory of incense, she was home again, sitting on the edge of her four-poster bed beside Lola, buckling their Sunday shoes.

When they were small, the sisters got themselves dressed for mass, and then they waited for Mamamía to inspect them. She'd straighten an earring here, adjust a hair clip there, and then kiss them each on top of the head. Their mother was always immaculate in a sleeveless shift, pearls at her neck, giant sunglasses, even in the house. Mamamía was prepared for the rigors of the late morning sun, prepared for the envy of every other woman at Parroquia Sagrado Corazón de Jesús. When they walked to mass, Rafaela enjoyed the promenade, the twirling of the parasol handle against her palm. She liked observing what the other girls were wearing, comparing the varying heights of their mothers' heels (no one's were ever taller than Mamamía's). Rafaela and Dolores giggled behind their fans whenever they caught a boy ogling their mother, which was often. In San Juan, mass was a team sport.

The memory made her feel even more alone, even farther away from home, and at the basilica, when she dipped her fingers into the holy water and blessed herself, Rafaela had the sensation that her body itself was a church, that the cavity of her chest was the tabernacle. She could feel her own heart beating inside. But then mass began, and the sounds were a balm, the Latin prayers flying up through the vault, echoing among the arches. There was something curative in the simple acts of sitting, kneeling, standing, kneeling, sitting. Reciting the habitual words. She imagined Dolores and her parents kneeling in their faraway pew, their voices blending with her own earnest prayer. By the time she took communion, Rafaela felt restored to herself. She felt prepared to endure another week in exile.

So it didn't feel like luck, exactly, when just at that moment, she opened her eyes and her gaze fell upon the back of a head she had seen before. She recognized the precision line just there above the collar where the jet-black hair faded into the strong, tanned neck. She stayed where she was, and that head inclined as Rafaela watched from her kneeler in the ninth pew. When the priest lifted the host, it must've been her imagination, because she couldn't have heard his voice from this far back. She must've used her own fancy to project the solidity of the single word there, into the ether. She gave it the hint of a Spanish inflection.

"Amen," Peter Brennan said, as he took the host.

And when he turned, she was able to study him in profile for the first time, from behind the protective shield of her folded hands. The startling thickness of those black lashes, the expressive eyebrows, the ruddy cheeks. His eyes icy blue, even in profile, even in the dim glow of the stained-glass shadows. He turned the corner to begin his walk back, and at that moment, his eye fell on Rafaela watching him. She squeezed her eyes closed as quickly as she could, but it was too late. He'd already seen her, and she'd seen him, the way his face changed instantly, before he could stop himself. The smile that looked like an escapee, the dimple, the recognition. If someone had asked her, in that moment, to name what it was she was feeling, Rafaela may have paused and given the matter real consideration. With sincere reflection and an honest accounting, she may have diagnosed herself as suffering from loneliness, longing, and an acute case of straightforward, unsophisticated lust. An acknowledgment of that reality likely would have tranquilized some part of the romantic commotion that was happening within her. But no one was there to ask. Rafaela cracked open one eyelid to watch him go and, indeed, it was too late. She felt the tabernacle of her breast fly open. She felt her heart move toward him.

When mass ended, she took her time in the pew, singing until the last verse of the last hymn was complete, and then kneeling once more in an effort to recapture the tranquility she'd experienced briefly before the appearance of the handsome young officer had disquieted her all over again. When she gathered her bag and hand fan from the stone floor, and blessed herself at the door, when she stepped out of the cool, consecrated hush and into the blazing Caribbean midmorning sun, she expected to find him loitering there on the steps, or nearby on a bench. She'd taken her time because she liked the idea of making him wait. She assumed he'd make small talk, remark on the service, the church, the weather, ask for her name, her story, her family background, and because she already knew he was a gentleman, she presumed he'd do all of this while trying not to gaze too long at her mouth, and trying not to glance at all toward the fixed buttons on the front of her dress. But when she shaded her eyes and scanned the plaza, that officer and his glorious head of hair were already gone.

Rafaela began to look for him everywhere. In the canteen during her lunch break, in the laundromat where she washed everything but her unmentionables (which she washed by hand in a basin in her room because she couldn't bear the idea of a sailor watching her fold her clean underthings in a public place under fluorescent lighting), on the brisk walks she and Clarisa took around base in the evenings to stretch their legs after working all day. Rafaela seldom ran into him, though, and when she did, the officer always acknowledged her with a smile and a friendly nod that was, Rafaela felt, far too courteous.

All of which is to say that, when at last they finally spoke, Rafaela was absolutely swollen with anticipation, straining to hold on for dear life. More than a month had elapsed since she'd seen him at the basilica that Sunday morning, almost three months since the day he'd rescued her in the canteen, and although she returned to the same mass now week after week, and sat in the same pew, and closed only one eye behind the tent of her folded hands when she knelt to say her prayers, she only saw him at the basilica on two other occasions, and both times, although she learned to sing with a little less devotion, and move herself more quickly toward the door after the recessional hymn, still, he was always gone by the time she got to the plaza.

So by that sixth Sunday, she wasn't surprised to find that he was nowhere to be found when she emerged from the church. She'd become as accustomed to the disappointment as she was to the hope. Still, in the plaza, she felt her shoulders slump within the starched fabric of her blouse. The bus stop was five blocks from the church, but she had almost two hours to kill before the bus would be back, so Rafaela had developed the habit of buying herself a pot bake, and then window shopping while she ate it, as if she were Audrey Hepburn in *Breakfast at Tiffany's*. The breakfast was the best thing she would eat all week, so she savored every bite, and took her time peering in the windows at the things she'd never buy: jewelry, clothes, hats, shoes. When it began to feel melancholy, when it reminded her too much of what her life had been like before, she allowed her gaze to soften, and she looked at her own reflection instead, and she recognized that she didn't need anything but this one body, the clothes she had on, the sweet warmth of the coconut bread wrapped in her paper napkin. Her family. She took a bite, sinking her teeth into the crust, and then smiled at her image in the glass.

There, just there, was the illusion of other teeth smiling back, the grin too large for her face. She fixed her gaze, readjusted her focus so she was looking past the glass instead of at its surface. And there he was at a table on the other side, a tiny cup of coffee on a saucer in front of him and a newspaper folded beneath one elbow. And was he ... was he laughing at her? He waved then, and she felt her cheeks redden and her mouth go dry, which made it difficult to chew and swallow the rather large mouthful of the pot bake she'd just crammed in there. Rafaela waved back, and then, once she'd managed to swallow the bread, she laughed too. And then he stood from his seat, leaving the cup briefly unattended, and swung the door open onto the sidewalk, alarming the waitress who chased after him, accosting him in the doorway.

"Oh no, I'm not leaving," he said to the waitress. "I just spotted a friend." He gestured at Rafaela.

The waitress eyed him suspiciously, but backed away, keeping her eyes on him in case he should try to run. He looked up then, and locked his own eyes with Rafaela's, by which time she had wrapped the pot bake back into its napkin along with her dignity.

"Come in!" he said.

Rafaela could barely respond. She stood on the sidewalk, momentarily frozen in her heels.

"Let me buy you a coffee?"

She nodded once, and as she approached the doorway, he didn't move himself out of the way. He stood holding the door open so she could brush past him as she walked through. She passed closer than she needed to, inhaling the scent of his neck along the way.

He bought her coffee, and then another coffee, and then a waffle with maple syrup and a fried egg and some bacon and a stack of toast with extra butter, and he very kindly did not mention her enormous appetite, although he could not entirely hide his admiration at how much she managed to pack into her tiny frame. Rafaela ate enough for a week, hoping he might buy her breakfast again next Sunday, and when she was finally finished eating, he bought her another cup of coffee, and she missed her bus.

"I'd offer you a lift, but I don't know how you'd manage the motorbike in that skirt," he said, which was the closest he ever came to remarking on her appearance. Rafaela was surprised to find that, as much as she abhorred those kinds of remarks from the other men on base, she longed to know what this one thought of her. She'd have gladly traded back at least one slice of that toast in exchange for a compliment about her eyes or her smile or her accent. But Peter kept his hands folded on the table between them and set the conversation very carefully in the direction of childhood, family, work, travel. He had an easy warmth, was quick to laugh, and she had the impression that he talked to her the same way he might talk to a friend, another man. It was both stirring and strange, especially when she found she had difficulty concentrating on what he was saying—not because of the swiftness or complexity of his English words, but because those words were coming from such an uncommonly lovely mouth. Rafaela leaned in. She tried to focus on the ideas instead of the lips.

They waited for the late bus together, and when it arrived, instead of seeing her safely aboard and bidding her good afternoon, he got on with her.

"But what about your motorbike?" she asked, as he slid into the seat beside her.

He waved a hand. "My duty hours start late tomorrow," he said. "I'll come back and grab it in the morning."

The next Sunday morning, when Rafaela turned up at the gate for the early bus to Port of Spain, Peter was already waiting, his black hair so thick that even the rigorous grooming of the Navy barber couldn't fully domesticate it. Rafaela noticed that when he wasn't in uniform, he wore it parted and swirled to one side like a dollop of whipped cream. He was wearing a lemon-yellow guayabera and khakis, and Rafaela had a hard time keeping her face neutral when she saw him there. She was engaged in that effort when she noticed that there were two other people already waiting at the bus stop as well, and one of them was a woman, and she was standing rather close to Peter actually, and she was leaning toward him, and as Rafaela watched, he said something to her, and she threw her head back in laughter, touching Peter's arm. She was touching his arm. So now the effort for Rafaela to keep her face neutral took an entirely new direction, and when she came to a stop, she gave him a perfunctory nod and said, "Good morning," in the same clipped way her math teacher at Las Madres used to say good morning to his students when he was hungover. Peter smiled at her, but Rafaela turned away, pretending to peer down the road in search of the bus, which was not due for another seven minutes. She felt like a fool; for all the times she had triple-checked his left hand for a wedding band, it had never occurred to her that the absence of a ring didn't mean he was available. No wonder he'd been immune to her presence. Despite the tumult of her feelings, there was a tickle up the back of her neck when he said her name.

"Rafaela, do you know Mindy?"

The girl removed her hand from Peter's arm and stuck it out toward Rafaela, who shook it reluctantly.

"I don't believe I do," Rafaela said.

"I'm Mindy." The girl pumped Rafaela's hand in her grip. "Oh, I guess he just said that!"

She laughed uproariously again, although it was not yet 7:30 A.M.

Rafaela found herself unable to muster a polite response, silenced by the scrutiny with which she was now studying her competitor. Mindy's hair was shiny, but her face was a little horsey, Rafaela decided. She glanced at Peter, whose expression was inscrutable.

"Mindy works in the officers' mess," he said.

Mindy dropped her voice behind her hand, and leaned toward Rafaela, "And boy, it really is a mess, wow!"

She laughed even louder this time, and Rafaela noticed that Peter moved his arm before Mindy could place her hand there again, whether for his own comfort or to save Rafaela from the spectacle, she couldn't say.

Because Mindy's joke had been overt and not at all funny, withholding a response would've been rude, so Rafa tried. She offered a limp little breath and a smile, a lukewarm expression of amusement. She felt it was more than sufficient.

"Rafaela's in the secretarial pool," Peter said, and Rafaela nodded.

But before she had to say anything more, the bus appeared mercifully early, and although she'd been the last one to arrive at the bus stop, Rafaela felt no compunction about being the first one to climb aboard. She flashed the base ID that allowed her free transport into town, and made her way to a seat near the back, where she turned her face toward the window and clamped her handbag across her lap. She felt the tingle of pressure behind her eyes and couldn't tell whether the prospective tears were from heartache or simple humiliation.

She liked him. Rafaela could've had a date with any single sailor or officer in all of Trinidad, but he was the only one who'd captured even a slip of her interest. She felt so stupid. Out of her peripheral vision Rafa watched Mindy slide into the second seat, right behind the driver, and scooch her weight quickly to the window, patting the seat beside her. Rafa turned her head farther toward the window, wishing she could shove it open and climb out. She slouched down in her seat. In her mind, she heard Mamamía telling her to sit up straight, but she ignored her faraway mother, who would surely make an exception under these circumstances. Rafaela closed her eyes, hoping her lids could hold back the mortifying tears she was brewing. She wished Lola was here.

And then she smelled him before she saw him, the mild spice of his aftershave. And then she felt him leaning his shoulder against hers, bumping his weight lightly into her frame.

"You okay?" Peter asked. He was sitting beside her.

Rafaela fluttered her eyes open, but looked only at the back of the seat in front of her. She sat up straighter and reached for an excuse for her behavior, her mood.

"I'm fine," she said. "Bit of a headache, I guess." She pinched the bridge of her nose between finger and thumb to illustrate her malady.

"Yes, well," he said softly, "Mindy's been known to cause headaches."

Rafaela felt her posture shift, her spine uncurl.

"Chilblains too," he whispered.

And then he executed an act of outright magic. Like a shaman, and without the slightest acknowledgment of the spell he was casting, he slipped seamlessly into Spanish as he explained that Mindy was not his girlfriend, that from what he could tell, she was good-natured and lonesome and a long way from home, and that it was a balancing act, as he'd gotten to know her a little bit, to conduct himself in a way that provided kindness and comfort without encouraging any false hopes on her part. There was only one girl on base, actually only one girl in all of Trinidad, or perhaps on the planet, with whom Peter felt no desire to keep his balance. For this one girl, he was ready to fall.

Rafaela listened to all of this without breathing, without moving, without lifting her eyes from the seat in front of her. She marveled at his beautiful Spanish, which changed his voice, changed the words he chose to express himself, changed her insides from solid to liquid so that, when she finally looked up, it was first to his mouth, to see the changing shapes of his lips as he formed those beautiful, homecoming words, and only then, only after, to his piercing blue eyes.

"I'm hoping that girl might let me buy her breakfast again, after mass," he said.

And then he set his hand open, palm up, on his own knee. And waited for her to take it.

Chapter Fourteen

~

New Jersey
1991

Ruth, who was unaware that her capacity to be deeply in love with two men at the same time was an inherited trait, met both of her college boyfriends at her off-campus job a few months after Titi Lola died. Her freshman and sophomore years of college had been an extended romantic drought, and her loneliness was only magnified by the weight of her sudden grief. So, during the early fall of her junior year, when she found herself faced with not one but two romantic prospects, Ruth was both pleasantly surprised and utterly unprepared. She handled it poorly.

She met Thomas first, on a Saturday afternoon in late September. No sign of autumn yet in New Jersey, and it was hot in the photo lab that day, so Ruth had propped the street door open with a brick because the owner of the building refused on principle to turn on the air-conditioning in September, regardless of actual weather conditions. Ruth had her hair pulled up in a scrunchy and her school bag was on the floor behind the counter. She worked here sixteen hours a week—four hours each on Mondays and Wednesdays, and a long eight-hour shift every weekend. Saturdays were always quiet, which had surprised her when she first started, but she soon understood that Saturday was the day people were out in the world *taking* pictures, not so much the day they earmarked to drop off their film or pick up their prints. So Ruth learned to bring her schoolwork with her on Saturdays, to run the day's prints early, and then pass the long hours reading or studying. She'd once asked her boss, Gus, if there was any hope of getting a more comfortable chair behind the counter, but he'd looked at her like she was crazy.

"I'm not paying you to lounge around in a comfortable chair," he said.

You kind of are on Saturdays, she did not say, because she liked the job and she liked the money, and she didn't want to give him the idea that maybe he should just close the shop on Saturdays and save himself her paycheck. So instead she said, "No, you're right, sorry. Just an idea." She perched herself uncomfortably on the hard, wooden stool behind the register, and longed for the beanbag in her dorm room.

It was just after two o'clock when Thomas came in, and of course she didn't yet know he was Thomas. The bell didn't jingle because she'd propped the door open, but Ruth sensed the way the light changed when someone walked in, and she looked up from her book. He seemed a couple years older than her, and was wearing his Wodsley T-shirt tucked into his jeans. The way he wore his shirt struck her as bizarre, because it indicated both a meticulousness about his appearance and a vigorous disregard for actual style, which gave him a self-possessed dork vibe she found strangely compelling.

"Hiya," he said without really looking at her.

She nodded at him, and quickly cleared her lunch away from the counter where its remnants had been sitting since she'd finished eating a half hour ago. There'd been too many red onions in her salad, so she was glad of the bright, sour odor of the photographic chemicals to cover her breath. He bent to examine the various envelopes below the counter.

"How come you're not at the game?" she asked.

He looked up, confused. "Game?"

She pointed at his T-shirt. "You go to Wodsley?"

"Yes."

This didn't seem to clear it up for him.

"Me too," she said. "I thought I was the only student in the whole school who couldn't go to the game today."

They were about three blocks from the stadium, and every few minutes she could hear a roar go up. In a few hours, when the game was over, there'd be a drunken parade back to the dorms, right past the open door of her photo lab. She would bring the brick in before then. Close the door. When she walked home later, she'd keep her eyes on the sidewalk in front of her, careful not to step in anything gross.

"Oh," he said. "I'm not really . . ." He shook his head. "Not really into basketball."

She looked at him blankly. "It's football," she said.

He grinned. And until that moment, Ruth had never understood what people meant when they said someone had a twinkle in their eye.

"Oh," she said.

"Yeah, I'm just messin'," he said.

"Very funny."

"But seriously." He shrugged. "Not that into football."

She nodded. "You have an accent."

"I do," he said.

"Where from?"

"From Ireland."

"Oh!" she said. "My dad's Irish."

He smiled, but didn't answer. Years later, he'd explain to her that usually, when people claimed their family was *Irish*, what they meant was Irish American, and so there wasn't a lot more to discuss there, because Thomas wasn't Irish-American. He was *Irish* Irish, from the village of Cong in County Mayo in the province of Connacht in the west of Ireland. And he didn't like to point this out to people because it was kind of a dickish thing to say, so he usually let them take the conversation wherever it might go. For his part, he was happy enough to return to the task at hand.

"Cool," he said, waiting just a beat to see if she had more to add on the Irish topic before asking, "Which one of these do I use? I don't need them back in a hurry."

"Lemme see your film?"

He dug into his pocket and pulled out two small yellow cannisters.

"Right," she said, leaning over the counter even though she already knew which envelope he should take. She pretended to look. "The red one, there," she said. "All the way on the left."

He pulled two red envelopes out of the stack and fished a pen out of the cup on the counter.

"You can put them both in the same envelope," she said.

And then she tried not to watch him as he leaned over to fill in his details in block capitals. She didn't want him to feel like she was looming in judgment over his handwriting. She had a bad habit of always trying to fill an uncomfortable silence.

"Actually my dad isn't really Irish," she said, just for something to say. "He's Irish-American."

Thomas stopped writing and stood up.

Years later, he'd also explain how unusual it was that she'd been the one to make that distinction. He'd say it was a distinction only an Irish person would make.

"Or a Puerto Rican," she'd counter. "From there and *from there* are not the same."

But that conversation wouldn't happen for another two years. That first day, in the photo lab, when Ruth clarified that her father was Irish-American, the declaration only gave Thomas pause to set the pen down. To straighten up. To notice that she wasn't just a pretty girl with dimples and curls. There was something different here.

"His parents are from Ireland, my grandparents, but even they came over when they were pretty young. My grandpa doesn't even have an Irish accent," Ruth continued, unaware of the shift she'd just provoked, and still just yammering on to fill the silence. She did notice his heightened attention, though, and leaned down to rummage in the front pocket of her backpack for a stick of gum, in case the chemicals weren't strong enough. She thought she could still smell a trace of onion, even though she'd sealed the plastic container and tied a double-knot in the bag before tossing it. "Both born in Galway."

"Oh, that's not too far from my neck of the woods," he said. "I'm from Mayo. Have you been?"

She shook her head.

"Someday," he said.

"Yeah, I hope so." She smiled. "I like your accent."

"Thanks. I like yours."

She felt herself take in a sip of breath, an ancient worry, well-buried and almost forgotten, and here he was like an archaeologist with a straw brush, gently excavating.

"I have an accent?" she said.

"Well, you don't sound like you're from New Joysey," he said.

"Oh," she laughed. "Got it. Yeah, I'm not."

"So where are you from?"

Where was she from, anyway?

"Well. My accent is probably from St. Louis, I guess."

"Ah, midwestern."

"Yeah, but I'm not really from there. I'm originally from Puerto Rico," she said. And that sentence brought Titi Lola to stand in the room beside her, absent and present both. For a moment, the swell of Ruth's grief was just as acute as it had been two months ago, beside her titi's open coffin in Parroquia Sagrado Corazón de Jesús. Ruth heaved it aside. "Born in San Juan," she said. "That's where my mom's from, too, her whole family. We moved to Missouri when I was like ten."

She'd found herself doing this lately, exaggerating the age she'd been when they left there, as if those three imagined years might redeem an authenticity she could no longer feel. Thomas nodded, but didn't answer. He tapped the end of the pen on the counter between them. And then finally he said, "I have so many questions."

She surprised herself with a laugh. "I know, it's confusing."

"No, it's great!"

"Well," she said. And then she made some kind of awkward, vague gesture. She wasn't even sure what she was trying to convey. Suddenly, his tucked-in T-shirt seemed so charming, so European, so out of her league. Ugh, why was she such a dork? No wonder she hadn't made out with anybody in months.

"So I'm going to need more time," he said.

"Time?"

"To formulate and ask my many, many questions, and for you to answer them."

"Oh."

"There are so many I don't even know where to begin. For example, did your Irish-American father live in Puerto Rico that whole time, or did they split up? And if he did live there, was he always, always sunburned, and if not, how? And then, for another example, is there, like, a big Puerto Rican community in St. Louis? Why St. Louis? Or is there an

Irish community in Puerto Rico? How did all of this happen, how did it happen, how did *you* happen?"

She laughed again, and felt the ghost of Lola flit from the room. "Oh, we are going to need more time," she said.

"So, then, dinner."

"What?"

"Have dinner with me."

Ruth shrugged, delighted, but eager not to show it. There had been one casual boyfriend in high school, and a couple of regrettable vodka-fueled hookups the summer before college, but nothing serious and nothing since. She would of course never reveal this truth to Thomas, not even after they were engaged, but the fact was that she was twenty years old and had never been on an actual date before. She worried she might blush if she didn't say something soon. "Okay," she decided. "Why not?"

"Tonight?"

"No, not tonight!" she laughed. She was working until six, and then had plans to go to a party with her three roommates. There was the distinct possibility the three of them would already be drunk when she got home, but it was too late to change her answer, and anyway it would have felt pathetic to go to dinner with him only hours after the suggestion had been made, even she knew that. Outside, she could hear another roar from the stadium.

He leaned on his elbows now, so his face was closer to hers. She chewed rapidly on her gum. She was sitting on the wooden stool, and she could see how the scruff of his beard would crowd his jawline if he didn't shave every morning. It was early afternoon and already there was a shadow there, a diagonal trail along his cheekbone, freckles across the bridge of his nose. His dark hair was cut short and his lips were very red. "Tomorrow night?" he asked.

She waited a moment before answering, "Maybe tomorrow night."

The phone beneath the counter rang, and she had to answer it. It was a quick one—no, they weren't open on Sundays. They closed at 6 P.M. today. When she hung up, he was again engrossed in filling out the form on the front of his envelope. He dropped his two canisters of film inside, and then slid it across the counter to her.

"You know, if we go out to dinner, and it doesn't go well, and then it's awkward, you'll have to go somewhere else to get your film developed," she said. "Are you sure it's worth the risk?"

He crossed his arms in front of him and mulled it over. "Are you planning for it to be a disaster?"

"Not necessarily." She shrugged. "But disasters are seldom planned."

He nodded in a serious way. "Well. There's that other photo place on Maple Avenue."

"They're expensive, though," she said. "And they do a good job with color prints, but if you ever have black-and-white images, you can forget it."

"I guess dinner better go well, then," he said.

"I guess so."

She wrote her phone number on the pad of paper she kept behind the counter, tore off the sheet, and slid it across to him. They still didn't know each other's names.

"By the way, I'm Thomas," he said.

"Oh!" She shook his hand. "Nice to meet you, Thomas. I'm Ruth."

He looked at her quizzically. "Ruth?" he said. "Is that a Puerto Rican name?"

"It is . . . not."

"It's not Irish either," he said.

"Nope. It's biblical."

"Are you somehow also Jewish?"

"Not that I know of."

"It's fine. We'll throw a few extra vowels and an accent mark in there. You'll be Irish in no time."

Dinner went better than well. Thomas didn't wear jeans or a T-shirt, so Ruth couldn't gauge whether the peculiar tuck-in had been an anomaly or was a regular habit, but she hardly cared. They went to her favorite Indian place where she only ever ate when one of her parents took her to dinner. She laughed so hard at the table she had to cover her mouth, afraid a piece of paneer would fly out and ruin everything by landing on his face. He walked her back to her dorm afterward and then before he leaned in, he asked, "Can I kiss you?" which Ruth thought all but killed the moment. But years later she would recognize that in fact, he was just decades ahead of his time. They made plans to see each other again the following weekend.

And then on late Wednesday afternoon of the following week, Ruth was at work again when Arthur came in. This time, she had the door closed, because even though it had only been four days, the arrival of autumn had happened in the interim, so the bell above the door did jingle when he pushed it open. Outside, the maple trees that lined both sides of Main Street had suddenly bedecked themselves in a blazing crimson. The sun was sinking low behind the shops across the street, giving the impression that the whole block was on fire. And against this splendid backdrop, he appeared.

Ruth stood up at once and her throat went dry. She had been watching this boy for two years, but they had never spoken. She knew they were in the same year because he'd been in the same freshman dorm building as her. He'd lived on the seventh floor, she knew, because she saw him press seven when he got on the elevator. Sometimes she imagined that his room was the one directly above hers. She saw him coming and going from the building at least a couple times every week. Once, she'd seen him turning his key in the front door lock just as she was getting on the elevator, and she'd pressed the door-open button for as long as she dared, hoping he'd get on, and it would just be the two of them. Her heart pounded imagining it, imagining that he'd turn to look at her, that he'd level his chocolate-drop eyes at her, and then pin her against the elevator wall and hit the emergency stop button and hike her skirt up around her hips and . . . she wasn't even wearing a skirt. And after perhaps thirty seconds of pressing the door-open button, she still didn't even hear his footsteps approaching, and she felt like a loser, so she let the doors slide shut without him. And still, she felt breathless all the way up to the sixth floor, all the way to her freshman dorm room, alone.

She knew his last name was Rodríguez, or at least she thought his last name was Rodríguez, because he played soccer, or at least she thought he played soccer because he was often seen around campus wearing various soccer jerseys with the last name Rodríguez emblazoned across the back. They'd never had any classes together even though at the beginning of every semester, when she walked into each classroom or lecture hall for the first time, she found herself surveying each table and desk to see if he was there. Once, when she'd stood behind him in line at the dining hall, sliding her cafeteria tray along the metal rails just behind his, choosing the same items that he chose from the servers, even though she didn't really care for green beans, just to give him something to remark upon, should he happen to turn and notice that they had selected exactly the same dinner—would you look at that!—she perceived that, unlike so many of their peers, he wasn't one for drenching himself in a cologne-bath of Drakkar Noir, but instead he smelled exceedingly clean, like fresh sheets and laundry detergent and sandalwood soap. She'd stopped herself just short of touching her nose to the back of his broad, lean shoulder to commit his scent to memory.

"Hi," Ruth said when he walked into the photo lab that Wednesday just at sunset. Just like that. *Hi.* Like it was no big deal, and like it hadn't taken her two years and the perfect confluence of circumstances for her to find the courage to finally unleash that single syllable.

"Hey," he said, and he looked right at her and smiled.

She sat down on the stool with a thump, grateful that it was there to catch her weight, grateful that she didn't fall off backward and into a legitimate swoon. His *voice*, my God. It was like soup and warm bread on a cold day. *Say more words*, she thought. To him, to herself. She needed to make more words exist between them. She found absolutely nothing in her mind, nothing from which to create more words.

"I didn't know you worked here," he said.

As if he knew plenty of other things about her, so it was strange that this one plain fact had slipped his notice.

"Oh," she said. "Yeah, I started last semester."

"Yeah, you go to Wodsley, right?"

"Yup," she said, and she could feel a tightness around her mouth, a giddiness that she prayed he couldn't sense.

"Yeah, I've seen you around, I think."

His dimples were like craters, you could fall into them. You could stick your whole tongue in there.

"Yeah?"

He nodded. "Yeah, definitely."

"Cool," she said.

"I think we lived in the same building freshman year," he said. "You were in The Dozens, right?"

"Yeah!"

"Yeah, me too."

She could not say *cool* again, she knew. But she could not think of any other words.

"Cool," she said. "Yeah. Yeah, you definitely look familiar."

"I'm Arthur," he said.

Arthur Rodríguez. It was not the name she'd expected. She thought he'd be Eric, maybe. Or Raúl or Javi. Something with four letters. Something suave, less geriatric. It didn't matter. He was Arthur, how wonderful.

"I'm Ruth," she said, and realized for the first time that her name was also extremely geriatric. Arthur and Ruth. They should be sipping lemonades through their dentures on a porch swing somewhere.

"So where are you from, Ruth?" he asked.

The dreaded question. She never knew how to answer.

"Oh, it's a long story," she said, pretending to busy herself with something very urgent beneath the counter because making eye contact with him was too intense, and she felt like her whole body was a neon sign advertising her sentiments. She was grateful for the moderate padding in her bra to disguise the morse code her nipples were determined to transmit. She crossed her arms in front of her chest anyway, just to be sure.

"I don't mean . . . I just mean, Puerto Rican or Dominican?" he asked.

She looked him right in the face. The question almost startled her. "What?" she said.

"Sorry—Cuban?" he guessed again.

"No, no," she said. "I mean, yes, I'm Puerto Rican."

"Yeah, me too. I mean, my Dad's Puerto Rican. And Dominican actually, half and half. My mom's white."

Do not say cool *again*, she thought.

"Yeah, I'm the same, half Puerto Rican, half white. But I was born there. In San Juan."

"Oh, word?" he said. "That's cool. I've never even been to Puerto Rico. Even my dad's never been. He was born in Paterson, where everybody just thinks he's black. I mean, African American. He explains to everybody that he's Domini-rican."

"Ha!" Ruth said by accident.

"He thinks it's more fun to say than Afro-Latino."

"I don't disagree."

"So, born in San Juan?" Arthur said, and Ruth had the feeling he was assessing all kinds of things about her in the context of this new piece of information. "Yeah, it's funny, I always figured you were Puerto Rican or Dominican when I saw you around. Or like, I knew you were *something*. But then I never saw you at the Boricua House or any of the events, so I wasn't sure."

Ruth felt herself hopping from thrill to thrill to thrill, like lily pads across a deep, still pond. He'd seen her. He'd noticed her. He'd had thoughts about her, about who she was or who she might be. And even more breathtaking, he had *recognized* her. Ruth had gotten so accustomed to confounding people that she never even realized she craved this kind of recognition. *His heart sees my heart.*

In St. Louis, when people bothered to take up the question of her ethnicity at all, they called her Mexican, in the same way they called the Vietnamese boy, two Korean girls, and one Chinese-American teacher in their school district all Chinese. Even the ones who cared, who knew they weren't supposed to say *oriental* anymore, hadn't quite made it to *Asian* yet. They were doing their best, Ruth thought, because that was what she wanted to believe. She seldom bothered to correct them.

All throughout her childhood in the Midwest, she had ingested the reality that the only thing that mattered about her appearance was the fact that she was almost, but not *quite* white. Even the forms she filled out when she was applying to Wodsley and other colleges gave her extremely limited options as far as those checkboxes were concerned. She'd had to choose one: White. Black or Negro. Indian. Asian. Other. Ruth had checked *other*, and her mother, leaning over her shoulder at the kitchen table, had literally smacked the pencil out of her hand.

"What are you doing?" Mama had asked.

Ruth bent down to retrieve the pencil from the floor.

"Just . . . filling out the forms?"

"I mean what are you doing checking *other*?"

Ruth had been unable to formulate a sensible response.

"You are white!" Mama said. "You check *white*!"

Mama tapped her finger impatiently on the appropriate box in case Ruth could not find it without her help. Ruth flipped her pencil around and started erasing her *other* checkmark, but then ventured a small opinion in her mother's direction. "You know, there may be scholarships available for—"

"White!" Mama had interrupted.

And so Ruth had checked *white*, but she'd felt a kind of slithering across her skin when she did it.

She'd hoped things would be different when she moved to the East Coast. It was one of the reasons she'd applied to so many colleges in New York, New Jersey, Maryland. She knew there were places in the world outside Puerto Rico where lots of Puerto Ricans lived. She knew there were communities, other kids like her whose experiences might have matched some of her own. Ruth hadn't been an unhappy child, not like Benny. She hadn't felt like a miserable outsider, hadn't felt homesick or super alienated, or like she was the target of persistent racism every day of her life. But there were little things, tiny things really, that Kathy and Jenny and Jennifer would never understand. The way the store clerks ignored her and fawned over her friends when they went shopping for prom dresses. Ruth had suspected that her appearance had something to do with that, but she couldn't prove it, not even to herself. There had been other moments, of course, when the ignorance was indisputable. Once, they'd all gone to dinner for Jenny's birthday, and the waitress had looked right at Ruth and said, "I hope french fries are okay with your burger, hon. Sorry, we're fresh out of rice and beans." And Kathy and Jennifer had both laughed, and Ruth's neck had gone hot. Jenny had squeezed Ruth's hand beneath the table, without saying anything. But those things didn't happen every day or even every week. For the most part, Ruth had been happy enough. She'd felt happy to be included in a friend group, to reliably have someone to sit with in the cafeteria. But she'd always hoped that in college, she might meet people who were different from the friends she had in St. Louis. She hoped to meet some kids who liked her without the attachment of the unspoken phrase *even though . . .*

So when she'd arrived here in Wodsley, she'd been aggrieved to immediately discover how self-segregating the campus was. Students joined fraternities and sororities that separated them not only by gender and race, but also by socioeconomic background, religion, grade point average, height, weight, level of attractiveness. Ruth found the sequestering creepy, but also personally troublesome, because what was she supposed to do? Where was the sorority for moderately attractive, island-born Puerto Rican–Irish girls of midwestern childhood and indeterminate race whose mothers insist they are white despite conflicting evidence? In the dining hall, all the white kids ate in the main room, while the students of color gathered into the smaller peripheral rooms that were partitioned from the main space by glass walls. Asian kids in this room, African American kids in this room, Latino kids over here. Ruth felt like a fraud no matter where she sat, so she ordered her food to go and ate at the desk in her dorm room.

Still, on her fourth morning on campus, Ruth burst into the Boricua House in a fever of naive optimism, determined to make some headway. She marched right in as if they'd all be waiting for her, her new group of would-be friends, waiting to embrace her. She was wearing the sticker name tag they were all supposed to wear the first week around campus. *Hello my name is RUTH BRENNAN.*

The girl behind the welcome desk was perhaps a year older than Ruth, and in no way welcoming. She was on the phone when Ruth walked in, and she looked right at Ruth, but did not smile or gesture or indicate that Ruth should take a seat and wait. She just stared at Ruth while continuing her conversation. So Ruth busied herself by wandering over to the bulletin board to review the flyers and upcoming events calendar while she waited. One flyer stapled to the board informed her in purple bubble letters that eight percent of the student population at Wodsley was Hispanic. Eight percent! That was almost one in ten! (Ruth was not a math major.) The Boricua House was a welcoming place for all Hispanic students, another flyer said, not only Puerto Ricans. Around the edges of the bulletin board, there were flags tacked up from Ecuador, Cuba, Mexico, Panama, Peru. Tuesday nights there was a potluck dinner. Saturday mornings there was a coffee club where people could practice conversational Spanish—*All levels welcome! No shaming!* the flyer said.

Behind her, Ruth heard the girl at the misnamed welcome desk hang up the phone. She turned away from the bulletin board, but before she could approach the desk again, Ruth realized another student had appeared, and they were both looking at her. The newcomer stood behind the other girl's chair. There was a tinfoil sign hanging from the front edge of the desk that said BIENVENIDOS.

"Ay, mira la blanquita," the newcomer said. "¿Qué quiere ella?"

Ruth was aware that she had lost some significant portion of her Spanish in the years since she'd left Puerto Rico. But she retained enough to understand that unmistakable hostility was being directed at her, and the accent was not island Puerto Rican. *Hey, check out the white girl. What does she want?*

Once upon a time, Ruth might have stretched her spine to its fullest height and replied in her pistol-whip Spanish, shaming them with her flaw-less Caribbean accent, a playground retort. *No quiero nada de ustedes come-mierdas. Estoy en el lugar equivocado.* But her mouth was dry, the linguistic stockpile of her mind long depleted. So the pit that opened in Ruth's stomach at that moment was exactly the same as the one that had opened at the St. Louis restaurant when that red-faced waitress had said *rice and beans.* It was the you-are-not-one-of-us pit. The chasm yawned open within her. And Ruth fell in. She never returned to the Boricua House again.

But then, two years later on a Wednesday evening at sunset in the photo lab, here was Arthur Rodríguez, single-handedly dismantling all of Ruth's disappointment, her heartache, her devastated optimism. Here he stood, resurrecting her hope of belonging. And my God, he was so good-looking. It was crazy that one human could be so many perfect things, and smell like that, and look like that. Crazy.

"Encantado de conocerte," he said with a formal little bow.

"Oh wow, you speak Spanish?"

He shrugged. "Of course. Don't you?"

"Yeah," she said. "I mean I used to. I lost a lot of it in Missouri."

He laughed. "Like you misplaced your luggage in Missouri?"

"Yeah, something like that."

"You left your heart in San Francisco?"

"Exactly." She was leaving her heart right here, in Gus's Pro Photo on Main Street, in Wodsley, New Jersey. "I mean, it was my first language, you know? But when we moved to St. Louis, my brother had trouble in school, so—"

"So your parents forbade Spanish at home?"

How did he know? She nodded.

"Ugh. That sucks," he said.

And she was mortified to find that she had tears in her eyes. *What the fuck, stop it.*

"So practice," he said. "It's still in there. You'll get it back if you try."

She shrugged again. "Who'm I going to practice with?"

He smiled at her, and his teeth were beautiful. She wanted to lick them.

"Conmigo," he said. *With me.*

Chapter Fifteen

~

San Juan, Puerto Rico
2023

Daisy.

There is a roar in her ears.

Daisy!

DAISY, can you hear me? Squeeze my hand if you can hear me, Daisy.

Her name is a beacon, a flare, would you look at that! The strength of it.

Daisy had never cared that much for her name, the simplest flower. She's never appreciated the plain, robust beauty of it before now. But it is hers. A talisman, with the divine power to pin her to this world.

Daisy!

Again. And behind the sound of her name, behind the roar, there are other noises. A cacophony, a whole percussion section in delight. A rhythmless drumbeat, loud and clamoring, a ruckus on the roof, far too raucous to be the nature of simple rainsplats striking the metal hood of an ambulance. Behind that, another discordant sound, though it all seems like music to Daisy. Euphoria, as her soul shoots into her body once more. Her name, her beautiful name.

Daisy!

And the tuneless wail of a siren.

Chapter Sixteen

~

St. Louis, Missouri
1980

On the surface of things, Rafaela and Peter were in lockstep over the plan to invite Eddie's family over: Benny would extend the invitation for Friday evening. Under no circumstances was Rafaela to cook. She would buy a cake from Morton's Bakery in town, and they'd serve coffee to their guests. Peter would buy a bottle of rum, too, in case they were cocktail drinkers. These things they agreed upon.

Benny was still in his room getting ready, and Ruth was in the den watching the opening credits for *The New Adventures of Wonder Woman*. Rafaela watched her daughter from the doorway, and suspected that Ruth was wearing her Wonder Woman Underoos beneath her favorite blue corduroy jumpsuit.

"Turn that TV off," Peter called from his station at the front window. "Our guests are arriving!"

"Do I have to, Mama?" Ruth whispered.

"They're in the driveway!" Peter yelled.

"Turn it off," Rafaela said.

When Rafaela and her daughter emerged from the den, the Morales y Reyes family were already seated on the blue-and-white flowered couch in the living room. So unaccustomed was Ruth to seeing people sitting on that couch that she gave a small gasp when she saw them there, and

Rafaela had to lightly pinch the back of her daughter's neck to quiet her. Rafaela had been worried that the couch might actually smell of dust. She'd beaten the cushions during the week and left them outside in the sunshine for a few hours to air them. She'd also boiled cinnamon sticks in a pot of water on the stove to create a welcoming aroma. Benny's friend Eddie looked miserable in a sport coat and tie.

"You must be Eddie," Rafaela said, reaching out her hand to the boy, who stood very awkwardly to shake it.

"Yes, ma'am," he said.

"It's nice to meet you, I'm so glad you all could come."

"Thank you, ma'am," the boy said, and then he half turned to indicate the presence of his parents. "This is my mom and dad."

The parents stood too.

"How do you do?" Rafaela said, shaking each of their hands in turn. "I'm Rafaela. So nice to meet you."

The parents both smiled and shook hands.

"Luis," said the dad.

"Consuelo," said the mom.

Rafaela could read nothing into their meticulously pronounced names, so she waited for them to say more as they returned to their places on the edge of the couch. They were a handsome couple, though their clothing seemed neither expensive nor particularly stylish. Rafaela could not find fault with their appearance, being neat and orderly on the whole, if perhaps a bit square. Square-jawed, square-hipped, squarely mannered, she thought. *Inelegant* may have been a credible appraisal, though not a generous one. And in any case, seated on the lap of Eddie's mother was the antidote to all those right angles, in the form of one gorgeous, fat, round, little baby with blinking, wet, black eyes. The baby would put everyone at ease. She'd give them all something to look at and talk about. Her wispy black hair was gathered together into a tiny curl that sprouted from a pink bow in the center of her head. Rafaela watched as the baby's presence pulled on Ruth like gravity. Her daughter made room for herself on the couch, squeezed in next to Eddie's mother, and put her face close to the baby's face.

"Hi there!" Ruth said to the baby.

The baby reached her chubby little hand out and grabbed Ruth's nose.

"Can I hold her?" Ruth said, leaning back and speaking to Eddie's mother.

The woman was bouncing her knees lightly beneath the baby's weight.

"Say hello first!" Peter said.

"Oh," Ruth laughed. "Sorry, hi."

Eddie's parents both nodded at her.

"I'm Ruth."

"Hello!" they said.

"What's the baby's name?" she asked.

No one answered her, and Rafaela began to understand why there was so little conversation. Benny was sitting in the wingback chair and, like his friend Eddie, he was also wearing a tie with a plaid shirt, but he'd outgrown his sport coat, so at least they hadn't had to fight that battle. Peter returned carrying their good silver tray with the silver coffee pot, and their china coffee cups with the gold rims. He crossed the room and set the tray down on the coffee table, careful to keep it out of swiping distance of the baby.

"What's her name?" Ruth asked again.

Again, Consuelo made no answer, and rather than intervening, Rafaela said to Peter, "I'll bring in the cake."

Peter began pouring out the coffee.

"Mi hija pregunta cómo se llama la bebé," Rafaela heard Peter saying in the living room behind her.

She turned in the doorway just in time to catch a smile falling across the face of Eddie's mother.

"Oh," Consuelo said. "¡Se llama Estela!"

"Estela," Ruth repeated. "Hi, Estela!" Ruth offered her finger into the squishy casing of the baby's grip. "Can I hold her?"

"Ask her in Spanish," Peter said to Ruth.

Ruth blinked at him rapidly a few times, and Rafaela, in the kitchen, held her breath. Did her daughter remember the forbidden Spanish words? Rafaela hadn't heard those beautiful shapes from the mouths of her children in over a year. There was a pang in the sound of Ruth's voice as she tried.

"¿Puedo cargarla?" Ruth said.

Rafaela dislodged whatever it was that had stuck in her throat with a quick cough, and then busied herself with the cake. Through the doorway she could see Eddie's mother shift the baby's heft onto Ruth's lap. The baby flapped her arms back at her mother, but didn't cry. Consuelo made noises and smiled at Estela, so the baby seemed quite content to stay there on Ruth's lap.

"I have Chinese checkers downstairs," Benny said to Eddie then.

Rafaela couldn't tell for sure, but she suspected Eddie didn't understand either. She noticed that Benny refrained from translating for his friend. He found simpler ways to communicate.

"You wanna go downstairs?" Benny pointed, and Eddie nodded, and the two boys got up, came into the kitchen, and squeezed past Rafaela, who was just transferring the cake onto a pale-blue ceramic stand. It was important to remove the little cardboard and foil disc from beneath the cake, too, before carrying it in to the guests, so it might be reasonably assumed that Rafaela had made the cake herself. As frequently happened whenever Rafaela was engaged with baked goods, she thought of Priti, which caused her heart to whip and stiffen like a speedy meringue. She still called Priti several times a year, always on Christmas and her birthday, but they hadn't seen each other since before Trinidad. It had been sixteen years, and in that time, Priti's role in Rafaela's maturing imagination had scattered, flourished, wilted, and grown anew. She still missed Priti like a second mother, and although they knew each other less intimately now than they once had, Rafa felt she had come to understand Priti in new ways. Rafa was a mother now, a homemaker, and a magnificently failed chef. She'd learned how hard these things were, even without the additional injustices Priti had faced. She felt ashamed when she thought back on it now, by how utterly she had failed to appreciate Priti's position, but Rafaela understood too well the futility of regret. With some effort, she shook her reverie into the garbage alongside the pretty pink box from Morton's Bakery, and licked a smear of icing from the knob of her wrist.

"Oh, wait." Benny paused in the basement doorway beside his friend. "Cake." Then to Rafaela, "Save us some."

The boys thundered down the stairs.

In the living room, Rafaela kept her eyes mostly on Ruth, who tickled the baby while the grown-ups ate and talked. If Ruth had any feelings about the sudden reappearance of the Spanish language as a permissible form of communication in their household, she gave no indication. She seemed interested only in the baby. Estela's heavy head swayed when she tipped it back to grin at Ruth with her gums, and Ruth held on tighter so the baby wouldn't topple over. There were four dimples between them, and it seemed clear to Rafaela that they were deeply in love, and that nothing else mattered at all.

Peter's Spanish was rusty too, Rafaela noted, but whatever he lacked in precision, he made up for in determination, and Rafaela, ever the dutiful wife, smoothed it over for him when he stumbled. Peter asked what part of the island they were from, and they answered Divisoria. He looked at Rafaela as if she could explain where that was, but she'd never heard of it before.

"It's a very small place," Luis explained.

"In the mountains," Consuelo added.

Which explains so much, Rafaela thought but didn't say.

They all sipped their coffee, and even the clinking of the cup back into the saucer sounded like a little alarm bell to Rafaela. She understood that whatever was taking place inside her was like a swollen droplet plinking into the dead center of a deep emotional reservoir. There was an outward furrow now, an emerging disquiet. She felt angry at Peter, but she knew he'd done nothing wrong. She had wanted to meet Eddie and his parents as much as her husband had, but she'd failed to ask herself why. Why did she want to meet these people, what did she expect of them?

During their time in St. Louis, Rafaela had become adept at maintaining an essential stillness. During their whole marriage, really—boiling cinnamon sticks wasn't the only trick she'd learned. Rafaela knew not to look below the surface, not to wonder what might be roiling underneath. When she did think about the broad strokes of her life, Rafaela knew, of course, that she was deeply unhappy. She didn't know why, but there were myriad possible reasons, and she suspected it was not only the quantity of those reasons, but also the precise combination of them that created this gulf between the empirical color she observed in her daily life and her ability to feel and experience that color as joy. In 1980, she didn't know that the name for this gulf was *clinical depression*, and she didn't know that no one was to blame. And then something about this evening with these very nice people had thrown her careful quietude off-kilter. Perhaps it wasn't a heavy droplet at all, but a stone. Now there were ripples in every direction, all the way out to every edge. Try as she might, Rafaela could not recapture her composure.

The cake was lemon chiffon, Ruth's favorite, but her daughter didn't even eat until the Morales y Reyes family left, because having a piece of cake would've required her to part briefly from the baby. Once they were gone, Ruth sat at the kitchen table with her slice while Rafaela and Peter cleaned up.

"Don't you guys want to have another baby?" Ruth asked, sinking her fork slowly into the yellow cake.

The response from Rafaela was a sound more bark than laughter, and she couldn't help but notice a hurt expression briefly cross her husband's face. He pinched it away.

"No more babies for us, pumpkin," Peter said to their daughter.

"I would take care of it," Ruth said. "You guys wouldn't even have to do anything. I would change its diapers and feed it and everything."

Rafaela knew she should make a joke or at least say something comforting. She should peel off the yellow rubber gloves and go to Ruth, place a hand on top of her daughter's head, and tell her that there was no need to make another baby because they already had the perfect little girl right here. She couldn't bring herself to do it. The bones in her shoulders felt hollow, her stomach twisted. She couldn't move. It occurred to Rafaela that part of her disturbance this evening was in observing the Morales y Reyes family's happiness, despite the many reasons Rafaela imagined they must have to feel unhappy. Each member of the family seemed so in sync with the others. There was a breeziness in the ways they accommodated each other, a simplicity in all their interactions. The way Consuelo handed the baby to Luis without a word while she wriggled into her coat, the way he reached for the baby even before Consuelo moved in his direction. They spoke the same language not just in their mouths or their thoughts, but in their muscles and bones, Rafaela thought. Perhaps that's what was broken between her and Peter. The thought flitted through her mind like a passing bird without alighting with any permanence there. But she knew without saying it to herself that the bird's name was Candido.

"You really weren't yourself this evening." Peter startled her out of her thoughts, his voice too close to her ear. She hadn't realized he was standing there.

"I know," she said. "I felt that too. I suppose I'm not feeling very well."

Peter's voice was lower than the sound of the running water, but Rafaela didn't stop clanking the dishes around in the sink to try to hear him. He was bent over, leaning his elbows on the counter while Rafaela did all the washing herself. His sleeves were rolled up, but it was unclear why.

"Really nice family though, right?" he said.

"They were perfectly nice, yes," Rafaela said.

"Why does it sound like there's a *but* coming?"

"I don't know, there's no *but*," she said. "Unless you expect me to have more to say about them?"

"Well, I thought you might," Peter said.

She was taking the clean plates out of the soapy water, and dipping them into the clear water in the second sink before stacking them in the drying rack. The lemon cake was still on the ceramic stand right in front of Ruth, and Rafaela knew without turning around that her daughter was going to sneak a second slice. They were already cut; it would be impossible to ask a child to sit there without taking a second slice. If Rafaela herself had the luxury of sitting down, she wouldn't even have bothered with a plate; she'd have pulled a chair and a fork directly up to the cake stand. She looked at Peter.

"Why?" she asked. "What more should I have to say about them?"

"I don't know." He sounded exasperated. "I mean, these are the first Puerto Rican people we've met since we moved back here. I thought that might be nice for you. I thought there'd be more to discuss than the dirty dishes."

"Well, I don't know why you thought that," she said. "They may be Puerto Rican, and yes, they seem lovely, but they may as well be from Pluto for all we have in common."

"How can you say that, Rafaela?" Peter said. "Be reasonable."

Which was almost as infuriating as when he told her to *calm down* or *relax*, both of which had become a blessedly rare utterance between them because, whatever Peter's faults, he was a man capable of learning. But in this instance, he seemed heedless to her growing unrest. How could he not feel what was surging through her? Wasn't it rising up from her skin in hot waves? He did not appear to be forewarned.

"Of course you have things in common," he was saying. "What a crazy thing to say. You have sons the same age, you're both Puerto Rican. You both live here, in St. Louis. Isn't that a lot of common ground right there, already?"

Rafaela stopped dipping the plates and turned to look at her husband.

"Do you have any idea how ridiculous that sounds?" she said.

"What's so ridiculous about it? It's true, isn't it?"

Rafaela heard their daughter's weight land into the chair behind her, and knew that Ruth had just committed the theft of the second slice.

"Put it back!" she said without turning around.

"What?" Ruth's voice was mostly a squeak. "How . . ."

When she turned to look, Ruth's mouth was standing open.

"Never mind," Rafaela sighed. "Go ahead."

"I can eat it?" she whispered.

"Quickly," Rafaela said. "Before I change my mind." Ruth wasted no time, so Rafaela returned her attention to Peter. "So. Your position is that we should be great friends because we come from the same country and we both ended up here?" she said.

"Well." Peter seemed to be examining Rafaela's statement for possible pitfalls. He couldn't find flaw, but neither did he want to commit. "I mean. It's not nothing, right?"

"It is nothing!" she said. "It's very close to nothing. You and Richard Nixon are from the same country. You want to go and be best friends with him?" She plunged her hands back into the water. "You see how silly that is? How presumptuous?"

"Rafaela, come on."

Peter tried scooting closer to her, tried bumping his hip against her hip, but the effort only calcified her. She didn't want to be like this, but she couldn't locate the switch that might turn off her anger and help her soften to him.

"Consuelo seems like a sweet gal," Peter said, as if that were the question. As if Rafaela hadn't noticed how lovely the woman was, and if Peter could only draw her attention to that, they could turn this whole thing around. "She's overwhelmed here too," he said, briefly leaning his cheek against her shoulder. "You remember how that felt, right?"

Rafaela breathed very slowly, in through her nose, out through her mouth, and when she'd completed the cycle, she was dismayed to find that the rage was still there, swift and uncertain of origin. Her fury became the prickle of threatening tears behind her eyes. How simple Peter made it all sound. How completely wrong he was about everything, how little he understood of her experience. He was still talking, and she was now doing him the kindness of not listening.

"And I don't think she speaks a word of English," he was saying. "You could help her, show her the ropes. It would be good for you both." His voice swam back to the surface, and he leaned a little closer, perhaps so their daughter wouldn't hear what he said next. "I know you're lonely here, sweetheart. You hardly talk to anyone outside of this house."

These words fell into Rafaela like into a dark pit, and she could not salvage them. He leaned against her once more.

"Wouldn't it be nice to have a friend?"

Her anger in this moment was unaccountable, so she tried to stifle it from her voice. She answered him coldly, "I do not need a friend."

There were many things she needed. She could provide him with a list. At the top would be a husband who would tell that country club manager to go fuck himself. Nowhere on the list would appear the friendship of Consuelo Reyes.

Rafaela could sense the shift coming over Peter, and it was this shift that sometimes caused her to back down, but not tonight. Tonight, Rafaela was a closed door, and soon Peter would be finished trying to pick her lock, to coax her open. He folded his hands into a tight knot in front of him while she watched, and Rafaela could see his growing impatience in the colors of his knuckles. She didn't care. She spent her whole life in this place tangled up in a knot like that. Let Peter feel it sometimes too.

Benny wandered into the room, already in his flannel pajamas. The feet of the jammies scuffed against the tile floor. And that was the antidote. Those footed pajamas cut through all of Rafaela's pain and resistance like an anchor through clean water. She felt herself return, and she was rinsed of dread. There was her sweet boy, in his last ever pair of footed pajamas. And there at the table was her beautiful girl. This was their one and only precious childhood and for better or for worse, this was the place they were doing it. Let them eat cake!

"Hey!" Benny eyeballed Ruth's plate. "Can I get another slice too?"

"Did you sneak a second slice?" Dad asked Ruth.

Rafaela looked at him. Where had he been just now, when she'd had that conversation with Ruth right in front of him?

Ruth looked at her mother and then shook her head just the tiniest bit. "No! It's my first." She tossed the lie like a frisbee, watching to see how it would land. "I'm just savoring it."

Dad winked at her.

"Liar," Benny said.

"Don't call your sister a liar," Rafaela said. "She's only fibbing."

Peter took one of the plates Rafaela had just washed out of the drying rack, wiped it with a dish towel, and handed it to Benny. "Just a small one," he said.

Benny sat down beside Ruth and chose the largest remaining slice of cake, right from the middle. They ate in contented silence.

"I don't understand why you won't just give her a chance," Peter said, returning to Rafaela just when she thought this might be over. Why wouldn't he let it go?

"I did!" Rafaela said. "I gave her a chance, she was just here for a whole evening! Didn't I feed her cake and serve her coffee in our good cups?"

Peter made his most perturbed, judgmental face. "Our good cups?"

"Yes." Well. She hadn't even known that sentiment was in there until she accidentally said it out loud.

"Our good cups," Peter repeated.

Rafaela wasn't usually one to double down, especially when she knew she was wrong. But there was something perverse about this whole conversation. She wanted to provoke him, to make him furious.

"Better than what she's accustomed to, I'm sure," she said, and felt immediately ashamed of herself. But only a little. That feeling was just one out of fifty-two cards in her shuffled deck. There was also a kind of wicked satisfaction when she observed how disgusted Peter was when she said it, the moment his face slammed shut as well. Maybe now they were even, equally sickened by each other, equally sure their spouse was a reprehensible person.

"Cake is good, right?" Benny said at the table.

It was so good Ruth didn't even answer. Just lifted another forkful into her mouth.

"You're being a snob, Rafaela," Peter said, not quietly enough that the kids wouldn't hear. They were sitting right there.

Rafaela was holding a plate in both hands. She lifted it, and for a long moment thought about smashing it over her husband's head. Ruth and Benny were both staring at them, still eating their cake. Rafaela averted her almost-violence and instead slammed the plate back into the sink. The edge of it caught on the tap, and a chip flew off and plinked against the window. A small tidal wave swamped out of the sink and up onto the backsplash. Then it made a return trip and sloshed over the lip of the counter and onto the floor, soaking her and Peter both, their stomachs first and then their shoes. The sound that came out of Rafaela in that moment was a caustic yelp, a noise only loosely related to human speech.

"She's a jíbara!" Rafaela said. "That whole family, jíbaros!"

In the silence that followed, Rafaela had a choice to make. If she consulted her emotional map, there'd be an exit ramp in there somewhere, she knew. If only she could locate it, she could take that emergency turnoff. This was her last chance to reverse course, reach for her husband, melt into him, and seek comfort there.

"That woman would not have been fit to sweep my father's floors in San Juan," she said instead.

She hated herself immediately.

But she hated Peter just a little bit more.

She didn't even mean it, she thought. Or at least she didn't want to mean it. Peter's response was a visible curdling of feeling. He shrank away from her, horrified. He grabbed the dishrag he'd just tucked into the door handle of the fridge, and leaned down to wipe the spreading puddle from the floor.

"Oh how the mighty have fallen," he muttered.

Then he deposited the soaked rag on the counter and left the room.

§

After the argument, Ruth and her brother found themselves alone in the kitchen with their mother's anger, but also with her other emotions, the whole palpable range of them. Ruth could feel that some of those emotions were the same as hers, in different situations. There was rage, yes. And snobbery, yes, that was undeniable. But there was also fear. Homesickness. The tremendous frustration of being misunderstood. There was grief. Why couldn't Dad see that? Where was his loyalty for Mama, why was he pushing her like that when it was so obvious she was hurting and needed him to be gentle? Ruth would help him understand.

When Mama was finished at the sink, she removed her apron and took herself back into the living room, where she sat quietly within the glowing halo of the floor lamp. She didn't read. She didn't pull her cross-stitch out of her sewing cabinet. She just sat quietly there beside the lamp, still wearing her wet shoes and her jewelry. She smoothed and smoothed the already-smooth skirt of her dress while Ruth watched from the doorway.

When Benny was done eating, Ruth washed her own plate and his too. Then she went into the living room and sat next to Mama for only a minute. She leaned her head on Mama's shoulder, and couldn't tell if Mama even knew she was there, which gave Ruth an eerie, unsettled feeling.

"It's okay, Mama," she whispered. "I love you."

Ruth waited for a response, watching the pearls at her mother's throat moving softly on the tides of her breath. Three cycles of breath before Ruth stood up and kissed her mother's cheek.

Ruth changed quickly into her nightgown, brushed her teeth, washed her face, and then went looking for her father in the den. Dad was sitting in his usual recliner, but without the footrest up. He was leaning on one elbow, his body all crumpled with tension.

"Will you read to me, Dad?" she asked.

He was watching *Fantasy Island*, the volume up loud.

"Dad?"

"What?" He turned toward her.

Ruth would never know Dad the way she knew Mama, even though he was simpler, easier to grasp. She'd never understand if he was truly malleable or just better at pretending, but it didn't matter anyway, because when his eyes moved away from the screen and landed on Ruth's face, she saw the way his features changed, the way his expression softened. Even though she hated the way he sometimes talked to Mama, *this* was still true. The way he loved them was uncomplicated and pure. The television lit one side of his face with its cold blue light, and he reached a hand out to her. Ruth took a step forward.

"Will you read to me?" she repeated.

He grabbed her hand and squeezed.

"Of course I will, sweetie. Go climb in bed. I'll be there in a minute."

In her room, she chose *Little Egret and Toro* from her bookshelf because she knew it was one of Dad's favorites. She turned on her daisy night-light, and then climbed beneath her quilt to wait.

"All ready for bed?" Dad said from the doorway, forced brightness in his voice.

"Yep."

He came and sat down on the edge of the bed, and then he flopped back onto the pillow beside her, so she flopped back too.

"Did you have fun tonight?" he asked.

"Yeah."

"You liked that baby, right?"

"I love her!" Ruth said.

"You were very good with her."

"Maybe you and Mama really should have another baby," she said again.

Dad snorted.

"Babies make everything better," she whispered.

Dad was quiet then. "I'm not sure it really works that way."

"It might, though."

"You liked the cake too," he said, changing the subject.

"Lemon is my favorite."

Dad was looking up at the ceiling, his hands laced behind his head. Ruth started raking her fingers through his hair, mussing his part, pushing it forward onto his forehead. She smoothed it in different directions until he closed his eyes.

"Dad?"

"Hmm." He didn't open his eyes.

"I think I know how Mama feels." She was nervous because she felt like this was important, and the moment was right, but she was unconvinced she'd be able to name what she was feeling, or to make him understand.

"Oh?"

She was grateful he didn't open his eyes. "It's like. The other day? On the playground? When Benny and Eddie went riding bikes, that day . . . when they came to the playground . . . Kathy called Eddie *foreign*."

"Oh." Dad's voice was sad.

"And, like, I didn't even really know what she meant by it. But . . ." Her own voice had dropped to a hesitant whisper. "Just—I didn't want her to think I was foreign too."

God, there was so much shame in that sentence. It bloomed up through her throat and she could feel it in her ears, in the echo of Mama saying *jíbara*. She didn't know what that word meant exactly, couldn't have guessed that years from now, righteous Puerto Ricans would reclaim and honor that word, fold it proudly into their sense of themselves. She only knew that tonight, when Mama used that word to describe Eddie's family, there was a sour curl to it. Ruth recognized the stink.

Dad's eyelids were open now, and Ruth was blinking furiously. For a moment she thought she'd be able to blink them away, but no. Her eyes were too full and wet, and one fat teardrop escaped down each cheek. Dad reached up and brushed them away with the back of his hand.

"Oh, sweetie," he said.

He sat up and put his arm around her, pulled her against his chest, and kissed the top of her head.

"Listen," Dad said softly. "This is important."

Ruth curled into him, her ear against his chest. She could hear the voice of his heartbeat in there, and she believed it said Mama's name. His voice was as soft as the lamplight.

"That girl Kathy?" he whispered.

"Yeah?" Ruth said.

"She's an idiot."

Chapter Seventeen

~

San Juan, Puerto Rico
2014

Daisy had just turned thirteen the first time Tío Benny and Tía Pamela called to ask if their niece could spend the whole summer with them in San Juan. Daisy and her mom took the call on speakerphone.

"It would be great for Stefani to have her cousin here for the whole summer," Benny said to Mom.

"They're such a good age for it," Pamela said. "And the boys are so busy at this age, they're hardly around anymore."

Stefani had three older brothers who were all close in age, and then there was a five-year gap before she was born. Two of the boys were in college, and the youngest was heading to the fire academy in Miami right after his high school graduation, so their house was emptying.

"Please, Titi Ruth!" Stefani said. "I need the company or I'll cry all summer!"

"Can I, Mom?" Daisy asked.

Benny reminded Mom of their own teenage summers returning to San Juan with their mother. Back to their grandparents and friends, day trips hiking up waterfalls in El Yunque with Lola, playing cards with Mamamía on the patio while Papamío marinated steaks. Long afternoons filled with golden laughter and the tangy aroma of meat sizzling on a grill. It was during one such summer, when Mom was thirteen herself, that she and Benny realized how much earlier and more suddenly the sun set in Puerto Rico than it did in St. Louis. At night they took a blanket to the rooftop and, lying on their backs on either side of their mother, they counted the stars in the inky black sky, pointing out the constellations they knew. Tío Benny was good at remembering and reminding. Mom couldn't think of a reason to say no.

On the last day of June, Daisy flew alone to San Juan, where Benny and her cousin Stefani were waiting for her in the arrivals hall. That first night, and every night afterward, Daisy stayed up late with Stefani baking cookies, watching scary movies, and only emerging from Stefani's bedroom around noon so they could drag themselves to the beach or go window-shopping in El Viejo San Juan. Sometimes they'd split a Coke, sitting on the old stone wall by the pier and watching the tourists disembark from their cruise ships for their few hours in the city. The girls would pass the Coke between them, scanning the crowds and picking out the boys they'd like to kiss. Texan, Nuyorican, Canadian, it didn't matter. When it came to imaginary kisses, the girls did not discriminate. On weekends they went fishing with Benny or shopping with Pamela. They passed lazy afternoons reading Suzanne Collins books side by side and then swapping, and then talking about the scandals they contained while lying on the sand without opening their eyes.

An odd thing happened to Daisy that summer: often, when the two girls left the house, Daisy discovered she'd forgotten her phone. The fourth time it happened, Daisy began to feel the liberation of it, as if she'd broken a watery surface and emerged into the freshness of deep breath. How unexpectedly good it felt, to be separated from her phone. She decided to turn that feeling into an experiment. She talked it over with Mom first, who was reluctantly agreeable. Then she powered the phone off and stowed it in the bottom interior pocket of the suitcase she wouldn't open again until late August. When Mom wanted to get in touch with her, she called Benny or Pamela or the house phone, and someone would pass the receiver over to Daisy. Soon the absence felt normal, and Daisy felt new.

"You should try it," she said to Stefani as they were locking the door behind them one afternoon to venture out on their bikes. "Being out of touch is incredible."

Stefani paused with her key in the lock and gave Daisy a dubious look, so Daisy nudged her.

"Stefani," she said, as she began to enumerate the miracle across her fingertips. "In the last two weeks, I haven't heard of a single influencer using the n-word, no mudslides or wildfires or natural disasters of any kind. If there have been horrific train derailments with hundreds dead, I know nothing about them. And do you know what happened to me yesterday?" Stefani was staring at her like she was an alien. "When we went into the museum?" Daisy paused for dramatic effect. "I did not make an escape plan."

"You what?" Stefani removed her hand from the key and planted it on her hip.

"An escape plan?" Daisy said.

"What are you talking about?"

"Like, every time I go into a public place, I look around to find the emergency exits and I make sure to locate the best hiding places in case there's a mass shooting."

"What the hell, Daisy?"

Daisy paused again. "You don't do that?"

Stefani shook her head, momentarily speechless.

"Oh," Daisy said. "Well, maybe I won't do it anymore either, now that I'm not staring at a feed filled with horrific gun violence every day."

They were both quiet then, before Stefani twisted her key in the lock, swung open the door, and tossed her phone on the bookshelf just inside the door.

"Let's see how this goes," she said, closing and locking the door behind them again.

Tía Pamela was waiting for them when they got back that evening with a "Where the hell have you been without that phone?" which prompted a protracted discussion about what the phone was actually supposed to be for, and why Pamela paid the bill every month, and the future parameters around Stefani taking the phone with her whenever they left the house.

"It was my fault," Daisy said. "I told her to leave it."

Pamela stood up from the table.

"I'm glad you girls aren't on your screens all the time, don't get me wrong," Pamela said. "But let's aim for a happy medium."

The next day they rolled Yahtzee dice in a box top at dusk on the beach and took turns recording their scores, passing the single pencil between them. Stefani left the phone zipped into the side pocket of her beach bag. After Stefani annihilated Daisy at dice, they pulled out their picnic of bananas, bread, and cheese.

"I love the food here," Daisy said.

"What, you don't get bananas in New York?" Stefani teased. "No cheese in the Big Apple?"

"Not this meal specifically," Daisy said, chewing. "Though this is some extremely delicious cheese. I just mean the food in general, Puerto Rican food."

Stefani sighed. She was leaning back on her elbows, looking out across her toes at the darkening surf. "I dunno. I wish we could eat out more. There are so many great restaurants here I want you to try, but my mom cooks practically every night."

"Yeah, you're so lucky!" Daisy shook her head. "She's such a great cook."

"Your mom is a great cook," Stefani countered. "She always makes different things. We have the same stuff all the time, every week."

"Well." Daisy took a bite of her banana and shrugged. "Your lazy ass could cook, then."

Stefani shoved her, and Daisy fell halfway over in her effort to save the banana from the sand. "I'm just saying, pasta and stuff like that is easy. Your mom is making incredible home-cooked meals from scratch all the time."

Stefani sat up and clapped the sand from her hands. "Your mom never makes Puerto Rican food?"

Daisy shook her head. "Not really. I mean, not often."

Stefani was rummaging in the tote bag to see what else she could find.

"You know, Grandma is a terrible cook," Daisy said. "Like, really bad."

"Oh, I've heard the stories." Stefani laughed, pulling out a heel of bread and pressing a square of cold cheese into it.

"Yeah, so my mom only knows how to make a few Puerto Rican dishes because Grandma never taught her. I guess the ingredients were hard to find in Missouri when she was younger, and Grandma didn't like to cook anyway. So Mom only learned a couple dishes from Lola before she died. Whatever other Puerto Rican recipes she makes, which is hardly ever, she finds them on Pinterest. Who knows if they're even authentic?"

Daisy watched her cousin rip the bread with her teeth.

"I'll tell you how I really feel," Daisy said.

"How do you really feel?" Stefani squinted at her, chewing.

"I feel that your mother's cooking has made me understand the injustice of our grandmother's disinclination for cooking and the subsequent scarcity of Puerto Rican recipes in my mother's culinary repertoire."

"Good heavens!" Stefani said, and brought a hand to her chest.

Daisy nodded. "It is a solemn business."

But Stefani laughed. "So I take it all back then." She popped the last morsel of bread into her mouth. "About wanting to eat out more. Maybe we should learn how to cook instead. I mean. In between lying on the beach and reading and napping and talking about boys and playing games. Whenever we're not doing those things, we could ask my mom. Maybe she'd teach us some family recipes."

"Yes!" Daisy said, sitting up on her knees.

"I'm so smart," Stefani said.

Daisy stood and flung her towel out into the wind, shaking the sand toward the ocean.

"Where are you going?" Stefani asked.

"Home! To learn how to cook!"

"Right this second?" Stefani tried to coax some irritation into her voice, but she was already rolling up to her feet, gathering her own sandy towel into the bag.

"I'm starving!" Daisy said.

So Tía Pamela agreed to teach them one recipe a week, Saturday afternoons. Every Friday, Pamela gave them a shopping list and some money, and the two girls hauled the ingredients home in a wheeled cart. With Pamela's guidance and varying degrees of success, they learned to make, first, sofrito, and then: arroz con gandules, alcapurrias, pernil, mofongo, tostones, ropa vieja, and pasteles.

On their second-to-last Sunday together, Daisy and Stefani spent all day alone in the kitchen, wearing aprons and hairnets they thought were funny. They reserved the irony for their outfits, though. The food was serious. When the meal was finally ready and all the house smelled of savory meat and the tang of salt, the girls plated everything on the dining room table with cloth napkins and two tapered candles. Benny and Pamela were astonished. The girls studied the grown-ups while they tried everything, eager to determine whether or not the praise was genuine. It was.

Daisy dug her fork into the mofongo mountain on her plate and took her time curating the perfect bite, with just enough meat and just enough plantain. The textures were sublime.

"We are goooood cooks," Stefani said with her mouth full.

"You got that right!" Benny said.

The experience of being there that summer had changed Daisy, engendered in her a more elastic sense of the world around her and her place in it.

The week before Daisy had to go back to New York, she and Stefani went to buy pads just on the off chance one of them might have their period soon (an eventuality they were both expecting to happen any day now). Next door to the pharmacy, they discovered a little thrift store that Stefani had never visited.

"But it's so cute!" It was Daisy who paused outside, the bulky, light-weight bag dangling from the crook of her elbow.

She looked at their reflections in the window, and then hooked her cousin's arm and pushed open the door. There was the familiar scent, or perhaps the familiar conglomeration of scents that, when combined, became their own uniquely recognizable aroma, the same in every thrift shop the world over. It was dust and old leather and a heavy accumulation of memories, and it made the air inside the shop feel positively sticky with nostalgia, a swirling of particles in a sunbeam. Daisy filled up with the scent. There were typewriters and umbrellas and obsolete computer accessories and a pair of ceramic swan figurines. A propped-open hardback suitcase contained a whole collection of prescription eyeglasses. In the children's aisle, Daisy found a funky rainbow tank top and a pair of Thomas the Tank Engine pajamas that would definitely fit her. The women's clothing was even better.

"Sick, right?" Stefani said, as she squeezed past the rows of overstuffed hangers and arrived at Daisy's elbow. "Look at this Michael Kors handbag. Eleven dollars!"

"That's hot." Daisy pulled out a shirt made from a sheer, delicate material. It was a button-down with pointy collars, and a print of wild horses in a desert landscape.

"Um." Stefani looked dubiously at the shirt. "That particular shirt might be here because it's an abomination, though?"

Daisy shook her head at her cousin. "Stefani, I'm surprised at you. Where's your sense of adventure?"

Stefani lifted one sleeve, squinting at the blurry print. "Is that an Indian?" she asked. "Daisy, are these, like, cowboys and Indians?"

Daisy snatched at the sleeve and peered closer.

"It's just a guy riding a horse," she said.

"In a feathered headdress." Stefani pointed at an impossibly blurry figure woven into the fabric.

Daisy didn't see it.

"But I mean . . . feathered headdresses do exist, though. Is it wrong to celebrate their existence?"

"Daisy, that shirt is a hate crime," Stefani said.

Daisy felt very sad. But she put it back.

"Look at this one!" It was a cropped T-shirt that said PLEASE DON'T SQUEEZE THE CHARMIN and its price tag said two dollars.

"I don't get it," Stefani said.

Daisy added it to her purchase pile.

On Daisy's last night in San Juan, they took two collapsible camp chairs out to the backyard and set up a Parcheesi board on a folding table between them. When Stefani deposited her dice into the little cardboard tube, Daisy felt like it was her heart rattling around in there, making that understated racket. Stefani held it in her fist and shook it tenderly. There was a huge catalog now, between them, of shared songs and handclaps and jokes and stories, not to mention family recipes. They'd built new ideas and memories into each other's minds, and they had done all that without exchanging a single text message.

"This has been the best summer of my life by a mile," Daisy said, and there was a tight feeling in her throat. "I wish my mom had moved back here, like your dad did. I wish my brothers and I had grown up here with you guys, in Puerto Rico."

Stefani glanced up at her cousin and tried for bravado. "Are you kidding me? You live in New York! It's the greatest city in the world."

"Um, we live in Palisades," Daisy corrected, shaking her dice. "From where, on a clear day in winter, we can *see* the greatest city in the world. Downriver. In the cold, gray distance."

"Still." Stefani cast her dice across the board.

Daisy set down her shaker.

"I guess we'll have to start texting when I'm gone," she said. "Return to the land of technology."

Her cousin sighed heavily, counting out loud while she moved her yellow pawn around the board.

"Yeah," Stefani said. "We can talk on the phone."

"We can talk on the old-fashioned telephone machine," Daisy said.

"We can fax each other."

"Morse code."

"Carrier pigeons."

They laughed, and Daisy learned that sad laughter lands differently in the atmosphere than the regular kind.

When she opened her suitcase that evening and drew her phone out to charge it before the journey home, she worried briefly that she'd fall back into old habits as soon as she returned to New York. She weighed the small heft of that device in her hand, and when she plugged it in and powered it on, she knew immediately that this had not been just a temporary time-out. It was a permanent choice she was making. Without hesitation, she pressed her thumb against the apps until they began to wobble and, one at a time, she deleted each of them. Twitter, Instagram, Snapchat. Gone.

"Seriously?" Stefani said, peering over her shoulder. "You're going cold turkey?"

Daisy nodded. "I do not miss it one bit," she said. "I'm happier without it. Anyway, lots of kids our age are becoming, like, vegan or vegetarian, right?" She shrugged. "This is just like that."

"Opting out," Stefani said.

"Exactly. Unsubscribing."

"But, Daisy," Stefani said, falling back on the bed. "You know half those kids who declare themselves vegan on the first day of school are eating cheeseburgers by October."

Daisy set her phone on the nightstand with its little umbilical cord trailing down to the outlet beside her bed.

"Not me," she said. "I mean, I know my limitations, which is why I would never in a million years give up cheeseburgers." She tucked one hand behind her head. "But I want this phone-free life forever."

Stefani tucked one hand beneath her own head, too, and rolled over to face her cousin.

"Daisy Hayes," she said. "You are truly awake."

§

Eight weeks. That's how long it took Daisy to grow up, never mind that her period would not show up until October. When she arrived in San Juan at the beginning of that summer, she'd been an anxious, small-voiced child. She'd been a kid like all others, glued to her phone, almost entirely defined by a constant thread of worry she didn't even know existed. That worry was so continual, Daisy had failed to notice the way it sat heavy in her stomach in a fluttering pit. She hadn't known it was possible to evict that sinking, frenetic feeling. She hadn't known that the rod of tension usually bulleting down the back of her neck didn't have to be there, until it was gone.

Her first week back in New York, she tracked down a heavy, old rotary phone at the Salvation Army.

"This thing work?" she asked the lady behind the counter.

"Bring it over, we can plug it in and check."

The shop lady's hair was short and gray, and she wore a no-nonsense apron. Daisy appreciated this woman. The phone made a satisfying jangle when Daisy plonked it on the counter because it had actual bells inside. The lady turned and pulled the cord from the base of her modern, cordless landline. Then she clicked it into the little slot at the back of the rotary phone. Daisy lifted the receiver and smiled at the sound of the dial tone.

"I'll take it," she said.

She paid the woman seventeen dollars in cash, and carried the phone home in her backpack.

In her room, she had to hunt for the phone jack (behind her desk, it turned out—how convenient!) before plugging it in. Then she picked up her cell phone and dialed the house number, which she was surprised she could still remember, given that she hadn't dialed it in at least two years. The noise of that old rotary phone announcing itself throughout the stillness of the house made Daisy's skin wash with goosebumps. She jumped, and then waited for it to sound again before she picked it up. There was a soft, satisfying crackle on the line.

"What the fuck was that?" she heard her little brother yell from his room. He was almost eleven, and experimenting liberally with the word *fuck* whenever Mom wasn't home. He was still Charlie then, not yet Carlos, but already entirely himself.

"Come look!" she said.

When he didn't, she hung up the phone, picked it up again, and then dialed his cell phone number, which she had to look up on her own cell phone, because she'd never dialed it before.

"Come to my room," she said when he picked up.

"I'm extremely busy picking out my first-day-of-school outfit," he said.

"You have three more days for that. This will take thirty seconds."

"Fine."

She hung up. Her little brother appeared in her doorway a moment later, and then she had to contend with how unimpressed her brother was by her new purchase.

"But why, though?" he kept asking.

"Just feel it!"

He picked up the receiver, stuck his finger into one of the number holes, and spun the dial plate clockwise.

"Daisy, there's a reason why nobody uses this technology anymore," he said. "It would take me like ten minutes just to dial. Plus, who am I dialing? How am I supposed to remember anyone's phone number?"

Daisy took the receiver from him and replaced it gingerly in its cradle, as if it were an actual baby.

"That's what your brain is for," she said.

Daisy made dinner that night, and as she doled arroz con gandules out of the pot and onto their plates, she told Mom that she didn't need her cell phone anymore.

"You what?" Mom said.

"I'll take it," Vic said. "Hers is newer than mine." He unfolded his napkin across his lap.

"She needs a cell phone," Mom said, taking the plate from Daisy. "Thank you."

"I don't though, Mom," Daisy said, sitting into her chair. "I bought myself a landline phone."

"It's like the triceratops of telephones," her younger brother said. "Can I have Coke with my dinner?"

"Water or milk," Mom said.

He frowned, but filled his glass with water and joined them at the table.

"You can't take a landline with you to school, Daisy," she said. "What if something happens? I need to be able to get in touch with you."

They all knew what the *something* was that might happen, and there would be lockdown drills their first week back, in case they had been tempted to forget. Daisy nodded.

"Okay, Mom."

After that, Daisy developed a kind of minimalist hybrid relationship with modern technology. She kept her cell phone charged, brought it with her to school, sometimes needed to use its camera to upload homework to her Google Classroom, but when she got home, she plugged it in beside the cabinet in the living room and forgot about it.

Three or four times a week, she called Stefani from the jangly, staticky rotary phone in her room. If she wasn't doing homework, Daisy would drag the phone as far across her bedroom as its cord would allow, and then she'd stretch the receiver over to her bed where she'd lie down on her back with her head hanging over the edge and her feet up on the wall. In this posture, she talked to Stefani as if it were fully 1985.

"I'm definitely moving to Puerto Rico when I'm old enough," she told her cousin, twisting the curly cord around her outstretched finger, unaware that she'd inherited this gesture from the universal teenage consciousness of Generation X.

"Don't do it," Stefani said. "You'll get so fat if you live here."

"Facts," Daisy admitted. "I'll have to take up running."

"Or salad?" Stefani suggested.

"Definitely running."

They both laughed.

"But seriously, next summer maybe I should come to New York instead," Stefani said. "Before you go deciding our whole future, let's weigh all the options."

"Palisades is really not a viable option," Daisy insisted.

"I'll be the judge of that."

Chapter Eighteen

∼

Palisades, New York
2023

Outside Mama's living room window, a fog crouches down across the Hudson River, straddling the water from shore to shore, and extinguishing the winking lights of Dobbs Ferry on the opposite bank. Ruth sits next to Mama on the couch as they dial Benny's number in Puerto Rico.

"Daisy." Ruth says her daughter's name quietly. A prayer. And stands up to pace the room. When Ruth was little, she knew by instinct that Mama's cues were the only ones that mattered. As an adult, she still watches for them without knowing that she does. Ruth monitors Mama's face, which can cause her own terror to shrink or balloon within her.

Rafaela, infinitely more self-aware than her daughter gives her credit for, despite the encroaching fog and the shock she is only beginning to process, notes Ruth's rising panic. She sees her daughter observing her, and immediately fixes her face. She puts on a neutral, determined expression to replace the fear. She adjusts her voice, too, turning it into the hum of heavy machinery. Reliable. Steady.

"It's going to be okay," she says to Ruth while the phone rings against her ear.

Sixteen hundred miles away, in a house already darkened by the inevitable power outage, Benny has a cell signal. For now, the cell tower still stands. Benny's phone glows to life on his coffee table, buzzing and rattling along the tabletop. Its blue light joins the flickering candlelight already blushing the room. He lifts the phone, presses the answer button.

"Hola," he starts with a joke, "thank you for calling the apocalypse hotline."

Rafaela tells her son everything, and quickly, all in a rush. She always has been a believer in ripping off the Band-Aid, hair and all. None of these trigger warnings the grandkids are always talking about. All of life should come with one big trigger warning. Isn't that the sloppy, dazzling beauty of it all? They're protecting themselves from the best parts, she thinks. Preventing themselves from healing. *Resilience!* Rafaela wants to shout. *Resilience!* Across a continent, and into her granddaughter's battered, unmoving body.

After Rafaela delivers the news, Benny's silence stretches just long enough for her to wonder if the signal has faltered in the storm. But she also knows that this is Benny's way. An extra beat, perhaps three, while he processes the awful information. And then when he is ready to reengage, his tires will not spin at all, he will find traction immediately, he will bolt into efficient action.

"I'm going." There he is already.

Rafaela imagines him standing from the red couch in his darkened living room, imagines his wife stirring from her book at the far end, alarmed, sitting up.

"Going where?" she can hear Pamela in the background. "You can't go anywhere in this storm."

Rafaela hears Benny muffle the mouthpiece, hears the rumble of his distant voice. In her small kitchen in New York, in her beautiful replica little home, Rafaela gazes at her wretched, beloved daughter. Ruth looks old, she looks ancient. Again, mother and child trading places in the cosmos.

"He's going," Rafaela says to her relic of a child. "Benny will be with her soon."

Ruth nods, returning to the couch and sinking back down beside her. "Tell him I said thank you."

"It may take me a little while to get there with the storm," Benny says. "It's really bad out, a lot of roads are already closed. But I'm leaving now. I'll call you when I get there."

"Okay."

He hangs up before Rafaela can say goodbye.

"Be careful," she says, though he's already gone.

Even after she hangs up, Rafaela can still hear the storm in her ears. Or is that tempest happening right here in this room, is it emanating from Ruth? The cataclysmic rage of the wind, the unkind lashing of water that doesn't feel like liquid at all, but a thing made of whips and chains. Rafaela can feel the very substance of that storm in her bones, she carries the DNA of this weather deep in the score of her memory. She has lived these storms.

Rafaela feels that perhaps it's quite natural, at her age, and especially when she's stressed, that the memory of an old storm might supplant the reality of the current one. She remembers a hurricane called Santa Clara when she was nine or ten years old. She remembers sleeping on the floor in the pantry with the whole family, Mamamía and Papamío and Lola and Candido and Priti, crammed in like sardines, feet in faces. Rafaela used a sack of rice as her pillow, and the wind made the whole house buzz and thrum, but she felt safe there in that closed-in place with everyone she loved. So it can be hard to hold the space between then and now, to reliably fix people and things on the timeline of her lifespan. Perhaps there shouldn't be anything quite so alarming about that, she thinks. Perhaps she's just made a scientific discovery, opened a wormhole where time has become irrelevant, where her life is all happening at once. She's created a kind of miracle. When facing a tragedy of possibly magnificent proportions, why wouldn't the mind be tempted to obliterate this moment in favor of some other trauma she's already survived?

Rafaela is lucid now, anyway, despite the frightening little blip with Benny earlier. It just took her a minute. But now she's aware, and her mind is clear, and she has an idea, but she waits for Ruth to stir, to open her eyes.

"I don't know what to do," her daughter whispers beside her.

"It's okay. I do." Rafaela stands up. "I have an idea." She walks to the door and opens it. "Go pack."

"Mama, there are no flights."

"Just pack," Rafaela says. "Call the boys, fill them in. This way you'll be ready the moment there's a flight."

Ruth looks as though she might argue, but for what? There's no energy for anything but fear. "Okay," she says. "What are you going to do?"

"I'm going to make a couple of phone calls," Rafaela says. "And then I'm going to pack, too. I'll come over as soon as I'm done. I'll stay with you tonight."

Her daughter stands up and walks to the door but does not go through it. Instead she stops and puts her head on Rafaela's shoulder. Rafaela feels the strength of her legs beneath her and knows that the power of her physical presence is what matters most right now. She makes herself into comforting bedrock, embracing her daughter while she cries. They stand like that for a long time, and Ruth heaves all her terror into tears.

Chapter Nineteen

~

St. Louis, Missouri
1981

On the morning of Rafaela's thirty-fifth birthday, she awoke to the sound of the telephone ringing. She heard her husband talking to someone in the kitchen, and before she could wonder who was calling so early, Benny and Ruth appeared in her bedroom doorway, singing. Benny carried a tray with toast and coffee, and Ruth carried a single yellow rose in a bud vase. They sang loudly while Rafaela stretched and sat up in bed, fluffed the pillows behind her. She felt none of her usual irritation at being awakened.

"Happy birthday, Mama," Benny said, settling the breakfast tray onto her lap.

"Oh, thank you, my two little bonbons!" she said. "Come here, all I really want for my birthday is a kiss."

They both came in for a hug, and Rafaela held her coffee safely to one side while she kissed them. Benny was all limbs at this age, clumsier than he'd been when he was a baby learning to walk. His spatial awareness couldn't catch up with how quickly his arms and legs were sprouting from the trunk of his body, filling the space around him. He was always stubbing a toe on a corner or knocking a glass off a table with an errant elbow. At thirteen, her son was already taller than her, and quickly gaining on Peter. It had all happened so fast.

"And where's your breakfast?" Rafaela asked, taking a bite of her toast.

"We ate already." Ruth climbed into Peter's side of the bed and flung the comforter across her knees.

"Open the cards, Mama!" she said.

Benny sat on the end by their feet.

"How's the toast?" he asked.

"Perfect," she said. "Buttery."

"The trick is to butter it all the way to the edge," Benny said. "None of this slop-it-in-the-middle laziness."

"The cards, Mama!" Ruth said again.

"Yes!" Rafaela set her toast down and picked up the cards from the tray. One purple envelope in Ruth's tidy handwriting, one yellow in Benny's hurried scrawl. Two cards only.

Peter came into the room then and opened the curtains. "There you go," he said. "Bit of sunshine for the birthday girl. Ready, kids? Gotta get you to the bus!"

Rafaela glanced over at the digital alarm clock on her nightstand.

"We have to wait for Mama to open her cards," Ruth said.

"Don't want you to miss it!" Peter called from the hallway.

Rafaela lowered her voice. "You have at least four more minutes before you have to go."

Peter popped his head back inside the doorway. "Almost forgot," he said. "Your parents called. I told them you were sleeping in for your birthday, so they said they'd call back in a little while."

Rafaela nodded but didn't answer. She was busy peeling open the seal on her first card. Ruth's had a baby wearing big googly glasses and some headband antennae. Benny's was in the shape of a dachshund, and it unfolded four times so the dog got longer and longer. *I hope you're birthday's a real wiener!* it said.

"Oh!" She tipped her head back against the pillow. "I wish you could both stay home for my birthday."

"Can we, Mama?" Ruth asked.

Benny was already standing. He leaned over and kissed Rafaela on the cheek.

"Kids, let's go! You're going to miss it!" Peter called from the kitchen.

"I love you, Mama," Ruth said, sitting up on her knees and kissing

Rafaela once more on the cheek. "Happy birthday." She climbed out of bed and padded across the carpet in her tights.

Rafaela listened to the attendant cloud of noise as her children rumbled down the hallway, scrambled for their backpacks, scraped kitchen chairs, slammed the refrigerator door.

"I can't find my shoes!" Ruth whined.

"They're right here."

And then the louder slam of the back door that signaled the beginning of her daily solitude. She lifted her coffee cup from the tray and looked down at the two sweet cards. Two cards.

Peter would've driven the kids to the store to pick them out. He'd have paid for them, and for the yellow rose as well. Had the flower been his idea or Ruth's? He'd have helped Ruth retrieve the little bud vase from the hutch, made sure she didn't overfill it with water. So her husband hadn't forgotten her birthday. He'd participated just enough so that she felt the slight exactly the way he had intended it: he had chosen not to get her a card. He had chosen not to kiss her cheek that morning, not to say the words *Happy Birthday* to her. He had perfectly dismantled her capacity to complain.

You didn't get me a card would seem petty.

"The cards were from all three of us," he'd say. "Who do you think bought that rose?" he would say.

In fact, she couldn't blame him. Hadn't she done the same on Father's Day? Their marriage had become a battleground of minimal effort, littered with the corpses of their better selves. The blast of the phone ringing startled her from her thoughts, and she scampered out of bed, grabbed her robe, and ran to the phone in the kitchen.

The heavy not-quite-silence indicated Puerto Rico even before Papamío began to sing down the line, first in English, then in Spanish. She stood by the back door and watched a cardinal alight on the dogwood tree while her father sang. She held the phone in the crook of her neck while she tied the satin belt at her waist, and when the cardinal took off again, she closed her eyes so that, past the soft distance of the phone line, she could almost feel like she was there—a whoosh and a tumble— and just like that, she could be standing in her parents' kitchen in Puerto

Rico instead of here in St. Louis, where she'd wear a sweater in the house all day and still wouldn't manage to feel warm. It was November 16.

"Ah, thank you, Papi," she said, smiling into the phone. "It's good to hear that nothing has changed. You still can't carry a tune!"

"Only in a good, strong basket!" He laughed.

"Is that Rafa?" Mamamía's voice behind him. "Why didn't you wait for me!"

"I couldn't wait, I couldn't wait, Rafaela, listen," Papamío said. "We have a big surprise for you. We need you to come down."

"Down where?" Rafaela said.

Papamío laughed. "Down where! Down to Puerto Rico, what do you think? Down to Hades? You need to come down to Puerto Rico right away!"

"Oh, Papi." Rafaela ran a hand over her curls, twisting the blanket frizz out of them. "I wish I could."

"You can! You have to come," he said. "It's important."

She moved across the kitchen to look at the calendar stuck to the wall beside the fridge. It was Tuesday today, and Thanksgiving was early this year. Next week she'd have to undertake all that dreadful cooking. Oh, she didn't want to think about this on her birthday.

"Is she coming?" This was Mamamía again.

"She's coming!" Papamío said. "She has to come!"

A flutter of noise while her mother wrested the phone from her father.

"You're coming, Rafa?"

"Hi, Mamamía!"

"Did your father explain everything to you already? You know Peter has to come, too, he has to be there to sign the papers with you."

"Don't tell her, you crazy woman, stop talking, you're going to ruin the surprise!"

A struggle and then the loud hum of their competing voices behind the muffled barrier of someone's hand across the mouthpiece. Then Papamío's voice returned, bright and cheerful and crisp.

"So when are you coming?" he said.

Rafaela shook her head. "I guess maybe we could come down on the kids' Christmas break? Before New Year's," she said. "I'll have to talk to Peter and see—"

"No, Rafaela, you don't understand."

She arrested her reasoning because she could hear it in his voice now, the urgency. She frowned into her calendar, flipped the leaf up to December, and then let it fall back again.

"Next week is Thanksgiving," she said, but really she was only thinking out loud.

"Ah," he tutted at her, and in her mind she could see Papamío waving her off with one hand, dismissing her concerns. In her youth, that gesture had driven her batty. Now she found it endearing. "So come this week, then. Come tomorrow!"

She went. Since her decision to marry Peter (from which her parents had tried only gently to dissuade her), Mamamía and Papamío had almost never made any insistence upon Rafaela's person. So when they told her to come, the way they told her to come, she felt compelled to go. Peter made some reluctant noises at first—his job, the kids—but when it came to visiting Puerto Rico, he was easy. It was true that Peter had been the one to insist that the family leave San Juan and move back to St. Louis, but his reasons had been mostly pragmatic: there were better jobs for him in the States and, he believed, better opportunities for the children. But Rafaela knew that her husband missed the lifestyle in San Juan nearly as much as she did. So she dropped a scattering of verbal reminders about sunshine, food, and rum, and although Peter never voiced his compliance, he did open a suitcase on his side of the bed.

Rafaela went down to the travel agents the next morning and booked the tickets, Peter's cousin came from Jefferson City to stay with the kids for three days, and by noon on Thursday, she and Peter were sitting at Mamamía's kitchen table with a plate of coconut shortbread cookies in front of them.

"But what's this all about, Rafael?" Peter asked his father-in-law.

Papamío sat back in his chair and folded his hands across his stomach. A smile spread beneath the gray broom of his moustache. "All will be revealed in due time!" he said.

"Due time will be tomorrow at nine in the morning," Mamamía said, pouring lemon water from a pitcher into glasses of ice.

"What happens tomorrow at nine?" Rafaela asked.

They had an appointment with Don Julio Dorado y Beltrán, as it turned out, at his law offices in Hato Rey. Papamío drove, and there was something strange and satisfying about Peter sitting in the back seat with Mamamía, who insisted Rafaela sit in front. Rafaela knew it would annoy Peter to sit in the back while his wife reposed in front, that he'd consider the arrangement to be a mild affront to his masculine pride, and because it was not a real indignity (not like the kind Rafaela endured without complaint almost every day in St. Louis), it caused in her a spreading gladness. And yet, she knew it wouldn't help him to understand how she felt when people heard her accent and responded by shouting slowly at her like she was an idiot. Or how it felt when the teller at the bank asked if her house down in Porta Rico had a toilet. Or how it felt when she attended her one and only PTA meeting, to find there were no empty seats at any of the tables because they were all being saved for a friend. Peter would never know, because he didn't care to fathom how it felt Every. Single. Time. she walked through the members-only door into the Short Hills Babylon Country Club and descended the carpeted stairs to the staff locker room.

Don Julio's office was on the third floor of a large glass building, where a receptionist showed them straight to a gleaming conference room. Another receptionist delivered coffees to the long wooden table before Don Julio appeared with a large file jammed with papers. He wore an expensive gray suit and his moustache was as ample as Papamío's. Rafaela turned to look at the naked top lip of her husband sitting beside her, clean-shaven. His hair was still wavy, thick and black, his eyes blue as the ocean. She didn't look at him very often anymore, she realized. He was still so handsome. And then a flash of belated insight: how little that mattered in the end.

"Rafael!" Don Julio said, sticking his hand out to Papamío. "So great to see you! You look good."

Papamío half stood from his seat for the greeting, clapping Don Julio on the shoulder. Don Julio turned to Mamamía then and performed a small bow.

"María Teresa," he said, kissing her on both cheeks. "How is it that he's aged and you haven't? More beautiful than ever!"

Mamamía waved him off, unimpressed by the flattery.

"You must be Rafaela," he said then, training his attention on her. "How lovely to meet you after all this time."

Rafaela offered her hand and he shook it.

"And you." Don Julio stuck his hand out toward Peter. The indignities mounted. "Must be the lucky husband?"

"He is indeed!" Papamío said.

Peter shook the man's hand. "Peter Brennan," he asserted his name.

Don Julio plopped into one of the red leather chairs and landed his substantial file folder on the table with a thump, a small whoosh of air.

"I suppose your father has told you why we're here today?" Don Julio smiled, leaning back in his chair, one arm draped across the matching chair beside him. "Congratulations are in order!"

Rafaela shook her head and opened her mouth to respond, but Papamío beat her to it.

"We haven't told her yet," he said, clapping his hands and sitting forward. "Today's the day."

"Oh wow." Don Julio leaned forward, too, elbows on the table, gold watch winking out from beneath the cuff of his shirt, his delight rising to match Papamío's. "Big day! Big surprise then, right?" He opened the folder in front of him, drew a gold pen out from the inside pocket of his jacket. "Well, are you ready?" he said to Papamío. "You want to do the honors?"

Papamío held out his hand, palm up. "Please. You."

"María Teresa?"

Mamamía shook her head.

"Okay!" Don Julio took a deep breath, lifted three copies of a contract out from inside the folder, and slid them across the table. "You'll see here from these documents that your father locked a considerable sum of money into a trust for you on the day of your first birthday."

Rafaela had been staring at the paper, but now she whipped her head up to look at Papamío beside her.

"Papi?" she said.

He could barely contain himself, his nostrils flaring like he couldn't get enough air. He nodded. "Yes, mija. When we still had money, we locked some of it away for you and some for Lola."

"It was untouchable all these years," Mamamía said beside her. "Just locked into those trusts and growing. Until now."

"But why . . ." Rafaela began to tremble.

"The way the trust was structured, we weren't allowed to touch it," Papamío said.

"Good thing, too," Don Julio said. "Because that meant the creditors couldn't touch it either. Your dad is a smart man, putting this aside for you the way he did."

"We may have locked it up *too* tightly in fact," Papamío said then. "Back when you were still in school, we tried to draw payments just so you could stay in Las Madres, but the trust wasn't structured to allow for that. It was bulletproof!"

Beneath the table, Rafaela reached for her mother's hand, returning her attention to the papers in front of her.

Don Julio continued, "The initial sum is . . . here." The lawyer leaned across the table and tapped at a figure about halfway down the page.

Rafaela gasped, brought a hand briefly to her mouth, returned it to her lap, cleared her throat.

"That initial sum was exceedingly well invested over the course of the years," Don Julio said.

Rafaela lifted the stapled papers, flipped to the second page, placed it flat in front of her. She was aware of Peter's hovering presence, but he was vague and blurry.

"The ultimate term of the trust was to be thirty-four years, and here," said Don Julio, pointing to a staggering number near the bottom of page two, "is what can either be paid out to you in a lump now, or transferred, to remain within the investment strategy, as you wish, once we sign these documents today."

Mamamía was squeezing Rafaela's hand now, and Rafaela felt tears prick the corners of her eyes. Papamío's tears had come loose already and were streaming down his face unchecked. They gathered into his dampening moustache.

"Papamío?" she said.

"Happy birthday, my beautiful girl."

Her body felt rigid with confusion. Rafaela had never actively wished for a moment like this, because it seemed impossible. But now here it was, and mostly she just couldn't believe it was true. How could it be true?

"But you . . ." Rafaela didn't know how to catch one of the many questions swarming through her brain, to pin it down and then force it out through her mouth. "What about Lola?"

"Lola got her share already," Papamío said. "Almost two years ago, on her thirty-fifth birthday."

Rafaela shook her head, her empty mouth standing open. It was unthinkable that her sister had been able to keep something like this from her. And then almost immediately, it wasn't. Of course Lola would just carry on as if the money meant nothing.

"But then what about you?" Rafaela said.

"What about us?" Mamamía said. "We are old. And we are happy."

"You're not even sixty!" Rafaela said.

"This year!" Mamamía shrugged. "But anyway, we have done well in our second act. We have everything we need."

"But this is your money," Rafaela said. She turned to her father. "It's yours."

"It was never mine." Papamío shook his head. "Not since 1947."

"But—"

"It's yours, Rafa," Mamamía said, and then, "*only* yours. Do you understand? It belongs to no one else. Just you."

Rafaela had nearly forgotten Peter was here, but now she heard him making some rackety breaths in his chair nearby. Hyperventilating, maybe.

"Breathe, Peter!" Mamamía instructed.

Don Julio then whipped out a second folder, much slimmer, with a loose collection of asset protection documents inside, the gist of which seemed to be that, now that Rafaela's secret irrevocable trust had reached maturity, now that the money contained therein belonged to Rafaela alone and was no longer protected by the trust, Peter was to agree that this account would be kept separate from their combined marital assets. He would make no personal claim on Rafaela's money. Perhaps it was only the pressure, the weight of expectation and propriety, and the sense of overwhelm that led him to do it. Or maybe Peter didn't fully understand the Spanish documents he was signing, was too flummoxed to resist. Whatever the case, Rafaela was flabbergasted when, without any hesitation whatsoever, her husband uncapped the pen Papamío placed in his hand. And he signed.

After the initial jolt of this day passed, Rafaela would come to a more robust understanding of the money, of what it could and could not do for her. The sum would one day cease to amaze her the way it had on that first impossible day in Don Julio's office. It was a good sum, a large sum, yes. But eventually she would come to understand that it was not a return to the heady opulence of her youth, but rather a sum that would provide her freedom. If she was careful and managed it properly, it could last the rest of her life.

But that first day, as she sat at the long wooden table in that glass office building in Hato Rey, counting the digits on the contracts in front of her, Rafaela was astounded. Inexplicably, one of her first thoughts was of Candido. She remembered the two of them sitting side by side at the dining room table, their math books spread out in front of them, Candido leaning close, bumping his shoulder against hers. They were perhaps nine years old, and the pages of their math notebooks were covered in digits like these. Big, sturdy, challenging numbers. They swapped problems and strategies, raced to see who could come to the answer quickest. And then she was dumped from that memory immediately into another, a few years later. She was sitting in the front seat of the Buick Roadmaster, Candido driving her to Ponce to say goodbye.

She had begged her parents and Lola not to come. "It will be too hard to get on that ship if you're all there," she explained. So Papamío had loaned Candido the car, its last outing before they would sell it, and they loaded Rafa's trunk and two suitcases into the back. In those days, it was a six- or seven-hour drive to Ponce from San Juan. She wore a pale yellow linen dress, and they barely spoke, but Candido held her hand the whole way.

And now her life was shifting unexpectedly yet again. A blink and a gust, and her fortunes had entirely changed.

"You're happy, mija?" Papamío leaned over to whisper in her ear. "I know this doesn't make up for anything, but—"

Now it was her turn to interrupt, to intercept his misplaced feelings. "Don't be silly, you gave me the most beautiful life. There is nothing to make up for," she said. "There never was." She loved her father so much, she even believed it.

She stood from her chair then, and Papamío struggled to move the other chairs out of the way so he could wrap his arms around her. She could smell the sweet spice of his cologne as he hugged her, all her childhood rushing back. All the loneliness and sorrow of the intervening years extinguished, like they had never happened.

And just like that, she was rich again.

And just like that, she could leave him.

Chapter Twenty

~

Palisades, New York
2019

Rafaela told no one when she started to forget things, not even herself. She had always been a relatively private person, but this was different because it wasn't secrecy that drove the concealment but terror first, and then, a close second, the forgetfulness itself. She didn't tell her children because, in fact, she forgot that she was forgetting.

In the beginning it was only individual words, and it only happened when she was very exhausted or stressed out. She would look at a chair for a full minute and think, "Dammit, it's the thing you sit in! What is it called?" before the word would finally come back to her: *silla*. And then sometimes another full minute before she could retrieve it in English. The next thing to slip were her tasks. She would drive to the mall, park her car in the same lot where she always parked, walk inside, all the way through Macy's and out into the mall, on a mission toward a specific destination . . . and then her steps would slow beneath her. And she would stop, one thumb tucked beneath her purse strap, her keys still dangling from her hand. She'd stare down at the floor, eyes clicking through the spatial files in her brain where she stored her tasks. And she would come up empty. No recollection whatsoever of why she was here or what she was meant to do. She might go to the food court and order a salad, and then midway through her meal: A new dress for Carlos's big show! That was it!

But increasingly often, the forgotten task would not reveal itself until she returned home and discovered the empty toilet paper roll or the remnants of the broken bowl in the garbage. Sometimes, the forgetfulness moved in the other direction and presented as hypervigilance. She gave herself no credit for having already completed a task, so she would perform the task several more times, and then before she knew it, four additional copies of Oprah's latest book club pick would arrive in the mail. She'd pretend she'd ordered copies for Ruth and the kids as well, a family book club.

Rafaela told herself it was probably normal, everyone was forgetful at her age. She was seventy-two years old, and she'd probably squeezed a hundred years of living into those decades. She told herself it was because her life had not been linear or ordinary, she'd jumped countries and cities and states, crossed languages and cultures, populated the community of her brain with people from so many different places and backgrounds. There was also that long stretch of years when she was miserably sad almost every day, surely that must've had an impact. How could one human experience contain all that? It would be different if she'd stayed rich her whole life, she reasoned, if she'd married one of the boys she was supposed to marry. It would be different, she was sure, if she were still Puerto Rican.

Rafaela started writing things down the moment she thought of them. She kept a red spiral notebook full of things-to-do, which was very helpful as long as she remembered to consult it, and then to cross things off when they were completed. She suspected that Benny had noticed her slipping, because her son noticed everything, even though he was all the way down in San Juan. They spoke nearly every day by phone, just checking in, and FaceTimed at least once a week. Benny had always been attentive and patient, but recently Rafaela couldn't help noticing an irritability that crept into his voice when he said, "Yes, Mama, you already mentioned the new dental hygienist. Twice!" She found herself not answering his calls quite as often, whether to elude her own worry or just to duck Benny's exasperation, she couldn't say. Whatever the case, she knew Ruth and Benny were swapping notes about her because, within weeks of each other, they both started mentioning that now might be a good time to sell the condo and move in with one of them. It was a seller's market, they said. It annoyed her because she was forgetful, not stupid. She was perfectly capable of sniffing out their collusion.

When her kids brought up the idea of moving, Rafaela made the requisite forestalling noises because she knew they expected her to put up a fight, and she never did like to be too easy. But in truth, she'd had enough of solitude, and was ready to trade into the next phase. She liked the idea of eating dinner every night with her grandkids. That was the reason. Not the other thing.

"You know, the weather is great down here, Ma, and we've got plenty of room," Benny said over FaceTime.

Two of Benny's four kids had already graduated from college, and the third was a firefighter in Miami. Only the baby, Stefani, was still at home, and soon she too would go off to college in Florida on a softball scholarship. Their house would be empty. Plus, Rafaela liked Benny's wife, who was warm and funny and a great cook. She certainly loved the weather in San Juan. But Rafaela couldn't get past feeling like a guest when she visited them. She couldn't imagine sprawling out on their living room couch, watching television in her nightgown, her hair pinned into its weekly rollers.

"I'll think about it," she said, even though she had no intention of thinking about it.

She already knew she'd move in with Ruth and the kids, who lived nearby and had plenty of space. She had lived with them years ago when the kids were little, after Thomas died, so they already knew her rhythms and private eccentricities. Rafaela felt easy in their home. But she would make Ruth work for it, of course.

"I've decided to fix up the guest cottage, Mama," Ruth announced one Sunday evening over dinner on her back deck. "I've been meaning to do it for years, and I'm going to document it for *The Widow's Kitchen*."

"That sounds wonderful!" Rafaela said.

"I can do it as a before-and-after series," Ruth said. "Turn the cottage into a showcase, and then when it's done I might be able to do seasonal features. Holidays, things like that."

Rafaela nodded. Even though nothing about social media made sense to her, she knew it was Ruth's career and she'd learned to pretend it was normal.

"You want more wine, Grandma?" Carlos was always offering her more wine because he thought it was funny when she got tipsy. She thought it was funny, too, so she said yes.

"Why don't you pour yourself a glass, too, nene!"

"Mama!" Ruth said. "He's only fifteen!"

"And a half," he said. "Just a sip, Mom? Poor Grandma shouldn't have to drink alone."

"It's not very festive to drink alone, Ruth," Rafaela said.

"Go on," Ruth said, waving a hand in her son's direction. "But just a sip!"

Carlos was already out of his chair. "You want one, Daisy?"

Daisy was going to decline anyway, but Ruth beat her to it.

"Who's going to drive Grandma home if you guys are all drinking? I'm not doing the dishes and the driving!"

Rafaela didn't drive after dark anymore, so they all took turns.

"I'll drive her home, Mom." Poor Daisy was always the responsible one, and she was a good driver, but Rafaela didn't care for that patchouli smell of her car. It made her throat feel itchy.

Rafaela put her hand on her granddaughter's arm and leaned in. "Have the wine, dear," she whispered, "I'll sleep in Vic's room tonight."

Now that Vic was away at college, it was easy for Rafa to stay over and crash in his room whenever she liked.

"Oh good!" Ruth smiled. "I'm glad you're staying!"

"Daisy will have some wine!" Rafaela called through the sliding glass door Carlos had left open behind him. She could feel the blast of air-conditioning against her legs.

"Well, this is good timing, Mama," Ruth started. "Because I've been thinking."

"That's a dangerous habit!" Carlos called from the kitchen.

They all groaned. It was Papamío's favorite joke. It had never been funny, and then it became so timeworn that it *was* funny, and then eventually that wore off as well, and yet, it was still impossible for anyone in their family to confess they'd *been thinking*, without someone making the customary interruption. Carlos returned with three fresh wine glasses and the bottle tucked under his arm. He scooted the door closed with his backside and set the empties down in front of his mother and sister, but he topped up Grandma first.

"None for me tonight," Ruth said, pushing the empty glass back from her plate.

"Why, are you pregnant?" Carlos said.

"Gross!" Daisy said.

Ruth swatted her daughter with her napkin. "What's gross about that?"

Carlos and Rafaela snickered together.

"I still have work to do after dinner, and I need to be fresh," Ruth explained.

"I'm also not pregnant, in case anyone was wondering," Rafaela said.

"Same," Carlos said.

They all looked at Daisy, who said nothing. She sipped delicately from her wineglass.

Ruth cleared her throat and deliberated momentarily before jumping right in with her abrupt change of subject. "So, Mama. I'd like to feature you in this new series I'm planning."

"Me?" Rafaela said.

Daisy made a displeased face, but then checked herself.

"Sure, like old times. Like back when we first started," Ruth said.

Rafaela scooted her glass toward Carlos. "More wine!" she barked.

Carlos laughed.

"I'm serious, Mama, it could be really great. I have a whole plan."

"Oh. She has a plan." Rafaela raised her eyebrows at her grandkids.

Ruth ignored her. "We'd start with all the before shots, show how dated and underutilized the cottage is."

Rafaela could see that her daughter was keeping one eye on Carlos, whose "sip" was a solid three-quarters of a wineglass for himself and an even larger pour for his sister, but Ruth ignored the infraction. They all knew what teenagers got up to, and having a glass of wine next to your grandmother at dinner was the least of it.

"So we'd document the whole construction process," Ruth continued. "And you wouldn't have to come in until the very end of the project."

Ruth pushed her plate aside and leaned forward in her chair, elbows on the table. Rafaela's daughter wasn't aware that she was giving herself away. Her posture, her attentiveness, her refusal of the wine, and most damning, the fact that she'd left her phone inside for the duration of this meal—taken as a whole, that evidence belied her efforts to make this conversation seem casual and spontaneous.

"I know you've been thinking about selling your condo—"

"*You've* been thinking about me selling my condo." Rafaela played the role of recalcitrant aging parent very well. There was no question where Carlos had gotten his penchant for acting.

Ruth folded her hands. "Well, *we've* been thinking about you selling your condo then."

Rafaela sniffed, sipping from her glass. "Okay."

"So . . . what if we featured your condo too? We could show how beautiful it is, your immaculate taste, those spectacular views of the river—I bet it would bring in a ton of interest from prospective buyers."

Rafaela made a noncommittal humming noise while Ruth flattened her hands against the table in a way that signaled whatever she was about to say next would be the crux of the whole conversation.

"And then in the end, we could do a big changeover reveal . . . of your new home," Ruth said.

Carlos was seated between them, swiveling his head back and forth like a cartoon character. He gripped the bulb of the wineglass with both hands. "Grandma's going to come live with us?" he said. "In the guesthouse?"

Ruth pressed her lips together nervously. "If she wants to. Do you want to, Mama?"

They all turned to stare at her. Rafaela stared back.

"Let me think about it," she said.

"Here's to Grandma thinking about it!" Carlos raised his glass, and they all clinked. "Ooh, we're going to drink *so* much wine together, Grandma!"

They both caught a fit of the giggles then, while Ruth rolled her eyes and Daisy stood up to clear the table. In the end, Rafaela agreed to the cottage, but not to the inane, invasive chronicling of her life, because no one wanted to see an old lady's condo, or an old lady's moving van, or an old lady's reaction to some tastefully chosen soft furnishings with pops of color, no matter how devoted Ruth's legions of followers seemed to be.

But then she forgot she'd declined, so when Ruth asked again, suddenly there she was, grinning like an idiot on camera, Ruth and Rafaela standing shoulder-to-shoulder on the pool deck pavers in Ruth's side yard with Daisy and Carlos nearby.

Ruth instructed Rafaela not to look yet, but had stopped short of blindfolding her only because Rafaela had refused. Behind them, the Japanese maples ruffled lightly in the breeze. In the video they would watch later, Ruth's eyes would connect directly with the camera, but Rafaela couldn't quite locate the lens, so she appeared to be disoriented, gazing slightly off camera throughout.

"It's finally here, the big day! Ready, Mama?"

Rafaela nodded. "Ready."

"Just a reminder for you viewers at home before we go inside, here's what the place looked like before. This is the exterior" [PAUSE] "and this is what the interior looked like just four months ago." [PAUSE]

Her daughter had been doing this kind of thing for years, but Rafaela would never get used to hearing her talk like this.

"Where am I looking?" Rafaela asked. "I don't see the pictures."

"No, Mama, this is just audio for the B-roll we're going to add later."

"Oh."

[PAUSE]

"Okay, so here we go, Mama! Three, two, one!"

The background behind them slid past the glowing pool as Ruth maneuvered herself and Rafaela to a different angle, still focusing on Rafaela's face, her mouth gaping, her hands flying up to her two cheeks in a gesture of astonishment. It was late afternoon and the light was soft, golden.

"Ay, oh my God, Ruth," Rafaela gasped. Her eyes were wet.

And now there was Carlos in the background of the shot, recording with his own camera to get a different angle. There were the backs of their heads, and just a few feet beyond them, Rafaela's new home: a trio of symmetrical arches cut into thick, creamy stucco. Two broad steps leading up to the entrance matched the red clay on the Spanish-tiled roof. A miniature balcony of wrought iron embraced a half-story window cut high beneath the roofline. Two giant flowerpots had been placed beside the steps and planted with braided hibiscus flaunting their canary-yellow blossoms. There was Rafaela's rocking chair on the porch, a throw blanket draped over its arm. Beside it, the woven basket with her crosswords, her pencil and glasses waiting.

"Oh," she said quietly. "This was not what I expected."

A tiny replica of her home on calle Américo Salas, remarkable in its likeness. Remarkable.

"How?" she said, but did not finish the question.

It didn't make sense here, among the Craftsmans and Victorians, the modern farmhouse architecture of the lower Hudson River Valley, this stately and graceful little home.

It was a drug. A curative.

A time machine.

It teemed with her happiest memories, this small, new place. It was confusing, impossible. In a life filled with loss, so much had been restored to her.

"You like it, Mama?"

Rafaela blinked her wet eyes. "It's perfect," she whispered, her lips trembling.

Inside, there was red tile underfoot, accents of wrought iron. Handles, hardware, railings. Warm marble on the kitchen countertops. An over-stuffed white sofa, an oak table, a black bookcase with all her favorites, a mahogany sideboard littered with picture frames. Memories, all in black and white.

Rafaela could touch those memories. She could smell them, bed-rock. There was Mamamía in her emerald-green dress, Papamío in his tux. There was Benicio standing beside the Buick Roadmaster in his guayabera and slicked-back hair. Rafaela and Dolores standing on either side of Priti in their school uniforms on the front step in Mira-mar. Priti staring out with her dark green eyes, never opening her lips in photographs. The sisters again, wearing Bermuda shorts beside Can-dido, the sunshine rocketing down all around them, their mouths open wide with laughter, their fingers numb with cold, their shoes sloppy with melting snow.

"Are you okay, Mama?" Ruth had one arm around Rafaela's shoulders.

Carlos was still filming nearby, but Daisy's eyes were trained directly on Rafaela, intuiting her emotions, poised and ready to intercede. Steady. Rafaela could not speak. She waved a hand in front of her face.

204 • Jeanine Cummins

"Come on, Mom." Daisy stepped into the shot. "You too, Carlos—turn it off."

Ruth did not post the video because Rafaela, with Daisy's support, forbade her from doing so. Still, all of them were glad the video existed, even Daisy, and Rafaela most of all.

"You're right, Mama," Ruth said. "It's too intimate."

"But isn't that exactly what people want?" Carlos asked. "That kind of intimacy? Like they're getting a private look behind the curtain?"

"Don't be gross, Carlos," Daisy said. "We don't need Mom's whole throng of followers all up in Grandma's private business."

"I'm just saying. Grandma's so adorable she could go viral."

"I don't want to be viral!"

"It doesn't matter, I'm not going to post it!" Ruth brought an end to the discussion. "Some curtains should stay closed."

And Rafaela loved her daughter all the more for knowing that crucial truth. So many people had forgotten.

§

The day the truck came to transfer Rafaela into her new life across the river, she did not lift a single box. She sat at her kitchen table drinking coffee while the movers packed and busied themselves all around her.

In the months after the move, Rafaela felt a marked improvement in her mental function. In fact, she was so lucid in her new home that she began to wonder if she had perhaps imagined or exaggerated her previous forgetfulness. She was stable and comfortable, and she began to think that the move itself had helped, that it had forced her to engage parts of her brain that had been rusty from abandon. In the old condo, she'd become complacent in her routine, but now, each day was full and new, and her mind hummed like a well-oiled machine.

And then the pandemic came, and obliterated any hope of spontaneity. The sharp relief of Rafaela's life began to blur around the edges again, but still, she was able to feel grateful that she was here in this replica little home, separated by nothing more than a maple tree and a pool deck from her daughter and grandchildren. They formed a safe bubble so that no one was alone. At least twice a week Rafaela found herself thanking

God out loud that she had chosen to move when she did, that she wasn't stuck and isolated in her old condo across the river.

Still, as the days ground into an endless cycle of tedium, Rafaela felt the forgetfulness return. Not all at once, but in flashes. A zap and a tilt, and she wouldn't be able to hold her mind upright. She'd forget, for a moment, how to make toast. She would dial Lola's number, and then remember that her beloved sister had been dead for almost thirty years. The grief would return wholesale and unabated. These were vanishing days, vanishing days.

Rafaela began to catalog herself, forcing her way through her daily crossword even when she had to fudge a couple of entries. Or all the entries. Then she would pick up the picture frames from the sideboard one at a time and tell herself the stories they contained so she'd remember them: there was Mamamía's green dress. There was Candido in the snow.

When she watched the home-reveal video Ruth had made over and over again, she was able to hold her gratitude. Everything felt clear. So it was during a moment like that, a rational, crystalline, satisfied moment, that Rafaela cracked open her laptop and decided, at last, to face this thing head on.

In her old age, Rafaela had begun to grow a realization that she'd behaved as a passenger through most of her life. Things had happened *to* her with some frequency, but seldom had she made an effort to take control of the wheel and drive the bus herself. Even the biggest decision of her life, her divorce, had felt like an inevitable mutual dissolution, galvanized by her financial windfall, rather than a dynamic resolution that she herself set in motion. But despite all that, it had been a spectacular life, so far, and she was not ready to cede her memories of it to a slow-rolling extinction. There were experimental drugs, she knew, and clinical trials and all kinds of mental exercises. Rafaela would arm herself. She would fight.

§

Rafaela had always loved games. Board games, playground games, video games. When she was little, she played backgammon with Papamío, Snakes and Ladders with Priti, hopscotch with Lola. Candido taught her dominoes. Mamamía would join them for the occasional game of Clue,

but refused to play Monopoly on grounds that it celebrated the colonizers, a declaration that always made Papamío roll his eyes. In Trinidad,
Rafaela resorted to solitaire, which was no less satisfying than the other
games. She liked the snapping sound the cards made when she flicked
them down on the table in their tidy little rows. Years later, when Benny
had trouble learning English, it was Rafaela who suggested they start
playing charades after dinner each evening. When it was Benny's turn, he
was able to be his bright and goofy self without the pressure of grammar.

"Giraffe!" Benny would shout while Peter loped around the living
room. "Palm tree! Bicycle!"

The year she and Peter got divorced, when Benny was thirteen, Rafaela
bought their first Atari Video Computer System for Christmas. By the time
she upgraded him to the Atari 5200 a couple years later, they both knew
the gift was as much for her as it was for him. They took turns, playing
side by side on the old velvet couch in the den, their knees touching, Ruth
munching popcorn and reading comic books in the nearby recliner while
mother and son passed the joystick between them. They played all the
typical games, of course, *Centipede*, *Pac-Man*, *Space Invaders*. Benny loved
Donkey Kong, but Rafaela's favorite was *Q*bert*. The colors, the rhythm,
that cute little weirdo with his huge tubular nose. When it was Benny's
turn, he was all over the board willy-nilly, erratic, but Rafaela developed a
pattern from which she never deviated unless she got trapped. There was
something soothing in the repetition. She felt unstoppable.

So Rafaela was thrilled to discover that some doctors believed video
games could help support cognitive function in elderly adults. It felt like
a Saturday morning when she invited Vic over to help, but it could have
been a Tuesday, because every day of 2020 after mid-March was exactly
the same.

"I bought myself a Nintendo Switch," Rafaela said to Vic, indicating
the box on her coffee table. "I just need a little help setting it up."

"Nintendo Switch!" Vic said. "Get it, Grandma!"

Rafaela did a little shimmy.

"What games did you get?" he asked.

Rafaela reached into the envelope and pulled out the colorful plastic
casings one by one. "*Mario Kart, Super Smash Bros. Ultimate*, and *Assassin's Creed*."

"Ooh, which *Assassin's Creed*?" Vic sat down on the couch to inspect her selections. "I haven't played this one. *Black Flag* is off the chain, though. Graphics are sick."

"Well, dear," Rafaela said. "Your grandmother is nothing if not a sucker for some sick graphics."

"Ha!"

Vic was already behind the television plugging things in.

"This thing can go online, too, right?" she asked.

"You want to go online, Grandma?" Vic asked.

"Yes!"

"You know you can just play against the computer, right? Or we can get more controllers and we can play against each other."

Rafaela tried not to glare at her grandson. "You understand that I've been playing video games since before you were born, correct?"

Vic laughed. "I know, Grandma, I'm just making sure. Like, you don't have to go online."

Grandma spoke more slowly this time, to make sure he understood her. "I want. To go. Online."

"Yes, ma'am!" He picked up the controller and started to set up her account. "I just need your email address."

She moved closer to him and watched the screen in case of typos. "It's bellarafaelabombon@gmail.com."

Vic laughed out loud again. "Of course it is."

"Don't you forget it."

"You meeting a boyfriend online, Grandma?"

She hesitated, and then decided that her life was too short for such hesitations. "As a matter of fact, I am," she said.

Vic was speechless in reply.

"An old friend," she said. "He plays online, too, and we thought it would be fun to play together."

"You are amazing," Vic said.

Rafaela sighed. "I know."

"I heard some of these games are supposed to be really good exercise for your brain, too," Vic said.

"Yeah, I think I heard something about that." She smiled.

"Okay, so what do you want your password to be?" Vic turned to her.

Rafaela spelled it out for him, indicating which letters to capitalize. "HotTamale47/Miramar."

Vic shook his head. "Incredible."

Rafaela got Vic to write down her username and password on the inside cover of her little red notebook, along with detailed instructions about how to get online and locate her friend using his username.

"But don't forget about me!" Vic said. "I'm stuck at home too. You can invite me over here to play sometimes, right?"

"Sometimes," she said. "And then other times I might want to sit here alone and play in my underwear!"

She kissed him on the cheek and then locked the door behind him when he left. Alone, Rafaela kicked off her shoes and curled up on the sofa with her new gaming controller in her hand. She was literally taking control, and if there was any part of her situation that was susceptible to will and determination, then Rafaela was going to win.

Start game.

Chapter Twenty-One

~

Palisades, New York
2019

"I've decided to stay in San Juan a little longer than usual this summer." Daisy had carefully planned the moment to reveal this information, waiting until Mom was in the driver's seat of her car and the vehicle was in motion. This would be Daisy's sixth year in a row spending July and August in San Juan, her sixth summer of wanting to stay there forever.

"What? But that's . . ." Mom glanced at Daisy, her face puzzled. "Surprising."

Daisy took a deep breath and nodded.

"You really think your freshman year of college is the right time for that? Wouldn't you rather come back early, make sure you're ready for move-in day?"

Daisy waited a beat before answering, took a moment to steel herself. "I talked to Tío Benny, and they don't mind me staying longer."

"*Tío* Benny?" Mom said. "Why are you saying *tío* all of a sudden?"

The irritation was predictable, but Daisy was confused by its target. She'd expected Mom to be laser-focused on the academics of this argument.

"What are you talking about?" Daisy said.

"He is *Uncle* Benny," Mom corrected her. "Since when do you call him Tío Benny?"

"Oh, I don't know." Daisy shook her head. "Since forever?"

Hadn't they always called him Tío Benny? It was true that Mom tended to call him "your uncle Benny," and it was also true that, when Daisy thought of him, she didn't think the word *tío* in Spanish. Benny was her *uncle* when she was speaking English. But he was definitely Tío Benny in both languages. She hadn't been trying to make a statement.

"Anyway, you can't say Uncle Ben anymore," Carlos piped up. "He's canceled."

Mom flipped her blinker on as she pulled up to a red light. They were heading to the mall to buy a dress for Daisy's graduation, even though Daisy wanted to find something at Salvation Army instead. She'd decided not to fight Mom on the dress because in the wisdom of choosing her battles, Daisy had selected this one instead.

"Anyway, he said I can help out with some of his properties until I find a real job," Daisy said.

"Oh," Mom said. "His Airbnbs, you mean."

"Well, sure," Daisy said, not sure why calling them *Airbnbs* was such a downgrade from *properties*, but feeling it nonetheless.

"Okay then," Mom said. "Huh."

"The woman who usually works with him is having a baby, so he needs extra help for a few months. Maybe longer." Daisy said this part very quickly, like a combatant who might lower her shield just long enough to strike a blow at her opponent before retreating again.

Mom glanced over at Daisy, and then with some effort, pulled her eyes back to the road. She was quiet for another beat while the new information settled in.

"But your first semester at Stony Brook starts in September," Mom finally said. "Move-in day is August twenty-second. How are you going to attend college on Long Island if you're working in Puerto Rico for *a few months*?"

"Well, that's the thing," Daisy said. "I thought it would be good to take a gap year."

"Wow!" Carlos said.

"Like hell it would!" Mom said.

"Listen, it's fine," Daisy said. "I'm still going to go to college."

"Damn right you are," Mom said. "After I worked my butt off all these years to pay for it, and spent a small fortune on your SAT tutor. Not to mention all the hours of applications, essays, financial aid packets. You better believe you're going to college!"

"I will, Mom, that's what I'm saying!" Daisy said. "The provost will hold my place for a year, I already talked to them. I can start next fall instead."

"You talked to the provost," Mom said.

"Yes."

"Before talking to the lady who's actually paying for the college."

"Well, I just wanted to have all the facts lined up before I brought it to you."

Mom did an alarming thing then, which she only ever did when she was so furious she couldn't speak. She clamped her lips together and puffed air out through her nose like a bull.

"The provost said this is actually becoming really common," Daisy said. "A lot of kids need to decompress after their senior year of high school and all the stress, so they take some time off. They do it all the time in Europe."

"This is not Europe!" Mom yelled. "This is Long Island!"

Mom pressed her lips back together while she sped up to pass an eighteen wheeler, and Daisy hoped there hadn't been a fatal flaw in her planning. Mom wasn't known for judicious driving at the best of times.

"Take it easy, Ruth," Carlos said from the back seat. "I'm too handsome to die."

"And you discussed all this with Benny, too, before talking to me?" Mom said. "I'm the last person on your list?"

"Well, no. We didn't discuss the details," Daisy said. "Just, again, trying to line things up before . . ." She trailed off, because it was true that she had talked to Benny first. And the provost second. And Mom third.

"Well, I'm going to give my brother a piece of my mind," Mom said.

"Mom, don't. I'm grateful to Benny." She could at least opt out of the tío/uncle portion of this fight. "You know I've always wanted to move to San Juan, or at least stay longer than just a summer break. This is my chance to finally do that, to try it out for real. It's a great opportunity."

"A great opportunity," Mom repeated.

"Yes."

"Which part, exactly?"

"I mean. All of it?"

Mom took the exit ramp for the mall.

"Puerto Rico is a mess right now, Daisy. It has never recovered from the storm. You know that. You've seen it."

Since 2017, "the storm" always referred to María, never mind that there had been a dozen terrible storms since.

"The only people moving to Puerto Rico right now are bitcoin crypto-monsters," Mom said.

"Colonizers," Carlos agreed.

"Everyone else with a brain is getting out," Mom went on.

"Oh my God, Mom, that's so offensive!" Daisy said.

Carlos cracked his knuckles behind them.

"It's not offensive, Daisy, it's a fact! It's one thing to go down there and visit, but to live, really? Why would you climb aboard a sinking ship?"

Daisy felt a buzzing in her solar plexus, something deeply troubling in her mother's words, but it was slippery. She couldn't pin it down. Mom pulled the car to a stop beneath another red light.

"I mean, a sinking ship, though?" Daisy said. "If you were paying more attention, you'd know the real problem is rich, tax-dodging mainlanders coming in and gentrifying the place. Pushing locals into service jobs and out of their homes."

Mom ignored this. "So your plan is what?" she said. "Instead of going to college, you're just going to up and move countries?" She said this like it was the most absurd thing she'd ever heard.

Daisy looked out the window at the ugly highway they'd just exited, with its Jersey barriers and its eight lanes of sluggish traffic.

"Yeah, I am," she said. "Lots of people move from one place to another, it's not a ridiculous thing to do. Grandma did it. You did it."

"Good grief, Daisy, that's not the same thing!" Mom's voice was almost frantic with anger.

Daisy heard her brother lock his phone screen in the back seat; TikTok could no longer distract him from the dumpster fire igniting up front. Ever since his name change in middle school, Carlos had made a meaningful effort to earn and honor the culture of his moniker, but after Hurricane María, when the whole world watched the United States president toss paper towels at the devastated citizens, Carlos experienced an uptick in rage that accelerated his learning. Now, at the age of fifteen, he was a fully politicized Boricua, and even though he didn't speak Spanish, he knew more about the history and politics of the island than Daisy did. Daisy could feel him stiffening in the back seat while their mother talked.

"When people leave Puerto Rico these days, they do it because they don't have a choice, Daisy. They can't get good paying work, as you just said. They can't afford to buy a house or raise a family, as you just said. They're being pushed out." She did not say *by people like you*, but Daisy felt the sentiment blooming like a time lapse of algae across a stagnant pond. "When my mother did it, she didn't have a choice either, by the way." The light turned green and Mom turned onto the ring road around the mall. "She was married, and my father made the decision to move back to Missouri for work and for our education. And I know this might seem impossible for you kids to understand nowadays, but at that time, the woman didn't have much choice. The husband made the money, so he made the decisions."

"All right, but what about you then?" Daisy asked.

"What about me? I was a kid when we left Puerto Rico. I didn't have a choice either."

"I'm talking about when you moved thousands of miles away to go to college," Daisy said. "You didn't technically move to a new country, but the East Coast is a whole different culture from where you grew up, right? You were exactly my age when you took off and left Missouri behind forever. You don't even go back to visit! You always make Grandpa and Trisha come here."

"They like coming here!"

"That's not the point! And anyway, Tío Benny did a big move, too, at my age."

"Uncle Benny."

"Oh my God, Mom!"

There was so much frustration in this car it was like a fourth passenger, strapped into the back seat with its earbuds turned up too loud. The conversation was going even worse than Daisy had feared.

"And anyway, what Benny and I did was *not* the same," Mom continued. "I moved to the East Coast to go to college, to get my education, to better myself, just like my dad wanted when he brought us here. I did *not* move to some poor Caribbean island to fix people's broken-down junkers."

Daisy gasped. Mom took a sharp breath too, but did not amend herself. They all knew Mom was capable of being mean when she was hurt, but she adored Benny. They'd never heard her talk about him like that before, not ever.

"Jesus, Mom," Carlos said. "It wasn't just some random island. It was Puerto Rico. It was home."

Carlos didn't even mention the *broken-down junkers*. They sailed right past that scornful mess, because there was too much at issue here to address all of it. Daisy shook her head and returned to the conversation she intended to have, changing tactics once again. With tremendous restraint, she ignored her mother's comments and corralled her voice.

"Anyway, I'm never going to be totally fluent unless I do the total immersion thing," she said. "When Stefani's gone—"

"To *college*," Mom said.

"When Stefani's gone, I won't be able to rely on her. I'll have to speak Spanish."

Except to tell Daisy that declaring a language major was a waste of time, that the technology was improving every day and would eventually do all the work for them, Mom never talked about the Spanish language. She never spoke Spanish with Grandma, wouldn't speak Spanish with Daisy or her brothers, and she'd never admit it to anyone, but they all knew that Mom had almost entirely lost her native tongue. Daisy was already more fluent in Spanish than her mother would ever be again. Mom pretended not to care. She pretended she'd chosen to jettison her language, that she preferred to devote her finite brain-space to more important things. In any case, whether Mom admitted it or not, Daisy knew this was a wound, and she should've been more careful. Already, a dart of tension quivered along her mother's jaw.

"Anyway, it's only for a year, Mom. It's not a big deal," she said. "You can come visit me. It'll be fun!"

"More fun than this?" Carlos asked.

They both ignored him. Mom was still snagged on the previous point, and her voice had grown bitter.

"So you think you're going to get language immersion in Puerto

Rico?" she said. "You're, what, you're going to go down there and become fluent in Spanish by talking to a bunch of vacationers who are renting your uncle's Airbnbs?"

Daisy shook her head but did not respond because they were past the point in this argument where they might achieve constructive dialogue, and had entered the part where they'd only say regrettable things. This was pointless. She was shutting it down.

"So you're going to hang around your uncle's gentrifying tourist traps on the beach," Mom continued. "In Condado and Isla Verde, where ninety-five percent of the people speak English. Good luck becoming fluent in Puerto Rico, Daisy. You'd be better off moving to Haverstraw and working in a kitchen. That's where you'll learn real Spanish."

Daisy winced, unable to extricate herself as she'd hoped, and the situation now desperate enough that she was willing to resort to technology for assistance. She texted her brother in the back seat. WTF do I say here??? Help.

Three dots appeared on her screen and then the bubble of Carlos's response. She cray. Abandon ship.

"You know, speaking Spanish won't make you Puerto Rican," Mom said now, breaking out the meaningful weaponry. "There's a little more to it than listening to Bad Bunny and eating mofongo."

You got that booty too, though. Carlos was quick with the texts from the back seat, but then out loud he added, "I prefer Residente myself. Bad Bunny's good, but he gets too much airplay."

Daisy cut his rumination short. "I don't need to *become* Puerto Rican, Mom. I *am* Puerto Rican!"

"Oh, really." Mom gripped the steering wheel, and Daisy could feel the emotion radiating off her.

This was also the moment that Carlos could no longer contain his irritation to pithy wisecracks. "You know, Ruth," he said. "Just because you drank the self-loathing-flavored Kool-Aid in Missouri doesn't mean you should expect us to drink it too."

Daisy turned in her seat just long enough to bug her eyes at him. *You aren't helping!*

"I am *not* self-loathing!" Mom's voice had grown to a loud warp, and she sat forward in her seat.

"Well, you ain't exactly proud," Carlos muttered.

"How dare you!" Mom yelled.

Carlos shook his head and stared out the window.

"You have no idea what you're talking about," Mom said, and then she glanced in the rearview mirror. "Both of you are obsessed with all this identity nonsense. And then what about the Irish part? You're more than half Irish, and you never even talk about that."

Daisy hated when Mom made a good point. Why was that, anyway, that they were so disconnected from their Irish side? "Maybe because Dad's gone," she said.

"Or maybe because we've never been there," Carlos said. "We don't know that much about it."

"Or maybe because it's unpopular to be white all of a sudden, so you're not interested in that part of your heritage?" Mom said.

"Wow," Daisy said. "That is unkind!"

"But not untrue," Mom said.

"How are we supposed to feel about it when we don't even have any family left over there?"

"Do we?" Carlos asked.

"No." Mom shook her head.

"But anyway, it's not an obsession and it's not nonsense, Mom," Daisy said softly. "I wish you wouldn't say things like that. It's perfectly legitimate and normal for us to be interested in our family's heritage. It's weird that you're so dismissive about it."

"I'm dismissive because it doesn't make sense," Mom said. "Why you kids try so hard to be *from* somewhere you're not actually from. Just be from here. This is where you're from." Mom pointed one finger into the steering wheel, as if insisting that Daisy and Carlos were from precisely that place.

"So our heritage means nothing," Carlos said. "Just because you decided, for whatever mysterious reason that is definitely not self-loathing, that you didn't want to be Puerto Rican anymore, we're all supposed to pretend we're not Puerto Rican?"

"You're not Puerto Rican! There's no pretending!" Mom jabbed at the radio button to turn it on and then immediately turned it back off. "It's not a special category, Carlos. People from Puerto Rico are exactly the same as people from anywhere else in the United States. Black, white, mixed-race, Asian."

Daisy's eyes got huge, but her mouth stayed shut.

"Anywhere else in the United States?!" Carlos made a windy bark of frustration. "Are you serious, Ruth? *In the United States?*"

Mom sniffed. "Technically."

"Actually, technically—"

"The bottom line is, I'm your mother," Mom cut him off and returned to Daisy. "So whether you like it or not, it's my job to take an interest in your future, and to advise against your inclination to make boneheaded decisions."

Daisy's phone buzzed against her thigh, and she pulled it halfway out to read her brother's text: REWD.

"Exactly, you're our mother!" Daisy clenched her fingers together, hoping to give her anger a place to go that was not her voice. "And whether you like it or not, *Mom*, you are Puerto Rican. Spending ten years in Missouri did not cure you of that condition. You didn't become a white Midwesterner just because you lived there for a while. So I hate to break it to you, but that means your kids are also Puerto Rican."

Mom shook her head. "I'm *half* Puerto Rican," she corrected. "And it means no such thing."

Daisy literally pressed her palm against her forehead, but did not respond.

"Anyway, if you want to abandon your education to go become a beach bum on a tropical island, I guess I can't stop you. But don't expect me to hold my tongue while you make stupid choices. And don't expect me to hold on to that college fund forever either."

The phone buzzed again. SO REWD!

Mom swung into a space and put the car in park, but didn't turn it off. Daisy hoped they could leave the conversation here, pick it up again later with more composure. The idea that they might now walk into the mall together and find a dress they could agree on seemed ludicrous.

"I don't think I'll ever understand you kids." Mom crossed her arms in front of her.

Buzz. Understatement.

"All this romantic nonsense about Puerto Rico, Puerto Rico." There was a crack in Mom's voice, maybe a softening, but she cleared it out of her throat and continued. "You know, things were never so great in Puerto Rico."

In the heartbeat that followed this contention, Daisy swelled with guilt. Not only because of the way she and Carlos ganged up on their mother in these conversations and steamrolled her emotions, but also because it was true that they couldn't understand Mom's experiences, what made her feel this way. What had it been like for her growing up in Puerto Rico with a white father, and then in St. Louis with a Puerto Rican mother? Maybe she felt adrift or unsettled in herself, Daisy thought. She wished her mom would open up to them instead of this.

"Do you even remember it?" Daisy asked.

The wrong question.

"Of course I remember it!" A new fury colored Mom's cheeks.

Daisy had been trying to reach for something soft in her mother, a place where Mom would pause. And then answer the question for real. With consideration. Did she remember living in Puerto Rico? She was six when they left.

What did she remember? *What did she remember?*

Did she remember walking to her grandparents' apartment on Sunday afternoons, the globe of the sun lodged like a peg in the clean blue sky? Did she remember piraguas, palm trees, Papamío's raspy laughter, tostones frying in oil? Did she remember the cabinet in the living room where they kept the hurricane lamps, the smell of the kerosene, the box of thick wooden matches, the swishing sound of wind through palm fronds? Or how good it felt to stand in the warm surf next to Benny, with the tinny sound of their father's shortwave radio playing salsa music on the towel behind them? Or clambering up the roots of the banyan tree behind their house, finding the place where the two great limbs came together in a kind of hammock, where she could lean back and cross her legs and lie very still to watch the sparrows and spiders and frogs, a whole kingdom of animals beneath the sprawling canopy? Was it possible for her to remember a time when almost everyone in her world was Puerto Rican, free from foreign definitions of what that meant, when they didn't have to prove anything about their humanity or qualifications to the non–Puerto Rican people in their midst? When they were uncompromised, uncompared, uninhibited, did her mother remember how it felt to be a person, just a person, without any qualifiers, how it felt to be a little girl named Ruth, living in a place she loved, with people she loved? Where community wasn't a thing she had to seek out and create—or fail to create—as a footnote to a larger experience, but was, in fact, her entire beautiful, glowing, golden, sweet, heady bubble of a world? The sound of el coquí outside her nighttime window—surely she remembered that.

Daisy might never know.

"It's okay if you don't remember, Mama."

Mom threw her head back against the headrest and ran her hands over her hair. "I said I remember!"

Buzz. She don't remember.

"I just." Mom's voice grew quieter. "I don't know why it's all so important to you. It's my childhood, not yours."

Daisy held her tongue, and Mom turned to look at her.

"Why does it matter so much to you, where I grew up?" Mom's voice was softer now, but the tempest was still there in her face. "I really do not understand."

Daisy wasn't sure how to explain it, but she wanted to try. Unfortunately, Carlos got there first.

"But it's more than just where you grew up, Mom," he said, unbuckling himself to lean between the seats. "It feels reductive when you say things like that."

Daisy frowned at him because they both knew how much their mother hated words like *reductive*, and just when they had almost gotten out of this mess. Daisy pulled out her phone and surreptitiously texted: STOP. TALKING. OMG ULL PUSH HER OVER THE EDGE. She heard his phone ding, but Carlos ignored it.

"You talk as if who you are has nothing to do with who we are. Like we have no access to our own identity or ethnicity."

Oh, this would not go well now, Daisy knew. How had they gotten so off the rails so quickly? The mall was only an eight-minute drive from home! This conversation had stopped being about her decision to take a gap year, or even about her decision to spend that year in San Juan. She leaned her head against the window.

"Good Lord," Mom said, surprising no one, making herself louder than Carlos so she wouldn't have to listen to him anymore. "Your ethnicity? Do I need to remind you that I'm white, for God's sake? Look at me!" She held her arm out as evidence, but whatever proof might exist there was covered by long sleeves. "Look at yourself!" she said. "This is all so ridiculous, it's so frustrating, so counterproductive!"

Carlos's voice remained calm. The louder Mom got, the more carefully he measured his words. "Well, it certainly is unfortunate that we can never discuss it without you flying off the handle."

"Carlos—" Daisy tried to interject, but he raised his voice to talk over her.

"Maybe if you were more open," he said. "If you'd talk to us instead of getting all nasty every time it comes up, we might understand why it upsets you."

Daisy loved her brother, but it was clear that his presence was actually the biggest flaw in her plan. Mom turned the car off, and reached across the center console to grab her purse from the floor by Daisy's feet.

"I am done with this conversation," Mom said.

She opened the door and climbed out, but Daisy and Carlos both knew that pronouncement usually indicated that Mom was *almost* but *not quite* done with the conversation. She typically employed that line as a way of indicating to the other party that she was about to have the last word. Indeed, she turned and ducked her head back into the car. She looked right at Daisy, ignoring Carlos completely, even though he'd been the one to push her to this point.

"If you are determined to waste your time in Puerto Rico learning Spanish or whatever, *fine*," she said. "Knock yourself out. Go to Puerto Rico, take your bikini, work on your tan. But don't pretend you're on some noble mission to reconnect with your roots, for the love of God. You're no more Puerto Rican than you are Japanese!"

She slung her purse over her shoulder and slammed the door.

"Wow," Daisy said. She felt her phone buzz.

Sayonara.

§

Daisy moved to San Juan. Vic drove her to the airport because Mom refused. But on the morning Daisy left, Mom did walk her out to the car and did give her a long hug in the driveway.

Nine months later, a global pandemic shut down the world, and Vic (from college) and Daisy (from Puerto Rico) both returned home to Palisades. Carlos was delighted to have them back, but to her credit, Mom gave no outward indication of gloating. She did not remark at all on the brevity of Daisy's gap year. Instead, she stocked up on jigsaw puzzles and wine.

For three weeks, Daisy spent most of her days in bed. She rediscovered her cell phone, downloaded the most mind-numbing games she could find, opened a TikTok account, threw herself headlong down every available rabbit hole. She scrolled through years' worth of posts on *The Widow's Kitchen*, hearting and commenting on every single one. Daisy stopped exercising and showering. On the twenty-third day, when she found herself embroiled in a Twitter battle about whether or not masks were a government conspiracy, she sat up in bed, and shook herself out from beneath the covers. She stood up in her socks and dirty sweatpants. She walked downstairs as quickly as possible and trudged into her mother's kitchen toward the sliding glass door behind the table. Mom looked up from her laptop and asked if she could fix Daisy something to eat.

"Sure, Mom," Daisy said, sliding open the door.

She stepped one foot through the open door onto the mat outside and, while her mother watched from her seat at the counter, Daisy drew her arm all the way back and launched her cell phone out into the yard. It skidded across the pool pavers, leaving shards of itself behind.

"Daisy!" Mom stood up from her stool.

Daisy slid the glass door shut behind her.

Mom sat down again. "Are you okay?"

Daisy locked the sliding glass door with her thumb and sat down beside Mom at the counter. "I am now," she said.

In September, Daisy couldn't bring herself to start Zoom college, and Mom, having witnessed both Daisy's plunge into, and resurrection from, zombieland, didn't press her. Their argument of the previous year remained unresurrected, unresolved, and the tacit understanding between them was that Daisy would go to college when the world reopened. She would do it her own way, in the dimensional world. She was not a kid who could survive screen-schooling. In fact, she was no longer a kid at all.

Shortly after Zoom college started without her, an idea asserted itself with some measure of clarity in Daisy's mind. Once it appeared there, it felt so inevitable, it was as though it had been there all along, and she'd merely cleaned the tarnish off it, shined it up, and stuck a price tag on it.

Secretly, she wrote a business plan (well, first she went online and ordered a reference book called *How to Write a Business Plan*). Then she wrote a business plan. Next, she started researching neighborhoods, rents, clientele, similar businesses that had succeeded, similar businesses that had failed. She researched competition, supply chains, pricing, hidden expenses. Daisy worked on this project with all the love and devotion the girls in her seventh-grade Family and Consumer Sciences class had devoted to the project of planning their imaginary future weddings. (Daisy had gotten a C+ on hers, the only girl in her class to score below a B.) She used everything she learned way back then about poster boards and glue sticks, but brought an enthusiasm to this new project that the seventh-grade wedding assignment could never have inspired. In her pandemic bedroom, Daisy clipped images from magazines and newspapers to create mood boards. She filled a whole binder with her ideas, and finally, she came up with the name. When she felt ready, she called Stefani from her rotary phone.

"I'm going to open a shop," she told her cousin.

"You what now."

"A vintage clothing and curiosities shop."

"During a global pandemic," Stefani said.

"Well, no, probably after."

Except for the static, the line was quiet.

"Hello?" Daisy said.

"Hi."

"Did you hear me?"

"You're going to open a vintage store."

"Yes! For chic and diligent people who want to avoid the twin transgressions of overconsumption and overspending," she read from her business plan. "Ultra high-end. Impeccably curated."

"Of course," Stefani said.

"In San Juan," Daisy said.

"Well, yeah, obviously."

"You wanna hear the name?"

"Hit me," Stefani said.

"I'm gonna call it the Double Down." Daisy held her hands out in front of her as if she could already see the name emblazoned across an awning.

A pause from Stefani, and then, "Girl, yes!" she said, whistling and cheering. She paused again. "But your mom is gonna freak."

Chapter Twenty-Two

~

St. Louis, Missouri
1982

The questions Ruth had about the end of her parents' marriage were entirely pragmatic. Where would they live now? How often would they see Dad? Would Mama still have to cook for them? What about the country club?

Her parents presented her with a unified set of answers. They would remain in St. Louis because the mediator suggested Mama could have primary custody as long as she agreed to stay. Ruth and Benny could help her pick out her new house. They would see Dad every other weekend, plus Tuesday evenings when Mama went to her personal finance class at the community college. Yes, Mama would still have to cook, because not every domestic problem could be resolved by the dissolution of an unhappy marriage. But certainly they could eat out more often, and when they went to Red Lobster, Ruth could order the crab legs. As for the Short Hills Babylon Country Club, Mama would never set foot in that godforsaken place again. But Ruth could still go on her weekends with Dad if she wanted to.

She wanted to.

Benny's questions weren't as straightforward, but nonetheless, Ruth observed that her parents answered them together, as a unit, which was more than they'd ever done when they were trying to stay married. They sat side by side on the couch, not touching each other, but listening carefully to Benny's questions. Then Dad grabbed Mama's hand, and they sat like that while Benny talked, Mama's fingers tucked into the ball of Dad's fist, which made Ruth wonder if they really had to go through with this.

"Why do we still have to live here if we're not even living together anymore, why can't we go back to Puerto Rico?" Benny asked.

"This is how it works, honey," Mama said. "Until you and Ruthie turn eighteen, and as long as Dad and I are sharing custody, we have to agree to live in the same place."

Benny picked at a loose thread on the arm of the couch. "Are you guys going to marry other people now?"

"No," they said in harmony.

Benny wanted to know if they were happier now, or if breaking up the family would make them happier in the future. He didn't ask this in a mean or accusatory way; he earnestly wanted to know because, if being apart would make his parents happier, that knowledge might help Benny find a way to be happy about it too. He also wanted to know if the divorce was partly his fault for being so miserable all the time.

"Of course it's not," they told him.

Ruth had her doubts. But in any case, Benny aside, everyone found the divorce suprisingly easy. Three out of four Brennans were happier when it was finished, and both of Ruth's parents suspected that, although Benny was deeply unhappy, he was not, in fact, any unhappier than he'd been before.

Dad stayed in the old house, which felt slightly depressing to Ruth. When she and Benny went back for their weekends, she noted the places in the carpet where furniture had been removed, and Dad hadn't bought anything to replace it yet, shapes that were bluer or browner than the neighboring carpet-fields where sunshine had bleached the fibers. Sometimes she stretched out on her stomach, leaned her weight on her elbows, and tried to encourage the holes left behind by the feet of Mama's love seat to fill themselves back in. She picked and pulled at the strands, trying to stand them back up to their original heights. She worried that those carpet-craters might make Dad feel lonely or sad, but he didn't even seem to notice them.

If Ruth had been old enough to wonder about finances, her parents would've told her it was none of her business anyway. But the truth was, the divorce was only scandalous because they were Catholic and it was the Midwest and it was 1982. In reality, it was a good divorce because of money. Dad suddenly had more of it because he no longer had to share it with Mama. And Mama suddenly had more of it because she was rich. (Even though Mama told Ruth not to say *rich* for the same reason she wasn't supposed to say *fat* regardless of a person's actual girth. Mama felt that both of these words were gauche, so Ruth didn't use them even when they were super obvious.) The fact was, Mama didn't have to work, and she'd still have enough money to maintain a comfortable lifestyle without having to rely on Dad. Her parents had agreed to a clean break in this regard: Rafaela would not seek alimony or child support, and Peter would not make any claim on Rafaela's trust. They were both to be immediately liberated and fully financially independent. So even though Ruth and Benny didn't know any of this precisely, they were spared the resentment that usually fills the voids created by division.

The third weekend they were supposed to go to Dad's house, Ruth called her father as soon as she got home from school. Mama had gone to the grocery store and left Benny in charge, which meant that Benny was in his room with his boom box turned up, and Ruth was alone in the kitchen with a half-eaten banana and a great idea. Her father's secretary answered and put her right through.

"Hey there, pumpkin!"

"Dad! I have the best idea!"

"What's up?"

"It can be pizza night!"

"Hmm."

"Friday night is always pizza night at Kathy's house." Ruth remembered too late how much Dad disliked Kathy, and therefore how unlikely this information was to appeal to him.

"Your mother isn't expecting me until seven o'clock," he said. "I'm sure she's already made plans for your dinner." She could hear him shuffling papers around on his desk.

"Yeah, Dad, it's an emergency, though," Ruth said, swinging the yellow phone cord like a hammock. "She's making that pineapple stir-fry thing," she whispered, checking the driveway to make sure there was still no sign of Mama's car.

"Oh God," Dad said. Ruth could hear the look on his face. "Is she there?"

"No. She's at the grocery store. Buying the canned pineapples."

Dad laughed. "Then why are you whispering?"

"I don't know!" Ruth groaned. The pineapple stir-fry demanded a certain gravity. "Please, Dad, be a hero. Make it pizza night."

Ruth could tell by the sound of the breath he expelled that she'd nearly won. She pushed him gently.

"Don't leave me alone with the pineapple," she whispered.

"Okay, okay," he said. "I can't get out of here until five, and then rush-hour traffic, it'll be five thirty at least before I get there."

Ruth bounced on her toes, and the weight of the phone cord danced beneath her, slapping the linoleum tile. "Yay! Thank you, Daddy!"

"Don't thank me yet," he said. "I'll have to talk to your mother when she gets home. Before she starts making that stir-fry."

"Yes!"

"So just tell her to call me as soon as she gets in."

"I will, I will! Thank you, Dad."

And so, every other Friday evening became pizza night at Dad's house, and once that was established, it was easy enough for Ruth to implement pizza night at Mama's house too. The tactic was different. She told Mama she deserved a night off from the kitchen, that it would be good quality time, they could all eat together on the couch and watch *Fantasy Island*. Ruth expected Mama to make noises about nutrition and decorum, but Mama was all too eager to kick off her shoes under the coffee table and eat with her hands. Sometimes she didn't even make them use plates. Ruth was impressed.

In fact, her divorced mother was full of surprises. For example, Mama bought leotards, leg warmers, and a VCR, and began pushing her brand-new coffee table to one side so she could do Jazzercise videos in the living room. Once she had mastered the moves, she signed up for in-person Jazzercise classes at the local Y, too, and she seemed so ebullient when she returned home with the soft glow of perspiration lighting her skin that Ruth wondered why she hadn't joined the Y years ago. After Mama wrapped up her personal finance class on Tuesday nights, she enrolled in a GED class, which was the biggest surprise so far, because Mama explained to them that GED stood for *General Education Diploma*, which she wanted to get because she had never finished high school. This little nugget was particularly astonishing because, though no one in their family ever voiced the information aloud, it was widely understood among the four of them that Mama was approximately one million times more educated than Dad, and they all knew Dad had a college degree in radio engineering from a university in Kansas City. Mama was not the least bit ashamed of it, though, and actually seemed surprised they hadn't known.

"How?" was Benny's one-word question.

"I had a stellar education at Las Madres in Puerto Rico, and I was a straight-A student," she said. "I simply never had the opportunity to finish."

Well! Mama decided that Benny and Ruth were old enough to look after themselves the two afternoons a week she'd be at class until suppertime. As a reward for proving their self-sufficiency and independence, Mama would buy them an Atari Video Computer System for Christmas. It was a good deal for all parties involved.

Mama didn't want a celebration when she passed the test and got her diploma. "All I want is to never be bored again," she announced. So she started a garden. Obviously, no vegetables—only flowers. But even then, she didn't really enjoy the dirt, so she started looking into more classes, but only one at a time, and never in pursuit of a degree. She took whatever interested her: First Aid and Interior Decorating and Personal Computing and then a Ceramics class. She didn't like the latter one at all, but she finished it anyway, completing all her projects on time (if not enthusiastically), mostly in order to show Benny and Ruth that she followed through on her commitments, a fact she was eager to illustrate after voiding her previous commitment to their father.

So in December, when Dad asked their surprising new mother if the kids could come to his house for Christmas morning, Mama's response was placid. As long as she had them for Nochebuena and Three Kings Day, she said, the twenty-fifth of December was no big deal. In exchange for that arrangement, Dad agreed that Mama could take them to Puerto Rico for six weeks during their summer vacation. He could have them for the other two weeks, and would book them a cabin at the Lake of the Ozarks for the last week of summer. Ruth could not believe her luck. It was like a thousand pizza nights had come at once. Even Benny was happy with the plan.

Titi Lola arrived from San Juan on December 20, and was so cold she threatened to immediately return to the airport. But Mama just piled on the sweaters and thanked her for coming.

"I could never leave you alone on Christmas," Lola said.

Anyone looking at Lola and Mama would've known they were sisters, but although the resemblance was distinct, they had learned from youth, as sisters always do, that one was slightly prettier than the other. And so, as Mama took care to emphasize and preserve her beauty, Lola set her mind to cultivating other qualities. Unlike Mama, Lola had become slightly thicker around the middle with age, and she seldom wore makeup except for her trademark red lipstick. But her hair still gleamed in black curls that were wilder and more abundant than Mama's, and she wore rings on every finger, bangles that clacked up and down both arms whenever she threw herself open for a hug, which she did with some frequency. Lola was spontaneous, droll, and a great cook, but perhaps her best quality, as far as Ruth was concerned, was the effortless way she could transform Mama into a firecracker of joy.

Lola had been planning their holiday menu for weeks, meticulously strategizing ingredients and substitutions, sending Mama repeatedly to different grocery stores to purchase what she needed ahead of time, or to report back to her in San Juan when she couldn't find the requested goods. What they didn't have in St. Louis, Lola brought with her from Puerto Rico. She brought one blue hardback suitcase with her shoes, clothing, and cosmetics. And a second smaller suitcase full of food.

The night she arrived, Benny hauled the luggage up the narrow staircase to the fourth bedroom, which Mama had insisted they needed, and which they'd christened the Lola Lounge.

"Oh, that small one could've gone straight to the kitchen," Lola said when she saw Benny arrive in the doorway with the bags.

"Now you tell me," Benny said, heaving the carry-on up onto the bed.

Ruth was stretched out there, too, and she felt the mattress bounce lightly beneath the weight of that case.

"What do you have in here, gold bricks?" Benny asked.

"Better." Lola flicked the two locks and opened the little suitcase like a radiant clamshell. Inside was a traveling harvest of plantains, yuca, gandules, taro, a plastic bag with several banana leaves kept moist between some dampened paper towels, and an assortment of herbs and peppers in smaller baggies. Ruth didn't recognize any of them, not because she'd forgotten them in the four years since they'd moved away, but because of her mother's binational propensity for canned goods. Lola reached in and grabbed a yuca, waxy and rough, which she tossed to Ruth, who caught it in both hands.

"El lechón refused to get into the suitcase," Lola said.

Benny laughed, but Ruth cringed. She'd always felt conflicted about eating those delicious baby pigs at Christmastime, so even though she knew Titi Lola was joking, she liked the idea that, right now, tottering through the streets of El Viejo San Juan, there was one little piglet who'd escaped his fate.

"Anyway, we won't miss him!" Lola said. "We'll have enough pasteles and florecitas to feed an army of parranderos."

"They don't have parrandas here, Titi," Benny said. "They have carolers instead. But it's not the same. You don't feed them. And they're . . ." Benny tried to find the words to describe the staid, red-cheeked Christmas carolers with their sheet music and mittens. "Different," he said.

"Well," Lola said, tossing Ruth a second yuca. "More for us then!"

Ruth examined the lumpy, hairy shapes and felt dubious. But within a few hours she was wearing an apron and standing beside her tía in the kitchen, surrounded by heavenly smells. There was oil in a pan on the stovetop, sizzling garlic, onions, peppers, tomatoes. Ruth was chopping the cilantro just like Lola showed her, carefully keeping her fingers tucked in and moving the knife blade straight up and down.

"Perfect!" Lola said, inspecting her handiwork. "Toss it in!"

"Right on top?"

"Right on top."

Ruth lifted the cutting board over the pan and slid the cilantro in while Lola stirred everything together. The aroma immediately changed, deepened, spiked into a pang that curled into the back of Ruth's throat and made her mouth water. It was an aroma Ruth didn't know she'd missed until she smelled it again, there in Mama's new kitchen. It filled the air, steamed the winter windows. Mama sat at the little table nearby with her coffee and magazine. She and Lola talked in Spanish while Lola cooked.

A long-buried memory made itself present in the bright little kitchen then: the peal of Mama's laughter, deep from the belly. It was a sound that had become shallow and discolored in recent years, and here it was again, and Ruth remembered it. Her mother's happiness. Ruth wiped her hands on her apron and ran over to the table where she looped her arm around Mama's neck and kissed her cheek. Mama pulled her onto her lap and hugged her. Benny laughed while Lola spun him under one arm and dipped him over her spatula.

"I refuse to dance another step until I get fed!" Benny said, pushing his face over the steaming pan. "Smells so good!" He switched to Spanish, and Ruth could understand enough to know that Lola was telling him how they made the sofrito, but after that she was lost because they were talking so fast. So she just laughed when they laughed, and decided not to be unhappy about it.

Ruth was still happy on Christmas morning, waiting for Dad to pull the Datsun into the driveway. She sat on her knees, draping herself over the back of the couch while she watched for him out the window. She'd been hoping for snow, a white Christmas, but so far the sky was holding out, a cold, heavy lid of white clamped above them that refused to give way to snowflakes. She figured Lola would love to see the snow, and it might even convince her to love St. Louis so maybe she'd stay. It would be amazing if Lola lived here, too, and if Mama could be this happy all the time (and they could eat like this all the time).

That morning, Mama added cinnamon and a drop of vanilla extract to her coffee to make it festive, and she let Ruth have hot cocoa instead of orange juice. Mama hummed while she helped Ruth pack her weekender duffel bag. Mama was still in her bathrobe and slippers, her curly hair gathered up on top of her head.

Benny was sulking because he didn't want to go to Dad's, but Ruth didn't pay her brother any mind. This was the fundamental difference between them, she'd learned. Benny made himself miserable by always wanting specific things he couldn't have. Ruth, on the other hand, was adaptable. She knew without having to learn that if you didn't waste your energy wanting too hard in any one particular direction, you could find yourself quite happy in a myriad of unexpected circumstances.

"He's here!" Ruth leaped up from the couch before Dad even pulled into the driveway. "Love you, Mama! Have fun with Titi Lola today!" She kissed her mother on the cheek and skidded out the door, hauling her bag behind her. Usually Dad would beep twice and wave at their mother in the doorway before backing out. But here was the first indication that today would be different. Dad turned off the engine and opened the driver's side door of the Datsun. He stood now in the wedge, one elbow up on the roof, the other on top of his door.

"What's this?" he said to Ruth. "Why aren't you dressed?"

Ruth stopped and looked down at herself. "What do you mean?"

"I mean, why aren't you dressed? You can't go in your pj's."

"Why not?"

"Rafaela, why aren't they dressed?" Her father spoke right past her to where her mother was leaning against the doorjamb behind her, coffee cup in one hand.

"It's Christmas morning," Mama said. "They wanted to go in their pj's, I didn't see the harm."

"Right." Dad stood out and slammed the car door. "Back inside."

Ruth dropped her duffel bag at her feet.

"But—"

"No buts, let's go, we're going to be late," Dad said.

"Late for what?"

He didn't answer. He was next to her now on the walkway, and he leaned down to grab her bag. Benny hadn't even made it to the door yet.

"You gotta put on something nice," Dad said. "Maybe that red corduroy jumper and the white turtleneck with the rose on the collar."

She did like that festive outfit, but it didn't match her vision for the day. How could she sprawl cozily on the carpet and tear into her presents, and stuff herself with Christmas cookies and hot apple cider, and play with her new toys, and watch cartoons and movies all day long in the restrictive discomfort of tights?

"But I have to wear tights with that jumper," she said.

"So then put on some tights," he said. He looked at Mama. "Her white tights are clean?"

"I think so." Mama stepped away from the doorway, and Dad followed her back inside.

The next fifteen minutes were a minefield of tense voices and exploding moods. Dad muttered about Mama sabotaging their holiday, and Mama muttered about Dad expecting her to be a mind reader. Benny shouted that he wasn't wearing that, and those shoes didn't even fit him anymore, and what kind of a masochist wears a tie on Christmas morning anyway, while Mama yanked Ruth's hair into merciless braids, and Ruth wondered when Benny had gotten so good at English.

"What's a masochist, Mama?" she asked.

"Hush, you'll wake Lola."

But Ruth wasn't the one hollering. She stuffed her still-warm jammies into the side pocket of her duffel bag and wondered how long it would be before she was able to put them back on. Benny was already in the passenger seat when Dad tossed her bag in the back.

"Why'd we have to get all dressed up?" Benny asked from the front seat. He had won the tie battle, but was wearing a pullover sweater and a scowl.

Dad pulled up to a stop sign and turned on his blinker. "We're going to mass with my family."

"But we went to mass with Mama last night!" Ruth whined. She wasn't typically a whiner, but an injustice on this scale warranted an elevated vocal pitch.

"Well, I don't know anything about that," Dad said. "Your mother doesn't tell me these things, so how am I supposed to know?"

"I'm telling you now!" Ruth said.

"It was a long-ass mass too," Benny said.

Dad jammed on the brakes. "Boy, did you just say *ass* in this car?"

"No! No, I said *mass*," Benny insisted.

Ruth giggled. Dad glared at her in the rearview mirror.

"We haven't been to Christmas mass with my family since before your mother and I were married. Not even after we moved back here. I tried every year, and now it's high time," Dad said. "Your mother's not the only one with a family, with traditions. You kids are going to learn some of my customs too. And I want you both on your best behavior. You hear me?"

"Okay, Dad," Ruth said. Benny didn't answer.

"None of this *ass* business," Dad said.

Ruth giggled again, and Benny tugged at the collar of his sweater. She could see the reflection of her brother's face in the side-view mirror. She crossed her eyes and tried to make him laugh, but it was useless.

The parking lot was jammed, every pew, jammed. Ruth spotted Grandpa Pete about halfway up on the left. She could see the bald circle at the back of his head, ringed by white hair.

"There's Grandpa," she whispered, pointing.

An usher looked sharply at her and put a finger to his lips.

"Sheesh," she said.

Dad pulled her by one ear over to a back corner, and she went up on tiptoe to alleviate the tugging pain, but she knew better than to make another sound. Benny slumped after them. They found a place to stand among all the other latecomers lined up along the walls at the back of the church. Benny folded his arms and leaned one heel up on the wall. Dad leaned across the top of her head and whispered directly into Benny's ear, but she could hear him clearly because he was four inches away.

"Are you chewing gum?" Dad was incredulous.

Benny shrugged.

"Out," Dad said. "Now."

Benny made an exaggerated gulping sound. "It's gone."

Ruth looked up to see a red hot flush crawling up Dad's neck, but she couldn't tell if it was embarrassment or fury or both. "No communion for you," Dad said.

Benny made a face like *big whoop*. He'd had communion less than twelve hours ago.

At least the music was good. Ruth sang all the Christmas songs at the top of her lungs while Benny rolled his eyes at her, and when it was time for communion, she stuck her tongue out at him before she went to take the host.

And even with all that, it still wasn't that bad. It was hardly hot apple cider and cartoons in your pajamas, but Ruth was happy to be with her dad and Benny. She was happy to sing the Christmas hymns, and she was already thinking about getting back to Dad's house after mass and stripping out of these tights, straight back into her jammies. Grandpa Pete winked at her from his pew when she went past for communion.

After mass, it was harder for Ruth to maintain her sanguine outlook, the main impediment to her optimism being the discovery that they were not going back to Dad's house to dive into their presents. Instead, they were going to Uncle Jim and Aunt Linda's house for Christmas dinner.

"Why is it called Christmas dinner if we're eating it at noon?" Benny grumbled.

Dad didn't even bother answering him. The worst thing about Uncle Jim and Aunt Linda's house was that they didn't have any kids, so there was no kid stuff there. And they were super protective of their non-kid stuff, always acting like kids were wrecking balls, even when they sat still and behaved like perfectly normal little humans. When Dad and Mama were married, they hardly ever went to their house, even though they only lived on the other side of the county. Uncle Jim came over a few times a year and had a beer in the backyard with Dad, but that was it. Uncle Jim and Dad had only one other brother, Paul, and he lived in Oregon with his wife and three nice kids. Ruth and Benny only met them once, and afterward, they talked for weeks about how they wished Uncle Paul was the one who lived in St. Louis, and Uncle Jim and Aunt Linda could go live in Oregon.

The house was full of people when they got there. Grandpa Pete was there with his wife, Pearl, who wasn't Dad's mom, but who had married Grandpa Pete after Dad's mom died. Pearl was nice, but smelled like medicine. And then Aunt Linda had about a thousand brothers and sisters, and every one of them had about a thousand kids, so there was hardly even anywhere to sit down. Ruth sat on Grandpa's lap for the first few minutes, eating liberally from his plate of snacks until it was empty. The men at the table talked across the top of her head and mostly about football, which Ruth found incredibly boring. Most of the kids had gone down to the basement where Uncle Jim had a pool table, so after the snacks, Ruth and Benny went down and tried to join in. The other kids were all cousins. They knew each other.

Benny hung back by the wall and examined the pool cues, waiting his turn, but Ruth stood beside the two other girls who were leaning on the edge of the pool table to watch.

"I'm Ruth." She leaned her chin in one hand. "What are your names?"

"I'm Lucy," the closer girl said. "That's Kelly."

Kelly did not look over, but in a faraway voice, she said, "Lucy, I'm hooome!" and everyone except for Ruth and Benny laughed.

It must have been an inside joke because Ruth didn't get it, but when Benny grabbed her by the elbow and led her toward the steps without explanation, she did not resist. There was some ugly feeling in that room. The oldest boy waited until they were halfway up the stairs before calling out, "¡Adiós, amigos!"

So Benny and Ruth ended up sitting quietly in the living room together, where there was an oval rug, some fancy chairs with wooden arms, and several glass cabinets filled with figurines. They made up a game that involved one of them copying the pose of one of the figurines, and then the other one had to guess which figurine they were copying. It was the perfect game because they were quiet and they didn't have to touch anything. Ruth was standing silently on one foot, with one arm drawn elegantly in front of her and the other tossed lightly over her head in imitation of a dancing lady, when Aunt Linda burst in and demanded to know what they were doing in this room.

"We're just playing," Ruth said.

"Come out of here," Linda snapped.

"We're just hanging out," Benny said. "We're not even touching any-thing."

"You'd better not be touching anything, young man," she said.

Aunt Linda was sweaty and frazzled-looking, and despite the fact that she was unfriendly and neurotic, Ruth felt bad for her that she had to run around cooking for and serving so many people on Christmas day when all anyone wanted was just to be sitting down in their favorite chair with good socks and something warm in a mug.

"You need any help cooking or setting the table?" Ruth asked. Now that she'd been helping Titi Lola all week, Ruth had some confidence in the kitchen. Plus, there was nothing else to do.

"Aw, aren't you a sweet little homemaker," Aunt Linda said. "Didn't get that from your mama, did you?" She tried to make her voice conspiratorial, but Ruth didn't know how to respond. Aunt Linda saved her the trouble. "Just run along downstairs with the other kids and stay out of trouble until the food's ready. I've got dinner covered."

Aunt Linda sealed up the living room behind them and swept back to the kitchen. Ruth and Benny followed her as far as the basement door. Neither of them wanted to go back down there. Ruth grabbed her brother's hand, and he didn't exactly grab back, but to her relief, he let her hang on there at the end of his arm. After a moment, he even pulled her in a little closer. Then Benny opened the basement door and the two of them stepped inside, but that's as far as they went. They sat down side by side on the top step without a word, and closed the door behind them so they could lean against it. It was dark here now, and they could hear the conversations going on both above and below. Ruth put her head on Benny's shoulder and allowed herself to cry. Just for a minute.

"This sucks," he said.

"I miss Mama," she whispered.

Benny was quiet for a long moment, but finally answered, "Me too."

"I miss Lola," she said.

"Me too."

Ruth sniffed. "It doesn't seem right that she has the same name as Lynda Carter."

"Yeah." Benny didn't love Wonder Woman as much as Ruth did, but he was highly attuned to injustice. "That is some real bullshit."

When dinner was served, there weren't enough seats. There were folding tables set up in various places so all the grown-ups had somewhere to sit, but the kids piled their paper plates with food and brought them back to the basement. Ruth and Benny waited until the staircase was clear and then took their dinner back to the top step. The food was good, but they weren't hungry. Benny ate his anyway because he could always eat, no matter what was going on. He ate Ruth's, too, when his plate was empty.

When they left the kitchen, Dad had been sitting with Uncle Jim and Grandpa at the table. There was some other guy, too, who they didn't know, probably one of Aunt Linda's brothers. Ruth and Benny could hear the men now, chatting across their dinner plates.

"Must be nice to have a proper Christmas dinner again!" Grandpa said.

"Linda's a great cook," Dad said.

"Long time since you had a meal like that, huh, Pete?" Uncle Jim said to Dad.

Ruth pressed her ear against the plywood door so she could hear better, because Dad was speaking quietly and Benny was chewing with his mouth open.

"Ah, Rafaela does her best." That's what it sounded like he said, something like that. "Maybe cooking's not her strong suit."

"I'm not sure anything's her strong suit," Grandpa said.

"Ah, that's not fair, Pop." This was Uncle Jim. "She's great at being uppity."

The men laughed.

"We tried to warn you, Peter," Grandpa said. "It's one thing to have a little fun when you're young, but you don't marry a girl like that."

"A girl like what, exactly?" Dad said.

"Ah, you know what I mean," Grandpa said. "What, you want me to say it?"

And now Dad was talking again, but he was sitting in a chair with its back to the basement door, and he'd dropped his voice so Ruth couldn't hear him at all.

"All right, all right, let's everybody relax before we say something stupid," Uncle Jim raised his voice.

"Bit late for that," Dad said, his voice rising too, and Ruth imagined him taking a swig of beer.

Her cheek felt warm against the wooden door, and even though she hadn't eaten much at all, she felt queasy. There was the jarring sound of a chair scraping across the linoleum floor, and Dad's voice was unmistakable now.

"You've made your point," he said. "Your collective point, as it turns out. I suppose you've been saying this to each other for years, what, behind our backs? Having a laugh every time we leave the room?"

"Don't be so sensitive, Pete," Uncle Jim said. "We're only trying to say we've been on your side this whole time."

"There're no sides," Dad said. "It's not a war. She's the mother of my children, of your grandchildren, Dad. And you didn't have to fawn over her, but you never even gave her a chance, never made her feel comfortable. You were ignorant from the first day you met her."

Silence. Even the background noise in the kitchen was suspended.

"You were always rude to her, all of you," Dad went on. "You too, Linda."

There was another loud clatter, a pot slammed onto a stovetop or a handful of cutlery tossed into the sink. No one else spoke. Uncle Jim could be heard clearing his throat. Ruth and Benny stared at each other in the half-light, and then the basement door was yanked away from Ruth's cheek, and her weight fell in, and Dad was standing above them there in the doorway in the sudden light.

"What are you doing, sitting there?" he asked.

Ruth only looked at him. Benny stood up and folded their paper plates in half, the plastic forks inside. He shook his head at their father, who seemed to understand everything at once. He pulled them both into a strong hug, kissed the tops of their heads.

"Let's get outta here."

In the back seat of the Datsun, Ruth wriggled out of the tights and tugged her flannel pants back up in their place while they waited for Dad to follow them out to the car. When he appeared on the front step, he was carrying a tinfoil shape with both hands and walking strangely, like a speed walk, and when he arrived at the car, he went to Benny's door instead of his own, and gestured with his chin in a clear indication that he wanted Benny to open it, but Benny pretended like he didn't understand. So Ruth said, "Open the door!" at the same time they heard Dad say it through the closed window, so Benny had no choice but to lean forward and open it, at which time Dad deposited the tinfoil onto Benny's lap.

"What's this?" Benny said, but Dad had already closed the door and, with a quick glance back at the house, was now racing around to the driver's side door. He was snickering when he climbed in.

"Dad, have you been drinking?" Ruth asked, because that's what her mother always asked when Dad seemed unnaturally giddy and was about to drive.

"Nah," he said. "I only had one beer."

"What's so funny then?" Benny said.

Dad turned the key in the ignition and used his chin to point at the shiny surprise in Benny's lap.

"I stole Aunt Linda's pie," he said.

"You what?"

Dad answered with a grin and put the car in reverse, checking his mirrors as they backed out of the long driveway.

"I figured it was the least they could do, after ruining Christmas."

Ruth laughed.

"What kind of pie?" Benny wanted to know.

"Caramel apple," Dad reported. "It's her famous pie."

"Yesssss," Benny said.

"She had two of them," Dad said, as if they needed to be convinced. "Plus, there were like four other desserts there that other people brought. They'll never miss it."

But secretly, Ruth liked the idea that they might, that in fact Aunt Linda might stand stock-still in the kitchen, a posture of indignant confusion, arms crossed, searching her brain for where she might have put the errant pie.

"I know I made a second one!" this fantasy Linda said, in Ruth's brain.

At home, Dad and Benny put their pajamas on too. Dad turned on the television and the lights on the Christmas tree, and then he pulled the foil off the top of the pie. It was still warm, and he set it in the middle of the coffee table alongside three forks.

"Ice cream?" he asked.

"Of course!" Benny said.

Dad brought the vanilla in from the freezer, dumped the whole quart in the middle of the pie, and they didn't bother with plates. They destroyed the pie, eating until all evidence of their crime had been consumed. Ruth licked her fork and a smudge of caramel carnage from one knuckle.

Chapter Twenty-Three

~

Palisades, New York, 1999

New Jersey, 1991

When the kids were really small and Thomas was still alive, Ruth occasionally googled Arthur Rodríguez. Not because she wished she had married him instead, and not even because she harbored any harmless fantasies about him, but because she was a frazzled young mother who remembered that she had once loved someone other than her husband, and because the internet was there. This was the first time in human history that an unwashed mother in stained sweatpants with clammy armpits could engage in a kind of Choose-Your-Own-Adventure experience while nursing her child in the middle of the night. She could sit in the glider beside the crib at three in the morning, and she could latch a baby onto her breast, and she could open Facebook and flip the pages back, just a chapter or two, to where she had made one choice. And imagine, just for a few minutes, what her life might be like if she'd made the other.

Arthur was not as handsome as Ruth remembered, which made sense, as they were both older now, but she was startled when she clicked through his older photographs to realize that, even during the years when she'd known him, perhaps his dimples hadn't been as deep as she'd recalled. Perhaps his chocolate-drop eyes were just some regular brown eyes that she'd romanticized in their degree of meltiness because she'd been young and naive and susceptible to infatuation. Arthur Rodríguez was moderately good-looking, but his wife was very pretty, and he gazed at her adoringly in photographs, which made him seem more attractive again. But then he also appeared to have a model car collection he was weirdly proud of, which brought her back to square one. Ruth studied the small Porsches and Mustangs and Corvettes with her mouth hanging slightly open and tried to reconcile her bewilderment. Had she dodged an Arthur-shaped bullet? No, this was endearing, she decided.

Arthur and his wife had a baby of their own, so perhaps his wife was also sitting in a rocking chair somewhere, nursing that baby, and scrolling idly through Facebook, feeling baffled by old boyfriends. Ruth knew that her life would not have been better with Arthur, and not only because he was maybe less dreamy than she'd made him out to be, and also not only because a different husband wouldn't change the fact that she would still have stained sweatpants and clammy armpits and a baby who needed feeding at three in the morning. But mostly because her life could not have been better with anyone than it was with Thomas. Because, despite the fact that he pretended to be inept at packing the diaper bag so she always had to do it, despite the way he left a heap of crumbs beside the toaster every single morning, and despite the fact that he'd been the safer, more logical choice, he was also, in the end, the choice her heart had made, and was still making. She loved him. She loved this life, even when she fell asleep in the glider and woke up to find her nipple shriveled by cold air, and her milk-drunk baby fast asleep with his mouth open.

In college, after they finally, finally met on that autumn afternoon at Gus's Pro Photo in Wodsley, Ruth didn't start dating Arthur Rodríguez right away. They were friends first, and initially, the thrill of being his friend was almost more than Ruth could handle all by itself. Then they became best friends, the kind of friends that can only happen in college. They started hanging out together every day, shopping together, eating their meals together.

Once their friendship was fully established, she stopped being unceasingly distracted by his hotness, so they began studying not-quite-together, but near each other. He was studious, which Ruth found contagious. In between chapters and essays, he would tell her about the girls he liked, even though he didn't like any of them enough to turn the plural into the singular, and Ruth would tell him about Thomas, how cute and interesting he was, how hard they laughed when they were together, and how refreshing it was that they enjoyed each other so much without rushing headlong into a commitment.

Thomas was three years older than them, which at that age seemed like an enormous gap. He was independent, never jealous, entirely self-possessed. Thomas was in graduate school, and didn't have time for nonsense. Thomas had a car and a paid internship and seemed like a man of the world, despite the fact that he still, on occasion and despite Ruth's influence, showed up with his T-shirt tucked into his jeans.

"So are you guys, like, boyfriend and girlfriend now or what?" Arthur asked.

They were sitting across the room from each other in the study lounge in Arthur's dorm because the one in Ruth's dorm was always full of girls who did handstands and push-ups and jumping jacks while they quizzed one another out loud. This lounge was usually empty except for Arthur and Ruth, so they spread out. They each took a whole table and bench to themselves, and when Ruth needed a break, she would lie down on the bench. When she yawned, she could do so very loudly without disturbing anyone but him.

"I don't know," Ruth said. "I feel like Thomas is pretty serious about me." She propped her elbows on the tabletop and focused her gaze on the paper clip she was mutilating. "But we haven't really talked about it. And I don't know if I'm ready for all that."

"You think he is?"

Ruth shrugged. "I mean, he is older. Seems like his partying days are behind him."

Arthur gave her a skeptical look. "Let's be honest, Ruth, do we think this guy ever had partying days?"

Ruth laughed. "Maybe not."

"Yeah."

"Do people still ask each other to be boyfriend and girlfriend?" Ruth said. "Is that a thing, to have a big conversation about it? Or is it just assumed?"

Arthur shrugged. "I wouldn't know."

"Do any of the girls you date ever ask to be your girlfriend?" she said.

"Hell no," he said. "But obviously I discourage that kind of behavior anyway."

Ruth laughed. "But maybe one of them could sneak-attack you and blurt it out when you're unprepared."

"Nah, I'm not that desirable," he said. "I'll be fine."

When Ruth laughed harder than she meant to, he grinned at her with his dimples and his teeth.

"Besides, it's super easy to make a girl stop talking as soon as she says something you don't want to hear," Arthur said, clicking the button on his ballpoint pen.

"Oh, really." She sat up from the bench where she'd been stretched out.

"Yeah." *Click click.* "You just put your mouth on her mouth."

Ruth held herself very still because if she controlled her breathing, then maybe her face wouldn't flush, and if her face didn't flush, maybe he wouldn't see whose mouths she accidentally pictured when he said *your mouth on her mouth.* She could feel her heartbeat at the base of her throat.

"Good God, you're a mess, man," she croaked out with a laugh.

"It's true," Arthur sighed. "I'm glad at least one of us has our shit together in the romance department. Even if he's not your boyfriend."

She smiled, thinking infinitely safer thoughts of funny, kind, smitten Thomas, who stared at her so intensely it sometimes made her eyes water, who always seemed to be aware of her grief, even when Ruth didn't say Titi Lola's name out loud. Thomas, who believed his attendance at weekly mass was in no way incompatible with his dazzling catalog of curse words. *Sure, that's just being Irish,* he would say, and Ruth wondered what liberation it must be, to know with such conviction that you could attribute your eccentricities to a single, uncomplicated origin.

"Would you ever want to move back there?" she'd asked Thomas on their fourth date, and his face had gone uncharacteristically still while he composed the breath to explain to her why, no, he would never move back to Ireland. That was the night he told her that his mother had died when he was twelve, and his father had more or less ceased to function as a parent around the same time. So Thomas had already had this life in mind for a decade or more: a faraway place, a solid education, a beautiful girl, a future less bleak than the past.

Ruth had suppressed her impulse to cry when Thomas shared all of this, but it was a battle not easily won. The result was an immediately deepened intimacy between them, a new lens through which Ruth now considered Thomas perhaps the most compelling person she'd ever met. She admired the way he carried his sadness, neither burying it nor indulging it. He lived well with his grief and turned himself toward happiness as a daily practice. On the days when Lola's absence tormented her, when Ruth walked through the hours with the creaking fragility of a glass figurine, she strived to be more like Thomas, to carry herself like he did, to live happily within the limitations of her sorrow. On those days, he made her laugh, he made her pepperoni pizza from scratch, he gave her the gift of his quiet presence as a barrier against loneliness. Ruth fell for him by inches and hours and, on some days, by galloping light-years. The only time she wasn't thinking about him was when she was thinking about Arthur.

"I mean, I guess Thomas might be my boyfriend." She shrugged, warming to the idea. She was playing with her highlighters now, standing them up like a colorful army, arranging them in rainbow order. "You wanna meet him?" she asked.

"Nope." Arthur surprised her by answering quickly. "No thanks, no need to go that far."

She tried knocking the highlighters down like dominoes, but only the first two fell. "Why not?"

"Do I want to meet the dude who's romancing my girl?" he said.

My girl. Again, she tried the trick of stillness. And again, she felt confident it didn't work. But for once, she did not say anything goofy or regrettable. She did not pretend to engross herself in some other task in order to divert him to an exit ramp. And in fact, beneath the tension, she recognized a new feeling: irritation with Arthur, because she did not want to imperil the giddy possibility of Thomas on the whim of this dimpled boy. She had no interest in belonging to a cadre of besotted girls. Ruth had to figure this out, to disarm it, whatever it was. She looked at her friend evenly, and Arthur met her gaze across the span of the quiet room. There was one empty table between them, and Ruth refused to indulge the image of herself sprawled across that table, flat on her back. She knew what his skin felt like now because she had touched him in the various ways best friends touch each other. She had grabbed his elbow, slung an arm around his shoulder, hugged him. He'd given her a piggyback one time when she wore new shoes and got a blister on her heel. Once, she'd run her hand along the soft fuzz at the back of his head after a haircut. Velvet.

So she already knew what his body felt like in these ways, and there was no need to imagine the feel of his shoulder blades beneath her hands as well. No good reason to do it. But he called her *my girl* and then looked straight at her with those chocolate-drop eyes, and the air in the room was absolutely dripping with it. She didn't imagine it. She knew he felt it too.

Ruth held perfectly still until it passed.

The plan for Arthur to help Ruth practice her Spanish never came to fruition because Ruth was too ashamed of the decrepit state of her first language. At the beginning, he tried speaking to her in Spanish, but she always answered in English, and sometimes he even had to repeat himself slowly when she didn't understand, and then before they knew it, their English habits were entrenched and there was no going back. He invited her, often and enthusiastically, to come with him to Boricua House events, but Ruth always declined for two reasons: One, she didn't need it. All the yearning she'd experienced before, to meet people who understood this part of her, had been satisfied by Arthur. And two, she was terrified. She and Arthur had only known each other seven weeks, and already he was the best friend she'd ever had outside her family. Better than Jennifer and Kathy put together. Better than Jenny, even. Ruth was terrified that if Arthur observed her in that Boricua House environment, he'd identify something fraudulent, whatever it was those girls had seen the first day she'd tried to walk in there seeking friendship. He would change his mind about her.

When they were alone together, Ruth didn't worry about any of that. When they shared stories about their families and childhoods, there was an exhilarating shorthand between them, feelings no one else except Benny had ever understood. All her life, Ruth had been searching for the means to articulate her experiences, and now she didn't need to. With

Arthur, she could rest and know that he understood. She didn't mind the desert-island quality of their friendship. Ruth was accustomed to some degree of isolation.

Now it was week eight of their friendship, the week before Thanksgiving break when Mama would come visit her on campus and take Ruth out for Thanksgiving dinner to a local Spanish restaurant and then announce over the pumpkin flan that, in the wake of Lola's death, she'd finally done what she should've done years ago: she'd put the St. Louis house on the market. But now with Lola gone, Mama couldn't bear the thought of going back to Puerto Rico alone, not even with Benny there, so she was looking at property here in New Jersey instead, in nearby Montclair. This eventuality thrilled Ruth, though she was loath to admit this to Mama, who, Ruth now realized, was definitely and pathetically her best friend in the world besides Arthur. Well, during that week eight, Arthur invited her to the Boricua House annual dance. Perhaps *invited* was not the right word.

"You're coming with me," he said. "Period."

"I don't have anything to wear," she tried.

"You don't have to get dressed up, it's not like that. You can wear jeans, Timberlands, whatever you want. And they'll have a DJ and some dope food and it's *so fun*. It will be awesome."

They were walking across the quad on a Sunday afternoon when he said this. The dance was two days from now, the night before the break. The sky was lodged above them, the color of slate, the color of autumn. Ruth felt like crying.

"I don't know how to salsa," Ruth said. She did, but only with Mama, only barefoot on Titi Lola's balcony in Luquillo, a memory that brought her ever closer to tears.

"I'll teach you," Arthur said.

She stopped abruptly and sat down on a passing bench. She was wearing a light jacket and her backpack because they were headed to the library to return some books. He sat down beside her and they both leaned their elbows on their knees.

"I get that you're nervous." His voice was soft, coaxing. "Help me understand."

She shivered, even though it wasn't cold. She felt like a recalcitrant child, but there was no way she could say the words that were beginning to form in her mind. They felt hazy, as if they were spelled out in a scattering of seeds, and she might make the choice just to blow across them and send them flying. *I've never had a Puerto Rican friend before. I don't know how to do community. I don't know who I am outside my family.* Troubling realizations all. She was embarrassed.

"You're worried about, what, about getting rejected?"

That was partly it.

"You worried you won't fit in?" he prompted.

It was both a salve and an irritation, the way he so often knew her thoughts before she said them, her feelings before she felt them.

"I don't know." She shrugged. "Maybe."

"Give yourself a chance." He nudged her knee with his knee.

"Did I ever tell you about the first time I went in there? The only time I went in there?" she asked.

"Yeah," he said. "That sucks, it does. I'm sorry that happened to you. But you can't let one bad experience ruin the opportunity to be part of something so amazing, something you've never had before."

She tucked her lips inside her mouth and rubbed them against each other. She sat up straighter and blew out a big breath as a happy couple strolled past them holding hands.

"I don't know, I guess nobody wants to be rejected twice, right?"

"Yeah, but that was just one girl," he said.

"It was two girls. The only two girls who were there."

"Okay, two girls. But still. It wasn't everybody."

"It was literally everybody who was there that day! And they called me *blanquita*."

A word Papamío had once called her in affection, now a slur. It was a word that described a thing about herself that was both true and not true, and that Ruth was powerless to affect in any case: her whiteness. Ruth hadn't changed, but the value of that word had, the world had, and Ruth felt the pointed end of it where it lodged in her skin, the color of which was arguably white and arguably not white, depending on who you asked. No one ever asked Ruth herself.

"That was horrible," he said. "So don't let them win. Show 'em who you are."

"Who am I, though?" She reached for a laugh.

"You have to come," he said. "It'll be great, you'll see. You'll wonder why you didn't do it sooner. You'll be so pissed you let one mean girl rob two years from you."

"Two mean girls," she said, but when she looked at him, she knew he'd won. He bumped his shoulder against hers and then tucked her whole body under his arm. "It's gonna be so fun!"

"Maybe you're right," she said.

"I am." He grinned.

Maybe it would be fine.

Ruth would never be able to say for certain whether it was the same girl who had (not) greeted her that day at the (un)welcome desk, because more than two years had elapsed, and in any case, Ruth had done her level best to eradicate the details of that memory from her brain. It's possible the girl at the dance just inspired such an identical feeling in Ruth that she had conflated them into one awful person. But in any case, the moment Arthur held open the door for her and she walked through it into the party room the Boricua House had reserved in the student union, there she stood, not ten feet away, giving Ruth a whole up-and-down swoop of eternal judgment. Ruth froze, of course, certain she'd made a mistake in coming here. But Arthur moved in behind her, put his hand on the small of her back.

"Gimme a sec," he whispered.

And then Arthur stepped past her, between Ruth and the girl. And her beloved Arthur hugged this loathsome person, who was still glaring at Ruth over his shoulder. Arthur whispered something in the girl's ear, and then all the shapes of her face melted in Ruth's direction. Arthur took the girl by the hand and pulled her over to Ruth.

"Ruth, meet Danielle," he said. "Danielle, this is my best friend, Ruth."

And despite everything, Ruth felt proud when he said *best friend.* She stuck her hand out to Danielle, but Danielle shocked her by stepping right past the outstretched hand and embracing her instead. "So nice to meet you, finally!" Danielle squealed. "I'm so glad you came, it's going to be such a fun night!"

Ruth's mouth opened, but nothing came out. Arthur elbowed her in the ribs, and then her voice emerged.

"Yes," she struggled to say. "Nice to meet you too."

"Any requests for the DJ?" She raised her eyebrows and grinned.

"Nah, not yet," Arthur said.

"Ruth?" Danielle grasped both of Ruth's hands in hers. She squeezed them, and Ruth didn't know how to disentangle herself from the dubious clutch of Danielle's sudden affections, but she felt certain the DJ question was a test. So she allowed a long moment to pass while she flipped through Mama's entire record collection in her mind.

"Anything by Willie Colón."

"Girl, yes!" Danielle said. But when she added "¡Wepa!" Ruth couldn't say why, but she felt sure the girl was making fun of her.

Danielle spun away, headed across the dance floor to the DJ booth, and Ruth leaned in to Arthur's ear. "What did you say to her?"

He stood up straight and looked her in the face. "What do you mean?" All innocent.

"When we walked in," Ruth said. "She was giving me such a dirty look, and then you talked to her, and all of a sudden she's my best friend."

Arthur laughed at Ruth's air quotes around *best friend*.

"I just told her you were all right," he said.

She looked closely at his face. "That's it?"

"And I told her you're Puerto Rican."

"Ah," Ruth said, but it rankled her, that Arthur had to vouch for her, had to present her bona fides. And it rankled her that, before Danielle knew she was Puerto Rican, she'd been so determined to make her feel unwelcome. And it had worked. Ruth had felt it down the back of her neck.

"Listen, these girls are sweethearts," he said. "I've known them all since freshman year. But they're protective, you know?"

The disco ball was spinning colors across the dance floor, and Ruth followed the lights with her eyes.

"What do you mean *protective*? Like, of you?"

"No, I mean. Yeah, maybe. But more, they're just protective of each other, you know? Of this community."

This community where I don't belong, Ruth thought.

"You'll understand when you get to know them."

"But how is anyone supposed to *get to know them*," (air quotes again) "if that's their standard greeting?"

Ruth and Arthur were skirting the dance floor while they talked, and now they had arrived at the drinks table, where Arthur snagged a plastic cup for each of them filled with something bright pink with a scent of artificial fruit.

"You have to understand where they're coming from. Most of them grew up here, they're from New Jersey or New York, right? And they're tight. It's a tight community. But a lot of them have never even been to Puerto Rico. They're a hundred percent Puerto Rican, both parents, all four grandparents, whatever." He sipped from his little red straw. "To people here in New Jersey? They're Puerto Rican. But then Danielle went down there for the first time last summer, to Ponce, and stayed with her Mom's cousin and her whole big-ass family, and she expected a warm welcome, like she was going to have a transformative homecoming experience or some shit."

"And?"

"And she got there and they treated her like garbage. They made fun of her accent. They told her Nuyoricans are a whole different breed."

"Oh." Ruth looked across the dance floor to where Danielle was stretched up on tiptoe, shouting up to the DJ, and her heart softened. But not enough.

So we are the same, Ruth thought. How unexpected. There should be a kinship between them, but instead, there was this. Ruth found that the new information, and the empathy it opened in her, made her feel even more annoyed on the back end.

"So then she should understand what it's like!" Ruth said.

"You're right, she should," Arthur said.

"And she should be nicer."

"A hundred percent."

Ruth bored her eyes into his, but she did not ask why he chose to be friends with such a bitch (it was 1991, and she still used the word *bitch* then, to describe girls who were mean to her) because she knew how that sounded, and after all, she was not Arthur's girlfriend. In fact, she might even be Thomas's. Ruth was swamped with longing for Thomas in that moment. The safe, simple way he adored her. The uncomplicated lines of their romance. There was nothing muddy between them, nothing that sounded a note of fear or loss. With Thomas, she was just happy. Herself.

"I think she might have a little thing for me," Arthur confessed then, above the increasing volume of El Gran Combo.

"Well, of course she does," Ruth said, sipping from her own skinny red straw.

Perhaps the reason for the animosity had nothing to do with anything else, Ruth thought. Wouldn't that be refreshing, if it was just the obvious thing? Ruth had arrived with the cutest boy on campus. Of course she'd find all manner of weaponry aimed in her direction.

"So then, if you want me to make friends with them," she said, "maybe all you need to do is let them know I'm not their competition." It was impossible not to notice the way various girls pretended not to glance at him from different corners of the room.

"Yeah. Good point," he said, finishing his drink.

Except later that night, on the way back to Ruth's dorm room, after he'd danced with her all night, and of course he was a great dancer (which reminded Ruth that in fact she *could* salsa, rather well actually, not to mention merengue, samba, and bachata), Arthur hit the emergency stop button in the elevator in her building. And then he backed her against the wall, and when he pressed his body against hers, and all the scent of him lit her up like a torch, and his tongue tasted like a maraschino cherry, it was exactly like Ruth had always known it would be.

She wasn't proud of the way it all happened, but Ruth told herself that she and Thomas had no agreement to be exclusive, even though she knew with relative certainty that he wasn't seeing anyone else, and that he likely believed she wasn't either. Ruth didn't want to stop seeing Thomas, even as her relationship with Arthur intensified, even as he suggested that she break it off with her other man. Arthur was cool about it. He didn't make demands. But even then, some quiet corner of her mind was whispering that maybe she loved Arthur for all the little gaps in her that he filled up, all the longed-for answers he provided, and because he was incredibly hot. And maybe that wasn't enough of a reason to really fall in love with a person.

Still, her feelings for Arthur were explosive, so it surprised her how tightly she clung to Thomas. The notion of breaking up with him made her feel sick with a low-grade panic; her every instinct was to cleave to him. Even as she fell in love with Arthur bit by bit, she realized in horror that she was also already in love with Thomas. More than a bit. And none of that had anything to do with similar childhoods or simple lust. Thomas could deliver her to hysterical laughter without uttering a single word. She felt smarter and safer and less worried whenever she was with him. When she was ready, Ruth knew she could reveal every unattractive piece of herself to Thomas, and those flaws would only endear her to him. Thomas hadn't yet said *I love you*, but Ruth already knew that he did, and what's more, she knew it was a feeling so deep and true that it could survive the ordeal of her future vulnerability. But she wasn't ready.

On the last Friday night in January, Ruth, who had definitely used the word *slut* before to describe girls in similar predicaments, feigned a headache and opted to stay home alone, rather than going out with either Thomas or Arthur. She bought a phone card in the student union and, from her dorm room, called Benny at home in San Juan. He'd gone back three and a half years ago, and if Ruth had any initial misgivings about her brother returning to Puerto Rico, the final remnants of those reservations had been dispelled during the week of Lola's funeral. Benny knew where he belonged, and he'd made it happen. Everything about him had expanded and settled once he took his place back home in San Juan, so Ruth's envy was overshadowed by admiration.

"How are Mamamía and Papamío doing?" she asked.

The silence on the long-distance phone line was never really silent. It crackled and hummed.

"Ah," Benny exhaled. "You know. Bien y bien mal." Good and terrible. "Mamamía keeps a smile on her face, food on the table. But she used to hum when she ironed Papamío's shirts."

Ruth wished she could take some further measure of their suffering and fold it into her own, distribute the collective load of their grief so it might weigh evenly across all of their shoulders. She felt tears gathering in her throat, but they felt selfish, so she washed them down with a sip of tea.

"You still dating that girl Pamela?" she changed the subject.

"Yeah," he said. "Ruthie, she's really great."

She smiled.

"What about you?" he asked.

She took another sip of her tea and tried to gather courage. She'd expected him to ask, she'd walked him into the question precisely so she could confess, but now that the moment was here, she was filled with shame, which, again, felt selfish. So she took one deep breath in and then told her brother everything. She spared no reprehensible detail, and Benny didn't flinch.

"That sounds really hard, Ruth," he said, without a glimmer of judgment.

His compassion made her feel even guiltier. "I have to figure this out," she said. "I feel horrible." There was some security in knowing her confessor was so far away.

"But you're so young," Benny said kindly. "Don't be too hard on yourself. It's not like you're married. Being heartbroken is part of growing up, think of it that way. Maybe you're just ushering these guys through a rite of passage."

Ruth snorted. "I'm sure they'll be enormously grateful."

"Well, they should be."

"Maybe you should come visit," she said. "And you can pick for me."

"Hey, that sounds super appealing, but no thanks." He laughed.

The lightness between them was not enough to temper the tide of Ruth's misery. She started to cry. She knew this was ridiculous, but she wanted Benny to understand that the situation was causing her real anguish.

"But how can I be in love with two people at once?" she asked.

"Well, you can't be," Benny said.

But she knew with every certainty and for the first time in her life that her big brother was wrong.

"There's only one of them you can't live without," he said. "Which one is it?"

It was both.

"I don't know," she said wretchedly.

"Then maybe you're not really in love with either of them."

He was wrong, wrong, wrong.

Benny was quiet for a long moment then, and Ruth noticed that her tears were flowing so freely her pillow was soaked beneath her. The headache she'd faked earlier was now real, her sinuses corked from all the crying.

"I don't know what to do," she whispered.

"You know what I think?" Benny said.

"Hmm."

"I think the reason this is so hard is that it feels like you have to choose between the two halves of yourself."

Ruth frowned in her bed beneath the covers. She wanted to reject this theory outright, but she couldn't.

"You think you're going to marry one of these guys?"

Ruth didn't answer. She didn't deserve to marry either of them. And besides, she was twenty years old, in love with the whole world. Marriage seemed an insane prospect altogether.

"So, let's say one day you marry one of these guys," Benny said. "Then you're going to have Latino babies or you're going to have Irish babies. So maybe it feels like this is your last chance to be one thing or the other."

She opened her mouth to say it wasn't that simple. There were arguments to be made here. She closed her mouth again without making them.

"Think about it. Is it just a coincidence you got yourself tangled up in this mess right after Lola died?"

Ruth sat up in her bed and reached for the box of tissues on her nightstand. She blew her nose.

"Maybe you feel like you've just lost this huge connection, this major part of yourself," Benny said. "So now there's even more at stake, and you have to choose."

She could feel her ribs quavering beneath her skin.

"It would be totally understandable if you felt like that, but it's not true, Ruth. It's a grief-illusion."

She flopped back on her pillow and tossed her spent tissue on the floor. "I don't think it's the whole story. But maybe that's part of it. I never thought about it like that before."

"Well, it's hard to psychoanalyze yourself when you're in the middle of it," he said. "Plus, who has time for self-reflection when you have ten boyfriends?"

"Oh my God, Benny, stop!"

He laughed. "They're both lucky, that's the main thing."

She smiled. "I wish you could meet them. They're so different."

"Okay, so then does one of them make you happier?"

Maybe? Ruth shook her head.

"Is it easier to be yourself around one of them?"

Thomas.

This was the first easy answer. Still, she didn't say it out loud because even as it came to her, simply and quickly, she was aware that there was some hypocrisy in the answer. She hadn't told Thomas everything; Arthur knew. And of course there was also the fact that, although the relationship with Arthur was more capricious, Ruth liked the ways he stretched her. So she didn't feel exactly like the person she wanted to be when she was with him, so what? She still *liked* the person she *wanted* to be when they were together. And there was a thrill in the striving she wasn't quite ready to relinquish.

"You just have to be honest with everybody involved," Benny said. "Starting with yourself."

Ugh. Benny's benevolence aside, Ruth hated herself a little bit. That was some honesty to start with.

"I love you, Benny," she said before they hung up the phone that night. She was sure she had said that to him before, but she couldn't remember when. "You're a good big brother."

"I really am," he agreed. And then, "Yo también te quiero."

And she cried all over again, starting from scratch.

In time, Ruth would come clean to Thomas. She'd explain how and when things with Arthur had shifted. Thomas would try to stop her midway through. He'd tell her that whatever he suspected, he didn't actually want to know, but she would need to unburden herself. And when she did, Thomas would break up with her and leave her bereft but certain, finally, in the way she hadn't been during those many months when she'd been torn between the two men she eventually came to think of as the two loves of her life. (Ursa Major and Ursa Minor. Greater and lesser Antilles. Dale Earnhardt and Dale Earnhardt Jr. Mama and Dad.)

Eventually, Ruth would manage to convince Thomas against all hope to take her back. She would do this by taking full responsibility, explaining the theoretical pitfalls of her grief and bisected psychology without making excuses, and then by being incredibly patient while he made her wait. She spent idiotic portions of her paychecks from Gus's Pro Photo to buy him flowers every week he wasn't speaking to her. She left them on his doormat or the hood of his car or stuffed into his mailbox without a note. Until finally, after eleven weeks, eleven bouquets, when she showed up at his apartment on a Thursday afternoon with a fistful of purple tulips, he opened the door, and he let her in. Ruth would love Thomas madly, and for the rest of his life, for giving her that second chance.

She would break it off with Arthur, of course, tenderly, but without much sorrow. Even their rousing, bounteous friendship had to go. Arthur would bow out sadly but gracefully, only to reappear with some regularity and try to change her mind, once with a ring, on bended knee. She would briefly imagine herself as Ruth Rodríguez. Of course she would, and the idea would cause her to flush with heat. But then she'd remember the intense heartache of her previous entanglement, and she'd know beyond all doubt that she was supposed to be Ruth Hayes. Not Rodríguez. Hayes.

But her faltering indecision had lasted far too long.

§

After she and Thomas were married, Arthur mostly stayed away. Eventually, with the exception of those middle-of-the-night internet searches, she seldom even thought of him anymore. When she did, she marveled at herself, couldn't imagine how she'd ever behaved so appallingly. In time (and *The Bachelor* notwithstanding), she almost believed what Benny had told her, that being in love with two people at once was an impossibility, nothing more than a grief-illusion.

It didn't matter anymore anyway. Arthur had played an important role in Ruth's life. He'd emboldened her to reconcile San Juan Ruth with

Missouri Ruth and East Coast Ruth, to merge all three of her disconnected selves into one authentic, self-assured person. He taught her to
find friendship in unexpected places, without preconceptions or embarrassment or worry. He ushered her across a threshold she'd failed to tra-
verse alone, and on the far side, she discovered a new way of moving
through the world that did not involve hiding anything. Arthur had been
her first of many Puerto Rican friends. Her first of many mixed-race
friends. He'd been her first real friend. So yes, it had been painful to let
him go.

But then they all grew up, Ruth and her not-quite-dueling boyfriends.
Whatever had happened in their lives before marriage and children was
lightness and folly when compared to the heft and scent of her baby in
the crook of one arm. One at a time, her children were born and made
a mockery of Ruth's forgotten heartache. From this vantage point, it
seemed ludicrous that she had ever contemplated these future babies
with any kind of scrutiny or torment, as if anything about them mattered
more than their perfect existence, as if these three babies weren't exactly
the three babies she was destined to have and to mother, no matter what.

And then thirteen years into their family, Thomas died.

After that, Ruth never googled Arthur Rodríguez again.

At her midnight laptop, on the night her eighteen-year-old daughter
announced she was moving to San Juan, for the first time in many years,
Ruth considered it. What would be the harm in a little escapism, a trip
to the other side? She opened Instagram, opened the search function,
and typed his name. Her pinky finger hovered over the *return* key. One
second passed. Two. Three.

She swatted the laptop closed.

Chapter Twenty-Four

~

San Juan, Puerto Rico
2022

In late April, Grandma came to visit, and on her second night in San Juan, she invited Daisy to dinner at the Vanderbilt in Condado.

"Wear something nice," Grandma said.

Daisy wasn't offended because she understood that her funky thrift-store style was unpredictable, and she appreciated the heads-up.

"Have you been to the Vanderbilt before?"

Daisy had not.

"Oh, it's just marvelous! You'll love it!" Grandma said. "Very classic, right up your alley. Think old Hollywood starlet."

"Ooh, nice!" Daisy said. "Are we talking . . . like Bette Davis? Or more Brigitte Bardot?"

"Well, it's still San Juan, dear," Grandma said. "Go for the bombshell, of course."

The Vanderbilt was categorically upscale, perhaps the fanciest place Daisy had ever been for a meal, and she felt perfectly dressed in a silver and cream brocade wiggle shift, vintage, of course, which she paired with black Converse. When the host showed her to their table, Grandma had already arrived, and was seated behind a glass of red wine.

"Oh, very mod!" Grandma said as Daisy leaned in to kiss her cheek. "You got it just right!"

Daisy stood back and did a turn so Grandma could admire the dress before she took her seat, which was a huge leather armchair, heavy enough that it required the assistance of the host to push toward the table.

"This place is amazing!" Daisy said, as the host placed the leather menu directly into her hands. He lifted the bottle of red wine from the table and showed Daisy the label before pouring some into her waiting glass. When he was gone, she leaned in to whisper across the low candle between them, "So luxurious!"

Grandma smiled and settled deeper into her own leather armchair. "This is the life!"

Daisy kept one eye on Grandma as they studied their menus. They all agreed—*they* being Daisy's mom and brothers, Benny and his family— that Grandma's memory issues seemed to have eased up in recent months, or at least the decline they'd witnessed before the pandemic had been arrested. Daisy suspected that her grandmother had gotten herself onto medication, but she didn't know for sure. Grandma still refused to talk about it, but whatever secret methods she was using to treat her symptoms, she'd managed to allay the worst of their collective fears. Still, she was seventy-four, and Mom and Benny didn't like her traveling on her own. They handed her off like a baton in a relay race when she insisted on flying solo, Mom getting her as far as the gate in JFK, and Benny waiting in the arrivals hall at Luis Muñoz Marín International Airport on the other end. When she was *in* San Juan, however, there was nothing they could do to curtail her independence. Grandma called friends, booked cabs, scheduled shopping trips, made dinner reservations, and almost never told anyone where she was going. They all watched the Find My dot on her cell phone map to provide themselves with the limited relief of that information. To Daisy, Grandma seemed as sharp as ever.

"What's good here?" Daisy asked.

Grandma looked up from her menu. "Oh, everything!"

Daisy laughed, running her finger down the menu and noting that the selections were not local, the cuisine not Puerto Rican. This restaurant could've been in any cosmopolitan city, Paris, Dubai, Tokyo. She felt a twinge then, a wish that this fancy place might assert its Puerto

Ricanness. Still, Daisy, who had taken to eating cereal at least two meals a day and who, since moving back to San Juan for her second try, occasionally made a whole cheap, lazy dinner out of carrot sticks and hummus, was very much onboard with the meal, which arrived on bone china plates covered with silver domes that the waiter removed at precisely the same second and whisked away. Grandma's was a curried swordfish with chickpeas and pancetta. Daisy's was a Berkshire porkchop with colorful lentils in a tomato glaze.

"Good, right?" Grandma said, after her first bite.

The whole experience of the meal was a delight, all five of Daisy's senses sparked and hummed.

"We used to eat here when I was a little girl, all the time," Grandma said. "It was Papamío's favorite place."

Daisy stopped chewing while she mulled this over. "It's been here that long?" She looked around, and realized that, though she hadn't given the idea any conscious deliberation, she had vaguely presumed that all of this old-world glamour was artificial, manufactured for the wealthy clientele.

"Forever!" Grandma stabbed a glazed mushroom onto her fork. "The Vanderbilt is a San Juan institution!"

And just like that, Daisy's mind hauled open yet again. It was a feeling she'd become accustomed to since coming back to live here this time. She thought she knew San Juan from her summers here, from her pandemic-shortened stint a couple years ago. But there was still so much she was learning about her new hometown. She recognized the feeling of an assumption being blown apart. The Vanderbilt, a San Juan institution. And why shouldn't it be? If Paris or Dubai or Tokyo had restaurants like this, then of course San Juan would too.

"You want dessert?" Grandma asked.

They ordered crema catalana with toffee popcorn, and it was perhaps the best thing Daisy had ever put in her mouth. When it was gone, Grandma grew uncharacteristically quiet, looking into her steaming cup of coffee as if trying to read some omen there. There was still half a bottle of wine on the table.

"You okay, Grandma?" Daisy asked.

Grandma smiled, gesturing to Daisy's empty cup. "You all done with your coffee?" she asked.

"Yeah, but take your time," Daisy said. "I'm in no hurry."

"Oh no." Grandma chuckled. "You misunderstand me, dear. It's time for you to run along. I'm meeting a friend for a drink."

"Oh!" Daisy laughed. "Well, aren't you full of surprises!"

"You don't know the half of it!"

"But how are you getting home afterward?" Daisy asked, hearing her own mother's voice coming out of her mouth.

Grandma used her face to visibly disapprove of the question. "I have spent a good few decades on this planet, and some number of those decades right here in this beautiful city! I am well capable of getting myself home!" she admonished Daisy.

"Sure, until you go and drink three bottles of wine," Daisy said, gathering up her tote bag. "I know what you get up to, young lady."

Grandma laughed. "Yes, well. It's a hotel. Worse comes to worst, I'm pretty sure they have beds upstairs."

Daisy laughed, wrestling herself out of the enormous armchair and leaning over to kiss her grandmother's cheek. "All right, try to stay out of trouble," she said. "And thank you for the most amazing meal I've had in a very long time. Maybe ever."

"You're welcome, dear. Now scram before my boyfriend shows up and feels obliged to entertain you."

"Boyfriend!?" Daisy said.

"Shoo!"

§

Daisy's days in San Juan had taken on an erratic but comforting rhythm in the months since her return. Once she found the perfect space, and negotiated and signed an excellent lease, she spent every available hour preparing for the grand opening of the Double Down, and as little time possible worrying about the rupture this decision had caused with her mom. She was too busy and exhausted to actively fret about it, but Daisy missed her mother, and felt hurt that Mom was too stubborn to support her. They still talked every week or so by phone, but their conversations were stilted in a way they never had been before. Daisy spent most of her energy trying not to talk about the store, but because her whole life right now was the store, she had little else to say. On the far end of the phone line, she could sense her mother sifting through possible topics, searching for something safe to discuss. What could they talk about that wouldn't tip them back down the same old chute? Daisy's refusal of college, her doomed future, her mother's intractable disappointment. The conversations either blew up or petered out. There was never a happy, healthy end.

"I'll call you next week, Mom," Daisy would say.

"I'll be here."

Daisy still worked with Benny, managing the properties that were closest to her apartment, but she now thought of that job as her side hustle. The Double Down was her calling. Her new space was large and airy, more warehouse than shop, in a low-rent neighborhood full of nightclubs. She'd procured two major investors, a half dozen micro-investors, and a small business loan with Grandma on board as cosigner (under the condition that she never reveal her cosigner's name to her mother). Her Kickstarter campaign had also been a success, and Daisy applied every single dollar to her budget. Friends helped her install the new lighting and replace the cracked toilet in the tiny bathroom, but she had to hire a contractor to refinish the concrete floors. By early spring of 2022, the space was nearly ready. Next she had to fill it, and for that, she would need a truck. She called Benny to see if he had any leads on something cheap through the garage.

"Yeah, Mama's friend Candido has a huge fleet of trucks and he replaces them pretty frequently," Benny said. "He's always got something for sale. Let me give him a call."

By the end of that week, Daisy was the proud owner of a rusty 2002 Chevy Silverado of indeterminate previous color. The truck was a year younger than she was, and she drove it to every corner of the island, filling its bed with castoffs, the occasional gem hidden among the detritus. She hauled everything back to her new space, cleaned it, polished it, and arranged it artfully. At the end of each day, she was physically sore from manual labor. Her hands were chapped from scrubbing and washing, and she felt like she was now permanently covered in a thin layer of sticky dust. Sometimes, after a full day's exhausting work, she would have to drive herself back to Condado and spend the whole evening cleaning bathrooms and changing sheets at one of Benny's apartments, getting it ready for visitors arriving the next day. Occasionally she'd fall asleep on the couch in one of those apartments waiting for the towels to come out of the dryer. Through every hour of it, she was aware of her good fortune.

Late at night, Daisy retreated to her own little apartment, her paradise, where she'd kick her shoes into the closet and drag her bare feet along the shag carpet while she waited for her toast to pop. Then she'd spread the newspaper out across the table and cover a yellow legal pad with notes about upcoming estate sales, auctions, foreclosures, going-out-of-business sales. She called and visited literally every single hotel, big or small, in Puerto Rico (she believed), where she worked hard to ingratiate herself to any willing party who might tip her off when they were about to refresh their decor. Now she had a lead on a sick chandelier in Ponce. Daisy had never been happier or more exhausted. She imagined this was how a newly ordained priest must feel. She'd found her calling, and thrown herself in with abandon. Sometimes in the quiet of those nights, she thought about the choices she'd been making, and she reflected on the fact that she was only free to make them because hers was a life of privilege. On the nights when she felt clear enough to broach this conversation with her mom, to acknowledge her entitlement and lay herself open to honor her mother's grievances, Daisy invariably looked at the clock and realized it was too late to call home. *Maybe tomorrow*, she would think.

Meanwhile, her final decision would be when to open. Carlos thought a soft opening would work best, would allow her to begin recouping some of her initial investment even while she worked on finishing touches. Then again, Carlos had also suggested that she call the shop the Other Cheek, so his ideas weren't necessarily dependable. Daisy knew she'd only get one chance to impress her first-time customers. She had to wow them. Her forays to Arecibo, Rincón, and Humacao had turned up treasures, but not enough of them. Daisy's inventory wasn't quite there yet. She needed a line on more old people. Stylish old people. She wondered if hitting up the nursing homes was too macabre.

One of Stefani's friends had come through with an antique cash register that still functioned, and which weighed about a thousand pounds. Daisy was in the shop late, fiddling with the buttons and trays, figuring out how everything worked, when her phone rang. It was an ancient landline, of course, with the same shrill jangle Daisy had come to expect from a telephone, but it still scared her enough to send a wash of goosebumps up the back of her neck when it rang late at night in the quiet shop.

"Hello?"

"Daisy!" It was Grandma. She'd been here almost three weeks and, between Daisy's grueling work hours and the rigorous demands on Grandma's dance card, they'd hardly spent any time together at all since their swanky dinner at the Vanderbilt.

"Grandma, hi!" Daisy said, wiping sweat from her forehead. She was trying to save money on air-conditioning until the customers came.

"Hello, dear," Grandma said. "Listen, I know you're busy. Are you at the shop?"

"Yes!" Daisy decided not to tell her that she'd just called the landline at the shop. "Getting ready to head home for the night," she said instead.

"Such a hard worker!" Grandma said.

"Tell that to Mom, would you?"

"She'll come around, dear. Give her time."

Daisy sat down on her stool.

"I hope I'll get to see the shop before I head back?" Grandma asked then.

"When do you go?"

"Tuesday."

Daisy looked around the space, tried to see it through someone else's eyes. What would it feel like to walk in here for the first time? A friend had made paintings for the walls, all of which were gorgeous, La Perla at dusk, a cascade of ruffled skirts in the motion of bomba, a gap-toothed child holding a mound of bright red beans in the bowl of his cupped hands. The colors were warm and vivid, and the lighting all around the shop was opulent. The merchandise gleamed from salvaged bookshelves and dressers and tables. Every imaginable color of chintz, gauze, gingham, and lace draped from hooks and hangers. A dressmaker's form wore a tangerine jumpsuit and a silk scarf. All the treasures of a bygone world surrounded Daisy, everything restored and repurposed and made meaningful again because of her efforts and imagination, her ability to illuminate the magic in ordinary things. She turned in a full circle, surveying this sanctuary she had created out of nothing, and she literally swelled with pride. It came in through her lungs and stood her up a little taller. So she wasn't ready to open just yet, but in that moment Daisy decided she was ready to share it with her grandmother. Her first customer.

"What about tomorrow?" she said.

"Oh!" Grandma said. "Is it ready?"

Daisy shrugged. "Close enough."

"Oh, I can't wait! That sounds perfect," Grandma said. "But there's something else I need you to help me with first."

Daisy caught El Suspiro before it escaped from her lips. So she had a lot to do, so what? Her grandmother would be leaving for New York in three days, and Daisy's heart would ache from stretching after her.

"Of course," she said. "Name it."

Grandma gave her an address in Luquillo, and Daisy jotted it down.

"Can you meet me there around noon tomorrow?" Grandma asked.

"Sure thing." Daisy studied the address in her own handwriting. She thought she recognized it. "Isn't that one of Benny's apartments?"

Daisy had keys to all of Benny's properties, even the ones that weren't on her roster, so she let herself in when she arrived. Grandma was already there, sitting quietly at the round dining table in front of the sliding balcony doors. She must have arrived only a few minutes before, because the air conditioner was running but it was still warm in the room.

"Hello, sweet girl!" Grandma stood up and kissed Daisy on the cheek.

"Hi, Grandma!" Daisy dumped her bag on the table. "Do you really have to go back on Tuesday?" she asked. "Can't you stay a little longer?"

"Oh, stop fussing," Grandma said, walking into the kitchenette and drawing a glass out of the cabinet, which she promptly filled with water from the tap. She handed it across the counter to Daisy. "Drink this, you look overheated."

Daisy resisted the urge to smell her own armpits. Hygiene had been minimal lately. There was no time. She gulped the water and tried to blow her sticky hair off her forehead. Grandma emerged from behind the counter.

"Have you been to this apartment before?" she asked Daisy.

"I don't think so. I'd remember that view." She moved back toward the table and stood beside her grandmother, looking out at the ocean.

"It was my sister Lola's apartment," Grandma said.

"Oh!"

"She left it to me, and I gave it to Benny to manage. That's how he got started in the property business. He saw there was good income in it, good potential."

"Wow, I had no idea," Daisy said.

"Lola lived here, though, she didn't rent it out," Grandma went on. "But she had a great mind for things like that. She knew how to make smart investments."

Daisy nodded. "I've heard so many stories about her from Mom over the years, I feel like I knew her."

Grandma nodded. "Come," she said. "I want to show you something."

She turned and wandered back through the living room and down the short hallway that led to the bedroom and bath. Daisy set her drained glass on the counter and followed. At the end of the hall was a locked door. Grandma drew a key out of her pocket and fitted it into the lock, which was sticky from disuse in the salty seaside air. Eventually, the key turned with a squeaky scratching sound, and Daisy stepped back to give Grandma space to haul the door open. Inside, the closet was much bigger than Daisy expected, almost the size of another small bedroom, and it was stacked floor to ceiling with boxes and bags.

"What is all this, Grandma?" Daisy had become an expert in assessing a possible mother lode of old stuff. Her heart quickened.

"Storage," Grandma said. "Help me. Grab that one."

Daisy lifted the cardboard box Grandma indicated and pulled it down from the top of the stack. Its flaps were tucked in on themselves, but it wasn't sealed.

"Go ahead, open it."

Daisy did as she was instructed. Inside was a collection of cloth drawstring bags with names printed on the outside that Daisy recognized. Dior. Louis Vuitton. Chanel. She forgot to breathe as she pulled out the first bag and opened it. Inside was an unassuming camel-colored handbag with navy trim and a gold buckle. Daisy pulled the bag out and examined it. She opened the clasp and found there was still a receipt inside. Someone had paid an ungodly amount of money for this Gucci handbag in January 1951, and it was in mint condition. It did not have the tag still attached, but it did appear to be barely used. Every item in her shop taken collectively might not match the value of this single handbag. She placed it carefully back in its bag and pulled the drawstring closed. Her hands shook as she opened the next bag to discover a pair of black slingback heels with a crusting of jewels across the toes, size eight, also like new. Daisy examined the immaculate, unscuffed soles. The tag inside the left shoe said Prada.

"Gorgeous," Daisy whispered reverently.

"You like them?" Grandma asked. "They don't really seem like your style."

"Maybe not," Daisy laughed. "And they wouldn't fit me anyway." She held the right shoe at arm's length and watched the way the jewels shifted in color beneath the light. "But so beautiful," she said.

"Well," Grandma said. "I'm glad they're not your size, so you won't be tempted to pilfer the merchandise."

Daisy glanced up at her grandmother's face. "Merchandise?"

Grandma ignored her. "Grab that one." She pointed to another box, and again, Daisy hauled it out. Again, she found treasures inside.

"But where did all of this come from?" Daisy asked.

"It was Mamamía's," Grandma said. "My mother's. When she died and Benny went to clean out their apartment, I couldn't decide what to do with all of it, so I asked Benny if he could just store it for me until I had a chance to go through it. He brought it here."

"But wait, I thought Mamamía and Papamío were broke?" Daisy said. "How did she afford all of this?"

"Well, they weren't always broke," Grandma said. "Some of it was from before, when they were rich. But the rest . . . this is how Mamamía got them back on their feet."

"What do you mean?" Daisy asked. There was a grainy *shhh* sound as Daisy pulled another heavy box out of the closet and into the light. "Didn't she have to sell all this when they lost their fortune?"

"No, on the contrary, she used it to start her own business."

"What?"

"You think you're the first hustler in this family?"

"I just, I had no idea. I've never heard this story before. What did she do?"

"Well, Mamamía had always been known for her style," Grandma said, reaching into the box at her feet and retrieving an evening bag in the shape of a seashell. "Look at this one. So beautiful. I remember she wore this to Easter mass one year." She set the bag aside. "She was such a beauty in her day, and so charming. She was friends with all the big designers, and they would give her things, just like they do now with A-list movie stars on the red carpet. They knew that if Mamamía wore a gown to a dinner at La Fortaleza, they'd get a half dozen orders for the same gown before the end of the season. All the society ladies would copy Mamamía's style, and then, when they went abroad to Paris or Madrid, they'd strut around looking like a pale imitation—literally a pale imitation, ha!—of my mother. We'd see them sometimes in the society pages, wearing a shift Mamamía had debuted the year before. And then in New York, word got around that Mamamía was the ticket. She was the tastemaker for a whole new market."

"Amazing," Daisy said, picking through the treasures while they talked. "But then, it seems like it would've made perfect sense for her to sell all this stuff when they needed the money."

"Yes, but she decided to rent it instead."

"What!" Daisy stood straight up out of a box, and put her hands on her hips.

"Yep," Grandma said. "There was no word for what she did back then, but she became a kind of stylist. She got new pieces every season, began to expand her library of sizes. But more than that, even, she became a kind of matchmaker between the designers and the ladies."

Daisy was astonished. "Well, what a little genius!"

"I know! And it was all very hush-hush back then, pure word of mouth. Everyone wanted to pretend the impeccable eye for fit and color was their own. But for years, Mamamía was dressing every wealthy woman in San Juan."

"I can't believe I've never heard this before."

"Well, she kept it quiet. Both because her success depended on discretion, but also because she never wanted to take credit. She didn't want to hurt Papamío's pride."

"But he got back on his feet, too, didn't he?"

"Of course, yes! Once they straightened all that mess out, he got a good job in the private sector. Cleared his name, too, though they never got back to the kind of lifestyle Lola and I grew up with," Grandma said. "I don't think they wanted to. It wasn't easy when it happened, not for any of us. But eventually, when they got used to it . . . I think Mamamía and Papamío were happier being liberated from all those expectations."

"Well, amen to that!" Daisy said. She wanted to ask Grandma if she'd been happier too, after she got used to it, but she worried about the answer. So she stayed quiet, watching while Grandma picked up the seashell bag again, and flicked open the clasp to examine its silken interior.

"Think I'll keep this one for myself," Grandma winked at Daisy.

"So then." Daisy folded her hands into a prayer-knot and used her chin to gesture at the rest of the boxes. "What about the rest of it?"

"Well," Grandma said. "I think we should invest it."

Daisy nodded, gritting her teeth.

"Think you can use it in the shop?"

In that moment Daisy, who wasn't usually a crier, understood that it was possible for a person to change. All her words lodged in her throat, and she threw her arms tearfully around her grandmother. This was the culmination of a dream that had been dormant within Daisy since childhood, one that had only recently begun to sprout and grow. Here was fertilizer, sunshine, rain. Here was inheritance, approval, a direct line that ran through her mom and all the way back to Mamamía. All Daisy had ever wanted was to forge a meaningful life without doing anything to make the world worse, both of which seemed almost impossible given the current parameters of how to be a human being on planet Earth. This closet full of riches would change everything. Maybe even for Mom, maybe it would help her understand.

"I've been reading up since you showed me your business plan," Grandma said, disentangling herself from the hug. "You have to begin with the most dramatic, most splendid inventory, right? This is the perfect way to launch your brand."

Daisy nodded, then stepped into the dark bathroom for a tissue. She blew her nose and tried to get herself together, to meet Grandma's professionalism. She couldn't believe her grandmother was using words like *launch* and *brand*. Maybe any fear at all about her cognitive function was preposterous.

"If I start out like this, super upscale, like Mamamía, then my reputation will be established from the jump," Daisy said.

"And then finding good inventory is easier if you have that reputation?"

"Of course, once you're established like that, the inventory comes to you." Daisy folded her tissue and blew into it again, a honking sound.

"Just don't do that in front of your customers, dear." Grandma gestured at the rumpled tissue.

Daisy laughed, and then turned to survey the abundance of boxes once more. "I'm going to be the go-to place for luxury consignment in San Juan," she said.

"You should put that on your sign." Grandma elbowed Daisy in the ribs.

Daisy hugged her again. Grandma squeezed and let go.

"We can't stand around all day hugging and weeping," she said. "Let's get this to your shop!"

Daisy stood back and surveyed the bounty once more. On tiptoe, she couldn't quite see the back of the enormous closet. It would take several return trips in her Silverado to retrieve it all. She glanced at Grandma, an undeniably fit seventy-four-year-old.

"Why don't we just take these first couple of boxes for now?" she said. "I know you're not big into manual labor."

"You got that right. Never was."

"I'll find out from Benny when his next booking is. Then come back later today or tomorrow and get the rest."

"Suit yourself." Grandma curled her biceps to show off her muscles. "But let the record show that I offered to help."

"You did," Daisy laughed.

"Which means you owe me lunch."

Daisy was broke, and knew Grandma had expensive taste in lunch, but a single shoe from this closet would pay for a month of meals.

"Lady, you got yourself a deal."

Chapter Twenty-Five

~

San Juan, Puerto Rico

2023

Daisy can't move or speak or communicate in any way, yet she notes a new feeling that her soul has been loosely stitched back into her body. It doesn't feel as though the stitch will hold if anything happens along to test the strength of the seam. But neither does it feel, any longer, as if her soul is in danger of flitting away on each passing gust.

She hears the word *stable* in her hospital room, but just as often she hears the word *critical*, and she knows that these words are about her, about her condition. Daisy presses herself into the reassurance of her soul being united to her body, of that body being confined to a relatively comfortable hospital bed in the physical world. She tells herself to focus on that security, and knows instinctively that this is the way to heal herself, to focus all her energy on strengthening that reborn bond with the earthly world.

Daisy cannot differentiate between day and night, or between Spanish and English. She can't tell if the storm has passed or if it's still rocking the wet world outside the window. But she does learn to differentiate, vaguely, between her caregivers, and she develops a favorite. A woman whose name she does not know, but who smells faintly of lavender, and whose hand feels dry and cool against Daisy's forehead, a woman who hums sweetly when she comes in to check Daisy's vitals or change her position in the bed or refill whatever is dripping into her body from various hanging bags.

At some moment, during what could be Daisy's one thousandth year or second hour in the hanging Babylon of that bed, the nurse begins to speak, and Daisy is briefly able to latch on to the human sound of her words. The woman's voice is like a flotation device, her words, Spanish.

"Your mama's coming, Daisy girl, you hang in there."

She can feel a sort of fastening at the mention of her mother. Daisy's presence feels more . . . present. Suddenly she can feel something catch, as if she's swinging through space on the flying trapeze and just there, the dependable slap of skin on skin as the catcher grabs the flyer's wrists, and the flyer grabs the catcher's wrists, and suddenly they are locked and swinging, arcing. Just like that, Daisy's brain engages, her thoughts engage. She kicks in, and there she is. In that room. In that bed.

"Your mama's on her way, just you hang tight."

Daisy grips on with all her strength and this is the moment when she remembers everything, all at once, with the same startling speed and blur and whoosh as the crash. There is a click or a pop or a bang, and Daisy remembers the phone call from the obnoxious guest, the storm. She remembers the scooter, the rain, the cat. The car, oh God, the dark and terrifying speed of the car. And before all that, the mail, the steps, Mrs. Fernández, Daisy's own cozy apartment, her home. And something else, something nebulous. What was it?

Before she can grasp the thing that eludes her, the unreliable arena of her brain warps and lurches and deposits her elsewhere, a different sensation. Everything's changed. A memory then, sharp and tactile: She is six years old in the backyard, and the light is sweet, golden with bees. Her father is chasing her with the garden hose, the water warm and metallic. Daisy squeals and shrieks and squeezes her eyes against the spray. She launches herself at her dad, a wet cannonball into his softening belly. Her brain lurches and spins again, and delivers her into another recollection. Hide-and-seek in the house after dark, the sound of her mother doing dishes while Daisy searches for her dad and brothers. She checks the pantry, the laundry room, under her bed. When she can't find them, small Daisy feels lonely and melancholy, and just when she's about to report her failure to Mom in the kitchen, she spies them: six sock-feet sticking out beneath the trembling blue drapes in her parents' bedroom. She approaches with stealth, stretches a dimpled hand toward the edge of the curtain.

Her brain lurches again and again, and each new scene restored to her is a like a hint, a reminder that she might find her way home. This is who she is, she remembers, Daisy Hayes, daughter of Thomas, daughter of Ruth. *Spin.* Daisy Hayes, college mutineer, *spin*, explorer of Puerto Rico, *spin*, purveyor of curiosities, *spin*. She gains traction, and speed, and although the lurching and dropping now has the terrifying quality of a whirling gun barrel, although Daisy herself has no agency in this game, is not herself choosing when to spin, when to stop, when to pull the trigger, the gathering breadcrumbs of self are exhilarating nonetheless. And then.

The next lurch drops her down a lightless tunnel, a repository of nothing but blackness. Daisy staggers and gropes and finds no purchase. In the room around her, the beeping machinery increases in tempo.

Chapter Twenty-Six

≈

San Juan, Puerto Rico
1991

During the course of the ensuing years, whenever Rafaela and Dolores discussed the change in their family's circumstances, they did so obliquely, in a code that developed without intention. They occasionally spoke of *before* or *after*, but never specified before or after what. Privately, they both worried that their sister had taken the change in their family's fortune particularly badly, and they both felt lucky (and slightly guilty) to have escaped their sister's fate.

Here is what Lola saw when she considered her sister's choices: that Rafaela had been entirely unable to accept their new station in life, so she had sought out a man, a yanqui, who she believed could deliver her back to their previous social status. Rafaela had been seduced by that hair and those eyes, so she'd failed to notice that her beau was not, in fact, rich. (Though Lola could acknowledge that Peter was charming and he was kind.) But Rafaela had also failed to see what Lola did from the start: although Peter loved her, he would be a terrible match for her. He wouldn't rescue Rafaela from the prosaic life into which she'd fallen. On the contrary, he'd be unable to settle himself in Puerto Rico at all, so he would take her away, and this time, Rafaela's exile would be permanent. In his own foreign, faraway home, Peter would bequeath to Rafaela some mostly white children, without the ability to extend that whiteness to her. So he'd be marginally ahead of his time in matters of race, but solidly oblivious to the weight of his own chauvinism, or what Rafaela would endure as an outsider in the American Midwest. In the end, Peter would fail, not only to restore Rafaela to the social status she still believed was her birthright, but most important, he would utterly fail to understand her at all.

And here is what Rafaela saw when she examined her sister's choices: Lola had immediately and entirely given up. When, at the urging of his family, Lola's high school sweetheart dumped her and then shortly thereafter married her former, still-rich best friend, Lola had taken that indignity like a cloak, wrapped herself in it, pulled it up to her chin, and never emerged again. Or if that interpretation was overstating it, at least it was true that Lola had decided at age nineteen that love was a treachery, that she would rather live in loneliness and sorrow than risk that kind of heartache ever again. Fortunately for her, there was a third option that entailed neither torment nor risk, so she'd thrown herself into her studies instead. She'd become a math teacher and dedicated spinster well before she cracked her first wrinkle. "I prefer the term *bachelorette*, if you don't mind," Lola frequently admonished her sister. But as far as Rafaela was concerned, it was a life of romantic promise entirely wasted.

Both sisters were a little bit right. But both sisters were also a little bit wrong. Because their assessments of each other were skewed by the natural sibling habit of self-comparison, as well as by their tremendous love for each other, by their ardent wishes for their sister's happiness, and of course, by their failure to imagine happiness as a fundamentally distinct prospect. They wasted an awful lot of time feeling sorry for each other, then, and failing to recognize that, in the end, they were both (eventually) quite happy in their adult lives, never mind some questionable decisions along the way. Rafaela did not appreciate this fact until the summer day of her sister's funeral, and it struck her as absurd, that she had never realized the fullness and pleasure of Lola's life.

In the years after Rafaela left Puerto Rico for St. Louis, she spoke to Lola by phone every Sunday evening for at least an hour, and they visited each other no fewer than three or four times a year. So Rafaela knew about Lola's book club, supper club, and weekly card games. She knew there was one friend she went dancing with from time to time, and another friend who liked to hike or swim or go on long drives around the countryside, visiting the chinchorros. Lola attended mass every Sunday at their old church in Miramar, even after she moved all the way out to Luquillo, where there were at least a dozen closer churches. She spent holidays with Mamamía and Papamío, but also took real pleasure in solitude. Sometimes Lola eschewed her parents' dinner invitations because, truly, she wanted to stay home and bake a glazed pineapple cake in the shape of a bird.

If Rafaela had a bad day or exciting news, and tried calling her sister before the appointed hour on a Sunday evening, she was unlikely to find Lola at home. But despite all that evidence, it had never occurred to Rafaela, what Lola had discovered: that a full and satisfying life did not require wealth any more than it required a husband.

There was a quality to Lola's funeral that made Rafaela feel more awake than she had in years, a kind of drugged lucidity, as though she had absorbed her sister's life force, and its sudden presence in her body had heightened her senses. Thus supernaturally endowed, Rafaela stood trembling in front of the altar at the church where she'd been baptized and married, breathing through her open mouth so as to protect herself from recognizing any odor of death that might drift from Lola's open casket a few feet away.

"She looks so beautiful," Mamamía kept saying, and Rafaela tucked their mother's wrist through the crook of her elbow, and patted her hand.

Lola, who had once been beautiful, had not appeared so in many years, not because she lacked the capacity, but because she lacked the desire, and she most certainly did not look beautiful now. Her illness had been swift, grotesque in its simplicity. In May, Lola developed what she insisted was a summer cold. By June it became bronchitis, then pneumonia, then sepsis. She was dead before the end of the month, so along with their grief and shock, her family also had to contend with a good measure of incredulity. It was unreasonable, that a life force as vivacious as Lola's could be dismantled like that, without fanfare or warning, without even a good story.

Against the cream-colored lining of the coffin, Lola looked waxen and primordial, as dead people always do after their bodies are no longer animated by what once made them beloved. Lola's body, now deserted by its inhabitant, was pale and bloated. The expression that had been embalmed onto her face was too winsome, it had none of Lola's wit. Rafaela did not say any of this to their mother, of course. Instead, she frowned, joking silently with her dead sister because, in the absurdity of this moment, there was nothing else for her to do.

"No offense, but you actually look like shit," Rafaela said to the Lola in her head.

"Well, yes," said Lola's ghost. "But I'm dead. What's your excuse?"

Rafaela snorted, but she was able to disguise the sound with the context of expectation. She covered her face with one hand, and the mourners who were filing through the church presumed the outburst to be a spontaneous expression of grief, which, of course, it was.

"Mamamía looks good though," the Lola-ghost said.

"Always," Rafaela agreed.

"Leave it to Mamamía to bring the glamour to her own daughter's funeral." A beat. Then, "Is she wearing Louboutins?"

Rafaela peered down to examine their mother's heels against the stone church floor.

"Ferragamo, I think."

The Lola-ghost had no eyes to roll. Rafaela took a deep breath in and blew it out, thinking she might expel her sister's ghost on the exhale. At the far end of the receiving line, her young adult children, Benny and Ruth, stood on either side of Papamío, whose face was as gray as his suit. Ruth kept leaning slightly out of the line, turning her heart-shaped face toward her mother at the other end. She was both sail and anchor, that girl. Benny was tall beside her, the first one in line, a buffer for the rest of the family. In profile, in silhouette, Benny was the double of his father. Whatever regrets Rafaela may have had about her ill-conceived marriage, the unhappy years had produced these children, and that made every moment worthwhile. In the receiving line, Benny knew everyone, greeted them all by name.

"Papamío, you remember Adelita Cruz?" he said. "She taught at Titi Lola's school with her. Science, isn't it, Señora Cruz?"

Papamío nodded and extended his platitudes with his hand. "Thank you for coming. It would mean so much to Lola that you're here."

Benny had waited until the day after his last final exam, and then skipped his high school graduation to hop on the first flight back to San Juan, leaving a brokenhearted Amanda pining behind him in St. Louis. When he first left, Rafaela had supported the move, predicting it would be temporary, that he'd soon discover the rosy nostalgia of his childhood belied a hard island life. There was nothing easy here except the weather, and even that had its price. He'd find out. But Benny had been back for nearly three years now, and it was like he'd never left the island at all. He'd rented a house in Carolina with Tiago and a boy from Mayagüez, and even though Papamío griped constantly that he was wasting his big Acuña brain by not going to college, he helped Benny get a job anyway, at a body shop where he could apprentice to become a full mechanic. Benny was good at every part of it—fixing the cars, fixing the prices, fixing the relationships with the customers who adored him. The women all remarked on his eyelashes and tried to set him up with their daughters. Within six weeks, his Spanish was as fluent as the native he'd once been. Within six months, he was running the business end of the shop, and the owner, whose own sons had taken the guagua in the other direction, started asking Benny if he might take over the business one day. Her son was broader every time Rafaela saw him, and she marveled at the man he'd become, unlike anyone she'd ever known. He was not bookish or debonair like Papamío, nor was he gregarious like his father. Benny was steady, resolute, even when all his friends didn't understand why he'd come back to San Juan right when most of them were trying to get out. Benny had always known who he was, what he wanted, and he wasn't susceptible to other people's opinions about his life. He'd fixed his sights on his own clear future, and made himself into a secure man. He'd done all that without resentment.

During Rafaela's first visit after Benny had moved back to Puerto Rico, he'd taken her out for lunch, insisted on paying for everything himself. Across a plate of bacalaítos (not her typical fare, but delicious nonetheless), he'd let her off the hook for his entire childhood.

"You know, I really never got used to St. Louis," he said. "I guess I didn't want to. Maybe I thought if I was miserable enough, if I could make Dad feel guilty enough, he'd bring us home."

Rafaela kept her eyes on the food because it was unusual for Benny to be so emotionally forthright, and she didn't want to scare him off by being too attentive. She dipped her fritter into the garlicky sauce they were sharing, and took a crispy bite.

"But I've been thinking lately, maybe Dad did us a favor, taking us there," Benny said.

It was such a startling departure from his usual refrain that Rafaela stopped chewing midbite. All his life, he'd been bemoaning that move they made when he was nine years old. He'd been complaining of homesickness, threatening to run away back to the island, blaming his every passing sorrow on the geography of that exodus. She looked up at him, her hand still clutching the golden-fried remnant of her food.

"If we'd never left, maybe I wouldn't know," he explained. "Maybe I would never have appreciated this place, how great it is here."

Oh.

"I mean, I missed a lot. But then, I also gained a whole different perspective that I wouldn't have if we'd stayed here. Like Tiago, for example. He talks about moving to New York all the time. Won't shut up about it." Benny sucked Coke through his straw and rattled the ice in his paper cup. "He thinks everything is gonna be easier if he can just get off the island. He doesn't know it's the same over there as it is here, hustle and grind, and maybe, yeah, you might make more money, but it's worse too, because suddenly everybody treats you like you're *Porta Rickan.*" Rafaela laughed softly while Benny crunched into his food. He didn't speak again until he'd swallowed. "So maybe all those years of yearning were the great gift of my life, Mama. Because now I know all that."

Rafaela set the unfinished corner of her bacalaíto back on her plate, and wiped her fingers on the grease-stained napkin. Her boy was never coming back.

"Well, you're welcome," she said dryly. "This was always my plan."

Benny laughed.

And now she heard him again, laughing lightly at the other end of the receiving line, that bright, sacred sound echoing gracefully among the stone arches. How did he do that, her son? She leaned ever so slightly past the shrinking shape of Mamamía so she could see him, the tall elegance of Benny, his muscular frame contained neatly in his clean suit, his hand gripping another man's hand, drawing him in for a hug, clapping him on the shoulder. His voice was effortless as he turned the man toward Papamío, passed the man's hand into Papamío's hand.

"Pa, you remember Candido."

"Ay, oh my God, Candido," Papamío said. "Look at you, my boy!" Papamío stepped into a hug.

Rafaela felt her breath still within her. *My God, Lola*, she thought. *Candido is here.* But all was in silence, and that was the worst moment for Rafaela. Because here was Candido, after all these years. And she couldn't tell her sister.

He was still slender, and his green eyes were just as clear and arresting as she remembered them. He had a neat moustache and there were strands of silver in his thick hair, but mostly, he still looked like her friend, that same boy who had kissed her on her parents' couch almost thirty years ago.

Papamío's hand was on Candido's cheek now, and the intimacy of the gesture startled Rafaela. She wondered at that touch, at the feel of Candido's skin beneath the warmth of her father's palm. She found herself momentarily distracted from greeting Señora Cruz, who was now standing in front of her, talking about how lunch in the staff room wouldn't be the same without Lola and her Tupperware stuffed with tostones and beans, her crazy weekend stories. Rafaela smiled at Señora Cruz, nodding and shaking the woman's hand, but in fact she was entirely absent from the exchange, her whole body attuned instead to the nearby presence of Candido. Rafaela straightened her shift, smoothed her curls behind one ear. She could almost hear her sister's urgent whisper as he approached, *He's here for you, Rafaela, not me. He is here for you!*

Rafaela spotted the wedding ring immediately, as Candido covered both of Mamamía's hands with his. It wasn't a surprise, not really. She'd heard of Candido's marriage. But still, the visual impact of the ring was startling.

"I'm so sorry," he was saying, and his voice was just the same, and Mamamía pulled him into a hug then as well, and Rafaela felt the world tilting beneath her, because in all the childhood years they'd shared a home, Rafaela had never seen her parents embrace Candido, and yet here he was, mourning for her sister like a brother. Here they were exchanging the visceral comfort of family. His eyes were closed, and Mamamía's hair was a puff of gray curls beside his pinched face, and when at last her mother pulled back, she held onto his shoulders before she let him go.

He turned to Rafaela then, and she saw the real tears in his eyes, though he refused to give them leeway. His voice was a croak, a single word, her name. "Rafaelita."

He opened his arms and she sniffed quickly, but it was too late. All her grief had arrived at once, and Candido didn't wait, he embraced her, and just like that, they were children again, all three of them together, bright and intact, flying through the quiet, airy rooms of the big house on calle Américo Salas. Hide-and-seek. Potted palms. The aroma of Priti's quesitos cooling on the stove. Rafaela didn't worry about the makeup she was smearing onto the shoulder of his suit while she cried.

§

She met him for lunch at the Vanderbilt in Condado, which had been Papamío's favorite spot during the flush years. Rafaela thought it was a bit much, but Candido insisted, so she went. She hadn't been back since her girlhood, and didn't remember much about it until the doorman tipped his hat to her at the entrance. Rafaela stepped into a memory.

The click of her shoes, once patent leather, against the gleaming tile of the floor. The swooping grandeur of the double staircases, the cool hush of luxury. The staff gliding quickly and soundlessly around the lobby on unspecified errands for the wealthy clientele. The blush of golden light dripping from enormous chandeliers, the canopy of symmetrical arches echoing through the lofty silence. But mostly, it was the scent, an aroma Rafaela had no idea she would recognize until she inhaled it, and it charged across the decades of her life to pull her back. It was the oiled wood of the mahogany bar, the clean shine of leather sofas and tufted velvet seats, the towering bundles of fragrant orchids overflowing their crystal vases, and behind all that, the rich aroma of a five-star kitchen. Further still, from the bank of tinted glass that lined the back wall of the lobby, the distant hint of the salty surf winking in the noonday light.

Only then did Rafaela remember their annual tradition, that once a year, between Christmas and Three Kings Day, Papamío brought them all here for a long lunch, not just Mamamía and his girls, but Candido and Priti and Benicio as well. A holiday ritual, and the single time each year all seven of them dined at the same table together. Priti would wear her best dress, and Candido would wear the new clothes Mamamía had inevitably given him for Christmas. Another scent then: the ruby tang of something jewel-colored in the grown-ups' glasses, and the pillowy, salty zest of Rafaela's favorite beef Wellington, which Priti never made at home. She understood at once why Candido had chosen this place, the long balance of its relevance across the span of their lives. It felt as though Rafaela were seated at one end of a seesaw with Candido sitting opposite. The Vanderbilt was the fulcrum between them.

She was too early, she realized, so she hurried into the ladies lounge to retouch her lipstick and powder. She wished she'd had time to visit the hairdresser, to shop for something new to wear. She dawdled in the stall until she felt confident he would've arrived, that he'd be seated and waiting for her.

He was, and when he stood to greet her, he kissed her on both cheeks, which unsettled her even though she'd expected this greeting. She was bedeviled by the ancient memory of their jawlines grazing and withdrawing, the feel of his skin against hers. This was not at all how she wanted to begin, flustered and flushed. But then a waiter arrived with their thick leather menus before the host had even finished pushing in her chair. The moment quickly receded, and Rafaela composed herself again. Candido was married, she knew. Happily, she hoped. She smiled briefly at him before turning the bulk of her outward attention to the menu.

"No more beef Wellington, I'm afraid," Candido said.

"Oh heavens, remember the beef Wellington?" Her mouth filled with anticipation.

"That was your favorite," he said.

How strange that he remembered.

"It's probably just as well," she said. "It's fine to have beef Wellington for lunch when you're ten. Probably less so in your forties."

Candido laughed. "Oh, you can allow yourself the occasional beef Wellington, I'm sure."

Rafaela pressed her lips together and said nothing.

"The salmon is excellent," Candido advised. "And the lobster salad."

She nodded and closed her menu. "Lobster salad it is."

Candido ordered a bottle of expensive wine, which deepened her feeling of disquiet, though she couldn't exactly say why, and not enough for her to refuse the glass he offered when the bottle arrived. The wine was excellent.

Rafaela had been divorced for almost ten years, and she hadn't dated. At first she'd been too busy with the logistics of untangling her life from her husband's. She'd been overwhelmed by the task of shepherding her children through the minefield of divorce, distracted by the terror and thrill of her sudden independence and everything she had to learn in order to maintain it. And then later, after she'd found her balance, she realized that, like Lola, she rather enjoyed her solitude, her own interests. Peter took the children every second weekend, and at first she worried that those weekends would gape with loneliness, but on the contrary, Rafaela found those empty days to be sumptuous. Not since childhood had she encountered the luxury of unscheduled hours. She took long baths, read frivolous novels and serious novels. She mashed up avocado with honey and vinegar and slathered the goop all over her face to ward off wrinkles. She slept late, and when Peter returned the children after dinner on Sunday evenings, she felt restored enough to greet Benny's moods with patience.

The years passed, and despite her lack of interest in romance, still she took great care with her appearance, was always impeccably tailored, would rather be late than leave the house with a chip in her nail polish. She enjoyed the dependability with which she could turn men's heads. But the head-turning was itself enough for her. She discouraged what sometimes came after. She didn't like the approach, the smile, the cheesy pickup lines. She typically responded with such arrogant reproach that her would-be suitor left feeling not only rejected but also thoroughly humiliated. So in truth, this lunch with Candido was the closest she'd come to entertaining a romantic prospect in a very long time. She felt this truth encroaching on her mind, but she dismissed it by glancing once more at his wedding ring. It was all in her mind.

"So," he said, after the waiter had taken their order and delivered warm bread and herbed butter to the table. "Tell me everything."

Rafaela laughed. "Everything?" She tried a joke. "After four hundred years of Spanish occupation, Puerto Rico was ceded to the United States in 1898 like a spare toothbrush."

It worked. He laughed. "I mean, you know I kept up with Lola over the years," he said. "I saw her once in a while, we'd have her over for dinner, or I'd run into her at mass. She always filled me in."

Rafaela snagged on the *we* but shook her head. "I didn't know."

In fact Rafaela was quite well informed because her sister kept her apprised of Candido's every move, or tried to. But over the years, whenever Lola mentioned his name, Rafaela moved to change the subject. It was too painful for Rafa to contemplate that after she and Peter moved to St. Louis, she alone was the missing piece. But now here they were, sitting together in the Vanderbilt, where Lola would never be again, and the chance of reuniting those kindred parts of herself was gone forever.

Candido took a sip of his wine and replaced the glass on the white tablecloth, swirling the stem beneath his fingers. "I see Benny a good bit, you know. He has the contract for our fleet, so I deal with him a lot. Great kid."

Rafaela smiled, proud. "He is."

"Takes after his mother," Candido said.

"Thank God!"

They both laughed again, and then there was a prolonged beat of awkward silence.

"To be honest, he reminds me of myself at that age," Candido said. "Ambitious, always working. Full of ideas. Some people will haul themselves up the ladder no matter what. You can see that in him, that drive."

Rafaela nodded. "He was always like that!" she said. "Even when I hoped he'd find contentment closer to home. Well, closer to me, I mean."

"Well, he's thriving here, Rafaela. He really is," Candido said. And then, rather abruptly, "I was sorry to hear about your divorce."

Rafaela flashed her eyes at him, but then shrugged. "I wasn't."

"I just mean I didn't like to think of you unhappy," he said.

Her next sip of wine was more accurately a gulp, followed by another gulp. Finally, she spoke.

"I didn't like to think of me unhappy either." She smiled sadly. "But here we are. I didn't plan to bury Lola so young either."

When he reached over to squeeze her fingers, it didn't feel alarming or romantic, but there was an unlingering tenderness in it. She rubbed the back of his hand, and remembered it was the same hand that had folded hers into that fresh bag of snow all those years ago. She did not want to let go.

"I still can't believe she's gone," he said quietly.

"I can't believe she's gone," Rafaela repeated, shaking her head. "How can she be gone?"

A surge of grief swelled up between them, but Rafaela let it wash over her and roll out toward the surf. She breathed with the tide until the deepest part of the swell had passed.

She felt relieved when the food arrived, not because she was hungry in the least, but because it provided them with a gap, an opportunity to shift their attention in a new direction. She turned the subject first to the perfectly structured and seasoned lobster salad, and next to Candido himself. She skipped past the parts she already knew well, and went directly to the topic she'd long endeavored to avoid. She hoped for courage when she opened her mouth.

"And how is your wife? A better marriage than mine, I hope?"

"Oh. Well. My wife is a wonderful woman," he said. "Yasmina. From Fajardo. You'd like her very much."

She could sense his restraint, but couldn't determine its source. A hope to spare Rafaela's feelings, or some muddled confusion about his own? It didn't matter why, she knew. Rafaela would open the door graciously and usher him through it. So they had known each other since they were children, so they'd loved each other, so what. They were not children now; they were adults who cared deeply for each other, whose shared home and history were now welded by the bond of grief. They would be fine, they would negotiate their impediments with dignity.

"Lola said as much, and I would expect no less for you!" she said. "And how did you two meet?" She skewered a morsel of lobster onto her fork.

"In New York," he said.

"Oh!" This information nearly startled her out of her composure. She felt it land, felt it furrow her brow, and she hoped, in that moment, that recognizing one's own hypocrisy might be a sort of virtue. She had met and fallen in love with Peter at that same time, of course. Candido read every single thought on her face even before she could unpack them herself.

"We didn't date then," he explained. "It wasn't until years later when we'd both moved back home."

Home. There was a clarity to that word when he said it, a comfort and intimacy she'd long forgotten, rather than the sloppy mess that ensued whenever that word issued from her own lips. Rafaela nodded, as if to encourage him to continue, but he faltered on where to go next.

"It was after you and Peter left and moved to St. Louis with the kids," he said, nonchalantly leaning over to spear a cherry tomato from her salad with his fork. "Maybe a year after you left?"

Rafaela hated how relieved she felt to receive this reassurance, but she was also distracted by the theft of the tomato. What difference did it make, where or when he met his wife? Some, apparently. She watched him roll the cherry tomato in dressing and then pop it into his mouth.

"I ran into her at a friend's birthday party, and we started to reminisce about the bad old days in New York. We'd worked at the same hotel, but she was already saving up to move home when I arrived. She's a few years older than me. And ambitious! She was determined to return with enough money to get a nursing degree."

An older woman! Rafaela was intrigued. "And she did get that nursing degree, right? Didn't Lola tell me she was a nurse?"

"She is." Candido couldn't suppress a proud smile. "She's in neonatal care at UPR."

"That's great."

Rafaela felt a pang then that she refused to admit was jealousy, but which was very obviously jealousy in several forms. Peter had never been proud of her like that. Not once to her knowledge had her husband ever chased any measure of pridefulness from his voice when describing her to someone. Never had he thanked her for leaving her family, her island, never had he admired her improving English or remarked on her acclimating to a new culture. Hadn't she done those things relatively well? Hadn't she borne two bright, beautiful children and raised them to be happy, thoughtful, well-adjusted young adults, despite their growing up in a place where their mother had no family, no friends, no support, where she couldn't even buy a plantain? So there, beneath some jumble of muddier feelings, it was a miraculous ribbon of joy that Rafaela felt to know that marriage could still look like this. Joy, to see how happy Candido was in his life. The smile that lit her face was unexpected and genuine, but so were the tears that gathered behind her eyes. This was such a humid swamp of feelings she couldn't isolate a single, coherent one.

"And I heard you have kids?" she asked, hoping to barge through the rest of it by sheer force of will.

"A boy and a girl, same as you. Ten and eight."

The boy ate, slept, and breathed baseball. The girl loved books. There was a second assault on her plate then, a crouton this time, and the sight of it leaving her salad on the tine of Candido's fork unearthed a forgotten memory: a thousand such burglaries from their childhood, Candido forever filching food from her plate when no one was looking. Not because he was hungry or underfed, but because they both thought it was hilarious. When they were little, they ate only breakfast together, and then dinner once or twice a week when Mamamía and Papamío were out. The thievery was a game between them, but not even Priti was allowed to know, not even Lola. It was their secret. So whenever the purloined item was something of great value (her last tostone, for example), Rafaela was unable to lodge a verbal complaint without ruining the game. She resorted to pinching or kicking him under the table instead.

Candido reached into his back pocket then, and drew out his wallet. Inside were pictures of his children. He was still chewing her stolen crouton.

"They're beautiful," she said. "I hope they have better table manners than their father."

He laughed, and when he reached for her cucumber, she slapped his hand. She ate the cucumber before he could get to it.

"Remember, you used to get in trouble for guarding your food?" He laughed.

She'd forgotten that too. Priti chastising her for sitting with her arms outstretched around her plate like a goalie.

"This is not a zoo!" Candido said in his mother's voice. "Get your elbows off that table this instant!"

Rafaela joined him in his laughter.

"Your mother had no idea what I was up against!" She shook her head.

"You'll be happy to hear that I don't tolerate that kind of tomfoolery at my own dinner table. It was one of our first rules when the kids were little: Keep your hands to yourself at the table! No touching other people's food!"

"Well, I suppose you knew the dangers better than most." Rafaela sipped from her wine. Then, "I bet those kids adore you," she said. "When you become a parent, when you have a family like that, it changes everything."

"Well," he said, looking her straight in the eye. "Not everything."

Holding his gaze felt like barring the door against an onslaught, an invading army, a hurricane, but she did it. Rafaela didn't even blink.

"But yes, most things," he conceded. "You were obviously a great mother, Rafaela. Your own kids . . . Ruth—" He interrupted himself to sip at his wine. He shook his head then, and tried clearing his throat, but he couldn't seem to push any volume back into his voice, couldn't get breath into the words. "Your daughter . . . I obviously don't know her the way I've gotten to know Benny." He breathed then. "But she seems remarkable too, like Lola. And like her mamá."

Rafaela nodded, and a single tear escaped to darken the red linen of her napkin.

"You've done a great job with them, you know. You should be really proud. I don't imagine that was easy."

Rafaela folded her napkin onto the table, and reached across once more to hold his hand. All the years that had passed, all the people she'd been since she'd last heard the timbre of his voice. Their common language was two whole families ago, and still. There was not a single locked cupboard in her heart to which he did not have the key. She said none of this, of course, as she felt the gold band that encircled his fourth finger with her thumb. Instead, she squeezed. She smiled.

"Thank you," she said.

Because that was all she had. The rest of the meal was uneventful. They talked about Rafaela's recent move from St. Louis to the East Coast, Priti's exuberant second act living in Miami, where she was married to a middle school principal and taught step aerobics at the local gym. When Candido asked if Rafaela ever thought about moving home, she didn't reveal that San Juan could not feel like home now, not with Lola gone and himself happily married to some very lucky woman Rafaela did not want to meet.

She felt a familiar prickle then, a long-buried resentment she'd always done her best to ignore. Candido had a way of conducting all manner of emotional archaeology without even opening his mouth. The feeling within her was laid bare from one moment to the next—he had only to turn his head, a certain angle of light across his cheekbone, and she was flooded with it: *Why, why, why had Rafaela been the one to go to Trinidad? Why hadn't she thrown a tantrum, refused to go, insisted on a better solution? And why had Lola been allowed to remain home in Puerto Rico, close to everyone they loved, while the whole trajectory of Rafaela's banished life had been set in motion the very day she boarded that cursed boat out of Ponce? Why had she gone without a fight?* Rafaela never blamed Lola. She barely even blamed Papamío. But there were times when she felt her life had been stolen from her.

Candido sat across from her. They were middle-aged. He was married.

Rafaela drank wine and moved the conversation along to his freight business, how many employees and government contracts he had now, how rapidly they were expanding their fleet. His humility couldn't mask his overwhelming and hard-won success. She was proud of him, but it would've felt condescending to say so.

"Priti must be so proud of you," she said instead.

He grinned. "So she often reminds me."

"I think of her so often," Rafaela said. "Especially after the divorce, I thought of her every day, what it must have been like for her, raising you on her own, and without all the advantages I had."

Candido nodded.

"I called her once when Benny was in a snit," she said. "I mean, he was always moody when he was younger, but this was a particularly awful day. I remember crying after he stormed off to bed. And then the next day, as soon as he left for school, I called Priti to apologize for what we put her through when we were teenagers."

"She told me," Candido said. "That meant a lot to her."

Rafaela shook her head, embarrassed. "It shouldn't have taken me so long. When I think back to our childhood now, it seems so strange, so lop-sided. I can hardly believe it ever felt natural to me, the way we lived."

Candido shrugged. "It was just how things were then."

A generous interpretation, Rafaela thought. She gazed at him as he lifted the almost-empty wine bottle from the table, tipped the last of it into her glass.

"Should we order another?" he asked. "I feel like Lola would want us to have another."

She was tipsy enough to laugh, but not tipsy enough to sanction more wine.

When they parted ways at the curb in front of the Vanderbilt, Rafaela to return to her sister's apartment by taxi, and Candido to return to his office by foot, she realized that her grief was not only for Lola but also for herself, for everything she'd lost years ago, and then continued to lose, year after year. Even now.

Rafaela didn't often think back on her wedding, a day that did not lead to the happy marriage she'd hoped for. But when she did reminisce, she preferred only to reflect on the inherent beauty of the day: her gown, her mantilla, the decadence of the orchids, the stained-glass light of the church. Her beautiful groom, so handsome in his dress blues. There had been love there. But as she sat in the back seat of the taxi that afternoon outside the Vanderbilt, and Candido shut her inside, as she buckled herself in and he stepped back, waving from the curb, it was impossible for her to push the other memories away. What had always been repressed there, she now realized, beneath the honorable veneer of her wedlock.

She'd been in love with Peter the day she married him, it was true. But not exclusively. And not fully. It was Candido whose face she'd searched the pews for when she stood beside her darling groom in the church. When the priest asked if anyone present knew any reason why Rafaela and Peter should not be joined in holy matrimony, when Lola had cleared her throat lightly but said nothing, it was Candido's impossible voice that Rafaela imagined might ring out from the back of the church. Candido who accidentally crossed her mind just as she stepped forward to slip the band onto Peter's shaking hand, just before she whispered her vows before God.

It was always Candido who'd been too good for her. Never the other way around, not for a single day of their lives. How foolish she had been, with her antiquated notions of propriety and rank. How had she ever believed in such nonsense? Rafaela was so many lifetimes removed from the girl she had once been, she could no longer inhabit a brain where those ancient choices made any sense. All this time, she could've been here where she belonged, with Lola, with Candido.

And there he was, tall and broad in the shoulders, the wedding ring gleaming from his hand as he waved her goodbye, his green eyes mossy in the sunlight. This time she waited until her car pulled onto the highway before she gave in to the tears.

Chapter Twenty-Seven

～

San Juan, Puerto Rico
1991

Ruth and Mama walked together into the beachfront building in Luquillo the day after they buried Titi Lola. Ruth couldn't remember ever seeing her mother sweat as much as she had on this trip, her grief like a fur coat in summer.

"Ay, it's so hot!" Mama rummaged in her handbag for a fan while Ruth hit the appropriate button in the elevator.

When they opened the door into Lola's living room, the air inside was even warmer, and Ruth was briefly afraid her mother would swoon.

"Sit down, Mama," she said, and then she went straight to the AC window unit and turned it on high.

Mama sat down for only a minute before going to stand in front of that air conditioner with her eyes closed, turning her face at different angles, stretching her neck so the cold air could reach into the new folds she was developing there. Mama hadn't dyed her hair since the news of Dolores's sudden death, and it wasn't like her to return home with her roots on display. Such slovenliness went against her mother's sense of herself as a glamorous woman of the world, a swanning sophisticate who visited Puerto Rico much the way a sitting pope might occasionally visit the fond, distant, native country of his pre-papal life. But grief will shuffle and transfigure. The parent and child switch places. So Mama seemed unconcerned about the grayness of her roots as the blast from the air conditioner flung the curls away from her head, pushing them behind her like a whipping flag.

Ruth moved back to the doorway and closed the portón behind her. From across the hall, she could hear the soft patter of merengue music and smell something garlicky in a frying pan. Mama sat down on the couch.

"You okay now, Mama?"

Ruth had always considered her mother to be somewhat immune to weakness, even when Ruth was little, before her parents' divorce. Even during those years when Mama seldom laughed, it didn't occur to Ruth to worry about her mother, because there was some way in which Mama always seemed to hover just outside the reach of vulnerability. She was stalwart, impregnable. But whatever Mama-fortress had once existed, whether real or imagined, it was demolished the very instant Lola died. Mama looked smaller now, adrift on Lola's couch, and Ruth felt a new urge to protect her, to make her own arms into scaffolding and shore up whatever disintegration was afoot.

"Close the big door too," Mama said.

Ruth locked the portón and then swung the main door shut behind it. The music and garlic disappeared. They were alone in the quiet.

"Was it always this hot here?" Mama tipped her head back and closed her eyes.

"It didn't use to bother you so much," Ruth said, dropping the keys on the kitchen counter. "You didn't even notice it when we were little."

Ruth crossed to the sliding glass doors and pulled back the curtains, felt herself catch a gasp in her throat just as she did every time she took in this view after a long absence. Beyond the white railings and plastic patio furniture, it was impossible to discern where the turquoise sea separated itself from the turquoise sky. Below them, a hot apron of sand was studded with palm trees tossing their hair in the wind.

"We used to just open the windows," Ruth said, flipping the lock with her thumb and rolling open the slider. "Remember?"

The wind came into the room and splayed the curtains, knocking over a vase of dead daisies on the end table behind them.

"It's too strong," her mother complained, plopping herself on the couch. "Close it, close it. You'll let the cold air out."

She waved a hand toward Ruth, and within moments, she was asleep sitting up on the couch, her mouth drooping slightly, the wicked, persistent exhaustion of grief. It was one of Ruth's first lessons in obliteration. She was nineteen years old, and though she'd faced some challenges in her life—leaving Puerto Rico, learning English, getting used to her father's new wife—she liked to think of those events as character-building. All those experiences had taught her things, made her stronger. But this time felt different, there was no life lesson here. Lola was gone. She was too young to be dead, and yet dead she was, and Mama's annihilation was so absolute, it felt as though most of her had gone with Lola into that other place.

Ruth cleaned up the dead daisies and went out for a walk alone while her mother slept sitting up on the couch. She strolled the length of the crescent sand barefoot while the sun traveled west and low, her legs moving at a pace only this island could generate while the heat seeped out of the ground beneath her heels. She met a gathering of dogs on the beach, their humans standing well back from the shoreline, chatting while the dogs chased and nipped and rocketed through the surf together. Ruth listened to the familiar shapes of the humans' accents, and felt the weight of how much she'd lost, how much language she'd forgotten. She'd been so young when they left. Almost three quarters of her life, she had called another place home.

Maybe Ruth wasn't from anywhere anymore, she thought. Or maybe she just had to keep looking. She'd been in New Jersey for almost two years now, and though she had no boyfriend (and not for lack of trying), she did have friends, roommates. She had fun. Maybe this feeling of internal drift was just part of growing up, maybe everyone felt like this until they found their way. She didn't like dwelling on any of it. It was gut-wrenching to think Lola was gone; why did it also have to transform her mother into this relic of herself? And why, on top of everything else, did grief have to punch holes in Ruth's already-shaky sense of herself? It was hard enough to get through the abyss of these days without fielding new questions about who she was and where she belonged. She wanted to evict all of this nonsense from her brain. She did her best to breathe through it. Ruth asked those questions to leave her alone.

At the western curl of the beach where the land protruded before turning back to itself, where the water changed color in the rocky shallows, Ruth plopped her denim bottom down right in the sand. She rested her elbows on her propped knees and watched the colors saturate the early evening sky. The wind carried the scent of someone's balcony barbecue. There was a calming hypnosis in the rhythm of the waves, a slowness in Ruth's breath that she forgot every time she left here and remembered again every time she returned. She experienced this forgetting and remembering, this rolling amnesia, as a kind of spiritual atrophy. Each time she returned, she had to face the sharpening truth that she could no longer access the simple concept of home. She both belonged and did not belong at all, no matter where she was.

Why did we leave here? she thought, looking out at the colors, sinking her fingers into the cool sand.

A treachery, though: she thought it in English.

⸙

They spent the rest of that week cleaning out Lola's apartment to prepare it as a vacation rental. Mama complained about the heat every day, so Ruth left her in the front rooms, where she could work in the artificial cold from the air conditioner.

"I'll start in the bedroom," she told her mother.

She marked boxes for keeping and donating, and kept an open bag for garbage. Ruth took care of the bedroom closet first, and then the dresser and nightstand before tackling the paperwork. Lola's desk was a rolltop, small and tidy, with different cubbies to keep everything organized. Stamps here, envelopes here, pens here, extra staples. There was a single deep drawer where Lola kept her paperwork, minimal and orderly. Only one folder bulged with aging keepsakes, which Ruth saved for last because she expected it to be the most difficult. She sat cross-legged on Lola's bed and took a deep breath before opening the folder. Inside were some report cards from grade school, an old black-and-white photograph of somebody Ruth didn't recognize, a Playbill from the original Broadway production of *West Side Story* at the Winter Garden Theatre, and several ancient letters, which Ruth felt momentarily conflicted about reading.

But then, a memory: her mother and Titi Lola sitting together at the round wooden table in the kitchen in St. Louis, maybe five years ago. Ruth was around fifteen years old, Benny seventeenish. The two women were sitting in perfect quiet when Ruth walked in and found them sipping coffee.

"What's this?" Ruth said, immediately suspicious of their silence.

"Shhh!" They waved her into their cloud of secrecy, and she realized they were eavesdropping. In every slope of their shared posture, the rigid spines, the hovering hands, the cones of their ears trained eagerly toward the bottom of the staircase.

Mama pointed overhead. "Benny's talking to that girl Amanda again," she whispered to Ruth, and brought a finger to her lips.

Ruth hesitated for only a moment. "You know there's a more effective way to do this, right?"

Both women turned to look at her across the tops of their coffee mugs while she dragged the tabletop phone from its stand beside the back door.

"But he'll hear the click!" Lola warned.

"Not if you hold down the mute button," Ruth said.

The women were gleeful, bouncing lightly in their seats while Ruth pressed the mute button and carefully lifted the receiver. She held it up between them so they could all hear. There was almost no reward for this coordinated betrayal. The conversation was dull. Amanda talked about her lacrosse practice and her split ends, and Benny didn't even pretend to care. They could hear him maneuvering the joystick on his Atari. Ruth remembered how they all tried not to laugh when Benny came down in his socks to grab a Coke from the fridge. Titi Lola pretended to study her split ends, and their mother nearly fell off her chair laughing.

"All right there, Mama?" Benny asked, popping the tab on his drink.

In Lola's bedroom in Luquillo, Ruth spoke out loud in case her tía's ghost was listening. "It's not like you placed a ton of value on privacy, let's be honest." Then she unfolded the first letter.

Three of them were bona fide love letters from the young man in the black-and-white photograph whose name turned out to be Alejandro and who, in his final letter, declared his intention to marry someone else. Over the years, Ruth had caught snippets of the story about Lola's teenage beau, who'd dumped her and married her best friend after Papamío's demise, but Ruth had never heard that scoundrel's name, had never seen his asinine face before. Ruth hated that Titi Lola had kept Alejandro's letters; she wanted to punch him in the throat. But knowing that Lola had preserved them, for whatever reason, Ruth found that she was unable to toss them either. She slipped them back into the envelope and felt the sadness close around her like a caul.

The remaining letter in the folder was addressed to Papamío, and it was unusual because it was written in English.

"I know this handwriting," Ruth said quietly. She recognized it from the annual birthday and Christmas cards, which constituted the majority of her relationship with Grandpa Pete since that one disastrous Christmas when she was eleven years old. *Why did Titi Lola have a letter from Grandpa Pete?* Ruth didn't even think they knew each other. She opened the letter without thinking and read it in a blaze. Then, in swelling turmoil, she read it again more slowly.

"What the hell?" she said out loud.

Ruth read the letter once more, and then flipped it over to see if there was anything else, anything to help her reconcile this piece-of-shit letter with her grandfather, anything to help her loosen the stone it had lodged in her gut. She'd always known that Grandpa was sort of racist, but because she loved him, she'd wanted to believe it wasn't really his fault. It was his generation, his family, the way he grew up. In the twenty years of her life, there'd been a handful of times when Ruth had felt like she was on the cusp of discovering exactly what it was that Grandpa felt toward Mama. She remembered the word *uppity* from the Christmas dinner, perhaps only because she'd had to ask Mama later what it meant, and when Mama had arched an eyebrow and declined to answer, Ruth made a special trip to the school library to look it up. It wasn't in the dictionary, either, so she'd resorted to asking the librarian.

"Oh, it just means when somebody's too big for their britches," the lady had said unhelpfully to Ruth.

"Britches?" Ruth asked.

But the lady shooed her along back out to the playground.

Even after all that, after witnessing a number of inexplicable, impatient exchanges with waitresses over the years, after hearing Grandpa use the n-word once to describe a Chicago Bears running back whom he also deemed *uppity*, Ruth still hadn't fully put it together. Because she had some complicated feelings about how she thought of herself (mostly white) (but still Puerto Rican) (but still, almost totally white) (and also, completely Puerto Rican), and because Grandpa had always treated her with love and affection, Ruth had never accepted that her grandfather's bigotry might really extend to Mama, and might even extend to *her*.

Now, with the letter shaking in her hand, Ruth felt like an idiot. Because of course it extended to her. She read the letter one more time, stretching her synapses, trying to force it to make sense. But no, there were the words quite plainly, meant to describe her future self, meant to describe Benny. The room was suddenly too hot with the window open and the breeze rummaging through. Ruth lay back on Lola's pillows and breathed through her mouth.

When they'd moved to St. Louis, it was Grandpa Pete who had bought Ruth her first winter coat, white and puffy with a chevron of blue-and-pink stripes. He held her hand at the checkout counter, and said some coarse words to a woman behind them in line who'd gestured at Ruth and made a comment Ruth hadn't understood.

On Lola's bed, the cog and wheel were reluctant to turn in Ruth's mind. It felt like a visit to the eye doctor, like someone had just changed the lens in front of her eye and suddenly everything looked different. Ruth longed to return to the previous blurry lens, but it was gone, replaced by the malignant scrawl on the page in front of her, snapped into focus. So many things suddenly made sense.

Ruth stood up from the bed and moved toward the door with the letter in her hand. She touched the doorknob, but then it occurred to her that maybe Mama didn't know about this letter. Perhaps Ruth could spare her mother the painful sharpening of that blurry lens. Ruth stood with her hand on the doorknob and looked again at the date it was written, April 1968. Just a few weeks before her parents' wedding. Mama had enough grief right now.

Ruth had no way of knowing why the slanting script was smudged, but the blue ink had never quite recovered from that hot June day in Lola's bra. The softness of the paper belied the sharpness of the words it contained.

April 18, 1968

Dear Mr. Acuña & Torres,

I trust all is well in Porto Rico. By now you may have heard from my son Peter that he intends to ask for your daughter's hand, despite the strident advice and misgivings of his family. We obviously have not met your daughter, who I'm sure is a lovely girl, but Peter did send us a picture from Trinidad, and I'm sure you'll agree that this match, though sweet, is ill-advised in the long term.

I don't know how things are done down there, but here in the States, decent people don't mix races. Not because we have anything against Porto Ricans or any other race of people, but because the mixing isn't natural, and it provokes awful hardships for those involved, especially the poor half-breed children. This is why mixed race marriage is still illegal here, and it's my understanding that the laws of this land apply to your people as well.

I have thus far failed in my efforts to convince my son that his heart has led him astray. He's quite bewitched by your charming Raphaella. I urge you to provide our children with the guidance they need, to remind them that marriage endures long after the blush of desire has gone. It's as much for your daughter as for my son that I make this appeal, for neither one of them will be long happy in a marriage that so defies convention. What can they possibly have in common? It's only the foolhardy bravado of youth that compels them.

At heart, my son is a respectful young man who will require your blessing in order to marry your daughter, so only you can convince him to desist from this reckless plan. I expect that, as a father and fellow Catholic, you share my concerns. If we fail to prevent this engagement, then I must insist that you provide evidence that their union will be a lawful one. Please send documentation of your daughter's lineage, along with your personal reassurance that she is not sullied by negro blood, though the photograph my son sent along seems evidence enough to the contrary.

It is my fervent hope that we can resolve this affair between us without having to seek legal recourse in the aftermath.

Yours,

Peter Brennan Sr.

St. Louis, Missouri

Keeping the letter from Mama felt like the most grown-up decision Ruth had ever made, choosing to bear the hardship of it herself and spare her mother whatever pain it might arouse. Ruth did not extend that same consideration to her father, not because she cared less about him, but because it simply didn't occur to her. Because her father was a good father, because of his generation and his bearing and the way he conducted himself with his children, Ruth almost never considered Dad's feelings. In fact, she was only vaguely aware that he might have them.

As Peter saw it, his job as her father was to execute the function of cornerstone, column, and buttress. His role was to receive his daughter's distress with unflappable calm, and to provide her with solutions. The prospect of his own possible anguish was not typically a factor in the arrangement of their affairs.

Ruth waited until fall, until Dad came from St. Louis to help move her out of mama's new house in Montclair where she'd spent most of the summer, and back into the dorms at Wodsley. There was really no reason for him to come because, although Mama didn't love move-in day, Ruth didn't have that much stuff, and it was a half hour drive. Ruth could borrow Mama's car and do the move herself in two trips. But Dad came every year because he liked to see where she'd be living.

"I'm paying for half of it!" he'd say. "Need to make sure I'm getting my money's worth." And he'd flop down on the bed to check the mattress.

His visit became part of each semester's ritual, and after each move-in day, Ruth would discover a funny picture her father had hidden somewhere for her to find. He called them *inspirational portraits*, and they were of Gandhi or Jesus or Oprah, tucked inside Ruth's pillowcase, or slipped into the back pocket of her favorite jeans, or taped beneath the battery compartment of her keyboard. In Sharpie, he'd have added a ridiculous caption like, "Jesus is confident you'll make the dean's list this semester!" or "Oprah knows you've got this in the bag!"

On the evening of move-in day her junior year, Dad and his wife, Trisha, took Ruth to her favorite restaurant for dinner, and the letter, which Ruth kept in her handbag the whole time, was so distracting, Ruth could hardly enjoy her chicken tikka masala. But she waited all the way through the meal because she didn't want to talk about it in front of Trisha.

After dinner they went back to the Radisson, where Trisha, who insisted she was suffering from jet lag and who'd yawned all the way through dessert, went up to bed even though it was only 9:15 P.M., which meant it was only 8:15 in St. Louis. Ruth and Dad had managed not to make eye contact any of the four times Trisha mentioned the jet lag, and waited until the moment the elevator doors slipped shut behind her to collapse into hysterics for several minutes.

"Oh, she must be so exhausted." Ruth wiped a tear from one eye.

"It's not easy being an international jet-setter, Ruth," Dad said, and then he pulled an honest-to-God handkerchief out of his back pocket and used it to mop up the evidence of his laughter.

They found the quietest corner of the lobby then, and sat down in two chairs facing each other. There was a low orange table between them, where Ruth set the offending letter.

"I found this," she said. "Earlier this summer, when I went with Mama to clean out Lola's apartment."

Dad looked at Ruth's face, and then at the letter. There was the memory of laughter still clinging around them, and for this, Ruth felt grateful. A safety net for a fraught conversation. Ruth was sure Dad would recognize his father's handwriting immediately, but she couldn't tell right away if he'd ever seen the letter before. She watched him carefully as he leaned over to pick it up, as he read it, as the shame and horror of it fell across his face. When he was done reading, he placed it face down on the table between them. He tucked his lips into his mouth and there was a quiver on his features that Ruth had never seen before. Or maybe she had never really looked. His eyes were as blue as they'd ever been, lined with crow's feet now at the corners, and his hair was shot through with sparks of silver.

"Well." Dad cleared his throat. "They always were set against us. I'm very sorry you had to find that."

Ruth blew all the breath from her lungs. "Me too," she said, and waited for him to say more.

"I'm sorry it exists in the first place," he said. He leaned back in his chair, then immediately leaned forward again, elbows on knees.

"Well, obviously it's not your fault it exists," she said. "You didn't write it. But did you know about it?" She assessed him carefully to see if she could find the truth on his face, independent of whatever he would say.

"Yes and no," Dad said.

Ruth made her face into a question.

"I knew the letter existed at one time," Dad said. "I didn't know Lola had saved it."

"Had you read it before?"

"No."

"So when you say you knew it existed—"

"I knew my father had written to Papamío. Expressing concerns."

"Expressing concerns," Ruth repeated.

"Well," Dad said. "I know my father, so I had some idea the letter would've been offensive, but . . ."

Ruth waited for him to continue, but he'd stalled out. Ruth wasn't sure what she expected him to say here anyway. He wasn't even married to Mama anymore. They'd been divorced for almost a decade, and he had a whole new life now. A functional, happy marriage this time. Still, it was Dad who brought her up. He used his fingers to pin the letter to the orange table.

"Did you show this to your mother?"

"No," Ruth said.

Dad breathed, and in the swing of his breath, Ruth saw what he'd been so careful to protect her from all these years. She saw that he had *feelings* about this. Ruth had never seen him cry, and it would not happen tonight either, but the tears were there, nonetheless.

"You did the right thing," he said, finally, shaking his head. "Your mother went through enough when we were married. She doesn't need to be reminded of this after all these years. It's disgusting."

They had never talked about Mama, never discussed the marriage or the divorce, or Ruth's early years in Puerto Rico. This was the first time, a hallmark.

"You know, I will never love anyone the way I loved your mother," Dad said. He pushed a catch out of his throat and glanced lightly toward the elevator before the second half of the confession. "The way I will always love her."

His face was crumpled with emotion, and Ruth was baffled. "But. What about Trisha?"

"Oh, sweetie. One has nothing to do with the other." He smiled sadly.

"Trisha makes me *happy*. So happy. That's a totally different kind of love. It's easy. What your mom and I had, those sweet, domesticated years, she was my family, my everything. We made you! And Benny. That's the best thing I ever did. So yeah, the marriage was hard. But my God, that was love. It was priceless."

Ruth could hardly believe what she was hearing. "But then why? If it was that precious, why didn't you make it work, do whatever it took?"

"It just . . . the love we had for each other, the foundation." Dad felt his way carefully through the sentence, word to word. "It couldn't withstand the pressure of what she had to endure." Dad looked down at the table between them as if he could watch the memories of their life together play out across its surface. "For me, it wasn't hard." He paused, remembering. "I mean, the cooking was bad."

Ruth laughed. "Oh, I remember!"

"I mean *bad*," Dad said. "But I didn't care much about that, not really."

Ruth nodded.

"The only hard part for me was seeing how unhappy she became," he said. "It hurt that I couldn't keep her happy. I couldn't shield her from everything she went through out there. I tried to be upbeat, keep her positive, protect her. But people were mean to her. Eventually, she just curdled to our life. To me, too, I guess. I don't blame her. None of it was her fault."

Before tonight, Ruth had always presumed that Dad couldn't see it, the way people in St. Louis had treated Mama. Because he'd grown up there, because Missouri was what he was used to, because maybe he was in a little bit of denial about who Mama really was. And maybe Ruth had also given him a pass because Mama was not an easy woman. She was funny and smart and lovable, sure. But she was also arrogant, vain, too aware of her own beauty. She was quick-tempered, haughty, demanding, irritable. Ruth knew all of this to be true. But maybe Ruth had also given her father a pass simply because he was her dad. And she loved him.

So the notion that he *had* been aware of the hostilities, but hadn't been able to help . . . that notion was new to Ruth. And now she realized there'd been a certain comfort in presuming her father was merely oblivious. The alternative . . . Ruth shifted in her seat. She could see his remorse. But he'd chosen this, it occurred to her for the first time.

"You took us there," she said softly.

It wasn't an accusation. It was just a statement of observation, and Ruth said it out loud the very moment it occurred to her. Dad winced nonetheless. Perhaps she expected him to produce a list of reasons, his family, the job, the schools, the quality of life. But instead, he was quiet. They both were, remembering.

For Ruth, it was the country club, the manager with the pink eyelids, the locker in the staff room. She could only guess which memories might present themselves to her father. His regrets were private. But he knew them intimately.

And so his next words were not an excuse, Ruth understood. They were a truth, softly spoken.

"I just didn't realize," he said.

Ruth would think back to this moment frequently in the months ahead, her father's admission, his broken proclamation of love, the torment all over his face. The words he didn't say, perhaps wasn't able to say. She would ponder this memory without quite knowing why it lingered so haphazardly in her mind. Something in the mystery of her father's unspoken regrets. His rangy, comprehensive, unapologetic, imperishable love for Mama. And his deep, uncomplicated contentment now, with someone who wasn't her. The questions all this engendered about the qualities and varieties of love. Who felt most like home? What kind of happiness mattered most?

Because like her father, Ruth would fall in love once. And then twice. Like her father, she'd tell herself that one thing had nothing to do with the other. The great difference of course was that Ruth's two great and disparate loves would overlap, would swarm and crowd her heart. The entanglement would contain all the hallmarks of a heist: velocity, misdirection, duplicity, unimaginable payoff. Ruth, like most anyone who's ever fallen in love, would fail to appreciate that she was felon and victim, both.

When Ruth returned to her dorm late that night, she peeled off her clothes and pulled a nightgown over her head. As an upper classman now, this was the first semester she'd have her own room, the luxury of her own sink and toilet. In her private half bath, she switched on the light and lifted the lid of the toilet. Taped there, on the underside of the toilet lid was a close-up of a smiling George Washington, a message in her father's distinctive script. *You go, girl!*

Chapter Twenty-Eight

~

Palisades, New York

2023

Back in her own kitchen, Ruth finds that she cannot move beyond the counter, the scene of the crime, the inception of her nightmare. Her bottom is glued to the same stool where she'd been sitting when that stupid antique phone rang. Ruth weighs ten thousand pounds, and her bones are toothpicks inside the burden of her skin. One really bad phone call can waken and set loose the sleeping demons of the soul. Ruth knows this, has always known it. And yet that knowledge offers nothing in the way of assistance. In her lifetime of collected griefs, there has never been a moment worse than this one. Her dead or living daughter is sixteen hundred miles away, and she is stuck here. On this stool.

She calls the boys and then her father, commits the domestic atrocity of relaying the news. She surprises herself with the strength of her voice, the composure of her tone. She does not know that this is a direct maternal inheritance. Carlos, who's in Manhattan at rehearsal, she instructs to get an Uber home immediately. Vic, who found a good job at a Boston architectural firm after college and is still at his desk working late, she asks to book a flight directly to San Juan and meet them there as soon as the weather clears, as soon as he can. She stops herself from adding "just in case." Ruth is almost relieved when her dad doesn't answer, and she can type the worst of it into a text message instead. *Daisy was in an accident. Call me back.*

When the calls are finished, Ruth tortures herself by remembering every horrible thing she's ever said to Daisy. She replays every inane argument, every regrettable utterance. When they'd finally gotten their COVID vaccines and the world had reopened, when, instead of finally going to college, Daisy had announced that she was going back to Puerto Rico, their already heated, tenuous relationship hit a new low. Some months later, when Daisy confessed that she was starting a business, opening a store down there, Ruth feared her daughter would never come back, that they would never recover from this folly.

Now Daisy's store has been open for over a year, and by all accounts (both anecdotal and financial) it is thriving. Still, Ruth is the only member of the family who hasn't been to see it. Even Vic, who's always been the outlier, whose independence takes him farther from his family all the time, even he went to San Juan for a long weekend in December, to see Daisy's shop and support his baby sister. Ruth alone has been too stubborn in her disappointment, too judgmental, too exacting. She has refused to accept that Daisy has the right to forge a nontraditional path, and that path might be legitimate. Admirable, even.

Ruth drops her elbows onto the counter and lowers her forehead onto the knot of her folded hands. She knows with sudden clarity that this is her fault, all of it. Daisy's accident, the very fact of her daughter being in Puerto Rico to begin with. Maybe this is partly why Vic is so distant too. Carlos will follow, she thinks. He will flee as soon as he's able. Her children are leaving, and not just in the growing-up way. Because there's so much Ruth has refused to share with them, because she has kept this door sealed against them, Daisy went looking for the key herself. That is why they are here, at this terrible moment.

There are so many conversations Ruth needs to have with her kids. So many buried things she now wants to unearth.

"Please God," she says out loud. "Don't let it be too late."

§

Ruth does not exactly sleep, but she leans back on the couch momentarily, performing the kind of restful absence from her body that's only possible in times of grief or catastrophe. She closes her eyes, and the obliterating blackness flows into her mind like merciful ink. She stays like that for some number of minutes, and when she opens her eyes again, she is filled with a determination to make good use of the wicked, cavernous stretch of hours ahead.

She gathers her wallet, her insurance card, her laptop, and her glasses before calling the insurance company and following the prompts. It takes her seventeen and a half minutes to get a live human being on the phone. The live human being's name is Yvette, whose first order of business is to inform Ruth that their conversation is being recorded for training purposes and to ensure customer satisfaction. But as the customer in question, Ruth feels already unsatisfied because her daughter may or may not be still alive, and it took Yvette seventeen and a half minutes to answer her call. Ruth doesn't know where to begin.

"Member ID number?" Yvette suggests.

Ruth recites the number.

"Can you verify your name and date of birth, please?"

"Mine or the patient's?"

"Oh, you're not the patient?"

"No, the patient is my daughter."

"Okay," Yvette says. "So then your daughter's name and date of birth."

"Daisy Hayes. April 17, 2001."

Ruth can hear typing, which stops abruptly.

"Oh," Yvette says. "Your daughter is not a minor?"

"No," Ruth says. "She's twenty-two."

"I see."

More typing.

"I just need to check with my supervisor," Yvette says. "I'm not sure I'm permitted to discuss her care with you."

"She's my daughter," Ruth says impotently.

"I understand that, Ms. Hayes, I'm sorry. But there are HIPAA laws in place to protect the privacy of all our patients. Typically we can only discuss a patient's care directly with the patient herself. Is your daughter available?"

Ruth closes her eyes and breathes as slowly as she can.

"No," she says. "My daughter is not available."

"Just hold on one second," Yvette says, and then before Ruth can respond, there's a click, and a dreadful swarm of smooth jazz that interrupts itself every twenty seconds to reassure Ruth that her call is very important. After six minutes, the smooth jazz expires, Yvette returns, and Ruth makes the sign of the cross.

"Okay, good news!" Yvette says chirpily. "My supervisor says it's fine to discuss certain elements of your child's care because there's a previous note on Daisy's file indicating you as her emergency contact."

"Okay, great," Ruth says, and then she tries to tackle the absurd reality that she is now twenty-five minutes deep into this phone call and has not yet managed to tell Yvette that her daughter is in an emergency room in Puerto Rico, and that she may or may not, in fact, still be in a condition to require medical insurance at all.

"So what can I help you with today?" Yvette asks.

Ruth tries to stand back from the question and assess it much the way a mountain climber might plan the best route to the summit.

"My daughter was in a serious accident," Ruth begins.

"Oh, I'm so sorry," Yvette says.

"She was walking, I guess. And she was hit by a car."

"Oh gosh."

Yvette's responses fall like obstacles into Ruth's path, and Ruth wishes Yvette would stop interjecting so she can get these awful words out. She cannot abide the interruptions.

"I received a call this evening that she's, Daisy, she's in the hospital. And they said there was some kind of problem with her insurance. They said I should call just to verify her coverage."

"Oh my gosh," Yvette says again, "I'm so sorry."

"Right. Thank you."

"Let me see what I can figure out here," Yvette says, typing. "Let's just see what we have going on here."

In the machine-quiet that follows, while Yvette types, Ruth begins to shudder, from her core and up through her collar bones and out to the tips of her fingers, which, she realizes now, are freezing. The tip of Ruth's nose is also freezing. She knows it's not cold out. She touches the speakerphone icon and sets her phone on the arm of the couch so she can tuck her cold hands into her armpits. After a few moments, the shivering subsides.

"Oh. This is . . ." Yvette doesn't finish her sentence at first. She types a little bit more. "This is from Río Piedras Trauma Hospital in San Juan?"

"That's right." Ruth begins to shudder again, but she breathes through it this time.

"Right, I see the note here, that they called," Yvette says. "Where is that, the Dominican Republic?"

Ruth blinks. "Puerto Rico."

"Okay."

Ruth can hear Yvette sucking air through her teeth.

"But still, out of the country," Yvette says.

"Well, not really," Ruth says. "Not technically."

Yvette is silenced by this. Ruth reads the silence as quizzical.

"You said Puerto Rico?" Yvette finally manages.

"Yep," Ruth says. "Which is technically a United States territory."

She does not say *colony* because she's in enough trouble with Yvette already. Yvette does not immediately respond.

"It shouldn't be any different than if she went to an emergency room in Connecticut," Ruth says, somewhat desperately.

"Well," Yvette says, and Ruth can read every measure of the woman's significant reluctance in that single, stretched syllable. "I . . . it looks like, right, I do see that we have a couple of in-network providers in Puerto Rico. But unfortunately, the Trauma Hospital is out of network."

Ruth hears these words, but they make no impact.

"Okay," she says. "What does that mean?"

"It means her medical care at that particular hospital is out of network."

Now the words begin to make light, sporadic contact, like raindrops on dry pavement.

"But it was an emergency," Ruth says with utter futility.

"Yeah," Yvette says, with matching futility.

"So. What are we supposed to do?"

Ruth does not yet know the extent of Daisy's injuries. She knows that Daisy is sufficiently injured that she could not call home herself to announce her injuries. She knows that Daisy is, at best, unconscious. At best, when she is stable enough, Ruth hopes they will move her to the intensive care unit. Ruth's faculties regarding Daisy's medical care have thus far been engaged in the direction of praying that her daughter does not die. Her only wish is for Daisy's survival. There is literally no part of her brain that can care, at this moment, about the financial cost of that survival. *What are we supposed to do?*

Yvette does not have an answer.

"Okay." Ruth has to try. "Okay, so what is our out-of-pocket limit?"

"It is . . ." Yvette seems relieved to be typing again, to be retrieving the answers to simpler questions. "Eight thousand seven hundred dollars for Daisy individually. Nineteen thousand three hundred eighty dollars for the family."

That is a large number. Ruth does not care. She will sell her car. Whatever. She will empty Daisy's college fund.

"Okay," she says.

"But that's for in-network care."

Ruth shakes her head. "So?"

Yvette makes her finish the question.

"So then what's the out-of-pocket limit for out-of-network care?"

Yvette hesitates for a moment. "There isn't one."

This time it lands, the information really, really lands. It is a cataclysm. A meteor striking the Earth. Ruth begins to shudder again.

"Can she move to an in-network hospital?" Yvette asks then.

The shuddering stops, and as soon as it's passed, Ruth notes the appearance of an enormous, thundering headache in its wake.

"I don't," she says. "She's."

Yvette is typing.

"She's in a coma," Ruth says, not knowing whether this is strictly, medically accurate, but needing to impart the gravity of Daisy's condition to Yvette, needing her to understand the absurdity of the suggestion that maybe Daisy should get herself into a cab and head on over to an in-network hospital.

"It looks like there's one . . ." Yvette says. "Oh."

"Where?" Ruth asks.

"In Saint Thomas."

"Saint Thomas," Ruth repeats, wondering if Yvette will hear the insanity of it.

"Yes," Yvette says.

"The island," Ruth says. "Of Saint Thomas."

"I think so, yes," Yvette says. "It's actually not that far. It's within the hundred-mile radius."

"So, to be clear, you're telling me there is no in-network hospital in the United States territory of Puerto Rico?"

"Correct."

"And my daughter should go instead to the in-network hospital on the separate island of Saint Thomas, which is less than a hundred miles away. In the US Virgin Islands."

"Well," Yvette says. "I mean, obviously that's not a great option."

"No," Ruth says, but then she remembers something else Yvette said, and she throws her mind back to that detail with unreasonable hope. "But you said there were a couple of in-network providers?"

"Yes." A pause while Yvette retrieves the appropriate information. "There's a dermatologist in Carolina." Another pause. "And looks like an endocrinologist in Ponce."

They are both quiet for a moment while they consider this additional information.

"And a hospital on Saint Thomas," Ruth says quietly.

"Not very helpful, I guess," Yvette acknowledges.

And then, like a maniac, Ruth begins to laugh. It goes on for some moments, until the shuddering returns to displace it. Yvette clears her throat.

"So." Ruth gathers what feels like every remaining bit of strength in her body and she funnels it through the mess of her brain, and then out of her mouth in the form of words. "Please stop me if I have any of this wrong, but I think what you're saying is that, despite the fact that I pay more than thirty thousand dollars a year so that my children will have health insurance, and despite our exorbitant copays and deductibles, and despite the fact that I have never missed a payment, never been late on a payment, and despite the fact that Puerto Rico is a US territory, you're saying now that my comatose daughter is basically uninsured in Puerto Rico."

If there was any part of Yvette that had started to soften to Ruth, this is the moment that stops all that.

"Your daughter is still insured," Yvette says. "She's just currently out of network."

"You won't pay for her care, is what you're saying."

"We will pay for her care at any in-network facility," Yvette says.

"But there are none in Puerto Rico," Ruth says. "So she's not covered."

"She's out of network." Yvette repeats it now like it's a mantra, like it will save her from eternal damnation. "I'll be happy to send you a list of our in-network facilities if that would be helpful."

"That would not be helpful."

Ruth tips her head back on the cushion behind her, and feels the pain spread like a band behind her eyes and across her scalp. The silence becomes uncomfortably long, and then Yvette is the one to break it. She reverts to her script because what else is she going to do?

"Is there anything else I can help you with this evening?"

In this moment, Ruth's rage manhandles her feeble humanity.

"Yes, just one more thing, Yvette," she says. "You can go fuck yourself."

§

When Carlos arrives, he shows Ruth a hurricane app on his phone, and a churning spiral fills the screen.

"What is that?" she asks.

They are standing at the foot of her bed, in front of her half-filled suitcase.

"Real-time satellite imagery." Her son turns the screen so she can see it more clearly.

She squints, but can't make sense of what she's looking at. "Where is Puerto Rico?"

Carlos pinches the screen, zooms out so she can get her bearings on the map. There is Cuba. There is Hispaniola. Where is Puerto Rico?

"I don't see it," she confesses.

Carlos zooms in again. "It's under there."

But there's nothing to see. No visible land beneath the twisting roil of the behemoth storm.

"Oh my God," she whispers.

"It's bad, Mom."

§

Mama is at the kitchen door, and Carlos gets up to let her in.

"Did you pack?" she says to Ruth, who's back in the kitchen putting water in the kettle.

"I started, Mama."

"We can't go anywhere yet anyway, Grandma." Carlos shows her the app, but his grandmother waves it away.

"There have always been storms," she says.

"But like this, Grandma?"

"You have no idea," she says. "There were frightful hurricanes, truly. I think the only difference was, we didn't have a twenty-four-hour news cycle, no cell signals to go dark. The world wasn't watching—so when we got annihilated, we got annihilated. We were on our own!"

"Some things don't change, I guess," Carlos says.

"Anyway, I know how this works, okay?" she says. "I remember this much: you just have to hold on."

Ruth remembers too. Only one major storm that she can recall with any clarity from her own childhood. She must have been five years old or so, the year before they moved. But then dozens of storms since, waiting down a fragile phone line for word of Papamío, Mamamía, Lola, Benny. In fact, they all know how this works, at least from afar: it will be some ghastly, yawning chasm of hours. The trick is only to endure them. Those hours will march by at a deadening pace, but march by they will. They should play Uno or Monopoly. They should eat junk food and tell stories. They should sleep when they can, but without leaving one another's sides, without bothering to brush their teeth or change into their pajamas or slide their exhausted bodies between the sheets of a bed, because therein lie nightmares. But if they hold on to one another very tightly and fill the waiting hours with color and warmth and light, then eventually, eventually the storm *will* lift, it will. And that is where hope lives, in the quiet hours after Puerto Rico is left behind. There will gradually emerge, during those lurching hours, some clarified picture of destruction. It will be catastrophic or manageable. Whoever is left will roll up their sleeves as

316 • Jeanine Cummins

they have always done and begin the work of recovery. And in that bright yellow time, there will be birdsong. The phone will ring. And Daisy will be there, she will be there. She must.

Ruth presses her eyes closed as she wills herself to the other end of this coming press of hours.

"So, I made some phone calls," Mama says. "And I got us a flight."

Ruth opens her eyes again, and she and Carlos both turn to look at Mama. "What?" they say at the same time.

And then Carlos adds, "That's impossible, Grandma. There are literally no flights."

"It's not a commercial flight."

"But how, what—" Ruth cannot formulate the appropriate question.

"I called your father—"

"Dad?" Ruth's confusion consumes her whole face. "He didn't answer when I tried—"

"Not your father." Mama shakes her head, slaps a palm against her temple. "Not your father, what am I saying? I called my friend, you remember my friend Candido?"

Ruth is puzzled. "The boy you grew up with? The housekeeper's son?"

Now Mama frowns, baring her bottom row of teeth, and Ruth experiences a familiar flare of worry about her mother's cognitive function, her slipups, her confusion, but for all that, she seems to have gotten better recently. And anyway, Ruth has no space for that fear right now. It bounces, but doesn't stick.

"My friend, yes," Mama confirms. "Well, *the housekeeper's son*, as you call him, now happens to own the largest freight company in Puerto Rico."

"Holy shit, Grandma!" Carlos says.

"He has already mobilized a plane for us in New Jersey," Mama says, "and he assures me we will be the first flight to land when the airport in San Juan reopens."

"Baller," Carlos says.

Mama cocks her hip at him.

Ruth is already back at her son's shoulder. "Open that hurricane app again. Can you tell what time it'll be past, or mostly past?"

Carlos clicks and scrolls. "It's impossible to say exactly, but they're estimating most of the rain will stop by midafternoon tomorrow."

Ruth looks at her mother. "So depending on the damage, the airport could reopen by what, tomorrow evening? We could be in the air by late tomorrow."

"We could be with Daisy by tomorrow night," Carlos says.

"It's possible." Mama nods.

Now they're all thinking the same reverent thought. They're already in the prayerful quiet of that distant room. Whatever will happen next will happen there. They will face it together.

"We'll be ready," Ruth says.

Chapter Twenty-Nine

~

San Juan, Puerto Rico

2023

Daisy can feel pain now. Dull at first, and imprecise. But then it gathers itself, asserts itself. Makes brief but rigorous appearances in her physical body. There, in the hospital bed in Río Piedras, the pain is a corporeal thing. It feels encouraging. But she worries vaguely that the pain might be a staircase, and if she wants to emerge back into the waking world, which she very much does, the only way to get there is to mount that staircase and climb. She stands at the bottom of it and peers up. She doesn't know if she's strong enough. She's not sure she's ready to try.

Grandma is there sometimes. Carlos and Vic might be there, too, Daisy isn't certain. But Mom is there, she is there, and she is always there. She jokes with the nurses. She sings to Daisy. She tells Daisy stories of her childhood here in San Juan, and then stories of her childhood in St. Louis. These are stories Daisy has never heard before, and they play like movies in the cinema of her brain. There is a banyan tree, a strangler fig, in the backyard of Mom's house. Mom is a little girl with curly black pigtails and chubby knees. There is a lush, green kingdom in the branches, frogs and insects and birds, and little-girl Mom is the Queen and the King. *Yes, Mom,* Daisy thinks. *This is my way back, you are the lighthouse. Speak to me of home.*

"Have you noticed the banyan trees, Daisy? Have you seen them?" Mom says from her station at Daisy's bedside. "With their multitude of trunks? Do you know there's one right outside this hospital window? Open your eyes, and you'll see it. Go on, Daisy. Open your eyes."

Daisy's eyes do not open. The machine beside her bed clicks and hums and breathes for her. On a digital screen, Mom watches Daisy's heartbeat. She holds her hand.

"When I was little, I thought those trees had a thousand roots, a thousand trunks, but they're actually not trunks at all. Do you know how they work?" Mom says, her voice just loud enough to be heard above the noise of the life-making machinery. "Those trunks are actually the branches. The branches stretch up and up and out, and then they just drop." Mom raises Daisy's wrist just two inches from the hospital bed and then lets it drop. "Just like that," she says. "They drop and then they burrow into the ground, and that's how they become the roots. Isn't that the most magical thing you've ever heard? The roots become the trunks become the branches become the leaves become the roots. And on like that forever."

This image materializes and repeats on a loop on the movie screen in Daisy's mind A time lapse of leaves budding and unfurling and then curling, elongating, dropping, burrowing, growing anew. A tree recycling itself. Mom keeps talking in this way. For hours and days she does not leave that chair. She gives Daisy every story, every memory, every affirmation she can reach. Every intimate history she ever withheld. Every miserly, unacknowledged slip of pain, she shares. She tells Daisy that these traumas are her traumas, too, that she was wrong to deny them for so long. She asks Daisy to wake up because she needs to apologize properly. There is so much more Mom needs to tell her.

§

During their prolonged bedside vigil, the family members' various roles are established early, because they are mostly extensions of the same roles they occupy at home. Benny, Pamela, Stefani, and Candido come and go with delicate regularity, too, often enough to demonstrate their love and concern, but careful not to intrude. Among the others, Ruth is the cog at the center, and her mother and children wheel around her. Rafaela's movements have taken on a sort of stoic grace. She is able to smile and talk warmly to the hospital staff despite her devastation, so she fills the role of translator between the doctors and Ruth, not so much linguistically as emotionally. Vic has made himself into the indispensable son, as he always does. He drives everyone back and forth between Benny's house and the hospital. He takes food orders and then goes out to get the food and bring it back. Then he watches his mother to make sure she eats, before he collects all the trash and takes it down to the street where he stuffs it into the dumpster so it won't stink up the hospital room.

Carlos struggles the most to find his place without Daisy. For the first time in his life, his waggish irreverence fails him. So during the early afternoon of the fifth day of their vigil, Carlos retreats to his phone. He clears text messages, checks emails, wastes time on social media. He reads about the cleanup and recovery efforts that are ongoing around the island. San Juan was spared the worst of the damage, but a half a dozen small towns on different parts of the island were completely obliterated.

In one newscast, an old man sits in a folding chair outside the front door of his simple one-story, concrete home. According to the text at the bottom of the screen, the man's name is David Pedrosa y Mulero. The house itself appears intact, but the man's waterlogged belongings are strewn all over the yard around him. His furniture is bloated, caked with mud. He makes eye contact with neither the camera nor the reporter, who holds a microphone too close to Mr. Pedrosa y Mulero's despondent face.

"Sir, can you tell me how you fared with the storm?" the English-speaking reporter asks. "It seems like there's a lot of damage to your belongings, but the house?"

The old man looks up from his chair but then shakes his head. The reporter tries to help, prompting him.

"I don't see a high watermark on the outside wall as we've seen in other nearby communities." The reporter points to an exterior wall, causing the camera operator to pivot. "So that's an indication the water didn't come up so high, yes? It seems like you were lucky."

The camera pans back to the Mr. Pedrosa y Mulero, who shakes his head. When he answers, he holds his voice at an even tone, an act of grace that makes Carlos think of a lion tamer at an old-time circus, a man who could bring all that strength and ferocity to heel with a snap of his fingers.

"There's no high watermark," he says, "because the water was over the roof."

Mr. Pedrosa y Mulero looks away, and for a moment the reporter has nothing to say. There are thirty-seven confirmed deaths so far.

Thirty-seven people.

So far.

And everyone knows that this number is wrong, that it does not yet include the hardest-hit places, the destroyed places, the impossible-to-reach places, where the bereaved are already burying their unrecorded dead without aid or government accounting. Everyone knows that some portion of those lost will never be counted. Carlos looks at Daisy and feels this fact land in his chest, in his neck, across his clavicles. He is sitting in the deep window well beside Daisy's bed with one sneakered foot drawn up beneath him and the other one dangling down. Their mother is silent, watchful, taut. She strains forward out of her chair and toward Daisy, as if she expects Daisy to return to them any second, and she doesn't want to miss it, she wants her eyes to be the first thing Daisy sees when she wakes up.

Carlos blinks at their mother. He blinks at Daisy lying pale in the bed, her hard-fought tan fading rapidly. Soon she will fade to the color of the blankets, the sheets. Soon she will disappear entirely. Carlos needs to get out of this room. Instead, he returns his attention to his phone and closes all the news articles. It's only because he urgently needs something to do with himself next that he finds the voicemail. He never listens to voice-mail. Who listens to voicemail? Who even leaves voicemails these days? Only very old or very eccentric people.

Only Daisy.

He sees her name there at the top of his voicemail list, the little blue dot beside it, and his heart contracts. All of her voicemails have the blue dots beside them—he's never listened to a single one of them. Whenever she leaves a voicemail, Carlos does what all normal people do, he just picks up the phone and calls her back. He drops down from his spot in the window well.

"You want a coffee, Mom?" he asks.

She nods her head, and Carlos steps out, pressing his thumb to Daisy's name on the screen as soon as he's out of the room. He takes a deep breath to steel himself before putting the phone to his ear. The first voicemail is three seconds long, and all it says is: *Don't worry, we're still related.* She left it at 6:57 P.M. last Tuesday evening.

Carlos stares at the phone. There's a row of chairs lining the hallway across from the nurses' station, and he sits down in the nearest one with a thump. Last Tuesday evening was the night of the storm. The night of the accident. Daisy was here at the hospital by eight o'clock, just an hour after she left this voicemail. What if she was on the phone leaving this message when she got hit by that car? What if Carlos is the reason Daisy didn't see it coming? He shakes his head. He's being dramatic. This isn't about him, for crying out loud. Anyway, there was no sound of an accident on that voicemail. Just his sister, the brightness of her voice. The never-ending wackiness of her dispatches. *Don't worry, we're still related.* Carlos looks back to the voicemail list and realizes that the previous message is from the same minute, also from Daisy. He opens it.

Carlos, this is the weirdest thing, you're not going to believe it. Obviously, I couldn't wait for you and I opened the DNA results and HOLY SHIT, I'm still trying to wrap my head around it. Call me the moment you get this! Call me, call me, call me!

The feeling that shoots through his body at that moment is exactly how Carlos imagines a bell must feel after it's been struck by the clapper. It's an overwhelming vibration that obliterates any capacity for thought beyond the vibration itself. He rises from the chair and goes to find his mother a cup of coffee.

"I think I'll go by Daisy's apartment," Carlos says, after he deposits the cup into his mother's hand.

She takes her eyes off Daisy's face long enough to look at him. "What for?"

He makes his voice casual. "See if she has any plants that need watering. I'll take her mail in, let her neighbors know what's going on. Do they know? Has Benny filled them in?"

Mom shakes her head. "I don't know."

"I know she's close with Mrs. Fernández and Mr. Kurtzweiler. They're probably worried about her." He leans down and kisses the top of his mom's head. "I'll bring her some nice pajamas and a fresh change of clothes too," he says. "For when she wakes up."

Mom blinks at him. "Good boy," she says.

Mrs. Fernández has a spare key, but she's not going to let just anyone into Daisy's apartment. Carlos produces identification, but she's still hesitant, even after Carlos asks her how many Puerto Ricans she knows with the last name Hayes. So he calls his uncle Benny, who vouches for him over the phone.

"Carlos, you know I have a key," Benny says after Mrs. Fernández hands his phone back. "You could've just asked me."

"My brain isn't functioning the best," Carlos admits.

His sister's apartment is hot and stuffy. The storm shutters are still down so he opens the balcony sliders and raises the shutters to let in light and fresh air. He's been here three times before, and he thinks of it as the most Daisy apartment on the planet, yet somehow, each time he visits, she's managed to make it even more her own. He notes a canary yellow birdcage on an end table with a collection of glass bottles inside, all in different shapes and colors. On Daisy's nightstand, a feather sticks out of an inkpot. There are dirty clothes in a heap on the floor and clean clothes in a heap on the bed, but apart from that, the place is tidy. Her sole plant, a succulent on the windowsill, is doing just fine without his help.

"She was ready for the storm, I guess," Carlos says, looking around. The bathtub is no longer full, but more than half the water remains, and Carlos can see the high watermark from where she'd filled it in preparation. He reaches into the tepid water and pops the drain. She also has three cases of water stacked beside the front door. Carlos unpacks a few of them and puts them in the fridge because it will be nice for her to have cold water when she gets home. He wanders into her small bedroom and finds a tote bag left hanging on her closet doorknob. He rummages through her drawers and puts a good deal of care into selecting an outfit for her. He settles on a loose-fitting, wide-legged jumpsuit covered with toucans and palm trees and jaguars. He adds a set of pink silk pajamas, a soft-worn Mars Volta concert T-shirt, and a couple changes of underwear. He brings the book from atop her nightstand too. There's a bookmark—she was only on chapter three. He can read to her. He folds the clothing carefully and stows everything in the tote bag.

All the while, he searches for the DNA results, but there's nothing here. There's no desk in the bedroom, but he checks the nightstand drawer. Nothing. Back in the living room, he checks the bookshelf, the sideboard, the couch cushions, under the couch. He finds a drawer in the coffee table where she keeps paperwork, but his excitement dips as he flips through all of it without finding what he's looking for. He opens the cabinet where she keeps her garbage and finds a few envelopes and junk mail stuffed into the recycling bin, but it's not there.

"Dammit." He stands up, leaning both hands on the counter while he surveys the small apartment once more. He sweeps his eyes across every possibility, any nook where a stray envelope might hide. He goes back into the bathroom, checks the vanity, looks beneath the sink. There's nothing in the oven, fridge, microwave, freezer. The clock on her bookshelf is analog, because of course it is. It ticks loudly, taunting him.

"Daisy Hayes, you better not die without coughing up those results," he says.

He knows as soon as he says it that it's the worst joke he's ever made.

§

Ruth's stories are endless. She tells them until she is hoarse. She knows now, because of the gruesome things she's learned over the last month about the vanity of stubbornness, that these stories belong to her children. She can no longer afford to withhold them. She's wasted too much time wrapped up in her own muddy feelings about Puerto Rico. Or rather, not about Puerto Rico at all, but about her own experience being an island-born, mixed-language, ambiguously complexioned person in the wider world outside of Puerto Rico. She has projected these knotty feelings onto her children without explaining why. She was only vaguely aware she was doing it all these years, and she can admit now that she unwittingly withheld their father's heritage from them too. This withholding was only partly because she was preoccupied being a single mother, earning money, bandaging scrapes, packing lunches, reading stories. It was also partly because she didn't want her children to reach beyond the realm of their own comfortable lives, to sink roots into distant soil. That feeling was proprietary, yes, but it was also protective. She wanted her kids to have an identity that was easier than hers, easier than Thomas's, even. Her kids had lived in one place their whole lives, or most of their lives at least, and Ruth had hoped that would be enough for them. She wanted them to feel the kind of belonging she had always yearned for and could never achieve. But she hadn't told them that. She had never explained.

Well, she will tell them now, and she will let her children decide for themselves who they want to be. She will not be the one to exclude them; that was never her job or intention. She will mine her own life and extract treasure; she will wield the pickax of language, will relearn her own stories using words her children understand, words that aren't natural to her vocabulary. Ethnicity. Inclusion. Identity. Race. Complicity. Ruth will face her own discomfort and she will learn.

She will share this with Vic and Carlos too. She'll be generous with the details, will not flinch from the hard parts. She will start with Puerto Rico, then St. Louis, then Wodsley and Palisades. She will resurrect their father as well, in every story she can summon, his own faraway home, the hymn of his accent, his cultural perplexities, his mother's early death from cancer and his father's resulting descent into alcoholism. Ruth isn't even sure she's ever shared this with her kids, why they're only half a family now, why there are no living roots left for them on the Hayes side. Why this family meant everything, absolutely everything, to their father. The way Thomas had rolled out a sleeping bag on the floor of Daisy's room when she was a baby with croup. He slept with one hand tangled through the slats of his daughter's crib just to be close to her until she was well again. Ruth wants them to know all of it, every detail. She will share with her children the imprint of their messy, magical inheritance.

But Daisy first. Daisy first.

"Wake up, Daisy," she says.

Ruth weaves her stories into a rope, and this rope she tosses down the staircase of Daisy's pain to the bottom. It lands with a soft, dusty poof at Daisy's feet.

It is sixteen more days before Daisy feels ready.

She sidles up to the rope where it lies in a coil. She circles around it, testing her courage, and then she reaches out and takes the rope in hand, rough and strong, woven from many fibers. At last, she hauls her weight up onto the first step.

And she begins to climb.

§

Mom is telling a story. A playground in St. Louis. A boy named Eddie, a girl named Kathy. A bewildering wound inflicted. She is deeply involved in the telling of this story, and Daisy wants to listen. Has her mother ever told her a story like this? Daisy is reluctant to interrupt. Her vision is fluttery, feathered. Her eyes have been closed for a long time. There's a mask on her face. *Oxygen*, Daisy thinks.

"Mom?"

Her mother stops telling the story. She shrieks. She stands over Daisy. She screams for the nurse.

"She's awake, my daughter is awake!" Mom yells.

And there is pain everywhere. Most noticeably in her face, in her right temple, in her left arm, her left thigh. The pain is a searing, obliterating thing, and suddenly there are two nurses and a doctor there, and they move Mom away, and they come to stand in the place where Mom was before, and they are asking her questions, and they are adjusting all of her machinery, and one of the nurses removes the mask from her face, so they can all hear Daisy when she says quietly, "It hurts."

But they all laugh, and the doctor says, "I bet it does, sweetie."

And then one of the nurses promises to give her something for the pain after the doctor examines her.

§

It might be morphine.

Whatever it is, it works.

Daisy is in and out, but not like before.

In and out.

Out and in.

The stitching will hold.

She is here.

§

Daisy is aware that the days are passing. She knows this because some-times it's dark when she wakes up in pain, and other times, when she wakes up in pain, it is light. Then one day, she wakes up in the kind of pain that allows her to sit up in her bed and take a drink. The next day she eats. Jell-O at first, and then broth, and eventually actual food. Her mother and brothers are always there. Grandpa and Trisha are there for a few days. Grandpa insists on holding the fork and feeding her the scram-bled eggs just like he did when she was a baby. While Grandpa feeds Daisy, his wife, Trisha, compliments every passing nurse on either her fingernails or her eyelashes, which makes Carlos giggle uncontrollably. Grandma and Benny and Stefani continue to rotate through on a reg-ular schedule until Stefani has to go back to Tallahassee. She leans over Daisy's bed on her way to the airport, kisses Daisy on the forehead, and says, "Good job not dying."

Carlos tells Mom to please go home and take a shower, for the love of God. "She's not dead," he says. "But I've heard poor hygiene can be a killer."

"All right, I'm going!" Mom says, because Mom takes everything in her stride now. She never stops smiling.

And then predictably, Carlos gets bored sitting by Daisy's bed. He does mild calisthenics while he keeps her company. Jumping jacks, push-ups, crunches. He props one foot up high on the window sill and does some runners' stretches. He does some pliés and then flips through the channels on the television and calls Daisy a drama queen, and she tries not to laugh because it hurts to laugh.

"What happened to the driver?" Daisy asks this question with the same suddenness with which it appears in her mind. She's ashamed it hasn't occurred to her before.

"What?" Carlos says.

"The driver of the car that hit me."

"Oh." Carlos stands up and opens the locker behind her bed. "He's fine. He suffered a seizure while he was driving, but the airbag saved him. Or I guess he used your body to break his fall." Carlos begins to rummage through her personal belongings in the locker. "I can't believe I've been sitting in this godforsaken room for weeks and I never noticed this cabinet before."

Daisy's bloodstained clothes are long gone, cut to ribbons by the surgical team that wasted no time getting to the meat of her body that first night the ambulance delivered her to their care. But her backpack is there. Her keys. Her shattered phone.

"What's this?" Carlos pulls a sheaf of papers out of the bag, then answers his own question. "Holy shit, the DNA results!" He drops the backpack on the floor and sits down in the room's lone chair. "I went looking for these! Couldn't find them."

He is silent while he studies the papers. And then he looks at Daisy, her unwashed hair strewn out across the pillow, and the first thing he says is, "Maybe that smell wasn't Mom." And he feels more like himself than he has since the night of the accident. But then he waves the papers in front of her and says, "What the fuck, Daisy? What the fuck?"

"I know," she says, her voice rusty and raw. She points to the cup of apple juice on the tray table, and Carlos hands it to her. She sips. "Imagine if I'd died without getting to the bottom of this?" She hands the cup back and Carlos sets it down.

"Unthinkable," he says. But then he spreads his hands across the papers in his lap and suggests, "Maybe now isn't the time for all this, though? Maybe we should wait until you're a little stronger."

Daisy looks at him, aghast. "Carlos, don't be insane."

He looks back, deadpan. "I don't know any other way to be."

So, when their mom returns an hour later, her hair still damp from the shower, Daisy and Carlos are waiting for her.

It's an ambush.

§

Ruth reads the papers as best she can and then gropes around in her handbag for her reading glasses, because something must be wrong here. "This doesn't make any sense," she says quietly.

"Mm-hmm, we noticed," Carlos says.

Ruth glances up at her son, but he can't hold her attention; her eyes are drawn immediately back to the papers. She flips through them again and again.

"You gotta lotta 'splaining to do," Carlos says in his racist Ricky

Ricardo accent, an impression he's always insisted isn't racist when he does it because he's Latino.

He is Latino, Ruth catches herself. No air quotes this time. Her son is Latino. Recent epiphanies aside, it even says so, right here on the page. Her children are just as Latino as she is, apparently, which makes no sense at all, fifty percent. Half Puerto Rican, as far as she can tell. Half some-Caribbean-flavor-that's-definitely-not-Irish, anyway. They should be three-quarters Irish.

"This can't be right," she says.

Both Daisy and Carlos are quiet, perhaps wrestling with all the new information. Perhaps shifting and juggling everything they thought they knew about themselves, although of course whatever is written on this paper changes nothing. It's just as Ruth feared, the very reason she has always opposed DNA testing, especially for Caribbean Latinos—it's too ambiguous and it causes people to needlessly lose their balance.

Daisy has yellow bags beneath her eyes, a collage of unbeautiful colors that covers one whole side of her face, a deep wash of blood beneath the skin. Her voice is still scratchy from the machinery that kept her alive until just a few days ago.

"There must be some explanation," Daisy says quietly.

Carlos scowls at Ruth just the same way he did when he was a toddler with tantrums, his face so expressive she had difficulty taking him seriously, even when he was in a red fury. Her baby child, her little clown. But the question he poses now comes with real venom. He asks it with all the simplicity and heartache of a child who does not remember his father.

"So was Dad our real dad?"

Ruth stutters. "Of, of course he was! What? Carlos!"

"Carlos!" Daisy raises her voice to correct her brother, but the effort causes a spasm in her fragile throat, and a sputtering cough follows. The pain ripples through her body then, as all her muscles tense with the coughing. She pales from the pain, and Ruth stands up to hold a cup of water to Daisy's mouth. She feeds the straw between Daisy's lips, and waits for her daughter to swallow.

None of which dissuades Carlos. "You never slept with anyone else?"

For a moment, Ruth is speechless. In her life, she never dreamed she would field a question like that from her child. Her resulting anger threatens to incinerate everything she's learned about gratitude and regret during the last twenty-six days.

She turns her face to Carlos and says, "It is absolutely none of your business who I have or have not slept with. How dare you ask me a question like that. Who even are you?"

"That's what I'm asking you, Ruth! Who am I?" He throws his hands in the air like he's on a soap opera.

In the pit of Ruth's stomach, another storm begins to swell. Because there are other feelings behind her outrage, of course there are. It's too hot in this room. She feels sick. She could, perhaps, cure the feeling by retching, heaving, bringing it up. By blurting out one name into the room. But it can't be, it really can't.

Arthur Rodríguez.

No. Ruth needs to sit down, to breathe. She needs time to register this upheaval, but it's happening at warp speed.

"Carlos, take it easy," Daisy says. "Give her a chance to explain."

"Explain what?" Vic is in the doorway with Grandma. "We brought you an iced coffee. You allowed caffeine yet?" He sets the cup on Daisy's tray.

Ruth's mouth is a grim line.

"You gonna tell them, Ruth?" Carlos says, folding his arms across his chest. He is the only one of her children who calls her by her first name, ever since kindergarten, and Ruth has always found this habit funny, endearing. But not today. Her boy leans against the windowsill, and Ruth can see the banyan tree through the window behind him. When she holds the papers out to her mother, she sees that her hand is shaking. Mama looks through them with her head slightly tipped back and her lips pursed.

"What am I looking at?" Mama blinks at the papers.

Vic moves to her shoulder and dips his head down to see. "Looks like some DNA test results. Oh boy." He looks up at Daisy. "Yours?"

Daisy nods.

"And mine," Carlos says.

"Cool," Vic says, obviously not reading the room. "Can I see?"

Mama hands over the papers to Vic. "Be my guest—I can't make heads or tails of them."

Ruth sees that it's only a moment before Vic's expression changes too. And then his posture follows.

This family. This life. It's so much more fragile than Ruth ever realized before. Even after losing Thomas, she never felt this kind of vulnerability. On the contrary, that loss was like cement. It bonded them, made them impenetrable. But now this. This moment feels impossible, inconceivable, the way all three of her children are looking at her with the same expression of distrust. Like she's a stranger to them, and just at the moment when she'd finally learned what to do, how to correct the mistakes of her past.

Mama moves over to the chair, and Ruth stands out of it so her mother can sit.

"Wow," Vic says, his voice slung low as he flips through the pages. "This is really something."

"Well, what is it?" Mama asks then, lowering her weight into the chair. "What's all the hullabaloo?"

"Well." Vic clears his throat, unsure how to proceed. "It's not—" he glances at Ruth, who nods. "It's not what we would've expected. The DNA results."

Mama pulls a ziplock baggie out of her purse. Ruth watches while her mother opens it and reaches inside. How can she snack at a time like this?

"How so?" Mama asks, shaking the little baggie at Ruth. "Sunflower seeds?" she offers.

Ruth shakes her head. Vic clears his throat again.

"Well," he says, "Dad was from Ireland. And Grandpa Pete's family too, also Irish. And then you're from here."

"Right," Mama crunches on a sunflower seed, spits the shell out into a second baggie she appears to have brought for just that function. "And?"

"So out of the four grandparents, we have three Irish and one Puerto Rican. Which means we'd expect our DNA to be mostly Irish and then a quarter Puerto Rican."

"Okay, yes," Mama says.

Ruth is not looking at Carlos, but she can feel her younger son glaring into the side of her head. Daisy's hands are folded peacefully on top of her blanket. *She has survived, that's all that matters*, Ruth thinks. *Why are we even talking about this? Who cares?*

"But according to the test results, it looks like Daisy and Carlos are about half and half," Vic says, glancing around at the other faces in the room.

"Oh!" Mama says. "Half and half?"

"Half Irish, half Puerto Rican," Carlos says.

"Yeah." Vic pauses. "I wonder," but then he opts out of his sentence.

Carlos pushes him. "You wonder what?"

He commits slowly. "I wonder . . . if my results would be the same?"

"Well, of course yours would be the same!" Ruth throws her hands in the air. "You have the same parents, don't you?"

"Do we?" Carlos slings the question like a dart.

"Oh dear," Mama says.

But no one hears her, no one's listening. All eyes are on Ruth. Demanding answers. Ruth's hands are in the air, she's making the universal gesture for stop. She's trying to speak louder than her children, to be heard above their questions, but Carlos and Vic are both talking over her. Only Daisy is quiet, her eyes resting on her grandmother.

Rafaela reseals her ziplock baggie and replaces it in her purse. She clears her throat, then reaches for Daisy's iced coffee, and takes a sip. Then she performs El Suspiro, with a long, high note on the exhale. A wind song with her body, an effort to interrupt the chaotic din in the room, to bring the volume back to a place of harmony, where they can hear one another. It works. Ruth and her grandsons all turn to look at her. She clears her throat quietly.

"I think I can explain," she says.

Chapter Thirty

~

San Juan, Puerto Rico
1968

The first two years of the marriage were good. Well, okay, Rafaela is not one to exaggerate. The first two years of the marriage were fine once they made the necessary adjustments. As often happens, the couple's lofty romantic anticipation in courtship was met by the natural development of domestic torpor in wedlock. Nothing to be alarmed about. But Rafaela, who'd spent most of her early life on a pedestal, found that her transition into married life had other challenges in addition to those ordinary ones.

What Rafaela had learned in Trinidad was that her childhood had been downright aristocratic. She still behaved like a member of an elite social class in the ways she walked, spoke, and held herself, yes, but also in her ideas. Rafaela didn't realize she was a snob; she didn't mean to be. But she'd found it difficult to make friends among the other secretaries in Chaguaramas. Even her cousin Clarisa, who had plenty of girlfriends on base and whom Rafaela loved, sometimes struck Rafaela as uncultured, coming as she did from Mayagüez, which Papamío referred to as the stink-end of the island, even though it was Mamamía's hometown. But Rafaela also discovered, with tremendous indignation, that when she left Puerto Rico, people didn't even seem to understand who she *was*, or what set her apart from other girls. They treated Rafaela as if she were common, as if she were a girl who'd grown up buttering her own toast, and she should butter theirs too, and then serve it to them with hot coffee. In Trinidad, Rafaela learned to swallow indignities. She learned how to endure working for a boss who sometimes called her *pork chop*. She discovered that she had no choice.

But that was behind her now, thank God. She was a wife, for better and for worse—she was Peter Brennan's wife. And although that fact would never provide her with the same status she had once enjoyed as the daughter of Rafael Acuña y Torres, it was something. Peter was handsome and respectable and white, which Rafaela briefly mistook for being almost the same as being wealthy. So the great task of her adult life then, after spending her years first at the top and then somewhat closer to the bottom of the social order, would be for Rafaela to learn to inhabit the nuanced middle, to strip back the artificial layers of nonsense and expectation that had been heaped upon her through no fault of her own, and to discover who she was beneath the weight of her father's indulgence and an arbitrary system of social caste. That was a lot for a new marriage to bear.

In the late 1960s and early 1970s, the US Navy was ubiquitous in San Juan, and there was plenty of work for civilians, so after Peter was discharged from active service in Trinidad, he used his connections to land a good job as a radio technician at Isla Grande Naval Air Station. The newlyweds found a little house in Santurce with a banyan tree in the backyard that was an easy walk to nightclubs, restaurants, Rafaela's family, the beach. Peter could even walk to work, and Rafaela didn't have to go with him. She didn't have to spend her days typing or filing. She no longer had to hold her breath when her boss leaned over her desk after lunch, stinking of garlic and scotch. She was back home in Puerto Rico near her family, back in her own skin, her own language. She was happy.

In the spring, they took a honeymoon to Las Vegas, which was fun because of the sex and the gambling, but alarming because Rafaela could see that her husband loved this brazen, superficial place, and for the first time, she worried that Peter would get bored in a city as classic, Catholic, and colonial as her beloved San Juan. She tried not to think about it.

It wasn't long before Peter began coming home without greeting her.

Instead of coming to find her in the kitchen, he'd collapse on the couch in the living room or trek down the hall toward the bedroom, shedding his tie, his shoes, his belt. Sometimes he even dropped these items like a trail of breadcrumbs along the hallway, and left them where they fell until Rafaela picked them up and put them away. Once, she left them there overnight to see how long it would take before he cleaned up after himself. The next morning, he stepped over everything on his way to the kitchen for his morning coffee, which she had prepared for him along with a plate of scrambled eggs and bacon. Then he barked at her when he couldn't find his shoes on the way out the door.

"They're in the hallway," she said.

"Well, what the hell are they doing there?" he said. "That's not where they belong."

"No," she agreed. "It's not."

They glared at each other across the living room until he left, slamming the door behind him. Rafaela closed her eyes and called to mind how disgusted she'd felt every morning in Trinidad when her boss inevitably handed over her first round of memos stuck together with a glob of jelly from his breakfast doughnut. Who knew what Peter had to endure in his new job now that he was a civilian again? She wished he would tell her. But until he was ready, she'd have to be patient with him.

As their domestic routine hardened and set, they seldom went dancing or out to eat anymore. Peter wanted to save money for a car, which Rafaela thought was ridiculous since they could walk wherever they wanted to go. He began to relentlessly criticize her cooking, her housekeeping. And she knew he had a point—she was not great at these things. But when was she supposed to have learned these skills? And why would she even want to?

"It's not Peter," Rafaela said to Lola whenever they discussed it. "He's not the worst husband."

"So what's the problem then?" Lola asked.

"I think"—Rafaela shook her head—"I just don't like being a wife."

She did not say, although the demoralizing thought occurred to her with some frequency, that she was also sure she wasn't turning out to be the wife Peter thought he was getting. She felt like a disappointment

336 • Jeanine Cummins

to him. He had chosen her because she was beautiful and smart and charming, and because he felt lucky. She'd been a hot commodity on the naval base, despite her comedown, and she had refused all suitors until Peter. In hindsight, Rafaela realized that he hadn't piqued her interest because there was anything particularly special about him, but because he treated her with basic decency and kindness. He was different in just that way: he treated her like a person. (And, yes, he was good-looking.) This was, Rafaela realized far too late, not enough to build a marriage on.

She withheld these poisonous thoughts from her sister only because she mostly withheld them from herself as well. They were treachery. And they were folly. It was too late for these realizations. Rafaela had to make the best of it.

"It will be okay," she said to Lola. "I'll get used to it."

Lola sighed and gripped Rafaela's hands, and then she held Rafaela tightly in her arms until there was a loosening, a softening between them. In her sister's arms, Rafaela felt like she could wake up and try again the next day.

When Peter was at work, Rafaela was able to walk to her parents' apartment, where she drank coffee and read magazines with Mamamía, or helped Papamío with the pots of herbs and tomatoes he grew in the courtyard of the building where they now lived. Her parents had adjusted remarkably well to their new circumstances. Papamío had cleared his name and gotten a good job with a private accounting firm. Mamamía had her own income now, too, a flourishing business she was careful not to let overshadow the new pleasure she found in being a homemaker, a pleasure she hoped Rafaela might soon discover as well. At home, her mother wore diamond earrings and high heels when she was frying eggs, and her beauty was in no way diminished in the modest apartment. In fact, it seemed even more vivid, more remarkable now that it was removed from opulence and set apart by itself. Mamamía and Papamío were as happy as they'd ever been in the big house on calle Américo Salas. Her father's smile was quicker and more mischievous than in previous years. Rafaela took their example and did not complain, but Mamamía saw everything. She touched Rafaela under the chin as they sat together at the kitchen table with their coffees.

"It will be okay, you'll see," she said. "Once you have a baby, everything settles. Everything changes."

Rafaela sighed deeply.

"You'll see," her mother said again. "Love grows. It doesn't have to be fireworks all from the beginning. It can be steadfast. You will fall in love with him again one night when he kills a spider on the bathroom wall. And then again one day when he tells you a funny story about someone you both dislike. And then you'll fall in love with him all over again when you have a baby, and you see how he becomes a father. Every time he's patient with you, you'll fall in love."

Rafaela pinned her hopes to that idea. A baby would fill her days with affection and purpose, but would also unite them. A baby would bridge the gap she'd discovered in her marriage, would make their family whole by bringing one side into concert with the other.

In the meantime, such was Peter's dismay about Rafaela's domestic failures that she began to wonder if he'd gotten married not so much to find a companion and life partner, but more because he needed someone to do his cooking and cleaning. In her darker moods, she remembered how many of the housekeepers and cooks in Trinidad had been from Puerto Rico, and she wondered if her husband had mistaken her. He certainly seemed surprised by her lack of domestic skill and interest, and his impatience was palpable. He complained every single night across the dinner table, even on those rare occasions when Rafaela herself thought her effort had turned out rather well. He washed her dinners down with extra beer, and then groped for her in the dark at night. Eventually, she began to lose interest in that too. But afterward, when Peter slept against her skin in the lamplight, she traced a finger along his damp hairline and hoped their children would inherit the handsome arch of freckles along his forehead.

When Rafaela got pregnant with Benny, everything changed, just like Mamamía said it would. The night she told Peter the news, he stood up from the table, grabbed her by the hand, and pulled her out of her chair. He lifted her and spun her around just like the day he'd asked her to marry him and she, in a delighted sort of fugue state, had said yes. She laughed while they spun together in the kitchen, and then he caught himself midspin, and set her down gingerly beside the table. Her shoes were off, and the tiles were cool beneath her feet.

"Oh!" he said. "Oh, I probably shouldn't spin you! We need to be careful." And then he knelt down on the floor and took her hips in his hands and spoke into her belly. "Hello in there! I'm so happy you're here!"

Rafaela had never loved Peter more than she did that night, not even on their wedding day. Love grew, her mother was right. They both had tears in their eyes when he stood up and kissed her. And then he did a thing he had never done before in their marriage. He swept their two plates up from the table himself, and he dumped them in the sink.

"Let's go for ice cream," he said.

Rafaela failed to note the flaw in her current condition, however, which was that it would end in nine months. As long as she was the oven to their bun, Peter's patience and pampering were limitless. He stifled his complaints about her cooking as best he could, and after dinner most nights, he insisted that she lie on the couch with a book while he did the dishes. He kissed her and complimented her, and put his own shoes in the closet. He asked at least three times a day how she was feeling. She was feeling wonderful.

And she continued to feel wonderful after Benny was born, their perfect boy. Look what she had done! She had made this splendid child for them both to love! This was her most important contribution to their family, to their life together, this! Who cared about underseasoned skirt steak and overdressed salad? Who cared if she made the bed before nine in the morning on a Saturday?

The first few weeks were bliss. Rafaela spent most of her time staring at Benny's fluttering eyelids and puckering lips while Lola and Mamamía took turns cooking and helping out around the house. Peter was happy because the food was better, the house was cleaner, and he had a son! A perfect little boy. The little family developed a new rhythm. Rafaela got back on her tired but capable feet, and her sister and mother returned mostly to their own lives.

Benny seldom cried, and when he did, Rafa delighted in providing whatever comfort he needed, the bottle or the swaddle or to wrap his tiny fingers around her pinky and stare into her eyes. She always knew what he needed. Rafaela didn't even mind the cloth diapers, not even the disgusting ones. That odor was made by her very own baby, after all, so Rafaela honored the stink. Still, she wore rubber gloves when she ventured into the backyard with the hose to scrape the diapers clean before they made their way into the washing machine. She wasn't an animal. It turned out that her temperament was naturally suited to motherhood. Rafaela had always expected as much, but she was pleased to have that suspicion confirmed.

And so Benny became the sun, while Peter and Rafaela remained lowly planets in his orbit. Benny received the breadth of his father's attention, which pleased Rafaela, even when Peter fell into the habit of greeting her with only a dry peck on the forehead. Still, her husband's face transformed when he came in from work and dumped his briefcase and shoes by the door.

"Hey, kiddo!" He beamed, tossing his tie onto the discard pile, and swooping in to lift Benny out of her arms.

Rafaela's position in Peter's affections quickly retreated to its pre-pregnancy starting point, but it felt worse now, because for nine months, she'd experienced the warmth of his attentive care. Its withdrawal left a chill she hadn't noticed before, but she tried her best to ignore it. She was a mother now. She didn't have time to indulge such nonsense.

One night, Rafaela forgot to turn the burner to low before she sat down to nurse Benny, and she accidentally scalded the beans. At the table, Peter took one bite and made a face like he was going to throw up. He swigged milk and closed his eyes, and made a huge show of swallowing the food before he launched into his typical litany of grievances about her cooking. She stood up from the table without saying a word, walked into the living room where Benny was lying happily in his bassinet, and picked him up expertly with one arm. She held him against her shoulder while she slipped her feet into her sandals, and then she deposited him into his stroller, which was already sitting next to the front door. Peter came out of the kitchen and stood watching while she wrestled to get the stroller through the door.

"What's this?" Peter said.

"We're going out for a walk," Rafaela said, her voice full of the brightness it always contained when she spoke in front of Benny.

"Yeah, you'll have to walk since we can't afford a car in this city," he said.

"We don't need a car in this fantastic, pedestrian-friendly city!" This part of the argument was scripted, they'd had it many times. Rafa kept her eyes on Benny and her voice chipper while she launched the next part, which was new. "And you can cook your own goddamned dinner, I'm not your servant."

The stroller was stuck in the doorway. What was wedged there, under the wheel? Rafaela bent down to find one of Peter's shoes in the way.

"You got that right, if you were a servant, I'd have fired you by now," Peter said from across the living room.

She turned to look at him standing there, still in his work trousers and socks, his sleeveless undershirt still white, pristine white, because she bleached it and laundered it along with all the others. She did this every week although no one had showed her how, and after she laundered them, she folded them neatly and put them back in her husband's dresser drawer. Peter had never once said thank you for this. She was holding his shoe in her hand.

"What did you say?" she asked him.

He had the gall to repeat himself, although with slightly less conviction than the first time. "If you were a servant, I'd have fired you by now."

She pulled back like Roberto Clemente and pegged that wing tip at her astonished husband with all the force she could muster. Peter barely had time to lift his hands in front of his face before it hit him there, on the forearm.

"And put your goddamned shoes away!"

She opened the door, pushed the stroller through, and left.

It was at Benny's first birthday party, which they held in the little courtyard behind Mamamía and Papamío's apartment building, that she first heard that Candido was home from New York. He had been to visit her parents. Papamío was out when he came by, but Mamamía had sat with him for two hours, laughing, telling old stories.

"He's such a charming boy, so intelligent," Mamamía said. And Rafaela wondered, for the first time, if their family's misfortune had been good for her mother, if it had liberated her somehow, returned her to herself. She seemed more at ease now than she'd ever been when they were growing up. She spoke of Candido with naked affection where before, Rafaela was sure, there'd always been some measure of heedfulness. "He's grown so broad and tall!" Mamamía said. "You wouldn't believe it!"

Rafaela concentrated all her energy on making sure her face betrayed no emotion in response to this news or the way her mother delivered it.

"What about Priti? Is she coming back too?" Papamío asked, and Rafaela found that she was equally relieved by the change of subject and annoyed that the topic of Candido (and his broadened shoulders) had been so fleeting.

"No, she's staying in Miami," Mamamía said. "She loves it there."

"I heard she's getting married!" Lola said.

"Our Priti, getting married!" Papamío said with delight. He clapped his hands together. "Good for her, how wonderful."

"Where did you hear that?" Rafaela asked, sipping from her lemonade.

Lola was holding Benny on her lap, and Benny was tugging ineffectually at Lola's earring. Rafaela reached out to disentangle his chubby fingers from the hoop in her sister's ear. She wagged one finger at Benny.

"No, no," she said.

"No, no," Benny repeated.

Rafaela returned her attention to Lola. "About Priti getting married, where did you hear that? I just talked to her at Christmas and she didn't mention it."

"Oh, it just happened a few weeks ago," Lola said, readjusting her lopsided earring. "Candido told me."

"You saw him too?" Rafaela heard the jealousy in her voice, and hoped no one else noticed.

She glanced at Peter, who was on the other side of the courtyard with a group of young men playing horseshoes. He had a bottle of beer in one hand. It was remarkable to Rafaela, how attractive her husband was when seen from afar.

"I ran into him at church two weekends ago," Lola said, which made Rafaela feel a little better. Less snubbed. "And he invited me to lunch," which made Rafaela feel much worse. She couldn't stop herself from frowning.

"I'm sure he'll come visit you soon," Mamamía said, because it was obvious to everyone at the little table how distressed Rafaela was, that she was the only one who'd been left out of Candido's return. "He knows you've had your hands full with the baby."

"He'll be anxious to meet Peter too," Lola said, draining her glass. "Anyone else want more lemonade?"

News of Candido was hard to come by because, apart from Rafaela's family and his mother, they did not share any mutual friends. But Rafaela latched on to every piece of information her family tossed out. She remembered every slowly emerging detail: where he worked, where he lived, what he was studying in his night classes at UPR (civil engineering and business).

Without meaning to, and without even drawing this truth fully to her own attention, Rafaela began to widen the route she and Benny took on their afternoon walks to include a park near Candido's apartment building. Then she added a morning walk to their routine because, she told herself, Benny was getting to an age where he was resisting the morning nap, and the walk helped make him sleepy. This late-morning route took them past Candido's workplace. Rafaela walked so much, the soles of her shoes turned soft and scuffed, and when all those walks failed to produce the suppressed-desired result, she found additional reasons to visit that part of town. She made unnecessary dentist appointments, decided she needed a particular book that was only available from one bookseller in San Juan, discovered a dressmaker who stocked fabrics no one else had (for good reason, as it turned out). This went on for so long, that Rafaela was actually in danger of acknowledging her repressed hope by the time she finally ran into him.

Benny was a toddler, and Rafaela's habit of wandering the city to wear him out was so ingrained by that point, that she sometimes failed to lift her eyes from her darling boy while they tromped the streets together, sometimes with Benny asleep in the stroller, other times with him wedged into the space between Rafaela's outstretched arms, helping her push, his tiny fingers wrapped around the handle just inside hers, their pace slowed by half to allow for Benny's tiny legs to keep up.

They were at Benny's favorite playground in Chícaro, and she was pushing him on the swings when she saw Candido like an apparition, passing beyond the fence. She would have known him without looking up, would have known him just from the shadow he cast along the ground beside her feet, his shadow as familiar to her as her own, as her child's. She hadn't seen him in six years. And then it was all in slow motion. Benny's delight as he arced through the air on his swing, all dimples and wheeling arms and kicking legs. Rafaela threw one arm up overhead, her voice slow, her pulse loud.

"Candido!" She called out his name.

He slowed. And her heart staggered.

When he turned, there was a moment on his face like a precipice. A choice. He might have clamped it shut. Sealed it off. He might have tipped his hat to her and made polite small talk across the fence, and then slipped away as quickly as possible. But instead, his face slid open to reveal his heart.

"Rafa," he said. And he didn't walk across the small space that separated them. He didn't walk to the gate in the fence, swing it open, latch it carefully behind him, and then stroll casually across the mulch to where she stood. He jumped the fence and ran to her. And when he scooped her into his arms, and baby Benny's dimples deepened with surprise, there was a moment when, to any unknowing passerby, the man lifting the woman beside the swings could have been her brother. Her long-lost cousin. It wasn't immediately visible that sparks were shooting off beneath their clothes.

"Why didn't you come see me?" she asked after he set her down, but before he let go of her hands. "You've been back all these months? You visited my parents three times, Lola twice." She shook her head. Hurt.

He waited a moment before answering, before he pulled one hand

344 • Jeanine Cummins

away from her grip to shield his eyes from the sun, so he could lock his eyes on hers.

"You know why," he said.

The next Friday afternoon, Rafaela told Mamamía she had a luncheon in Bayamón, and that she wouldn't be back until evening. This was a lie, and it caused Rafaela a great deal of discomfort in her soul to tell it. She wasn't in the habit of duplicity. But Mamamía was delighted to take Benny for the day, and in fact, she would enjoy watching her grandson so much, that she would thereafter offer to make it a standing date. Why not leave him with her every Friday afternoon or evening? Perhaps she and Peter could spend the extra time reconnecting. They could go to the pictures or out for dinner in El Viejo San Juan, or for a walk around the lagoon when he got home from work. These were all good ideas for engendering romance, Rafaela thought. She would take them under advisement.

Then at three o'clock, Rafaela went back to that same park, where she had learned Candido passed on foot every afternoon around three thirty, in between work and his night classes at the university. Friday was the only evening he didn't have classes, so he would go home and grill himself a steak, and then he might head for the beach in Condado or out to play dominoes and drink a beer with some friends, or he might go out dancing with a young woman, a possibility that made Rafaela's heart throb with sourness.

When she arrived at the park, she sat on a bench facing the sidewalk where he would soon pass. She crossed and uncrossed her legs, and while she waited, she replayed the worst fight of their lives, worse than the time when they were seven and she teased him for the way he pronounced the word *puerta* with an L so that it sounded like *puelta*. Even worse than when they were thirteen and he failed to suppress his reaction to her extremely regrettable haircut. The worst one had been just two and a half years ago, when she'd called him at work in New York to announce her engagement to Peter.

"Why would you call me at work to tell me this?" Candido had asked.

She'd wanted to tell him herself. She didn't want him to read it in a letter or hear the news from Priti.

"You don't have a phone in your apartment," she said, which he took as a socioeconomic critique of his lifestyle, when all she'd meant was that she could only get ahold of him by phone at the hotel.

"Well, congratulations," he said that day before they hung up. "Sounds like he's everything you've been looking for." And though there'd been no identifiable sarcasm in his voice, Rafaela had received his regards like mockery.

They hadn't raised their voices or slung insults at each other or chased and slapped each other like when they were children. But something had turned that day, in that moderate exchange, and she feared the sourness remained between them until now, until last week. Rafaela didn't know if she'd ever be able to correct it. But then she saw him.

She didn't ask herself what she intended to do. She didn't make any plans or consider any ramifications. She simply put herself in his path because she could think of no other way to ease the suffering that had grown in her heart since his return. His brief presence would alleviate that agony. She thought no further than that until she was standing in his bedroom, unzipping the back of her dress, pushing the sleeves down over her shoulders, letting the soft fabric fall past the bones of her wrists and land at her feet. Candido sat in front of her with his face like a mirror, splintered with love and anguish and guilt and desire. When she stepped out of her dress and moved toward him, he said what she had always known.

"I've loved you since we were babies."

Rafaela would never accept the word *affair*, not during the time when it happened, nor in the years following whenever she thought back to it, which she would do with some frequency despite her efforts to avoid reminiscing. Her love for Candido would be so abiding and guiltless that the word *affair* would feel meaningless with its histrionics and moderation and suggestion of turpitude. Candido would remain pure, in her heart and mind, and Rafaela would experience no remorse whatsoever about the adultery, not even when she slid into the pew beside her husband on Sunday mornings, and got down on her knees to beseech God for an end to her torment.

It would take seven years before her deliverance would fall from the lips of her husband. "We're moving back to St. Louis, Rafaela," Peter said as she stood at the kitchen sink in their little house in Santurce one hot summer evening. "I can't take it here anymore. I'm done."

And she would wonder if he knew, if the move was his attempt to rescue her from herself, to salvage their sinking marriage.

They would argue. She would cry. And they would go.

She saw Candido one last time before they flew. She pressed her forehead into his, felt desperation in the way his hand encircled her wrist.

"I have to be with my family," she said.

"I'm your family."

"Candido, my children." She kissed his cheekbone and tasted salt.

Chapter Thirty-One

∽

San Juan, Puerto Rico
2023

"Dag, Grandma!" Vic says when Rafaela finishes talking.

"Get it, Grandma!" Carlos says.

Daisy smiles and sips from her iced coffee, but says nothing. Ruth, too, is speechless, her mouth slightly opened. Rafaela stands up.

"Sit down, dear," she says to her daughter. Ruth plops into the chair.

"Are you okay?" Rafaela asks.

"I don't know, Mama. I just. I'm shocked."

Rafaela nods, pulls her sunflower seeds back out of her purse.

"That's understandable," she says, once again offering the bag to Ruth who once again is stunned by her mother's capacity to snack at a time like this.

"No thanks," Ruth says, and then for a moment, the only noise in the room is the sound of Rafaela crunching the seeds.

She looks at her daughter, who can't muster a verbal response to the information she's struggling to take in. "You know it's okay, Ruth," Rafaela says, pausing her snack long enough to impart this. "We loved each other very much. We still do."

But Ruth is blinking and her face remains pinched, her breathing shallow. Rafaela puts the seeds down and leans into her daughter's face. She places one hand on Ruth's shoulder and the other under her chin, just like she did when Ruth was tiny, when she needed her little girl to see that the only important thing was right here, between them. The same signal she performed with Lola when they were small—the hook and reel. She brings her eyes level with Ruth's eyes.

"Listen, I made one big mistake in my life," she says, her voice soft but ardent. "And it most certainly wasn't you."

§

After the initial shock, the rest of the story emerges in a way that reminds Ruth of labor and delivery. It's intense and it comes in waves, and after each new revelation, everyone retreats to recover before the next swell appears. Ruth has so many questions she has to write them down, but she doesn't ask them all at once. Some of them she will never ask, because she will decide that, despite her curiosity, some things are truly none of her business. Some things are, though.

"Does Dad know? Does Candido?"

Mama's response to this most basic question astonishes Ruth.

"They likely knew as much as I knew. Which is to say they had their suspicions."

They have moved to the hospital cafeteria, where they are sitting in a corner booth, an attempt at privacy.

"Until today?" Ruth is incredulous. "You mean you never knew, until what, until these DNA results? But you must have known!"

"Well, of course I knew what was possible," Mama says. "But the opposite was just as possible. You and Benny look so much alike! And you both look like me."

This is true.

"Anyway, it didn't matter," Mama says.

Ruth's mouth falls open as if to protest, but before she can get there, the veracity of her mother's words strikes like a bell in her consciousness.

"What mattered was the family," Mama says. "I was Peter Brennan's wife, therefore, you were Peter Brennan's daughter. That was it."

"And I'm still his daughter," Ruth says, realizing as she tries these words out that they are true. There's no denying that she's always been closer to Mama. But what passes through Ruth in this moment is a hurricane of memories, her father on his knees at her bedside, in the soft glow of her daisy nightlight, saying her prayers. Her father holding a giant camcorder at her college graduation. Her father walking beside her down the long aisle of Saint Columna's where Thomas waited for her to say *I do*.

Her father is her father. Nothing has changed. Nothing about Ruth has changed at all. She's exactly the same person today as she was yesterday, and the same is true for her children. They are still who they've always been—the numbers mean nothing. They are quiet for a moment while Ruth catches up with the machinery of her mind.

"Candido seems like a nice man," she says. Generously, she thinks, given the circumstances. "Is he . . . is he married?"

"He was. Though not at the time we made you," Mama says. "He got married after we moved to St. Louis, and you know, I never admitted it even to myself, but I think that was a big part of my depression, moving away. Knowing that he was lost to me."

Ruth thought she knew every single thing about her mother. What a revelation! Even the utterance of the word *depression* feels like an epiphany. But of course. Of course that's what it was, how obvious now. "So he *was* married? Not anymore?"

Mama shakes her head. "She passed a few years ago. Cancer."

"Oh," Ruth says, and then other questions about Candido and his life appear in her mind, but Ruth isn't ready to ask them. "So, what do we do now?" she asks instead.

"Should we tell Candido, maybe?" Mama asks. "And your dad?"

Ruth shakes her head. "Not yet. Maybe later. I need to get used to it first. And Dad should hear it first, for sure, if we decide to tell them."

She wonders if there's any point in telling him, in telling either of them. She needs time to think.

"Smart cookie," Mama says. And then, standing out of the booth, "Speaking of cookies, they have chocolate chip. You want one?"

Ruth watches Mama walk back to the food counter, lean over the cookie display, and peer inside. Ruth tries to remember if she's ever seen Mama eat a cookie before. She's never known her mother to be such a carefree snacker, and so she wonders whether this is part of some larger personality change, another symptom of decline. Ruth runs her hands through her hair, pushes that worry out through her lungs because truly, she does not have space for it. Maybe, after seventy-five years of watching her figure, Mama has finally decided just to eat what she wants. Maybe it's as simple as that, Ruth thinks. And why not? Good for her.

Rafaela is standing in line to pay for her cookie when she recognizes one of Daisy's doctors in front of her. He's paying for his soup and Snapple when his pager goes off, which strikes Rafaela as comical. Who carries a beeper anymore, aren't those things obsolete? Certainly there must be a more dignified way to urgently contact a person whose job it is to save people's lives? She makes a mental note to share this observation with Daisy.

The man looks down at the pager, which is clipped to his belt, and then before he can even tell the cashier he'll come back for it later, she is already lifting his tray and setting it aside. She knows the routine. The cashier says, "Next," just as the doctor breaks into a run toward the elevator, and Rafaela watches him go. She pays for her cookie and rejoins Ruth at the table. She breaks the cookie in two, keeps one half for herself and slides the other across to Ruth on a paper napkin. They are finished eating, and Rafaela is imprinting crumbs onto the tip of her finger when Ruth's cell phone begins to ring in her bag. Ruth's bag is a mess, of course, and she can't find the phone, but Rafaela knows anyway, even before Ruth finds it in the third zippered pocket and pulls it out, before she can swipe the slider that will connect her to Carlos and the news he needs to deliver. Rafaela knows because during the second or third ring, it occurs to her that there was nothing comical about that doctor and his pager at all. That beeping, buzzing little contraption, that was a call for help, Rafaela knows, from someone in this very hospital. A plea to save someone's life. Daisy's life.

Over the many decades of her life, Rafaela can count on one hand the number of times her panic superseded her self-awareness and her animal instinct took over: Lola's death. Her parents' deaths. Thomas's death. Four times. This is the fifth. She doesn't register how she looks or how she sounds. She doesn't care if she's wrong, she hopes to God she's wrong, there's no potential for embarrassment here. There's nothing but urgency. Something in her gut tells her it's Daisy. And then Ruth's face confirms it.

They run.

§

By the time Ruth and Mama arrive back in Daisy's room, her bed has been wheeled out with her in it. Vic has his arms around Carlos, who is weeping heavily. Ruth has never known a feeling like this. There is a stampede of horror in her throat.

"Where is she?"

"They took her to surgery," Vic says.

"What?" Ruth turns in a circle, as if she'll find Daisy standing behind her. "How, why? How so fast?"

"They said it was a pulmonary embolism," Vic says.

Ruth doesn't really know what that means. She knows it's very dangerous. How dangerous? Where is the nurse?

"Nurse!" she yells, like a maniac. "Nurse!"

"She said she'd come right back, after they got her into surgery." Vic is such a grown-up.

Ruth maneuvers herself into position to take over the comforting of Carlos, who seems to have shrunk back to his preadolescent self. She wraps her arms around him, and Vic steps back, bumps himself against the windowsill.

"It's okay," she says to Carlos, although she has no idea if this is true. It's a mantra she will repeat until it happens. "It's okay, it's okay, she'll be okay."

She kisses Carlos's forehead and squeezes her eyes shut.

"What happened?" Mama asks, taking both of their handbags from Ruth and parking them on the chair. "She was fine when we left here."

"She was, she was fine," Vic says. "And then—" He takes a deep breath. "We were just talking. Carlos said something funny and we all laughed, and Daisy laughed. And then she coughed." Vic is crying now, too, but in a very somber way. The tears walk down his face. "She coughed and then . . . she couldn't get her breath after that."

"There was blood," Carlos says. "She coughed up blood." He lets loose a few quick sobs.

Vic nods. "That's right. And then, she was sort of clutching her chest. It looked like she was in pain. And then she just, like, fainted. Or something."

It's the *or something* that incites a horrid tingle from Ruth's scalp to the soles of her feet. "It's okay, it's okay," she repeats.

"Her lips were blue," Carlos whispers.

And then the nurse is there in the doorway, and it takes every morsel of psychic strength Ruth can muster in order to lift her face to what's coming, to square her shoulders to this woman. To ask the next questions.

The nurse warns them that the surgery can take up to four hours.

"But they'll have a better idea once they get in there and see what's going on. Your sons did an excellent job getting help right away." The nurse puts a hand on Vic's forearm and squeezes. "She was so lucky they were here."

Vic shakes his head, but the move is almost a spasm of emotion, and he can't really breathe. He gulps air and then hold it in. The nurse continues.

"We came with the crash cart right away, and we could see on the echocardiogram that she had a massive pulmonary embolus." There are many words in this sentence that Ruth doesn't fully understand, but she wants as much information as possible, so she nods her head, urging the nurse to go on. "She wasn't a good candidate for thrombolytics because of her previous brain bleed after the accident. So we had to take her to surgery right away. She's already under. It may be the fastest I've ever seen a patient get from embolism to operating table, which bodes very well for her."

"What's the surgery called?" Carlos asks, wiping his eyes. And Ruth knows that he's asking so he can google it after the nurse leaves the room. Ruth both does and does not want him to google it.

"The procedure is an open embolectomy. We have excellent surgeons here, Mrs. Hayes. Your daughter is in very skilled hands."

Ruth nods, but can't bring herself to say thank you.

"I will keep you updated as soon as I have more information."

Ruth nods again, and when the nurse turns to go, Carlos is already googling the surgery. "Up to twenty-nine percent." His voice is awed, reverent.

"What is that?" Vic asks. "What's twenty-nine percent?"

"The mortality rate." Carlos is crying again.

Ruth seals her eyes closed. She nods and then opens them again. "That means the survival rate is seventy-one."

"For Daisy?" Rafaela says. "I like those odds."

After Thomas died, Ruth stopped taking the kids to church. It wasn't a decision she made on purpose, but at first, after her husband's death, she had her own crisis of faith. And then, once she'd found her way back to the comfort of hope, she was simply overwhelmed. She had three small children. Vic played soccer on Sunday mornings. Carlos had dance recitals. Daisy was forever at a sleepover. Weekly mass became monthly mass, which eventually became Easter and Christmas. Ruth cannot remember the last time she prayed with her children.

In Daisy's vacant hospital room, she gathers her boys and her mother together. They stand inside the space recently occupied by Daisy's bed. There are black rubber marks against the linoleum from the wheels. The tile is slightly discolored there, in the rectangle where the bed should be, where Daisy should be. They huddle together inside this faded linoleum rectangle. They do not hold hands. They hold arms and necks and shoulders. They press their heads together.

They pray.

§

As the surgeon divides her breastbone and opens her pericardium, Daisy dreams of her father. In the dream, she remembers things about him that she'd long ago forgotten. The scar that dissected his right eyebrow. The curl of his lashes. The faint freckles along his cut cheekbones. His T-shirt tucked into his jeans. He doesn't speak in the dream, and neither does she. But they attend to each other in a way that's beyond words. She feels a warm comfort radiating from him. First, as they sit side by side atop the blue quilt in his childhood bedroom in Cong. Next, as they stand in the doorway of Daisy's own childhood bedroom in Palisades. Then, in the Double Down, Daisy on her stool behind the register while her father sits on the red velvet chaise longue someone brought in last month. He is smiling. He is beaming.

And then they're in a fluorescent room with broad windows and a banyan tree just outside the window. A curtain hangs from the ceiling, and when her father pulls it back, they're all there—her family. Mom is there, with a face like war. And there are her brothers, clinging so tightly to each other that their fingers dig, their knuckles whiten. There is Grandma, the infrastructure, brick and mortar. She holds them all together in her small arms. Daisy steps in among them but her body is loose. Vapor.

Chapter Thirty-Two

~

San Juan, Puerto Rico
2023

Benny will take Ruth to see the shop. He will park at a municipal lot two blocks away because it's a busy, narrow street. It's quiet in the early morning, and the whole street bears the unmistakable sticky-sweet smell of nightclubs and dance floors. Ruth will note bubbly graffiti on many of the walls and windows here, a flock of scooters on every corner. They will pass three nightclubs, a bar, a falafel joint, and a beauty supply store before arriving at a storefront with a wooden sign hanging from a wrought-iron post in front. It's eye catching, brightly colored in Caribbean turquoise and orange. It says THE DOUBLE DOWN. And then in smaller letters underneath: VINTAGE CURIOSITIES, COMMODITIES, & CONSIGNMENTS. In oil marker, the store name is repeated in huge letters across the top of the window, and in the corners, a tiny Puerto Rican flag on the right and a tiny Irish flag on the left. Daisy's handwriting in bronze marker across the bottom of the window declares: YOUR GO-TO PLACE FOR LUXURY CONSIGNMENT.

Displayed in the window is a starter selection of Daisy's merchandise. A golden chair with carved arms in a glowing, brocade upholstery. A silk scarf in magenta, an ornate bird cage in red, a pillbox hat with a peacock feather. A piano accordion sits atop a low, carved wooden stool. Tucked into the hollows are glittering shoes in every hue, and colored bulbs and baubles hang from above. Ruth catches her breath, reaches through the metal grate to press her palm against the warm glass.

Benny leans down to unlock the grate, roll it up, unlock the glass door. The spectacle continues inside—the space is large, and Daisy has filled it with treasures. Ruth breathes it in, whatever that humid smell is, and touches a few of the handwritten price tags that dangle from every lamp and vessel. It's hot inside, so Benny goes to turn on the air-conditioning, and just as he steps into the back room, the door behind Ruth swings open, and a breathless girl appears there with a hoop in her nose and one in her eyebrow, and she already starts talking before Ruth turns around.

"Where have you been? I've stopped by here like forty times. I'm dying to get my hands on that blouse—" Ruth turns in time to see the girl's face falter. "You're not Daisy," she says.

"I'm not," Ruth agrees.

But the girl doesn't pause for long. She brushes past Ruth, and goes straight to the rack where the blouse in question is hanging. It's silk. Black. Valentino. It swings from its velvet hanger like liquid stars. "Can I buy this anyway?" the girl asks. "Even though she's not here?"

Ruth breathes deeply, a habit she will never take for granted again. She notices her breath as it travels unimpeded around her body, into the folds of her lungs, and then back out again. She moves herself in behind the little counter, Daisy's counter, and does a quick assessment to determine that she doesn't know how to use the antique cash register. Luckily there's an iPad here, too, with a credit card reader. They've been plugged in this whole time. Fully charged.

"Seems like you can," Ruth says.

"Gorgeous, isn't it?" The girl places the blouse gently between them, and Ruth unbuttons the top button, removes it from its hanger, the fabric slippery and luxurious in her hands.

The price that Daisy has handwritten in her distinctive scrawl is $78, which seems to Ruth like both a bargain and an extravagance. She wonders how Daisy knew what prices to charge, how Daisy learned any of this, all of it, how she made this splendor out of nothing. Ruth marvels at this place that feels as though it's been here forever, an organic depository for local riches. And for a moment, Ruth feels like she's part of it. Like she's been here forever too. She works here. She belongs. She's woven into the fabric of this community, this blouse, spilling in among the liquid stars.

She feels ashamed that she waited this long to come see it, to take her place here.

While the girl waits, Ruth uses her lifelong knowledge of being a customer, of interacting with salespeople at shops, to finish the job of pretending to be a salesperson. She slips the gorgeous vintage blouse into a small paper bag with a handle. She hands the bag to the girl, who clutches it with greedy delight. Then Ruth takes her credit card and rings her up.

Ruth and Benny will be there for only forty minutes that first day. Ruth will make three more sales, and each time, a little flare of feeling will pulse through her. After the third sale, when she hears the electronic chime that signals a successful payment, Ruth becomes aware of the feeling, and she names it. It's precisely the same feeling she used to have all those years ago when she first started *The Widow's Kitchen*, when she would work to create something beautiful and meaningful, and then she would push it into the world without knowing how it would be received, and she would hold her breath until the validation arrived. *Ding ding!* And here it was again, in Daisy's shop. A different iteration of that same testimony. Her daughter had sought that feeling, too, and found a whole new way to create it for herself.

§

If the experience of emerging from the coma was like hauling herself up a long, harrowing staircase of pain, then Daisy's experience of surviving the embolectomy is like being dragged back to the consciousness of suffering by a team of mechanical horses. They have no patience for her resistance; they are not gentle. They come at her with hooks and straps and carabiners, and they attach her to the unrelenting machinery of life, and they wrench and yank her upward, banging her against every step along the way, and directly into a wall of pain. She awakes with a gasp. There. That is the thing she could not do before. She could not gasp. She could not breathe. And now she breathes! She breathes.

Daisy doesn't know what happened, or why she's in a different room now, or where her family is, or who the new nurse is. But she is alive, and she remembers that, just before she passed out, just as she coughed, and a bright spurt of red blood erupted from her mouth and sprayed across the blanket, she thought she would not be alive any longer. There had been a panicky pounding in her ears that sounded like death. The second time she's heard it in the last twenty-seven days.

Daisy will never be the same.

Mom comes into the recovery room and lays her cheek along Daisy's forehead. Daisy feels as though she's traveled back in time. All the progress she made over the last two weeks, gone. Daisy is set back like a haywire clock. She remembers the anesthesia dream and does not feel sure *dream* is the right word for it.

"Dad," she says, and her mom pulls back far enough to examine Daisy's face. Daisy registers her mother's alarmed expression.

Mom holds her hand while she and the recovery room nurse discuss Daisy's cognitive function, the possibility of brain damage, the timeline for determining impairment, best and worst case scenarios, elves, butterflies, demons, Daisy doesn't know.

She sleeps.

§

Although consignments come in all the time, Tuesday is the day Daisy has earmarked for cataloging and pricing new inventory, so Rafaela and her daughter are both on hand to get the work done, but they are overwhelmed. Well, Ruth is overwhelmed. Rafaela sits on the red lounger with one leg up and watches contently. Her daughter stands with her hands on her hips and surveys the merchandise all around her.

"I don't know where to start," Ruth says.

"Well." Rafaela leans forward and plants both feet on the floor. "Why don't we start by looking for a ring?"

Ruth steps gingerly among the bags and cartons, bends down and loosens the flap of a cardboard box to peer inside. "What kind of ring?"

Rafaela extends her own arms and examines her hands. "An engagement ring," she says.

Her daughter pivots on the balls of her feet to gape at her.

"I've decided to get married," she says.

Ruth's eyes pop wide, and a smile tiptoes onto her face. "Mama, that's wonderful!"

Rafaela sidesteps the emotion of the moment, walking over to inspect the glass jewelry case that separates the shoe section from the racks of clothing. "Life is short, right?"

"Too short." Her daughter steps over the stretch of bags on the floor to join her at the jewelry case.

"What about that one?" Rafaela points to a ruby with a halo of tiny diamonds around it, and a braided antique band.

Ruth unlocks the case, and Rafaela reaches in to lift the ring from its velvet pillow. She slips it onto the fourth finger of her left hand, a perfect fit.

"It's beautiful, Mama. But . . ." The subject of Rafaela's one true love is still new. Her daughter is shy in her words. "Candido didn't pick out a ring for you himself?"

Rafaela looks from her hand to Ruth.

"Oh, no, dear. He doesn't know about our engagement yet." She grins. "I'm going to tell him tonight."

Ruth laughs deeply, and it is exactly the sound Rafaela had been hoping to provoke. There were too many years without it. For her and her daughter both, there had been a dearth of laughter, lean years, a scarcity of joy. But now they are here and they are alive and they are together and they are home. Like a boomerang, Rafaela had sailed out into the world, out across Ponce and Trinidad and St. Louis and New York, across turmoil and strife and sorrow and growth, and she had tumbled and whipped and arced and flown, and there were times when she couldn't have said which way was up. It was a topsy-turvy route she had taken, yes, but wasn't this inevitable, in the end? Wasn't Rafaela always going to make her way back to where she belonged?

§

Ruth loses many hours to the insurance company. She talks to dozens of people and all of their supervisors. They assign her a special case worker. She writes letters and appeals and scathing social media posts. She rallies the ire of her followers to no effect. She documents everything. She contacts her congressperson, expresses her incredulity, but maintains her composure throughout the whole process, because her primary sentiment is relief, gratitude—that her daughter is alive. Ruth feels annoyed and anxious, yes. But she doesn't really feel angry.

By the time Daisy is discharged, her hospital bills total $578,432.63, and she is still in physical therapy. She got herself off the painkillers as soon as possible, but both Ruth and Daisy lost significant income, too, when their lives fell into the mouth of calamity. Nothing is the same now as it was before the accident, not their bodies or their souls or their bank accounts or the way they spend the hours of their days or the conversations they deem important or the relative locations of their bodies on the planet. Certainly not their priorities.

But when at last it becomes clear that Ruth will have to choose between selling the house or declaring bankruptcy, she no longer has difficulty accessing her rage. The feeling appears without her bidding and attends to her at night when she tries to sleep. It's as unrelenting as the tide, and equally vast.

Unbeknown to Ruth, when Mama becomes aware of the fiasco, she talks to her advisers about paying Daisy's medical bills. The advisers explain that her financial future will collapse wholesale if she tries to make a withdrawal like that from her long-term investment strategy. She will not have enough money to live on, they warn her. They tell her that the best way to provide a possible future inheritance for her daughter and grandchildren is to leave the money where it is, think about helping them on the back end instead. When Ruth finds out, she forbids Mama from touching the money anyway. She cannot abide the idea of a second insolvency. She cannot be responsible for that.

"We will find another way, Mama," she says.

The anger grows, and soon it occurs to Ruth that its presence is a cancer, that it will eat her if she doesn't find a way to evict it. She cannot hold it in her heart alongside the more important things she has learned. She spends one day screaming into the ocean, an exorcism. And then she sits down with the hospital administrator, who is kind, who has seen this nightmare before, who does everything in his power to help. Ruth negotiates the lowest possible rate, and a payment plan she thinks she can manage.

Then, she sells the house.

Ruth doesn't think for very long before deciding to stay in Puerto Rico. Daisy will remain here because this is her home; Ruth will remain here because Daisy is hers. Her job, such as it is, is portable. *The Widow's*

Kitchen can become *La cocina de la viuda* without any translation at all. Maybe it's time for a pivot anyway. There's a rich world of new material here, a collaboration maybe, in the next chapter of her career. Ruth doesn't yet know what they will be, but she can feel green shoots pushing through dark soil into sunshine.

She will find a little house close to Daisy, in the light-soaked neighborhood of her memory. Santurce will be both exactly as she remembers it and entirely new. It will delight and surprise her, to hear the variety of accents on her street as she pushes her little cart to the grocery store twice a week. Her Spanish will return, haltingly at first, and then she will clumsily improve. Ruth will become aware that her vocabulary is arrested to that of a young child, and then she will rejoice in learning new words, rolling them around her mouth, reaching for slang, jokes, idioms. Her timidity will fall away, along with other things she doesn't need anymore. She will remember a laughter that's been dormant so long she'd forgotten it ever existed. It will visit her often.

At night, Ruth will leave the windows open so the chorus of los coquís will sing into her dreams. She will hang yellow curtains in her kitchen and grow tomatoes in her courtyard. There will be hummingbirds in the garden.

§

Daisy and Mom are together in the Double Down.

With Benny's and Candido's help, they finally installed that enormous chandelier from the defunct hotel in Ponce. The new fixture sends a warm and fractured light all around the space. Daisy is a warm and fractured light herself. She still walks with a limp on her left side, and the scar that runs between her breasts will never fail to shock her. Sometimes the strap of her bra enflames it. Carlos and Vic have taken to calling her Frida Kahlo or sometimes Fri-Daisy Kahlo. But she is alive. She is alive.

In the evenings when they close the shop, sometimes Daisy walks with Mom over to Ocean Park. She's slower in her gait than she used to be, but she's getting faster week by week, and it doesn't matter anyway. Mom has a patience Daisy has never seen before. San Juan suits her. The warm Caribbean air does beautiful things to Mom's hair.

When they take off their shoes, Mom tucks them into a tote bag she carries for just that purpose, and then they make their way along the uneven sand toward the water. When Daisy feels unsteady, Mom puts a hand under her elbow. There is the surf rolling up toward their toes. There are some young people listening to bachata while they pop a volleyball back and forth over a net. Someday Daisy, too, will pop a volleyball over a net. Someday.

"Benny and I used to come to this beach with Dad when we were little," Mom says. "I don't know if Mama remembers."

They are all beginning to make room for this fear, because this is what they do now. They talk about everything, acknowledge every worry, every hurt. This is how they honor one another, how they create their new home in the world.

Mom broached their worries with Candido, too, privately and carefully. They wanted him to know what he might be getting into before he said yes to a wedding. Grandma's memory problems are unpredictable. They swell and retreat, but there is cause for real concern in the long term. His answer? A smile.

"I have waited a long time for the long term." He nodded. "I can serve as her memory."

Daisy tucks a strand of loose hair behind her ear. The tickle of that strand against her skin is a marvel. The sand beneath her toes is a miracle. She squeezes Mom's arm, and floats the idea that perhaps Grandma's forgetfulness doesn't matter. What happened decades ago, what will happen decades hence. What does it matter, if they are together?

Grandma and Candido planned a simple wedding, first—a Friday morning trip to the courthouse. But then she decided on a Friday evening beach wedding instead, just close family, a few friends. Priti is ninety-two now, and keeps insisting she deserves a reason to come to San Juan for one last party.

"I can't disagree, Ma," Candido says.

So they pushed the wedding to a Saturday, and the guest list currently stands at 134. It includes Peter and Trisha. Try as they may, no one can picture Rafaela getting married barefoot. They wait for her to announce that they're moving the celebration to the Vanderbilt instead. It's the only thing that makes sense. Carlos pesters her to create a wedding registry, which Rafaela deems the height of foolishness, but he won't let it drop, so finally, she relents. The registry contains a single item: *The Legend of Zelda: Tears of the Kingdom* for Nintendo Switch.

"The point is, she's happy," Daisy says. "She's right where she's supposed to be."

"About time," Mom says.

She kisses Daisy on the side of the head and wraps one arm around her shoulders. They stop together at the edge of the hot, bright Atlantic, and watch as the ocean folds itself up onto the land in turns. It kisses their toes, their ankles. It glistens in the sinking light as it recedes. Above them, a gull swoops silently through the yellowing sky, and Daisy leans her head on her mother's shoulder. She squeezes Mom's arm to remind them both that, no matter where they are, together, they are home.

Candido and his son stand beneath a banyan tree in a manicured courtyard beside the Vanderbilt hotel. It is evening, and there is nothing reasonable about the colors at his back, where the sky meets the sea on the untidy horizon. Beneath Candido's feet, the roots of that tree grip into the soil; they spread and hold, and Daisy can almost see it, in time lapse or memory: the roots become the branches become the leaves become the roots become the branches. The tree is its own unquestioning lover, its own family, its own history. It provides everything it needs for itself.

Beneath this paragon of splendor, Candido is waiting for his bride. Daisy sits between her brothers in the front row of folding white chairs, and experiences the gauzy, indistinct memory of a staircase she almost couldn't climb. And then a feeling of being ferried, lofted, borne. She is here now. She taps three fingers against her sternum to ground herself. She is here. Carlos squeezes her hand, and they turn to look.

Here is Mom in a navy tuxedo-gown, her arm tendered to her own mama, the beauty of love all over her face.

And here is Rafaela, all in white.

Acknowledgments

~

I am grateful to be surrounded, in life and work, by so many brave, compassionate, smart, and honorable people. Your encouragement sustains me.

To my US publishing team: Caroline Zancan, Caitlin Mulrooney-Lyski, Laura Flavin, Leela Gebo, Allegra Green, Chris Sergio, Meryl Levavi, Abigail Novak, Sonja Flancher, Amber Cherichetti, Hannah Campbell, Janel Brown, Peter Richardson, Emily Griffin, and Andrew Miller. And to my UK publishing team: Mary-Anne Harrington, Louise Swannell, Patrick Insole, Ellie Freedman, and Alexia Thomaidis at Headline. Thank you for making a home for me. Caroline and Mary-Anne especially, thank you for your courage, tenacity, and brilliance.

To the sales reps and booksellers, both at home and abroad, who have been my champions, and who quietly dedicate themselves to the daily defense of free speech and the power of the written word in a very challenging social climate. Thank you for making this life possible.

To Doug Stewart, who has become so much more than my agent, therapist, and friend, and all the rest of the stellar team at Sterling Lord, especially Szilvia Molnar, Tyler Monson, Maria Bell (we haven't forgotten about you!), and Amanda Price. To Rich Green at Gotham, thank you. And to my incredible UK agent Caspian Dennis at Abner Stein, who made me happy-cry after he read an early draft.

To my early readers: Carolyn Turgeon, Sabrina Claro, Karen Dukess, Katherine O'Connor-Ma, Jo-Ann Mapson, Tom Lopez, Valerie Young, Bryant Tenorio, and Sory Tenorio. Thank you for seeing what this book could become instead of what it was.

To these folks, who shared their insight and experiences with me as I uncovered the story I wanted to tell in these pages: Natalia Martinez Castro, Benjamin Davis, Agnes Caniza, Karl Katzaman Colón, Arlene Cabañas Berríos, Roberto Lucena Zabala, Denise M. Mullin, Aunt Lisa Cummins Thess, Aunt Sheila Cummins Oliveri, Tío Rafael Quixano Mendez, and Nora Mendez. For your meaningful personal encourage-ment and expertise in matters beyond me, special thanks to Virginia Sanchez-Korrol, Cecilia Molinari, and Carolina Sofía Quixano. To Mike Valdes-Fauli, you could get away with wearing a cape on the daily. Thank you to Emily Morina for your invaluable support.

It took me a long time to learn the word *hometown*, but no matter where I was born or where I roam, it's always you, Gaithersburg. To all my hometown peeps, thank you for holding me down and reminding me who I've always been. I'm proud to do you proud.

There are many people I won't name here, but without whom I would not have survived the last five years. You know who you are. For the kind of enduring friendship that makes life meaningful (and hilarious), thank you to Carolyn Turgeon, Evelyne Faye, Nikki Stapleton, Debbie Young, and Valerie Young. Ride or die.

To my extended families: Cummins, Kennedy, Lopez, Quixano, and Matthews. Thank you for being so attractive and funny that your shenan-igans retain the patina of glamour.

For my brother, Tom Cummins, and my sister, Kathy Lopez. Thank you for living so much of this book with me and for validating me at every turn. Together, we will serve as the memory. For my mama, Kay Cummins. Dad may have fashioned bedrock out of sand, but you were the reason he could do that magic. You were the secret ingredient.

To my daughters, Aoife and Clodagh. I know it's hard for a teenage girl to be proud of her mama. Thank you for doing that without fail. You two are my answer to every hard question. And to "the only man in Rock-land," my husband, Joe. I had no idea how lucky I was getting when I got you. Next time, I promise I'll try to write about puppies.

About the Author

Jeanine Cummins is the #1 *New York Times* bestselling author of *American Dirt*, which was an Oprah's Book Club and a Barnes & Noble Book Club selection, as well as a #1 Indie Next Pick. The novel has been translated into thirty-seven languages and sold more than three and a half million copies worldwide. Her other works include the memoir *A Rip in Heaven* and the novels *The Outside Boy* and *The Crooked Branch*. She lives in New York with her husband, their two daughters, and their dogs.

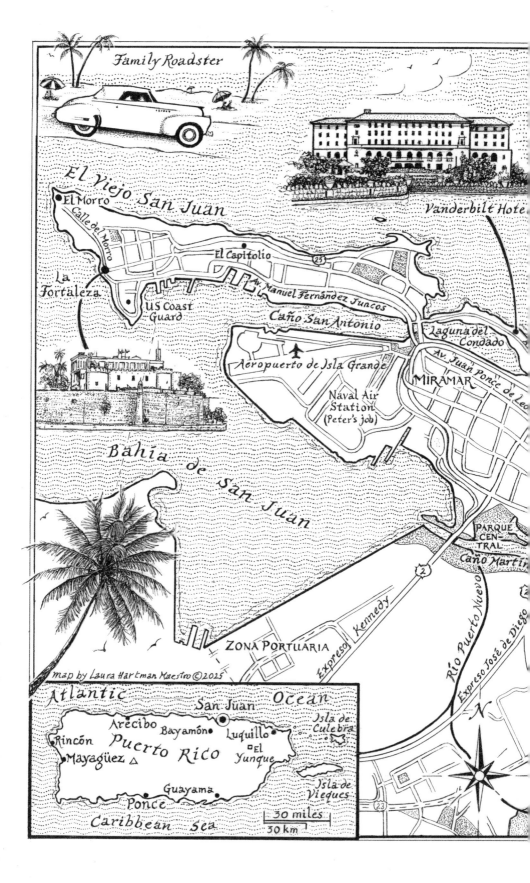

Family Roadster

El Viejo San Juan

El Morro

Calle del Morro

La Fortaleza

US Coast Guard

El Capitolio

Av. Manuel Fernández Juncos

Caño San Antonio

Aeropuerto de Isla Grande

Naval Air Station
(Peter's job)

Vanderbilt Hotel

Laguna del Condado

MIRAMAR

Av. Juan Ponce de Leon

Bahía de San Juan

PARQUE CENTRAL

Caño Martín

Expreso Kennedy

Río Puerto Nuevo

Expreso José de Diego

ZONA PORTUARIA

map by Laura Hartman Maestro © 2025

Atlantic   Ocean

San Juan

Arecibo   Bayamón•   Luquillo•

Rincón   Puerto Rico   □El
                                    Yunque
•Mayagüez △

Isla de Culebra

Guayama•

Ponce•

Isla de Vieques

Caribbean Sea

30 miles
30 km

N